SHOPAHOLIC
TO THE STARS

Sophie Kinsella

BANTAM PRESS

LONDON · TORONTO · SYDNEY · AUCKLAND · JOHANNESBURG

TRANSWORLD PUBLISHERS
61–63 Uxbridge Road, London W5 5SA
A Random House Group Company
www.transworldbooks.co.uk

First published in Great Britain
in 2014 by Bantam Press
an imprint of Transworld Publishers

A CIP catalogue record for this book
is available from the British Library.

ISBN 9780593070161 (cased)
9780593070178 (tpb)

Addresses for Random House Group Ltd companies outside the UK
can be found at: www.randomhouse.co.uk
The Random House Group Ltd Reg. No. 954009

The Random House Group Limited supports the Forest Stewardship Council®
(FSC®), the leading international forest-certification organisation. Our books carrying
the FSC label are printed on FSC®-certified paper. FSC is the only forest-certification
scheme supported by the leading environmental organisations, including
Greenpeace. Our paper procurement policy can be found at
www.randomhouse.co.uk/environment

Typeset in 11/13.5pt Palatino by Falcon Oast Graphic Art Ltd.
Printed and bound in Great Britain by
CPI Group (UK) Ltd, Croydon, CR0 4YY

2 4 6 8 10 9 7 5 3 1

To Patrick Plonkington-Smythe,
the best bank manager ever

CUNNINGHAM'S

Rosewood Center ◆ **W 3rd St.** ◆ **Los Angeles, CA 90048**

Dear Mrs Brandon

Thank you for your letter. I'm glad you enjoyed your recent visit to our store.

Unfortunately, I cannot comment on whether the woman shopping at the M.A.C counter on Tuesday was 'Uma Thurman wearing a long dark wig'. I therefore cannot tell you 'exactly which lipstick she bought', nor 'whether she's just as lovely in real life', nor pass on your note 'because she must want a friend to hang out with and I think we'd really get on'.

I wish you all the best for your forthcoming move to Los Angeles. However, in answer to your other query, we do not offer introductory discounts for new residents of LA to 'make them feel welcome'.

Thank you for your interest.

Mary Eglantine
Customer Services Department

INNER SANCTUM LIFESTYLE SPA

6540 HOLLOWAY DR. ∗ WEST HOLLYWOOD, CA 90069

Dear Mrs Brandon

Thank you for your letter – I'm glad you enjoyed your recent visit to our spa.

Unfortunately, I cannot comment on whether the woman in the front row in your yoga class was Gwyneth Paltrow. I'm sorry that it was hard to tell because 'she was always upside down'.

I therefore cannot pass on your query as to how she achieves 'such a perfect headstand' or whether she has 'special weights in her T-shirt'; nor can I pass on your invitation to an organic tea with kale cakes.

I'm glad you enjoyed our gift-and-lifestyle shop. In answer to your further question, should I meet your husband in the street, rest assured I will not tell him about your 'tiny splurge on organic underwear'.

Thank you for your interest.

Kyle Heiling
Achievement Manager (Eastern Arts)

Beauty on the Boulevard

9500 BEVERLY BOULEVARD

BEVERLY HILLS, LOS ANGELES CA 90210

Dear Mrs Brandon

Thank you for your letter.

Unfortunately, I cannot confirm whether the woman browsing at the La Mer stand was 'Julie Andrews in dark glasses and a headscarf'.

I therefore cannot pass on your comments, 'How hot was Captain von Trapp in real life?' or 'I'm sorry I sang "The Lonely Goatherd" at you, I was just very excited.' Nor can I pass on your invitation to 'come round for a fun sing-along with apple strudel'.

In answer to your further inquiry, we do not throw 'Welcome to LA' parties, nor offer free gifts to new arrivals; not even teeth-whitening kits to 'help them fit in'. However, I wish you every success with your imminent move to LA.

Thank you for your interest.

Sally E. SanSanto
Customer Services Consultant

ONE

OK. Don't panic. Don't *panic*.

I'll escape from this. Of course I will. It's not like I'll be trapped here in this hideous confined space, with no hope of release, *for ever* . . . is it?

As calmly as possible, I assess the situation. My ribs are squashed so that I can hardly breathe, and my left arm is pinned behind me. Whoever constructed this 'restraining fabric' knew what they were doing. My right arm is also pinned at an awkward angle. If I try to reach my hands forward, the 'restraining fabric' bites into my wrists. I'm stuck. I'm powerless.

My face is reflected, ashen, in the mirror. My eyes are wide and desperate. My arms are criss-crossed with black shiny bands. Is one of them supposed to be a shoulder strap? Does that webbing stuff go around the waist?

Oh God. I should never *ever* have tried on the size 4.

'How are you doing in there?' It's Mindy, the sales assistant, calling from outside the cubicle curtain, and I start in alarm. Mindy is tall and rangy with muscled thighs that start three inches apart. She looks like she probably runs up a mountain every day and doesn't even *know* what a KitKat *is*.

She's asked three times how I'm doing and each time I've

11

just called out shrilly, 'Great, thanks!' But I'm getting desperate. I've been struggling with this 'Athletic Shaping All-in-One' for ten minutes. I can't keep putting her off for ever.

'Amazing fabric, right?' says Mindy enthusiastically. 'It has three times the restraining power of normal spandex. You totally lose a size, right?'

Maybe I have, but I've also lost half my lung capacity.

'Are you doing OK with the straps?' comes Mindy's voice. 'You want me to come in the fitting room and help you adjust it?'

Come in the fitting room? There's no way I'm letting a tall, tanned, sporty Angeleno come in here and see my cellulite.

'No, it's fine, thanks!' I squawk.

'You need some help getting it off?' she tries again. 'Some of our customers find it tricky the first time.'

I have a hideous vision of me gripping on to the counter and Mindy trying to haul the all-in-one off me while we both pant and sweat with the effort and Mindy secretly thinks, 'I *knew* all British girls were heifers.'

No way. Not in a million years. There's only one solution left. I'll have to buy it. Whatever it costs.

I give an almighty wrench and manage to snap two of the straps up on to my shoulders. That's better. I look like a chicken trussed up in black Lycra, but at least I can move my arms. As soon as I get back to the hotel room I'll cut the whole thing off myself with a pair of nail scissors, and dispose of the remains in a public bin so Luke doesn't find them and say *What's this?* or, *You mean you bought it even though you knew it didn't fit?* or something else really annoying.

Luke is the reason I'm standing in a sports apparel shop in LA. We're moving out to Los Angeles as soon as possible because of his work, and we're here on an urgent house-hunting trip. That's our focus: real estate. Houses. Gardens. Rental agreements. Very much so. I've only popped to Rodeo Drive very, *very* quickly between house appointments.

Well, OK. The truth is, I cancelled a house appointment to come to Rodeo Drive. But I had to. I have a genuine reason for

12

needing to buy some emergency running clothes, which is that I'm running in a race tomorrow. A real race! Me!

I reach for my clothes, grab my bag, and walk stiffly out of the cubicle, to see Mindy hovering nearby.

'Wow!' Her voice is bright but her eyes are shocked. 'You look . . .' She coughs. 'Awesome. It's not too . . . tight?'

'No, it's perfect,' I say, attempting a carefree smile. 'I'll take it.'

'Great!' She can barely hide her astonishment. 'So, if you want to take it off, I'll scan it for you . . .'

'Actually, I'll wear it.' I try to sound casual. 'Might as well. Can you put my clothes in a bag?'

'Right,' says Mindy. There's quite a long pause. 'You're sure you don't want to try the size 6?'

'No! Size 4 is perfect! *Really* comfy!'

'OK,' says Mindy after a silence. 'Of course. That'll be eighty-three dollars.' She scans the barcode on the tag hanging from my neck and I reach for my credit card. 'So, you're into athletics?'

'Actually, I'm running in the Ten Miler tomorrow afternoon.'

'No way!' She looks up, impressed, and I try to appear nonchalant and modest. The Ten Miler isn't just any old running race. It's *the* race. It's held every year in LA and loads of high-profile celebrities run it and they even cover it on E! And I'm in it!

'How did you get a place?' Mindy says enviously. 'I've applied for that race, like, every year.'

'Well.' I pause for effect. 'I'm on Sage Seymour's team.'

'Wow.' Her jaw drops, and I feel a spurt of glee. It's true! I, Becky Brandon (née Bloomwood), am running in the team of a top movie star! We'll do calf stretches together! We'll wear matching baseball caps! We'll be in *US Weekly*!

'You're British, right?' Mindy interrupts my thoughts.

'Yes, but I'm moving to LA soon. I'm out here to look at houses with my husband, Luke. He has a PR company and he works with Sage Seymour,' I can't help adding proudly.

Mindy looks more and more impressed.

'So are you and Sage Seymour, like, *friends*?'

I fiddle with my purse, delaying my reply. The truth is, despite all my hopes, Sage Seymour and I aren't exactly friends. In fact, the real truth is, I still haven't met her. Which is so unfair. Luke's been working with her for ages, and I've already been out to LA once for a job interview, and now I'm out here again, finding a house and a pre-school for our daughter, Minnie . . . but have I even *glimpsed* Sage?

When Luke said he was going to work with Sage Seymour and we were going to move to Hollywood, I thought we'd be seeing her every day. I thought we'd be hanging out by her pink pool in matching sunglasses and going for mani-pedis together. But even Luke hardly ever seems to see her, he just has meetings with managers and agents and producers all day long. He says he's learning the movie business and it's a steep learning curve. Which is fair enough, because previously, he's only advised financial companies and big conglomerates. But does he have to be so resolutely non-starry-eyed? When I got a tiny bit frustrated the other day, he said, 'For God's sake, Becky, we're not making this huge move just to meet *celebrities*.' He said *celebrities* like he was saying *earwigs*. He understands nothing.

The great thing about Luke and me is that we think alike on nearly everything in life and that's why we're so happily married. But we have just a few, teeny points of disagreement. Such as:

1. Catalogues. (They are not 'clutter'. They're *useful*. You never know when you might need a personalized kitchen blackboard with a dinky little bucket for the chalk. Plus I like reading them at bedtime.)
2. Shoes. (Keeping all my shoes in their original boxes for ever is not ridiculous, it's *thrifty*. They'll come back into fashion one day and then Minnie can wear them. And meanwhile he should look where he's stepping.)
3. Elinor, his mother. (Long, long story.)
4. Celebrities.

I mean, here we are in *LA*. The home of celebrities. They're the local natural phenomenon. Everyone knows you come to LA to see the celebrities, like you go to Sri Lanka to see the elephants.

But Luke didn't gasp when we saw Tom Hanks in the lobby of the Beverly Wilshire. He didn't blink when Halle Berry was sitting three tables away at The Ivy (I think it was Halle Berry). He didn't even get excited when we saw Reese Witherspoon across the road. (I'm sure it was Reese Witherspoon. She had exactly the same hair.)

And he talks about Sage as if she's just another client. Like she's Foreland Investments. He says that this is what she appreciates about him: that he's *not* part of the circus. And then he says I'm getting overexcited by all the Hollywood hoopla. Which is totally untrue. I am *not* overexcited. I'm exactly the right amount excited.

Privately, I'm disappointed in Sage, too. I mean, OK, we don't exactly know each other, but we did speak on the phone when she was helping me with a surprise party for Luke. (Although she's got a new number now, and Luke won't give it to me.) I would have thought she might be in touch, or invite me round to her house for a sleepover, or something.

Anyway, never mind. It'll all come good tomorrow. I don't want to boast, but it's totally due to my own quick wits that I'm in this Ten Miler race. I just happened to be looking over Luke's shoulder at his laptop yesterday, when a round-robin email came in from Sage's manager, Aran. It was entitled *First come first served* and read:

Dear friends,
   There's a last-minute place available on the Ten Miler team due to an injury dropout – anyone interested in running and supporting Sage?

My hands were on the keyboard, pressing Reply and typing *Yes please! I would love to run with Sage! Best wishes, Becky Brandon* before I was even aware I was moving.

OK, so maybe I should have consulted Luke before pressing Send. But it was 'first come first served'. I had to act fast!

Luke just stared at me and said, 'Are you nuts?' Then he started going on about how this was a proper race for trained athletes, and who was going to sponsor me, and did I even possess any running shoes? Honestly. He could be more supportive.

Although, actually, he has a point about the running shoes.

'So, are you in the movie business too?' Mindy asks as she hands me the receipt.

'No, I'm a personal shopper.'

'Oh OK. Which shop?'

'It's . . . actually, it's . . . Dalawear.'

'Oh.' She looks taken aback. 'You mean, the store for . . .'

'Older women. Yes.' I lift my chin. 'It's a great store. It's really exciting. I can't wait!'

I'm being super-positive about this job, even though it's not *exactly* my dream. Dalawear sells 'easy-wear clothes' for ladies who rate 'comfort over style'. (It actually says that on the poster. I might try to persuade them to change it to 'comfort *as much as* style'.) When I went to the interview, the woman kept talking about elasticated waistbands and wash-able fabrics and not once about directional fashion. Or even fashion.

But the truth is, there aren't that many personal-shopping jobs popping up in LA at the last minute for a newly arrived Brit. Especially a Brit who may only be in the country for three months. Dalawear was the only store that had an opening, because of a maternity leave. And I rocked the interview, though I say it myself. I enthused about their 'all-purpose floral shirtwaister' dresses so much, I almost wanted to buy one for myself.

'Can I please buy some running shoes, too?' I change the subject. 'I can't exactly run in these!' I gesture at my Marc Jacobs kitten heels with a little laugh. (For the record, I did once climb an entire mountain in a pair of shoes just like these. But I mentioned that to Luke yesterday as proof of my athletic ability and he shuddered and said he'd wiped that whole incident from his memory.)

'Sure.' Mindy nods. 'You'll want our technical store, Pump! It's right across the street. They stock all the shoes, equipment, heart-rate monitors ... did you get a bio-mechanical assessment in the UK?'

I look at her blankly. A bio-what?

'Talk to the guys across the street, they'll get you set up.' She hands me a carrier bag holding my clothes. 'You must be super-fit. I've worked out with Sage Seymour's trainer. She's hardcore. And I've heard about the team regimen. Didn't you, like, go to Arizona for training?'

This conversation is unnerving me a tad. Hardcore? Team regimen? Anyway, I mustn't lose confidence. I'm perfectly fit enough to run a race, even if it is in LA.

'I haven't been on the regimen *exactly*,' I admit. 'But obviously I have my own ... er ... cardio ... programme ... thing ...'

I'll be fine. It's just running. How hard can it be?

As I head back out to Rodeo Drive, I feel a swoosh of exhilaration as the warm spring air hits me. I'm going to love living in LA, I just know it. Everything people say about it is true. The sun shines and the people have super-white teeth and the mansions look like film sets. I've looked at several houses for rent and they *all* have pools. It's as if a pool is a normal thing, like a fridge.

The street around me simply glistens with glamour. It's lined with expensive, shiny shopfronts and perfect palm trees and rows of luxurious-looking cars. Cars are a whole different thing here. People drive by in their colourful convertibles with the roof down, looking all relaxed and friendly, as if you might stroll up to them while they're pausing at the lights and start a conversation. It's the opposite of Britain where everyone's in their own self-contained metal box, swearing at the rain.

Sunlight is glinting off all the shop windows and sunglasses and expensive watches on people's wrists. Outside Dolce &

Gabbana, a woman is piling a whole load of bags into a car, and she looks just like Julia Roberts, except with blonder hair. And a bit smaller. But apart from that, just like Julia Roberts! On Rodeo Drive!

I'm just trying to edge closer to see what bags she's got, when my phone buzzes, and I pull it out to see *Gayle* on the screen. Gayle is my new boss at Dalawear, and we're having a meeting tomorrow morning.

'Hi, Gayle!' I say in cheerful, professional tones. 'Did you get my message? Are we still on for tomorrow?'

'Hi, Rebecca. Yes, we're all good this end . . .' She pauses. 'Except for one hitch. We still didn't get your reference from Danny Kovitz.'

'Oh, right.' *Drat*. Danny is one of my best friends and is quite a famous fashion designer. He promised to give me a reference for Dalawear, only it's been ages now and he hasn't done anything about it. I texted him yesterday and he promised he would send an email within the hour. I can't believe he hasn't.

Actually, that's not true. I can totally believe it.

'I'll call him,' I promise. 'Sorry about that.'

The truth is, I never should have asked Danny for a reference. But I thought it sounded so cool, having a top fashion designer on my résumé. And I'm sure it helped. They couldn't stop asking me about him in the interview.

'Rebecca . . .' Gayle pauses delicately. 'You *do* know Mr Kovitz? You have met him?'

She doesn't *believe* me?

'Of course I know him! Look, leave it with me. I'll get the reference. I'm really sorry for the delay. See you tomorrow.'

I end the call and instantly speed-dial Danny, trying to stay calm. There's no point getting cross with Danny; he just wriggles and becomes all plaintive.

'Oh my God, Becky.' Danny answers the phone as though we're mid-conversation. 'You would not believe what I need for this trek. It's like, who knew you could get freeze-dried lasagne? And I have the *cutest* little tea kettle, you *have* to get one.'

This is why Danny is even more distracted than usual at the moment. He's about to start training to do some celebrity charity expedition across the Greenland Ice Sheet. Every single person who knows Danny has told him he's mad, but he's adamant he's going to do it. He keeps saying he wants to 'give something back' but we all know it's because he fancies Damon, the lead singer from Boyz About, who's also doing it.

Although how you get it together with someone on a Greenland expedition, I have no idea. I mean, can you even kiss? Do your lips stick together in the freezing air? How do Eskimos manage?

'Danny,' I say sternly, wrenching my mind away from an image of two Eskimos stuck together on their wedding day, flailing their arms around to break free. 'Danny, what about my reference?'

'Sure,' says Danny without missing a beat. 'I'm on it. How many pairs of thermal underwear shall I take?'

'You're not on it! You promised you'd send it yesterday! I've got to go and see them tomorrow and they don't believe I even know you!'

'Well, of course you know me,' he says, as though I'm an idiot.

'They don't know that! This is my only chance of a job in LA and I have to have a reference. Danny, if you can't do it, just tell me and I'll ask someone else.'

'Someone *else*?' Only Danny can manage to sound mortally offended when he's in the wrong. 'Why would you ask someone else?'

'Because they might actually do it!' I sigh, trying to stay patient. 'Look, all you need to do is send a little email. I'll dictate it, if you like. "Dear Gayle, I can recommend Rebecca Brandon as a personal shopper. Signed, Danny Kovitz."' There's silence down the phone and I wonder if he's taking notes. 'Did you get that? Did you write it down?'

'No, I didn't write it down.' Danny sounds indignant. 'That is the crummiest reference I ever heard. You think that's all I have to say about you?'

'Well—'

'I don't give out personal references unless I mean them. Unless I've crafted them. A reference is an *art form*.'

'But—'

'You want a reference, I'll come and give you a reference.'

'What do you mean?' I say, confused.

'I'm not writing three crappy lines on an email. I'm coming to LA.'

'You can't come to LA just to give me a reference!' I start to giggle. 'Where are you, anyway? New York?'

Since Danny hit the big time it's impossible to know where he'll be at any moment. He's opened three new showrooms this year alone, including one in the Beverly Center here in LA. Which you'd think would tie him down, but he's always scouting out yet more new cities or going on 'inspirational research trips' (holidays).

'San Francisco. I was coming anyway. I need to buy sunblock. I always get my sunblock in LA. Text me the details. I'll be there.'

'But—'

'It'll be great. You can help me choose a name for my husky dog. We each get to sponsor one, but I may sponsor a whole team. It's going to be, like, such a life-changing experience . . .'

Once Danny starts talking about 'life-changing experiences', it's hard to cut him off. I'll give him twenty minutes to talk about Greenland, I decide. Maybe twenty-five. And then I *must* go and buy my trainers.

TWO

OK, I officially have the coolest running shoes in the world. They're silver with orange stripes and they have gel bits and mesh bits and I want to wear them all day long.

This sports shop is incredible! You don't just buy a pair of trainers here. You don't just put them on and walk around and say, 'I'll take them,' and then throw six pairs of sports socks into your basket as well, because they're on sale. Oh no. It's all very technical. You do a special running test on a treadmill, and they take a video and tell you all about your 'gait', and find the perfect solution for your athletic needs.

Why don't they do this at Jimmy Choo? They should have a little catwalk where you walk along to cool music and maybe strobe lighting, and they take a video. And then the expert would say, 'We feel the black and white stiletto perfectly suits your awesome supermodel gait.' And then you'd take the video home to show all your friends. I am *so* suggesting it, next time I'm in there.

'So here's the heart monitor I was telling you about . . .' The sales assistant, Kai, reappears holding a little metal and rubber bracelet. 'Like I said, it's our most discreet model, new to the market. I'm excited to hear your opinion.'

'Cool!' I beam at him, and put it on my wrist.

Kai has asked if I'd like to join in a customer study of this new heart monitor, and why not? The only sticky moment was when he asked what heart monitor I was using currently and I didn't like to say 'none', so I said 'The Curve' and then realized that's Luke's new BlackBerry.

'Would you like some more coconut water before you start?'

More coconut water. That's so LA. Everything in this shop is so LA. Kai himself is ripped and tanned and has exactly the optimum amount of stubble and bright turquoise eyes which I'm sure are lenses. He looks so like Jared Leto I wonder whether he went to a surgeon with a picture torn out of *US Weekly* and said, 'This one, please.'

He's already dropped into conversation that: 1. He's modelled for *Sports Illustrated*; 2. He's working on a script about a sportswear consultant who becomes a movie star; 3. He won Ohio's Best Pecs three years running and has had his pecs specially insured. He asked me within about thirty seconds whether I worked in the film industry and when I said no, but my husband did, he gave me a card and said, 'I'd love to meet with him to discuss a venture he might be interested in.' The idea of Kai and Luke sitting at a table discussing his pecs nearly made me snort out my coconut water.

'So if you'll kindly step up here.' Kai ushers me on to the treadmill. 'I'll be taking a record of your heart rate, so we'll raise it with some aerobic activity and then lower it with rest periods. Just follow the treadmill and you'll be fine.'

'Great!' As I step up, I notice a massive rack of exercise clothes being wheeled on to the shop floor by two sales assistants. Wow. They look amazing – all different shades of purples and greys, with abstract logos and really interesting shapes.

'What's that?' I ask Kai as the treadmill starts to move gently along.

'Oh.' He looks at it without interest. 'That's from our clearance fashion floor.'

Clearance fashion floor? No one mentioned a clearance fashion floor. Why didn't I know about the clearance fashion floor?

'Weird.' He peers at his computer screen. 'Your heart rate just spiked and we didn't even start the intense activity yet. Oh well.' He shrugs. 'Let's get going.'

The treadmill starts to move along more briskly, and I up my walking pace to match. But I'm distracted by the rack of clothes, because an assistant is putting sale tickets on every garment! I spot a '90 % off' sign and crane my neck to see what it's attached to. Is that a T-shirt? Or a mini-dress? Or—

Oh my God, *look* at that cardigan. I can't help gasping aloud. That is stunning. It's longline, in what seems to be grey cashmere, with an oversized, neon-pink zipper, all the way up the front and the back. It's *gorgeous*.

'So now we'll rest for a moment . . .' Kai is concentrating on his screen. 'You're doing great so far.'

The treadmill slows, but I barely notice. I'm feeling stabs of alarm. A pair of passing girls has seen the rail and fallen on it in delight. I can hear them exclaiming with glee, showing clothes to each other and dumping them in their baskets. They're taking *everything*! I don't believe it. The sale of the century is going on, ten yards away, and I'm stuck on this stupid treadmill. As long as they don't see the cardigan. I will them silently: *Don't look at the cardigan . . .*

'OK, this is strange.' Kai is frowning at his screen again. 'Let's pause the test.'

'Actually, I need to leave,' I say breathlessly, grabbing my handbag and shopping basket. 'Thanks. If I need a heart monitor I'll definitely get this one, but I must go . . .'

'Rebecca, have you ever been diagnosed with arrhythmia? Heart disorder? Anything like that?'

'No.' I'm stopped in my tracks. 'Why? Have you picked something up?'

Is he joking? No. His face is serious. He isn't joking. I'm gripped with fright. What have I got? Oh my God, I'll be in the *Daily Mail* health pages. *My one-in-a-million heart condition was picked up in a simple store exercise test. Shopping saved my life, says Rebecca Brandon—*

'Your heart response wasn't typical. It spiked, but not at the moments I was expecting. For example, it spiked just now when you were resting.'

'Oh,' I say anxiously. 'Is that bad?'

'Not necessarily. It would depend on a lot of things. Your general heart health, your cardio fitness . . .'

As he's talking, my eye wanders over to the sale rack again, and to my horror I see that one of the girls has picked up my cardigan. *No! Noooo! Put it down!*

'It's happened again!' says Kai in sudden animation, and points at the screen. 'Do you see? Your heart rate rocketed!'

I look at Kai, and at the screen, and then at the cardigan with the neon-pink zip, and it all falls into place. Oh God, is *that* why my heart rate zoomed up?

This is so embarrassing. Stupid dumb heart. I can feel myself blushing bright red and I hastily look away from Kai.

'Well!' I say in flustered tones. 'I have no idea why that happened. None! Just one of those mysteries. Mysteries of the heart. Ha ha!'

'Oh. OK.' Kai's expression snaps as though in recognition. 'Ooo-kay. I think I get it. I've seen this a couple times.'

'Seen what?'

'OK, this is a little awkward . . .' He flashes me a perfect smile. 'It was physical attraction to me, right? You don't need to be uncomfortable. It's normal. It's why I had to give up personal training. The clients became . . . I don't know, would you say "infatuated"?' He glances complacently at himself in the mirror. 'You looked at me and your response was beyond your control. Am I right?'

'Not really,' I say, honestly.

'Rebecca.' Kai sighs. 'I know it's embarrassing to admit, but believe me, you're not the only lady to become attracted to me—'

'But I wasn't looking at you,' I explain. 'I was looking at a cardigan.'

'A cardigan?' Kai plucks at his T-shirt, confused. 'I'm not wearing one.'

'I know. It's over there. It's on sale.' I point it out. *'That's*

24

what I was looking at, not you. I'll show you.' I take the opportunity to dash over and grab the cardigan, which, thank God, the girl has replaced on the rack. It's super-soft to the touch and the zip is amazing, and it's reduced by 70 per cent! I'm sure my heart is racing again, just from holding it.

'Isn't it gorgeous?' I enthuse, heading back towards Kai. 'Isn't it fab?' Suddenly I realize I'm not being very tactful. 'I mean, *you're* very good-looking too,' I add encouragingly. 'I'm sure I'd be attracted to you if it weren't for the cardigan.'

There's a pause. Kai looks slightly stunned, to be honest. Even his turquoise contact lenses seem a bit less sparkly.

'You'd be attracted to me "if it weren't for the cardigan",' he echoes at last.

'Of course!' I say, reassuringly. 'I'd probably get infatuated, just like those clients of yours. Unless there were any other amazing clothes to compete with,' I add, for honesty's sake. 'I mean, like a Chanel suit with ninety-nine per cent off. I don't think any man could beat that!' I give a little laugh, but Kai's face has gone a bit rigid.

'I never had to compete with clothes before,' he says, almost to himself. '*Clothes.*'

I'm noticing that the atmosphere isn't *quite* as easy and fun as it was before. I think I might just go and pay for my trainers.

'Thanks for the heart test, anyway!' I say brightly, and take off the bracelet. 'Good luck with the pecs!'

Honestly. What a big-head that Kai is. I know he has stunning turquoise eyes and a great body, but he doesn't have a neon zip, does he? Lots of men have stunning blue eyes, but only one cardigan has a cool oversized neon-pink zip. And if he thinks he's never competed with clothes before, then his girlfriends have been lying to him. Every woman in the world sometimes thinks about shoes in the middle of sex. It's a well-known fact.

Anyway. Don't think about stupid Kai. On the positive front, I've got the best, most whizzy trainers in the world. And OK, they cost $400, which is a lot, but I'll just have to think of this as an investment in my career. In my *life*.

'So, I'll box those for you,' says the sales assistant, and I nod absently. I'm imagining standing at the start of the race with Sage, and her glancing down at my feet and saying, 'Cool shoes.'

I'll give her a friendly smile and reply carelessly, 'Thanks.'

Then she'll say, 'Luke never told me you were such a serious athlete, Becky.'

And I'll say, 'Are you kidding? I love running.' (Which isn't quite true yet, but I'm sure it will be. Once I start this race, the endorphins will kick in and I'll probably become addicted.)

Then Sage will say, 'Hey, we should train together! Let's meet up every morning.'

And I'll say, 'Sure,' very nonchalantly.

Then she'll say, 'I train with some friends, but you'll love them. Do you know Kate Hudson and Drew Barrymore and Cameron Diaz and—'

'Will you be paying by credit or cash, ma'am?'

I blink at the assistant and fumble for my card. 'Oh. Right. Credit.'

'And did you choose your water bottle?' the sales assistant adds.

'I'm sorry?'

'We're offering a free bottle with every shoe purchase.' He gestures at a nearby poster.

Well. This $400 seems more and more of a bargain.

'I'll just have a look. Thanks!' I beam at him and head towards the display of bottles. Maybe if I'm carrying a cool bottle, Sage will notice that, too! There's a whole wall of them – chrome, matt black, and all sorts of silicon colours. As my eye travels upwards, I spot a label: *Limited-edition print*. I squint, trying to see – but they're on the fifth shelf. Honestly. Why would you put the limited-edition-print bottles on the fifth shelf?

There's a stepladder nearby, so I drag it over and climb to the top. Now I can see the bottles properly, and they're amazing: all with gorgeous retro prints. I can hardly bear to choose – but in the end I narrow it down to three: one with red stripes, one with amber swirls, and one with black and white flowers. I'll pay for the extra ones, I decide, because I can give one each to Minnie and Suze as souvenirs.

I carefully put the bottles down on the top step of the ladder and turn to survey the shop. I have an amazing view from up here. I can see all the aisles, and I can see that the woman at the cash register needs her roots touching up, and I can see . . .

What?

Wait a minute.

I stiffen in disbelief and peer more closely.

In the far corner there's a girl I hadn't noticed before. She's incredibly thin, wearing pale skinny jeans, a grey hoody up over her head, and dark glasses that hide her face. And no wonder she's dressed so furtively. Because she's stealing.

I stare in utter shock as I see her putting a pair of socks into her oversized handbag (Balenciaga, this season), and then another. Then a third. Then she looks around, kind of shrinks down into herself and walks swiftly towards the exit.

I've never seen a shoplifter in action before, and for an instant I just feel stunned. But next moment a boiling outrage is rising through me. She took them! She shoplifted! She shouldn't do that! People shouldn't *do* that!

What if we all did that? I mean, I bet we'd all like to have free socks, but we don't just take them, do we? We pay. Even if we can't really afford it, we *pay*.

My stomach is churning as I watch her leave. I feel really angry. It's *not fair*. And suddenly I know I can't just let her go. I have to do something. I'm not sure what – but something.

Leaving the bottles behind, I bound down the ladder and out of the shop door. I can see the shoplifter ahead of me, and increase my pace to a run, dodging pedestrians as I go. As I get near, my heart is thumping with apprehension. What if she threatens me? What if she's got a gun? Oh God, of *course* she's got a gun. This is LA. Everyone has guns.

Well, too bad. Maybe I will get shot, but I can't wimp out now. I reach out a hand and tap her on her bony shoulder.

'Excuse me?'

The girl whips round and I tense in fright, waiting for the gun. But it doesn't come. Her sunglasses are so huge I can barely see her face, but I make out a thin, pale chin and a scrawny, almost malnourished neck. I feel a sudden stab of guilt. Maybe she's on the streets. Maybe this is her only source of income. Maybe she's going to sell the socks to buy food for her crack-addict baby.

Part of me is thinking, 'Just turn away, Becky. Let it go.' But the other part won't let me. Because even if there's a crack-addict baby, it's just wrong. It's *wrong*.

'I saw you, OK?' I say. 'I saw you taking those socks.'

The girl immediately stiffens, and makes to run away, but I instinctively grab her arm.

'You shouldn't steal stuff!' I say, struggling to keep hold of her. 'You just shouldn't! You probably think, "So what? No one got hurt." But you know, shop assistants get in trouble when people shoplift. Sometimes they have to pay for the goods from their wages. Is that fair?'

The girl is wriggling desperately to get away, but I'm gripping on to her arm with both hands. Being the mother of a two-year-old, you learn a lot of immobilization skills.

'And then all the prices go up,' I add, panting. 'And every-one suffers! I know you might think it's your only option, but it's not. You can turn your life around. There are places you can go for help. Do you have a pimp?' I add, trying to sound sympathetic. 'Because I know they can be a real pain. But you could go to a safe house. I saw a documentary about it, and they're brilliant.' I'm about to elaborate when the girl's sun-glasses slip to one side. And I glimpse the side of her face.

And suddenly I feel faint. I can't breathe. That's—

No. It can't be.

It is. It *is*.

It's Lois Kellerton.

All thoughts of crack addicts and safe houses disappear from my head. This is surreal. It can't be happening. It has to be a dream. I, Becky Brandon, née Bloomwood, am clutching the arm of top Hollywood actress Lois Kellerton. As I peer at her unmistakable jawline, my legs start to shake. I mean, *Lois Kellerton*. I've seen all her films and I've watched her on the red carpet and I've—

But what—

I mean, *what* on earth—

Lois Kellerton shoplifted three pairs of socks? Is this some kind of candid-camera show?

For what seems like the longest moment, we're both motionless, staring at each other. I'm remembering her as Tess in that brilliant adaptation of *Tess of the d'Urbervilles*. God, she made me cry. And there was that sci-fi one where she got deliberately stranded on Mars at the end, in order to save her half-alien children. I cried *buckets*, and so did Suze.

I clear my throat, trying to gather my thoughts. 'I . . . I know who you—'

'Please,' she cuts me off in that familiar husky voice. 'Please.' She takes off her dark glasses and I stare at her in fresh shock. She looks terrible. Her eyes are red-rimmed and her skin is all flaky. 'Please,' she says a third time. 'I'm . . . I'm so sorry. I'm so sorry. Are you employed by the shop?'

'No. I'm a customer. I was up a ladder.'

'Did they see me?'

'I don't know. I don't think so.'

With a trembling hand she grabs the three pairs of socks from her bag and offers them to me.

'I don't know what I was doing. I haven't slept for two nights. I think I went a little crazy. I never did anything like this before. I never will again. Please,' she whispers again, shrinking inside her hoody. 'Take the socks. Take them back.'

'*Me?*'

'Please.' She sounds desperate. At last, awkwardly, I take the socks from her.

'Here.' She's scrabbling in her bag again and produces a fifty-dollar note. 'Give this to the employees.'

'You look quite . . . um . . . stressed,' I venture. 'Are you OK?'

Lois Kellerton raises her head and meets my eyes, and I'm suddenly reminded of a leopard I once saw in a Spanish zoo. That looked desperate, too.

'Are you going to tell the police?' she breathes, so quietly I can barely hear her. 'Are you going to tell anyone?'

Oh God. Oh *God*. What do I do?

I put the socks in my bag, playing for time. I should tell the police. Of course I should. What difference does it make if she's a movie star? She stole the socks and that's a crime and I should perform a citizen's arrest right now and march her off for justice.

But . . . I can't. I just *can't*. She looks so fragile. Like a moth or a paper flower. And after all, she's giving the socks back, and she's making a donation, and it sounds like she just had a moment of madness . . .

Lois Kellerton's head is bowed. Her face is hidden inside the grey hood. She looks as though she's waiting for an execution.

'I won't tell anyone,' I say at last. 'I promise. I'll give the socks back and I won't tell anyone.'

As I release my grip on her, her thin hand squeezes mine. Her dark glasses are already back on her face. She looks like an anonymous skinny girl in a hoody.

'Thank you,' she whispers. 'Thank you. What's your name?'

'Becky,' I reply eagerly. 'Becky Bloomwood. I mean, Brandon. I was Bloomwood but I got married, so my name changed . . .' Argh, stop gabbling. 'Um, Becky,' I finish lamely. 'My name is Becky.'

'Thank you, Becky.'

And before I can say anything, she's turned and gone.

THREE

Next morning, my head is still sparking in disbelief. Did that actually happen? Did I actually meet Lois Kellerton?

When I returned to Pump!, clutching the socks, it turned out they hadn't even noticed that the socks had gone. For an awful moment I thought they were going to accuse *me* of stealing them. But thankfully a sales assistant took over the incident, and called up the CCTV footage and we all watched as a thin girl in a grey hoody put the socks in her bag and slipped out. I was tingling all over as I watched. A tiny part of me wanted to yell, 'Don't you see who it is? Don't you *see*?'

But of course I didn't. I'd made a promise. Besides which, they'd never believe me. On the video you can't see her face at all.

Then we watched the footage as I chased her out of the shop. All I can say is, I am never buying an 'Athletic Shaping All-in-One' again. I wanted to *die* when I saw my bottom bulging through the shiny fabric.

Anyway. On the plus side, everyone was really impressed by what I did, even if they were more interested in arguing about whether the socks should have been fitted with security tags. My story was that the 'mystery girl' dropped the socks as I chased her down the street, and that I couldn't catch up with her. I didn't know what to do about the fifty-dollar note, so in the end I pretended that I'd found it on the floor and handed it over. I left my name in case the police needed a statement, then hurried back to our hotel, where I *finally* cut that awful all-in-one off myself. (I bought a pair of shorts and a vest from Gap instead.)

Lois Kellerton. I mean, *Lois Kellerton*. People would die if they knew! (Well, Suze would.) But I haven't told anybody. When Luke and I finally met up for supper last night, he wanted to hear all about the rental houses I'd looked at, and I didn't want to admit I'd spent quite so much time on Rodeo Drive . . . and besides which, I made a promise. I said I'd keep it a secret and I have. Today it feels as though the whole event was a weird little dream.

I blink and shake my head to dislodge it. I have other things to think about this morning. I'm standing outside Dalawear, which is on Beverly Boulevard and has a window display of mannequins in 'easy-wear' dresses and pantsuits, taking tea on a fake lawn.

I'm not meeting Danny for another twenty minutes, but I wanted to get here early and remind myself of the store and its layout. As I wander in, there's a lovely smell of roses in the air, and Frank Sinatra is playing over the sound system. It's a very *pleasant* store, Dalawear, even if all the jackets seem to be one style, just with different buttons.

I've gone through separates, shoes and underwear, when I come to the evening-wear section. Most of the dresses are full-length and heavily corseted, in bright colours like periwinkle blue and raspberry. There are lots of big rosettes at the shoulder or waist, and beading, and laced-up bodices, and built-in 'slimming' undergarments. Just looking at them makes me feel exhausted, especially after my 'Athletic Shaping All-in-One' experience. Some clothes just aren't worth the hassle of trying to get them on and off.

I'm about to get out my phone to text Danny when there's a rustling sound, and a girl of about fifteen appears out of the dressing room to stand in front of the full-length mirror. She's not the most together-looking girl. Her dark-red hair is in a fuzzy kind of bob, and her nails are bitten, and her eyebrows could do with a bit of a tweeze. But worst of all, she's wearing a jade-green, strapless, swooshy gown which totally swamps her, complete with a rather revolting chiffon stole. She looks uncertainly at herself, and hitches the bodice over her bust, where it really doesn't fit. Oh God, I can't bear it. What is she doing here? This shop isn't for teens.

'Hi!' I approach her hurriedly. 'Wow! You look . . . um, lovely. That's a very . . . formal dress.'

'It's for my end-of-year prom,' mutters the girl.

'Right. Fantastic!' I let a pause fall before I add, 'They have some pretty dresses in Urban Outfitters, you know. I mean, Dalawear is a brilliant choice, obviously, but for someone your age . . .'

'I have to shop here.' She shoots me a miserable look. 'My mom had some coupons. She said I could only get a dress if it didn't cost her anything.'

'Oh, I see.'

'The sales lady said green would set off my hair,' she adds hopelessly. 'She went to find me some shoes to match.'

'The green is . . . lovely.' I cross my fingers behind my back. 'Very striking.'

'It's OK, you don't have to lie. I know I look terrible.' Her shoulders slump.

'No!' I say quickly. 'You just . . . it's a tiny bit full for you . . . perhaps a bit fussy . . .' I tug at the layers of chiffon, wanting to trim them all off with a pair of scissors. I mean, when you're fifteen, you don't want to be dressed up like a Christmas cracker. You want to be in something simple and beautiful, like . . .

And then it hits me.

'Wait here,' I say, and hurry back to the underwear section. It takes me about twenty seconds to grab a selection of silk slips, lace slips, 'shaping' slips, and a 'luxury satin slip with boned bodice', all in black.

'Where did you get those?' The girl's eyes light up as I arrive back in the evening-wear section.

'They were in another section,' I say vaguely. 'Have a go! They're all in Small. I'm Becky, by the way.'

'Anita.' She smiles, revealing train-track braces.

While she's rustling around behind the curtain, I search for accessories, and find a black beaded sash plus a simple clutch bag in dark pink.

'What do you think?' Anita emerges shyly from the changing room, utterly transformed. She's in a strappy lace slip that makes her look about three sizes smaller and shows off her long legs. Her milky skin looks amazing against the black lace, and her short, stubby hair seems to make more sense, too.

'Amazing! Just let me do your hair . . .' There's a basket of complimentary water bottles on the counter, and, quickly opening one, I wet my hands. I smooth down her hair until it looks sleek and gamine, cinch her waist in with the beaded sash, and give her the pink clutch to hold.

'There!' I say proudly. 'You look fabulous. Now, stand with some attitude. Look at yourself. Don't you just rock?'

Once she's got a pair of heels on, she'll look a million dollars. I sigh happily as I watch her shoulders relax and a sparkle come to her eye. God, I love dressing people up.

'So I found the shoes in your size . . .' comes a trilling voice behind me, and I turn to see a woman in her sixties approaching Anita. I met her when I came for the interview before, and her name's . . . Rhoda? No, Rhona. It's on her name-badge.

'Dear!' She gives a shocked laugh as she sees the teenage girl. 'What happened to the gown?'

The girl's eyes slide uneasily to me, and I step in quickly.

'Hi, Rhona!' I say. 'I'm Becky, we met before, I'm starting work here soon. I was just helping Anita with her look. Doesn't that slip look great worn as a dress?'

'Well, goodness!' Rhona's rigid smile doesn't move an inch, but her eyes fix me with daggers. 'How imaginative. Anita, sweetheart, I'd love to see you in the green full-length.'

'No,' says Anita stubbornly. 'I'm wearing this one. I like it.'

She disappears behind the curtain and I step towards Rhona, lowering my voice.

'It's OK,' I say. 'You don't need to see her in the green. It didn't work. Too big. Too old. But then I suddenly thought of the slips and . . . bingo!'

'That's hardly the point,' says Rhona, bristling. 'You know what the commission on that green gown is? You know what the commission on a slip is?'

'Well, who cares?' I say indignantly. 'The point is, she looks lovely!'

'I'm sure she looked far lovelier in the green gown. I mean, a slip.' Rhona looks disapproving. 'To a prom. A *slip*.'

I bite my lip. I can't say what I really think.

'Look, we're going to be working together, so . . . shall we agree to disagree?' I hold out my hand placatingly, but before Rhona can take it, there's an exclamation from behind me and two arms twine themselves around my neck.

'Becky!'

'Danny!' I wheel round to see his pale-blue eyes shining at me through heavy eye-liner. 'Wow! You look very . . . um . . . New Romantic.'

Danny never puts on any weight or looks a day older despite leading the least healthy lifestyle on the planet. Today his hair is dyed black and gelled into a kind of droopy quiff; he's wearing a single dangly earring and tight jeans tucked into winkle-picker boots.

'I'm ready,' he announces. 'I have my reference. I learned it on the plane. Who do I say it to? You?' He turns to Rhona and makes a small bow. 'My name is Danny Kovitz – yes, *the* Danny Kovitz – thank you – and I am here today to recommend Rebecca Brandon as a personal shopper without parallel.'

'Stop!' I say, pink with embarrassment. 'This isn't the right place. We need to find Gayle, my new boss.'

'Oh,' says Danny, unfazed. 'OK.'

Meanwhile, Anita has reappeared from the dressing room and heads over to Rhona.

'OK, I'd like to get the black lace dress. And the pink clutch and the sash.'

'Well, dear,' says Rhona, her face still pinched with annoyance. 'If you're sure. Now, what about this fabulous pink stole? It would set off the black lace wonderfully.' She reaches for a length of pink tulle adorned with oversized white sequins, and spreads it out on the counter.

Anita glances at me and I surreptitiously shake my head.

'No thanks,' she says confidently. Rhona whips round in suspicion, but I give her an innocent smile.

'We'd better find Gayle,' I say. 'See you later, Rhona! Have fun at the prom, Anita!'

As I head away with Danny, I can't help wrapping an arm around him.

'Thank you for coming. You're such a star to do this.'

'I know,' he says complacently.

'I'm going to miss you when you go to Greenland! Couldn't you have chosen somewhere nearer?'

'What, some hike in the mountains?' says Danny dismissively. 'Some little day trek?'

'Why not? We would still have sponsored you—'

'Becky, you don't get it.' Danny gives me a serious look. 'This is something I have to do. I want to push myself to the limit. I have this great trainer, Diederik, and he's done the Greenland expedition. He says it's a mystical experience. *Mystical*.'

'Oh well. Mystical.' I shrug.

'Who *buys* these clothes?' Danny seems to have noticed the racks for the first time.

'Er . . . lots of people. Lots of very fashionable, stylish, um . . . chic people.'

'Chic?' He looks at me with a comically appalled face. 'Chic?'

'Sssh! There's my boss!'

We've reached the entrance to the Personal Shopping area, where I've agreed to meet Gayle, and there she is, looking around anxiously. Maybe she thought I wasn't going to turn up. She's a really lovely woman, in her forties – very pretty except her hair's too long, in my opinion – and I'm looking forward to working with her.

'Hi!' I wave to attract her attention.

'Rebecca.' She exhales. 'I was about to call you. This is very awkward. I'm sorry, I'm so sorry . . .'

She's about to tell me that Danny still hasn't come through with his reference, isn't she?

'No, it's fine,' I say hastily. 'He's here! Danny, this is Gayle, my new boss.' I nudge him. 'You can start now.'

'Excuse me?' Gayle looks baffled.

'This is Danny Kovitz,' I explain. 'He's come here especially to give you my reference! Go on, Danny.' I nod encouragingly, and Danny draws breath.

'My name is Danny Kovitz – yes, *the* Danny Kovitz – thank you – and I am here today to recommend Rebecca Brandon as a personal shopper without parallel. Where there is disaster she will find style. Where there is blah, she will find a look. Where there is . . . um—' He breaks off, pulls a piece of paper out of his jeans pocket and consults it. 'Yes! Where there is misery she will find happiness. Not just fashion happiness, all-round happiness.' He takes a step towards Gayle, who looks a bit shell-shocked. 'You *want* Rebecca Brandon in your store. The last person who tried to fire her faced a backlash from the customers, am I right, Becky?'

'Well.' I shrug awkwardly, feeling a bit overcome. I had no idea Danny would be so nice about me.

'You may have heard some strange rumours about Rebecca.' Danny has gone on to his second sheet of paper. 'Yes, she once deliberately trapped a customer in a dress. But she had a good reason.' He hits the paper emphatically. 'Yes, she's been known to disguise clothes as sanitary products. But she was helping her clients. Yes, she organized two weddings for the same day and didn't tell anyone, even her fiancé . . .' He peers at the sheet.

'Danny, shut up!' I mutter. Why is he bringing all this up?

'I have no idea why she did that,' Danny concludes. 'Let's

ignore that. Let's focus on the fact that Rebecca is a shining light in any personal shopping department and any store should be glad to have her. Thank you.' He gives a bow then looks up at Gayle. 'I'd now be glad to answer any questions, except those about my personal life, my beauty routine and my ongoing lawsuit with my former manager. For those topics I have Q&A sheets.' He rummages in another pocket and unfolds three lime-coloured sheets of paper, all headed *The Danny Kovitz Story*, which he hands to Gayle.

Gayle gazes at them in stupefied silence, then raises her eyes to me.

'Rebecca . . .' She seems lost for words.

'I didn't *mean* to organize two weddings,' I say defensively. 'These things happen.'

'No, no. It's not that. It's . . . Oh, it's too bad.' She shuts her eyes. 'This is all too bad.'

'What's too bad?' I say, with a sudden feeling of foreboding.

'Rebecca . . .' Finally she faces me properly. 'There's no job for you.'

'What?' I falter.

'I had a call just now from the group director. He's been doing a review, and we have to lose some staff.' She winces. 'I'm afraid that a personal shopping maternity cover is too great a luxury for us. We're going to have to get by with just Rhona for now. I would love to hire you, believe me.' She looks from me to Danny. 'But in this climate . . . things are so tough . . .'

'It's OK,' I say, my voice wobbly with shock. 'I understand.'

'I'm sorry. I'm sure you would have been a great addition to the department.' She looks so sad, I feel a pang of sympathy. What a horrible job, having to fire people.

'That's life,' I say, trying to sound more cheerful. 'Thanks for the chance, anyway. And maybe I'll come and work here when things get better!'

'Maybe. Thanks for being so understanding. I'm afraid I have to go break some more bad news.' She shakes my hand, then turns and strides away, leaving Danny and me looking blankly at each other.

'Bummer,' says Danny at last.

'I know.' I sigh heavily. 'Thanks for the reference, anyway. Can I buy you lunch to say thank you?'

By the time Danny leaves for the airport, two hours later, we've had a blast. We've done early lunch with cocktails, and a shopping spree for sunblock, and I've laughed so hard, my stomach muscles ache. But as I watch his car whisk him away along Beverly Boulevard, there's a lump of disappointment weighing me down. No job. I was counting on that job. Not just for employment, not just for money – but as something to do. A way to make friends.

Anyway. It's fine. It's all good. I'll think of something else. There are loads of shops in LA, there *must* be opportunities, I'll just have to keep looking . . . keep my ears and eyes open.

'Hey, lady! Watch it!'

Oops. I was so busy thinking about keeping my ears and eyes open, I didn't notice a great big crane-thing parked slap bang in the middle of the pavement. A man in a headset is directing people around it, and there's a bit of a buzz further up the street. As I go nearer to get a look, I can see glinting, and lights on stands . . . Oh wow! It's a camera crew! They're filming something!

I know I need to get back to the hotel and prepare for the Ten Miler race, but I *can't* just walk away. Even though I've been to LA before, this is the first camera crew I've seen. So I hurry along in excitement, heading towards the bright lights. The pavement is cordoned off with metal barriers and a guy in a denim jacket and a headset is politely asking people to step away, to the other side of the street. Reluctantly, I obey, keeping my eyes fixed on the action. There are two guys in jeans sitting on directors' chairs, and a burly man operating a camera, and several girls scurrying around with headsets too, looking important. I feel massive pangs of envy as I watch them all. I mean, *how cool*, to be involved in a film. The only kind of filming I've ever done was on TV, advising people how to invest their pension. (I used to be a financial journalist. I used to spend all day talking about bank accounts. Sometimes I get an anxiety dream where I'm back in that job and I'm on TV and I don't even know what an interest rate is.)

Standing on the pavement, all alone, is a woman who I guess is an actress, as she's so tiny and made-up. I don't recognize her, but that doesn't mean anything. I'm just wondering whether to get out my phone, take a picture and text **Who's this?** to my best friend Suze, when an older woman, in jeans and a black vest, comes up to her. She's wearing a maroon peaked cap and has long black braids, and the coolest high-heeled boots.

Everyone else in the crowd is pointing at the actress, but I'm riveted by the woman with braids. I know her. I've read interviews with her. She's a stylist called Nenita Dietz.

She's holding a see-through plastic bag containing a stripy, vintage-looking coat, which she carefully takes out and puts on the actress. She stares critically, adjusts it, then adds a necklace. And as I watch her, my thoughts are suddenly spinning in a new direction. Imagine having that job. Working on films; choosing outfits for actors; styling stars for appearances ... Forget department stores, I should aim higher! *That's* the job I should have. I mean, it's perfect. I love clothes, I love films, I'm moving to LA ... why didn't I think of this before?

Now Nenita Dietz is trying different pairs of sunglasses out on the actress. I follow every move she makes, utterly mesmerized. Nenita Dietz is amazing. She was behind that trend for boots with evening wear. And she's starting a line of underwear. I've always wanted to design my own underwear.

But how on earth would I get into it? How do you become a top Hollywood stylist? Or even a low-to-medium Hollywood stylist? Where do I even start? I don't know anyone here, I don't have a job, I don't have any film experience ...

Now people across the road are shouting, 'Quiet on set!' and, 'Rolling!' and, 'QUIET PLEASE!' I watch in fascination as the actress folds her arms and looks upwards.

'Cut!'

Cut? That was *it*?

All the film people are scurrying around again and I peer hard, searching for Nenita Dietz, but I can't see her. And people are starting to press at my back. So at last I tear myself away, my mind whirling with fantasies. A darkened cinema. My name rolling down the screen in white letters.

MISS HATHAWAY'S WARDROBE PERSONALLY SELECTED BY
REBECCA BRANDON

MR PITT'S SUITS SOURCED BY REBECCA BRANDON

MISS SEYMOUR'S GOWNS CHOSEN BY REBECCA BRANDON

And now, of course, it all falls into place in my head. Sage Seymour is the key. Sage Seymour is the answer. *That's* how I'm going to get in.

FRESH BEAN COFFEE SHOP
1764 Beverly Blvd
Los Angeles, CA 90210

• NOTES AND THOUGHTS •

Possible fashion trends to start:

- *Tartan dress with neon PVC accessories*
- *Fake-fur coat belted with three different belts (Yes! Signature look!)*
- *Pink hair and distressed pinstripe jacket*
- *Diamanté brooches pinned to wellies*
- *Jeans cut up and made into arm warmers*
- *Carry two designer handbags at once (Yes! Start immediately!)*
- *Full-length tulle skirt worn over jeans*
- *Mismatch shoes for quirky, kooky look. (Or will look as though have dementia??)*
- *Fresh orchids tucked into belt as corsage*
- *Bracelet made of fresh orchids*
- *NB: Buy fresh orchids*

FOUR

By 3 p.m., I'm standing in a crowd of runners, formulating a plan for my new career. All I need to do is meet Sage Seymour, start chatting about clothes, offer to style her for an appearance ... and I'll have an in. It's all about who you know, and Sage Seymour is the perfect person to know. And this is the perfect event to meet her! I mean, I'm actually in her team! I have every reason to talk to her, and I can easily edge the conversation on to red-carpet trends while we're sprinting along together. I haven't seen her yet, but my eyes are swivelling around, and I'm poised for action as soon as I spot her.

A bell sounds, and all the runners start pressing more closely together. The cocktails I drank with Danny are starting to creep up on me, and I slightly regret that last Malibu Sunrise now ... but never mind. The endorphins will soon kick in.

It's quite a spectacle, this Ten Miler race. It starts at Dodger Stadium and it goes along Sunset and then on to Hollywood Boulevard. According to the welcome pack, the route 'passes many Hollywood landmarks', which is brilliant, because I'll be able to sightsee as I run! I've already checked in, and I can't believe how many people are doing it. Everywhere I look, I see runners limbering up and jogging and adjusting their shoe laces. Music is playing through loudspeakers and the sun is shining hazily through the clouds and there's a smell of sun-screen. And I'm part of it! I'm standing in the middle of Group One, about ten feet away from a massive great metal arch which is the start of the race, with a number taped to my chest (184) and a special chip in my shoe. Best of all, I'm wearing the fab team baseball cap which was waiting for me at the hotel desk. It's bright turquoise, with TEAM SAGE in white letters. I feel like I'm in the Olympics!

Yet again I scan the crowd, searching for another TEAM SAGE turquoise baseball cap, but the runners are too closely packed together to see much. She has to be here somewhere. I'll just have to find her when we start running.

As I'm doing a leg stretch I catch the eye of a wiry black girl limbering up beside me. She looks at my baseball cap and her eyes widen.

'You're in the Sage Seymour team?'

'Yes.' I try to sound casual. 'That's right. I'm with Sage. We'll be running together, and chatting, and . . . everything!'

'Wow. You must be good. So, what time are you hoping to make today?'

'Well.' I clear my throat. 'I expect I'll take about . . . um . . .'

I have no idea. Ten miles. How fast can I run ten miles? I'm not even sure how fast I can run one mile.

'I'm just hoping to improve my personal best,' I say at last.

'I hear you.' The girl stretches her arms over her head. 'What's your race strategy?'

Meet Sage Seymour, talk about clothes and wangle an invitation to her house, flashes through my mind.

'Just . . . run,' I say with a shrug. 'To the end. You know. As fast as I can.'

She stares at me blankly, then laughs. 'You're funny.'

The runners are clustering together even more tightly. There must be at least a thousand people, stretching back as far as the eye can see. And despite my jet lag, I feel a sudden burst of exhilaration as I bounce lightly in my new hi-tech shoes. Here I am! Running in a high-profile race in LA! It just shows what you can do if you put your mind to it. I'm about to take a photo of myself and send it to Suze when my phone rings and it's Mum. She always calls last thing at night, just to tell me that Minnie's got off to sleep OK.

'Hi!' I answer the phone in delight. 'Guess what I'm doing.'

'You're on a red carpet!' exclaims Mum excitedly.

Every time Mum phones, she asks if I'm on a red carpet. The truth is, not only have I not been on one, I haven't even *seen* one. Even worse: Luke had an invitation to a premiere last time we were here, and not only did he not go, he didn't even tell me about it until it was too late. A premiere!

This is why I can't rely on Luke to get me into anything cool. He has completely the opposite view of LA from me. All he's interested in is attending meetings and being on permanent BlackBerry call – i.e., business as usual. He says the work ethic in LA is something he really relates to. The work ethic. Who comes to LA for the work ethic?

'No, I'm running in a charity race. With Sage!'

Mum gasps. 'You're with Sage Seymour? Oh, Becky!'

'I'm not exactly with her right this second,' I admit. 'But I'm going to catch up with her while we're running. I've got a TEAM SAGE baseball cap,' I add proudly.

'Oh, love!'

'I know! I'll take a picture of it. Show Minnie. Is she OK? Fast asleep?'

'She's fine, fine!' says Mum breezily. 'All snuggled up in bed. So, who else have you met? Anyone famous?'

Lois Kellerton flashes through my mind.

No. Don't even think about it. I love my mum, but if you tell her anything, it's all over Oxshott in a nano-second.

'There are loads of celebs in the race,' I say vaguely. 'I think I just saw a guy from *Desperate Housewives*.' It could have been him, or it could have been a different guy, but Mum won't know.

A klaxon is sounding. Oh God. Is that the race starting?

'Mum, I have to go,' I say hastily. 'I'll call later. Bye!'

That *was* the start of the race. We're off. We're running. I'm running too! Feet and arms are blurring around me as the runners jostle for position and I breathlessly try to stay with them.

God, they're fast.

I mean, it's fine. I'm fast too. I'm totally keeping up with the others. My chest is already burning, but that's OK, because the endorphins will kick in, any minute.

The most important thing is: where's Sage?

As the crowd thins out, I'm able to get a better view of my fellow runners. I'm scanning the heads desperately for a turquoise baseball cap . . . She must be somewhere . . . I can't have missed her, surely . . .

There! I feel a burst of joyous adrenalin. She's right up at the front, of course. OK, time to make my move. I'll sprint up to her casually, gesture at my hat and say, 'I think we're on the same team.' And our close friendship will begin.

I've never really considered myself an athlete before, but as I charge forward, it's like some invisible force is powering me. I'm overtaking the wiry black girl! I'm on fire! I'm exhilarated! But still the turquoise cap is bobbing along ahead of me, tantalizingly out of reach, so I put on an extra spurt of energy. Somehow I succeed in drawing level with her. My face is boiling and my heart is hammering in my chest, but I manage to point at my hat and gasp, 'I think we're on the same team.'

The turquoise baseball cap turns . . . and it's not Sage Seymour. It's some girl with a pointy nose and brown hair who just gives me a blank look and ups her pace. She's not even wearing a TEAM SAGE cap, either, just a plain turquoise one. I'm so disconcerted I stop dead, and nearly get knocked over by a horde of runners.

'Jesus!'

'Out of the way!'

'One-eight-four, what are you *doing*?'

Hastily I move to one side and try to catch my breath. OK, so that wasn't Sage. But never mind. She'll be here somewhere. I just have to keep my eyes open for turquoise . . . turquoise . . . Yes! Over there!

With a fresh surge of adrenalin I plunge into the race again and chase after another turquoise baseball cap. But as I draw near, I can see already that it's not Sage. It's not even a girl. It's a skinny, Italian-looking guy.

Bloody hell. Panting hard, I head to a water station and take a sip of water, still desperately scanning the crowd of runners, refusing to give up. So I've had two near-misses. Never mind. I'll find her. I will. Wait, there's a flash of turquoise up ahead. That *must* be her . . .

An hour later, I feel like I've moved into a parallel universe. Is this 'The Zone'? It feels more like hell. My lungs are pumping like pistons; my face is sweaty; I have blisters on both feet; I want to die . . . and yet still I'm moving. It's as if some magic force is keeping me going. I keep seeing turquoise baseball caps in the crowd. I keep chasing them. I've approached one blonde girl four times now. But none of them is Sage. Where is she? Where *is* she?

And where are these bloody endorphins? I've been running for ages and haven't had a single one. It's all lies. Nor have I seen a single Hollywood landmark. Have we even passed any?

Oh God, I *have* to drink some water. I head to the next water stand, decorated with helium balloons. I grab one paper cup and pour the water over my head, then gulp at a second. There's a crowd of cheerleaders in red costumes doing a routine nearby, and I look at them enviously. Where do they get all that energy from? Maybe they have special springy cheerleaders' boots. Maybe if I had glittery pom-poms to shake, I'd run faster.

'Becky! Over here! Are you all right?' I straighten up, panting, and look around in a daze. Then I spot Luke on the other side of the barricade. He's holding a Ten Miler flag and gazing at me in alarm. 'Are you all right?' he repeats.

'Fine.' My voice comes out rasping. 'All good.'

'I thought I'd come along to support you.' He eyes me in amazement as I stagger towards him. 'You're making incredibly good time. I didn't realize you were so fit!'

'Oh.' I wipe my sweaty face. 'Right.' I hadn't even thought

about how quickly I was going. The whole race has been a blur of chasing turquoise baseball caps.

'Did you get my text?'

'Huh?'

'About Sage pulling out.'

I stare up at him blankly, the blood still pumping in my ears. Did he just say . . .

'She sends her apologies,' he adds.

'You mean . . . she's not in the race?' I manage. 'At all?'

I've been chasing all those turquoise baseball caps for *nothing*?

'A friend of hers decided to take a bunch of pals on a trip to Mexico,' says Luke. 'She and her whole team are on a plane as we speak.'

'The whole *team* have pulled out?' I'm trying to make sense of this. 'But they trained! They went to Arizona!'

'Maybe they did. But they pretty much move in a pack,' he says dryly. 'If Sage says, "Let's go to Mexico," they go to Mexico. Becky, I'm sorry. You must be disappointed.' He touches my shoulder. 'I know you only ran the race to meet Sage.'

His sympathy hits a nerve in me. Is that what he thinks? I mean, I know it's the truth, but it shouldn't be what he *thinks*. Husbands should think the best of their wives, as a matter of principle.

'I didn't "only run the race to meet Sage"!' I say, drawing myself up tall with an affronted expression. 'I did it because I love running and I wanted to support the charity. I hadn't even *thought* about whether Sage was in the race or not.'

'Ah.' Luke's face flickers. 'Well, then, bravo. Not much longer to go.'

As it hits me, my heart plummets. I haven't finished. Oh God. I can't run any more. I just can't do it.

'It's four miles more.' Luke is consulting a race map. 'You'll do that in no time!' he adds cheerfully.

Four miles? Four whole miles?

As I look at the road ahead, my legs feel wobbly. My feet are aching. Runners are still pounding by, but the thought of getting back into the fray fills me with dread. A guy in a turquoise baseball cap powers by, and I scowl at him. I'll be happy if I never see a turquoise baseball cap again.

'I'd better limber up before I start again,' I say, playing for time. 'My muscles are cold.'

I lift up my foot to do a quad stretch. I count very slowly up to thirty, and then do the other side. Then I flop down and let my head dangle in front of my knees for a couple of minutes. Mmm. This is nice. Maybe I'll stay here for a while.

'Becky?' Luke's voice penetrates my consciousness. 'Sweetheart, are you OK?'

'I'm stretching,' I inform him. I raise my head, stretch out my triceps, and then do a few yoga-type poses I've seen Suze do. 'Now I'd better hydrate,' I add. 'It's really important.'

I reach for a cup of water and sip it slowly, then fill another and hand it to a passing runner. I might as well be helpful, while I'm here. I fill a few more cups with water, ready to hand out, and straighten a stack of energy bars. There are empty wrappers everywhere, so I begin to gather them up and put them in the bin. Then I re-tie a couple of balloons which have come loose and adjust some streamers. Might as well make the stand look tidy.

I suddenly notice that the guy behind the water stand is staring at me as though I'm insane.

'What are you doing?' he says. 'Shouldn't you be running?'

I feel a bit indignant at his tone. I'm *helping* him. He could be more grateful.

'I'm on a stretch break,' I explain, and look up to see that Luke is surveying me quizzically.

'You must be pretty well stretched out,' he says. 'Are you going to start running again now?'

Honestly. All this pressure to *run* the whole time.

'I just need to . . .' I interlace my fingers and stretch them out. 'Mmm. I have a lot of tension there.'

'Lady, you're gonna miss the whole thing,' says the water-stand guy. He gestures at the road. 'That's the last bunch.'

49

It's true: the race is thinning out by now. Only the last few stragglers are left. The spectators are drifting away, too. The whole atmosphere is kind of melting away. I can't put it off any more.

'Right.' I try to sound positive. 'Well, I'll just quickly run those last four miles, then. Shouldn't take long. Great.' I take a deep breath. 'I'll just get going, then.'

'Or . . .' says Luke, and my head jerks up.

'Or what?'

'I was wondering, Becky. If you didn't mind slowing your pace to mine, maybe we could walk it? Together?'

'Walk it?'

He puts his hand over the barrier and clasps mine. By now, we're practically the only people around. Behind us, workmen are beginning to dismantle the barricades and pick up litter with special sticks.

'Not often we get a chance to walk in LA,' he adds. 'And we've got the street to ourselves.'

I want to expire with relief.

'Well, OK,' I say after a pause. 'I don't mind walking. Although obviously I would very much have *preferred* to run.'

'Obviously.' He shoots me an amused little grin, which I ignore. 'Shall we?'

We start to walk along, picking our way through the paper cups and energy-bar wrappers left everywhere. I tighten my fingers around his and he squeezes my hand back.

'Come this way.' Luke leads me to the right, off the street and on to the pavement, or sidewalk, as I must start calling it. 'You know where we are?'

'Hollywood? Los Angeles?' I look at him suspiciously. 'Is this a trick question?'

Luke makes no answer, just nods down at the 'sidewalk'. And suddenly I get it.

'Oh!' I look down with a beam. 'Oh my God!'

'I know.'

We're standing on the stars. The Hollywood Walk of Fame, which I've seen a million times on TV, but never for real. I feel as though Luke has put it there especially as a present for me, all shiny and pink.

'Edward Arnold!' I exclaim, reading a name and trying to sound reverent. 'Wow! Um . . .'

'No idea,' says Luke. 'Someone famous. Clearly.'

'Clearly.' I giggle. 'And who's Red Foley?'

'Bette Davis,' says Luke, pointing at another star. 'Will that do you?'

'Ooh! Bette Davis! Let me see!'

For a while I do nothing but dart backwards and forwards, looking for famous names. This is the most Hollywoody thing we've done yet, and I don't care that we're being total saddo tourists.

At last, we resume walking along, checking off famous names every now and again.

'I'm sorry about your job.' Luke squeezes my hand. 'That's bad luck.'

'Thanks.' I shrug. 'But, you know, I've been thinking about it, and maybe actually it's for the best. Bob Hope,' I add, pointing at his star.

'I agree!' says Luke with sudden eagerness. 'I didn't want to say so before – but do you really want to commit yourself to a job when we're only here for such a short time? This is a wonderful place to explore. I'd just enjoy the healthy outdoor lifestyle with Minnie. Go hiking in the hills, play on the beach . . .'

That is so Luke. First the work ethic, now the *healthy outdoor lifestyle*? What's he on about? I haven't come to LA for the 'healthy outdoor lifestyle', I've come for the 'celebrity-big-sunglasses-red-carpet lifestyle'.

'No, you don't understand. I've got an even better idea. I'm going to become a Hollywood stylist!'

As I look up for Luke's reaction, I'm taken aback. OK, so maybe I didn't expect him to shout, 'Go girl!' but nor did I expect *this*. His eyebrows are raised and furrowed at the same time. His mouth is turning down at the edges. I've been married to Luke so long, I know his expressions off by heart, and this one is number 3: *How do I break it to Becky that I hate this idea?* It's exactly the same expression he had when I suggested painting our bedroom purple. (I still say it would have been sexy.)

'What?' I demand. 'What?'

'It's a great idea . . .' he begins carefully.

'Stop it,' I say impatiently. 'What do you really think?'

'Becky, you know Sage only hired me as a consultant on a short-term basis. If this whole venture works out, maybe Brandon Communications will open a media arm here and maybe I'll fly back and forth. But I can't imagine we'll relocate permanently.'

'So?'

'So, what will you do if you establish a whole new career here?'

'I dunno,' I say impatiently. 'Work it out.'

This is just typical. Luke always lets practical plans get in the way of creative inspiration.

'It'll be a lot of hard graft,' he's saying now, 'a lot of banging on doors, a lot of disappointment . . .'

'You think I can't do it?' I say, affronted.

'My darling, I think you can do pretty much anything you put your mind to,' says Luke. 'However, I think to get into the world of Hollywood styling in three months will be, let's say, a challenge. But if you really want to—'

'I don't just want to, I'm *going* to.'

Luke sighs. 'Well then, of course I'll help. I'll ask around for some contacts, see what I can fix up—'

'I don't need your help!' I retort.

'Becky, don't be silly.'

'I'm not being silly,' I shoot back, feeling outraged. 'I don't want to rely on my husband. I'm an independent woman, you know.'

'But—'

'What, you think I can't break into Hollywood on my own? You just watch. Katharine Hepburn,' I add.

We walk on for a while in silence, not even bothering to say the names any more, and gradually I simmer down. Actually, Luke's help would have been quite useful. In fact, really useful. But it's too late now, I've said it. I'll have to find a way to do it on my own and show him.

My mind starts working hard. Sage is still my most obvious way in. I'm bound to meet her soon. And meanwhile, I can plan a few outfits for her. Maybe I'll even buy her an accessory or two, just like a personal stylist would. Yes. Brilliant. And if Sage doesn't work out . . . well, I have other contacts, don't I?

'You know, Luke, I do have my own resources,' I say grandly. 'I have worked at Barneys, remember. I am a bit connected, remember. In fact, I think you'll find I'm even better connected than you.'

And it's true! I met loads of Hollywood people when I worked at Barneys. At least three producers, and a music consultant, and a casting director. I'll contact all of them, and *someone* will be able to give me an entrée, and then—

Ooh, Lassie!

From: Laird, Nick
To: Brandon, Rebecca
Subject: Re: Hi Melanie, how are you?!

_____

Dear Mrs Brandon

I am replying to your email to Melanie Young. I'm sure that Melanie does remember you from her shopping appointments at Barneys and am glad you still recall 'how fab she looked in that Moschino pencil skirt'.

Unfortunately Melanie has recently given up producing, moved to a commune in Arkansas and, according to her farewell speech, 'never wants to hear the word "movie" again'. She will therefore be unable to help you launch yourself as a celebrity stylist, nor introduce you to Sarah Jessica Parker.

I wish you every luck with your endeavors in Hollywood.

Nick Laird

Head of Development
ABJ Pictures

From: Quinn, Sandi
To: Brandon, Rebecca
Subject: Re: Hi Rosaline, how are you?!

Dear Mrs Brandon

I am replying to your email on behalf of Rosaline DuFoy, in my role as Rosaline's counsellor.

Rosaline does indeed remember you from her shopping appointments at Barneys and recalls well the 'amazingly slimming pant suit' you found for her sister's wedding.

Unfortunately, during the toast at that wedding, her husband came out as gay. Rosaline has always – rightly or wrongly – blamed her 'androgynous clothes' for his switch in sexuality and is currently penning an autobiography entitled 'If only I'd worn a f***ing dress'. As the memories are still raw and painful, she would rather not meet with you.

However, I wish you every success in Hollywood.

Best,

Sandi Quinn
Director
Quinn Clinic for Marital Therapy

FIVE

How can Hollywood people all be so flaky? How?

As soon as I got back to the UK, I looked up all my old contacts and sent off a stack of emails. But I haven't got anything out of it: not a lunch, not a meeting, not a phone number. Every single one of my former customers who worked in film seems to have moved jobs or had a nervous breakdown or something. The only one left was Genna Douglas, who was a customer of mine at Barneys and had the hugest collection of backless dresses. But after getting no reply, I Googled her, and it turns out she left her job at Universal a year ago to start a beauty salon. She's invented some treatment involving electric currents and honey and has been sued twice by disgruntled patients but is 'actively seeking investors'. Hmm. Don't think I'll be pursuing that one.

I'm so disappointed. I thought I'd be *swimming* in contacts. I thought I'd be fixing up lunches at Spago and meetings with producers, and saying to Luke casually, 'Oh, are you going to be on the Paramount lot this afternoon? I'll see you there.'

Anyway. On the plus side, I still have Sage. A genuine, copper-bottomed, A-list contact. And I haven't been sitting around doing nothing. I've started working on some looks for her, and I really feel I'm tuning into her personality. Her *world*.

'So, look.' I spread a pale-blue brocade coat out on the bed for Suze to see. 'Isn't this fab?'

Suze is my oldest friend in the world, and we're lolling on her bed in Hampshire with gossip magazines, just like we used to in the old days when we shared a flat in Fulham. Except that in those days, it meant lolling on an old Indian bedspread covered in cigarette burns and smelling of joss sticks. Whereas today we're lolling on a massive, ancient four-poster bed, with silk drapes and tapestry and wooden panelling that apparently Charles I carved his name in once. Or do I mean Charles II? Some Charles or other, anyway.

Suze is eye-wateringly posh. She lives in a stately home and ever since her grandfather-in-law died she's called Lady Cleath-Stuart, which sounds quite terrifyingly grown-up to me. *Lady Cleath-Stuart* sounds like a ninety-year-old battle-axe swishing at people with a riding crop and barking, 'What? What?' Not that I would ever tell Suze this. Anyway, she's pretty much the opposite of that. She's tall and leggy with long blonde hair, which she's now chewing in an absent kind of way.

'Lovely!' she says, fingering the coat. 'Really gorgeous.'

'It's a great lightweight coat that Sage can just shrug on over jeans or whatever. It'll really suit the LA climate. And then she can wear flats or those boots I showed you before . . .'

'Amazing collar.' She touches the grey frayed velvet.

'I know,' I say triumphantly. 'I found it in this tiny boutique. The label's new. It's Danish. Now, look at this skirt.'

I produce a minute denim skirt with ribbon edging, but Suze is still surveying the coat, her brow crumpled.

'So you've bought this coat for Sage? And all these other things?'

'Exactly! That's the point of being a stylist. I found the skirt in a vintage shop in Santa Monica,' I add. 'The owner customizes all the clothes herself. Look at the buttons!'

Suze doesn't even seem to see the buttons. She reaches for a T-shirt, which would be perfect for Sage to wear when she's hanging out at a coffee shop with Jennifer Garner or somebody.

'But, Bex, isn't all this shopping costing you a lot of money?'

'Shopping?' I echo incredulously. 'Suze, it's not *shopping*. It's investing in my job. And I usually get a discount. Sometimes I even get things for free. I just have to tell them that I'm shopping for Sage Seymour, and bingo!'

It's amazing how excited shop owners get when you mention Sage Seymour. They practically throw clothes at you!

'But you're not shopping for Sage Seymour,' says Suze flatly.

I stare at her, perplexed. Hasn't she been following what I'm saying?

'Yes I am! Of course I am! These things aren't even my size!'

'But she hasn't asked you to. She doesn't even know who you are.'

I feel a twinge of resentment. Suze doesn't have to remind me. It's not my fault I have the crappest husband in the world who refuses to introduce me to his celebrity clients.

'She *will* know who I am, as soon as Luke introduces us,' I explain patiently. 'And then we'll get chatting, and I'll have all these looks ready for her and become her personal stylist. Suze, I'm building a whole new career!' I can see Suze is about to raise another objection, so I carry on hurriedly. 'And anyway, I'm going to get double the use out of these clothes, because you're going to wear them and I'm going to take your picture and I'm going to build up a portfolio.'

'Ooh.' Suze perks up. 'You want me to be your model?'

'Exactly.'

'Cool!' Suze starts looking at the clothes with more interest and reaches for the coat again. 'Let's start with this.' She puts on the coat and I start adjusting the collar. Suze is so beautiful and willowy, she looks great in anything, and I feel a fizz of excitement at the thought of building up a library of amazing pictures.

I've been totally inspired by reading about Nenita Dietz on the internet. When she moved to Hollywood twenty years ago, she didn't know anyone. But she wangled her way on to the set of *Love's Breezing*, and marched into the office of the Head of Wardrobe, and wouldn't leave until he'd looked at her portfolio. He was so impressed, he employed her immediately. And then the star, Mary-Jane Cheney, hired her as a personal stylist, and it all snowballed from there.

Well, I can do that, too. I just need to put together a portfolio, and get on a film set somehow.

Suze is now wearing the brocade coat, a beret and a pair of sunglasses and posing in front of the mirror.

'You look fab,' I say. 'Tomorrow I'll do your hair and make-up and we'll have a proper shoot.'

Suze comes back to the bed and starts rifling through a bag of skirts. 'These are nice, too.' She holds one up against herself and looks at the label. 'Oh, they're by Danny.'

'I phoned his office and they sent a whole bunch over,' I explain. 'They're from the new collection. You know, Sarah Jessica Parker's assistant asked especially to see a sneak preview?' I add. 'Danny told me himself.'

'Ooh, SJP!' Suze's head pops up. 'Is she in LA? Have you met her?'

'No,' I say, and Suze sighs.

'Haven't you met *anyone* famous?'

This is what everyone has been asking me since I got back. Mum, Dad, our neighbours Janice and Martin, *everyone*. I'm tired of saying, 'No, I haven't met anyone famous.' And the truth is, I did meet someone famous, didn't I? I mean, I know I promised to keep it a secret. But Suze is my best friend. Telling a best friend doesn't count.

'Suze,' I say, lowering my voice. 'If I tell you something, you can't tell a soul. Not Tarkie, not anyone. I'm serious.'

'I promise,' she says, her eyes wide. 'What is it?'

'I met Lois Kellerton.'

'Lois *Kellerton*?' She sits straight up. 'Oh my God! You never told me that!'

'I'm telling you now! But I didn't just meet her . . .'

Suze is the best person to share stuff with. As I tell her about seeing Lois Kellerton shoplifting, and about chasing her down the street, she gasps and puts her hand to her mouth and says 'No *way*' several times.

'. . . and I promised not to tell anyone,' I conclude.

'Well, I won't blab,' says Suze at once. 'Anyway, who would I tell? The children? The sheep? Tarkie?'

We both start giggling. Tarkie probably has no idea who Lois Kellerton is, even.

'But it's so weird,' Suze adds, her brow creased in thought. 'I can't believe it. Why would a big movie star like that steal socks?'

'I haven't told you everything yet,' I say, and reach in my pocket. 'Look what arrived at the hotel.'

I still can't believe this happened. It was on the last day of our trip, when I was having a small private word with the front desk about the minibar bill. (I didn't necessarily want Luke seeing how many Toblerones I'd eaten.) The concierge caught sight of me and said, 'Ah, Mrs Brandon, this has just arrived for you.'

It was a smart white package, and inside was a small silver box engraved with three words: *Thank you Becky*. There was no note. But I instantly knew who it was from. She must have tracked me down. Or I guess her people did.

Now I hand it over to Suze, who turns it over in her fingers wonderingly.

'Wow,' she says at last. 'It's beautiful.'

'I know.'

'So this is, like, a bribe.'

Bribe?

'It's not a bribe!' I say, stung.

'No,' Suze backtracks at once. 'Sorry. I didn't mean "bribe". I meant . . .'

'It's a thank-you,' I say defensively. 'Look. It says "Thank you".'

'Exactly! That's what I meant. A thank-you.' She nods several times, but now the word *bribe* is circling around my brain.

'Anyway, what was she like?' Suze demands. 'What did she look like? What did she say?'

'Just thin, really. Stressed-out-looking. I hardly spoke to her.'

'She's not in good shape, you know,' Suze says. 'Apparently

her latest movie is beset with problems. It's millions over budget and the buzz isn't good. She's taken on the role of producer for the first time, but she's bitten off more than she can chew.'

'Really?'

'Oh yes.' Suze nods knowledgeably. 'Insiders on set claim the star's high-handed approach has made her enemies among the crew. No wonder she's stressed out.'

I stare at Suze in astonishment. Has she memorized every single gossip magazine?

'Suze, how do you *know* all this stuff? Have you been watching *Camberly* on cable again?' I say severely.

Camberly is the hottest show in the States right now. Everyone is saying Camberly is the new Oprah, and her interviews get huge press every week, and they show them on E4 in England. Suze twisted her ankle a couple of weeks ago and she got totally addicted, especially to the gossip segment.

'Well, I've got to do something while my best friend is in LA!' says Suze, suddenly sounding disconsolate. 'If I can't go there, at least I can watch interviews about it.' She gives a sudden gusty sigh. 'Oh Bex, I can't believe you're going to be in Hollywood and meet movie stars all the time and I'm stuck here. I'm so envious!'

'*Envious?*' I stare at her. 'How can you be envious of me? You live in this place! It's fantastic!'

Suze's husband, Tarquin, is even grander than Suze, and when his grandfather died, they inherited this monster house, Letherby Hall. It's seriously vast. They have guided tours and a ha-ha and everything. (To be honest, I'm still not sure which bit is the ha-ha. Maybe one of the twiddly bits on the roof?)

'But it isn't sunny,' objects Suze. 'And there aren't any movie stars. And all we do is have endless meetings about repairing eighteenth-century mouldings. I want to go to Hollywood. You know, I always wanted to be an actress. I played Juliet at drama school.' She sighs again. 'I played Blanche Dubois. And now look at me.'

I'm always very tactful about Suze's 'drama school'. I mean, it wasn't exactly RADA. It was the kind where your father pays huge fees and you spend the spring term at the school skiing chalet in Switzerland and no one actually goes into acting because they've got a family business to inherit or something. But still, I do feel for her. She is at a bit of a loose end, knocking around in this massive house.

'Well, come out!' I say excitedly. 'Go on, Suze, come to LA! Have a little holiday. We'd have such a laugh.'

'Oh . . .' Her face is torn a million ways. I can see *exactly* what she's thinking. (This is why she'd make a brilliant actress, in fact.)

'Tarkie can come too,' I say, to forestall her objections. 'And the children.'

'Maybe,' she says hesitantly. 'Except we're supposed to be focusing on business expansion this year. You know we're starting weddings? And Tarkie wants to create a maze, and we're revamping the tea rooms . . .'

'You can still have a holiday!'

'I don't know.' She looks doubtful. 'You know the pressure he feels.'

I nod sympathetically. I do actually feel for old Tarkie. It's quite a burden, inheriting a stately home, with your whole family looking on beadily to see if you manage it properly. Apparently, every Lord Cleath-Stuart has added something special to Letherby Hall, through all the generations, like an east wing, or a chapel, or a topiary garden.

In fact, that's why we're all here today. Tarkie's launching his first major addition to the house. It's called 'The Surge' and it's a fountain. It's going to be the highest fountain in the whole county and will be a big tourist attraction. Apparently he had the idea when he was ten, and drew it in his Latin book, and kept it ever since. And now he's built it!

Hundreds of people are coming to watch it being switched on and the local TV station has interviewed him, and everyone is saying this could be the making of Letherby Hall. Suze says she hasn't seen Tarkie this nervous since he competed in the junior national dressage when they were both children. That time he mucked up his half-pass (which is apparently bad) and his father, who lives for horses, nearly disowned him as a result. So let's hope things go better this time.

'I'll work on Tarkie.' Suze swings her legs off the bed. 'C'mon, Bex. We'd better go.'

The only disadvantage of living in a house like this is it takes you about six hours just to get from the bedroom to the garden. We walk through the Long Gallery (lots of ancient portraits) and the East Hall (lots of ancient suits of armour) and cut across the massive Great Hall. There we pause, and breathe in the musty, woody aroma. Suze can burn as many Diptyque candles as she likes, but this room will always smell of Old House.

'It was amazing, wasn't it?' says Suze, reading my thoughts.

'Spectacular.' I sigh.

We're talking about the birthday party that I threw for Luke, right here, what seems like no time ago. As if on cue, we both lift our eyes to the tiny first-floor balcony where Luke's mother, Elinor, stood hidden, watching the proceedings. Luke never knew she was there, nor that she basically funded and helped to arrange the whole thing. She's sworn me to secrecy, which makes me want to scream with frustration. If only he *knew* that she'd paid for his party. If only he *knew* how much she'd done for him.

To call Luke's relationship with his mother 'love–hate' would be an understatement. It's 'adore–loathe'. It's 'worship–despise'. At the moment we're on 'despise' and nothing I can say will shift his opinion. Whereas I've quite come round to her, even if she is the snootiest woman in the world.

'Have you seen her?' asks Suze.

I shake my head. 'Not since then.'

Suze looks troubled as she gazes around the room. 'What about if you just *told* him?' she says suddenly.

I know Suze hates the secrecy as much as I do, because Luke has totally got the wrong end of the stick and thinks she and Tarkie paid for the party.

'I can't. I promised. She's got this whole thing about not wanting to buy his love.'

'Throwing someone a party isn't buying their love,' protests Suze. 'I think she's all wrong. I think he'd be touched. It's so stupid!' she says with sudden vehemence. 'It's such a waste! Think of all the time you could spend together, and with Minnie too . . .'

'Minnie misses her,' I admit. 'She keeps saying, "Where Lady?" But if Luke even knew they'd been seeing each other, he'd flip out.'

'*Families.*' Suze shakes her head. 'They're just the end. Poor old Tarkie's in a total tizz about the fountain, just because his father's here. I said to him, "If your dad can't say anything positive, he should have stayed in Scotland!"' She sounds so fierce, I want to laugh. 'We must hurry,' she adds, glancing at her watch. 'The countdown will have begun!'

Suze's 'garden' is basically an enormous great park. There are huge lawns and acres of topiary and a famous rose garden and loads of special plants which I now can't remember. (I'm definitely going on the proper tour one day.)

We head down from the big gravelled terrace to find that crowds are already gathering on the lawn and setting up deck chairs among the trees. Music is playing from loudspeakers, waitresses are circling with glasses of wine, and a massive electronic countdown board reads *16:43*. There's a rectangular lake, directly in front of the house, and that's where The Surge is. I've only seen an artist's impression of it, but it's really pretty. It shoots straight up about a zillion feet and then falls down in a graceful arc. Then it swings backwards and forwards, and then at the end it shoots little droplets into the air. It's so clever, and there are going to be coloured lights in the evenings.

As we get near, we find a cordoned-off area for VIP visitors, where my mum and dad have commandeered a prime position, along with our neighbours Janice and Martin.

'Becky!' exclaims Mum. 'Just in time!'

'Becky! We've missed you!' Janice gives me a hug. 'How was LA?'

'Great, thanks!'

'Really, love?' Janice clicks her tongue disbelievingly, as though I'm putting a brave face on some personal tragedy. 'But the people. All those plastic faces and whale pouts.'

'Do you mean trout pouts?'

'And drugs,' puts in Martin ponderously.

'Exactly!'

'You need to be careful, Becky,' he adds. 'Don't let them suck you into their way of thinking.'

'Unhappiest city on the planet,' agrees Janice. 'It said so in the paper.'

They're both staring at me mournfully, as though I'm about to be carted off to a penal colony on Mars.

'It's a brilliant city,' I say defiantly. 'And we can't wait to get there.'

'Well, maybe you'll see Jess,' says Janice, as though this is the only possible ray of light. 'How far's Chile from LA?'

'It's . . .' I try to sound knowledgeable. 'Not far. Same general area.'

My half-sister Jess is married to Janice and Martin's son Tom, and they're out in Chile, where they're planning to adopt a little boy. Poor Janice is trying to wait patiently, but apparently it could be a year before they come back.

'Don't listen to them, love,' Dad chimes in cheerfully. 'LA is a fine city. I still remember the glint of the Cadillacs. The surf on the sand. And the ice-cream sundaes. Look out for those, Becky.'

'Right.' I nod patiently. 'Ice-cream sundaes.'

Dad spent a summer driving around California before he got married, so his version of LA is basically from 1972. There's no point saying, 'No one eats ice-cream sundaes any more, it's all about flavoured fro-yo.'

'In fact, Becky,' Dad adds, 'I've got a couple of favours to ask you.' He draws me to one side, away from the others, and I look up at him curiously.

Dad's aged a bit recently. His face is craggier and there are little white hairs tufting out of his neck. Although he can still vault over a gate quite athletically. I know this because he was showing off to Minnie earlier today in one of Suze's fields, while Mum cried out, 'Graham, stop! You'll do yourself an injury! You'll break a metatarsal!' (Mum has recently found a new daytime TV show, *Doctor's Surgery Live*, which means that she now thinks she's an expert on all things medical and keeps dropping words like 'platelets' and 'lipoproteins' into the conversation even when we're just talking about what to have for supper.)

'What is it, Dad?'

'Well, the first thing is this.' He takes from his breast pocket a small paper bag and pulls out an ancient autograph book with a picture of a Cadillac on the front and *California* in white swirly writing. 'Remember this?'

'Of course!'

Dad's autograph book is a family tradition. It gets pulled out every Christmas and we all politely listen as he tells us about all the signatures. They're mostly autographs of obscure TV stars from American shows that no one's ever heard of, but Dad thinks they're famous, so that's all that matters.

'Ronald "Rocky" Webster,' he's saying now, turning the pages fondly. 'He was a big star then. And Maria Pojes. You should have heard her sing.'

'Right.' I nod politely, even though I've heard these names a million times and they still mean nothing to me.

'It was my friend Corey who spotted Maria Pojes, drinking in a hotel bar,' Dad's saying. 'Our first night in LA. He dragged me over, offered to buy her a drink . . .' He laughs reminiscently. 'She wouldn't accept it, of course. But she was sweet to us. Signed our books.'

'Wow.' I nod again. 'Fantastic.'

'And so . . .' To my surprise, Dad presses the open autograph book into my hand. 'Over to you, Becky. Fill her up with some new blood.'

'What?' I stare at him. 'Dad, I can't take this!'

'Half the book's empty.' He points at the blank pages. 'You're off to Hollywood. Finish the collection.'

I look at it nervously. 'But what if I lose it or something?'

'You won't lose it. But you'll have adventures.' Dad's face flickers oddly. 'Oh, Becky, love, I am envious. I've never known anything like those adventures I had in California.'

'Like the rodeo?' I say. I've heard that story a zillion times.

'That.' He nods. 'And ... other things.' He pats my hand, twinkling. 'Get me John Travolta's signature. I'd like that.'

'What's the other favour?' I say, putting the autograph book carefully into my bag.

'Just a small thing.' He reaches into his pocket and produces a slip of paper. 'Look up my old friend Brent. He always lived in Los Angeles. This is his old address. See if you can track him down. Say hello from me.'

'OK.' I look at the name: *Brent Lewis*. There's an address in Sherman Oaks, and a phone number. 'Why don't you call him up?' I suggest. 'Or text him? Or Skype! It's easy.'

As I say the word 'Skype' I can see Dad recoiling. We once tried to Skype Jess in Chile and it wasn't exactly a resounding success. The picture kept freezing, so we gave up. But then the sound suddenly came back on and we could hear Jess and Tom having a row about Janice while they made their supper. It was all a bit embarrassing.

'No, you go and say hello,' says Dad. 'If he wants to, we can take it from there. Like I say, it's been a long time. He may not be interested.'

I really don't get the older generation. They're so *reticent*. If it were me getting in touch with my old friend from all those years ago, I'd be sending them a text instantly: **Hi! Wow, it's been decades! How did THAT happen?** Or I'd track them down on Facebook. But Dad and Mum just aren't into it.

'Fine,' I say, and put the piece of paper into my bag, too. 'What about your other two friends?'

'Corey and Raymond?' He shakes his head. 'They live too far away. Las Vegas, Corey is. I think Raymond's in Arizona somewhere. I've stayed in touch with them . . . at least, I have in a way. But Brent just disappeared.'

'Shame you didn't have Facebook back then.'

'Indeed.' He nods.

'Oh, thank you so much! They're a new present from my husband.' Mum's voice rises above the hubbub and I turn to look. Some lady I don't recognize is admiring her pearls, and Mum is preening in delight. 'Yes, lovely, aren't they?'

I grin at Dad, who winks back. Mum was so thrilled with her pearls. They're antique, from 1895, with a ruby clasp set in diamonds. (I helped her go shopping for them, so I know all the details.) Dad's BB was bigger than usual this year, so we all went a bit mad.

BB is our family shorthand for 'Big Bonus'. Dad worked in insurance for years, and now he's retired. But he still does consulting work, and it's amazingly well paid. He goes off a few times a year in a suit, and then once a year he receives a bonus cheque and we always get a treat. This year it was particularly good, because Mum got her pearls, and he bought me an Alexis Bittar necklace and Minnie a new dolls' house. Even Luke got a beautiful pair of cufflinks.

Luke always says to me that Dad must have some sort of niche, specialist knowledge that is really valuable, because he commands such high fees. But he's so modest about it. You'd never know.

'My clever husband.' Mum kisses Dad fondly.

'You look beautiful, my love!' Dad beams back. Dad bought himself a new tweed jacket with his share of the BB, and he looks really good in it. 'Now, where's this famous fountain?'

A few feet away, Tarquin is being interviewed for the TV. Poor Tarkie. He's not cut out to be a media star. He's wearing a checked shirt that makes his neck look bonier than ever, and he keeps wringing his hands as he speaks.

'Ahm,' he keeps saying. 'Ahm, we wanted to . . . ahm . . . enhance the house . . .'

'Bloody stupid idea,' comes a gruff voice behind me.

Oh God, it's Tarkie's dad, the Earl of Whatsit, stalking up. (I can never remember where he's earl of. Somewhere Scottish, I think.) He's tall and lanky with thin, greying hair and an Aran jersey, just like Tarkie wears. I've never spoken to him properly, but he's always seemed pretty scary. Now he's glowering at the lake and jabbing a weather-beaten finger at it. 'I said to the boy, that view's been unspoiled for three hundred years. Why on earth would you want to go messing with it?'

'They're going to do fireworks on the lake in winter,' I say, wanting to stand up for Tarkie. 'I think it will be beautiful!'

The earl gives me a withering look and turns his attention to a plate of canapés being offered to him. 'What's this?'

'Sushi, sir,' says the waitress.

'*Sushi?*' He peers at her with bloodshot eyes. 'What?'

'Rice and raw salmon, sir. Japanese.'

'Bloody stupid idea.'

To my relief he stalks off again, and I'm about to take a piece of sushi myself, when I hear a familiar, ear-splitting noise.

'Please! Pleeeease!'

Oh God. It's Minnie.

For a long time, my daughter's favourite word was 'mine'. Now, after intensive training, we've got her on to the word 'please'. Which you'd think would be an improvement.

I swivel around wildly, and finally spot Minnie. She's balanced on a stone bench, tussling with Suze's son Wilfrid over a red plastic truck.

'Pleeease!' she's yelling crossly. 'Pleeease!' Now, to my horror, she starts hitting Wilfrid with the truck, yelling with each blow, 'Please! Please! Please!'

The trouble is, Minnie hasn't really absorbed the *spirit* of the word 'please'.

'Minnie!' I exclaim in horror, and run towards her across the lawn. 'Give the truck to Wilfie.' Luke is coming towards her too, and we exchange wry looks.

'Please truck! Pleeease!' she cries, clutching it harder. A few people gathered around start to laugh, and Minnie beams at them. She is such a show-off, but she's so adorable with it, it's hard to stay cross.

'Hey, Becky,' says a cheerful voice behind me, and I turn to see Ellie, who is Suze's nanny and absolutely brilliant. (There's also Nanny, who looked after Tarkie when he was little and has never left. But she just potters around and tells people to wear vests.) 'I'm taking the other children to watch from the steps over there.' She points at a bank on the other side of the lake. 'They'll get a better view. Does Minnie want to come?'

'Oh thanks,' I say gratefully. 'Minnie, if you want to go to the steps with the others, you have to give the truck to Wilfie.'

'Steps?' Minnie pauses at this new word.

'Yes! Steps! *Exciting* steps.' I grab the truck from her and give it back to Wilfie. 'Go with Ellie, sweetheart. Hey, Tarquin!' I call, as I see him hurrying by. 'This all looks spectacular.'

'Yes.' Tarquin seems a bit desperate. 'Well, I hope so. There's a water-pressure problem. Whole area's affected. Terrible timing for us.'

'Oh no!'

'Turn it *up*,' Tarkie says feverishly into his walkie-talkie. 'Whatever it takes! We don't want a feeble little gush, we want a spectacle!' He looks up at us and grimaces. 'Fountains are trickier blighters than I realized.'

'I'm sure it'll be great,' Luke says reassuringly. 'It's a marvellous idea.'

'Well, I hope so.' Tarkie wipes his face, then checks the countdown clock, which reads *4.58.* 'Crikey. I must go.'

The crowd is getting bigger and there are now two local TV-news crews, interviewing people. Luke takes a couple of glasses of wine and hands me one, and we clink glasses. As we near the cordoned-off VIP area, I can see Suze talking animatedly to Tarquin's business manager, Angus.

'Tarkie must surely have business interests in the States,' she's saying. 'I'm certain he needs to do a trip out there. Don't you agree?'

'It's really not necessary, Lady Cleath-Stuart,' Angus says, looking surprised. 'All the US investments are taken care of.'

'Do we have any investments in California?' persists Suze. 'Like, an orange grove or something? Because I think we should visit them. I'll go, if you like.' She looks over at me and winks, and I beam back. Go Suze!

The earl and countess are making their way to the front of the crowd now, forging a path with their shooting sticks and staring critically at the lake.

'If he wanted to build something,' the earl is saying, 'what's wrong with a folly? Tuck it away somewhere. But a fountain? Bloody stupid idea.'

I stare at him angrily. How dare they come along and be so critical?

'I disagree,' I say coolly. 'I believe this fountain will be a major landmark in the country for centuries to come.'

'Oh, you do, do you?' He fixes his baleful gaze on me and I lift my chin. I'm not afraid of some old earl.

'Yes,' I say defiantly. 'Today will be unforgettable. You'll see.'

'Sixty! Fifty-nine!' The loudspeaker guy starts chanting, and I feel a sudden rush of excitement. At last! Tarkie's fountain! I clutch Suze's hand and she beams back excitedly.

'Twenty-three . . . twenty two . . .' The whole crowd is chanting by now.

'Where's Tarkie?' I say over the noise. 'He should be here to enjoy it!'

Suze shrugs. 'Must be with the technical guys.'

'Five . . . four . . . three . . . two . . . one . . . Ladies and gentlemen . . . The Surge!'

A roar of cheers breaks out, as the fountain spurts up from the middle of the lake, and hits the height of . . .

Oh. OK. Well, it's about five feet. It's not *that* high for a fountain called The Surge. But maybe it'll go higher?

Sure enough, it slowly rises up to about twelve feet, and there's renewed cheering from the crowd. But as I look at Suze, she seems horrified.

'Something's gone wrong!' she exclaims. 'It should be about five times that height.'

The water falls back down; then, as though with a massive effort, pushes itself up to about fifteen feet. It drops a little, then rises again.

'Is that it?' the earl is saying contemptuously. 'Could do better myself with a hose. What did I tell you, Marjorie?'

Now there's as much laughing in the crowd as there is cheering. Every time the fountain lifts, there's an outburst of cheering, and every time it drops down, everyone says, 'Aaah!'

'It's the water pressure,' I say, suddenly remembering. 'Tarkie said there was a problem.'

'He'll be devastated.' Suze's eyes are suddenly bright with tears. 'I can't believe it. I mean, look at it. It's pathetic!'

'No it's not!' I say at once. 'It's brilliant. It's . . . subtle.'

The truth is, it does look pathetic.

But then suddenly there's an almightly *Bang!* and a stream of water surges right up into the air, what seems like a hundred feet.

'There you are!' I yell, and clutch Suze in excitement. 'It's working! It's amazing! It's fantastic! It's . . . aah—' I break off with a strangled yell.

Something's gone wrong. I don't know what. But this isn't right.

A mass of water is falling at speed towards us, like a water cannon. We stare, transfixed – then it splats all over three people behind me, and they start screaming. A moment later, the fountain fires another waterbomb into the air, and we all start holding our hands above our heads. Another moment later and there's another *splat* and two more people are drenched.

'Minnie!' I call anxiously, waving my arms. 'Get away!' But Ellie is already shepherding the children back up the steps.

'Women and children to safety!' the earl is thundering. 'Abandon ship!'

It's mayhem. People are running in all directions, trying to dodge the falling water. I manage to get up the slippery bank, then suddenly see Tarkie, standing apart from the crowd, his shirt soaked.

'Off! *Off!*' he's shouting into his walkie-talkie. 'Turn everything off!'

Poor Tarkie. He looks stricken. He looks like he might cry.
I'm about to go and give him a hug, when Suze comes running
up, her eyes glowing with sympathy.

'Tarkie, never mind.' She throws her arms around him. 'All
the best inventions have glitches at first.'

Tarkie doesn't reply. He looks too devastated to speak.

'It's not the end of the world,' Suze tries again. 'It's just one
fountain. And the idea is still brilliant.'

'Brilliant? Catastrophe, more like.' The earl is stepping forward over the puddles. 'Waste of time and money. How much
did this fiasco cost, Tarquin?' He's jabbing with his shooting
stick as he talks. I feel like jabbing *him*. 'Thought your fountain
was supposed to entertain the troops, not drown them!' He
gives a short, sarcastic laugh, but no one else joins in. 'And
now that you've bankrupted the place and made us a laughing
stock, maybe you'd like to take a few lessons in running a
historic house *properly*? What?'

I glance at Tarquin and flinch. He's turned puce with
humiliation and his hands are nervously rubbing against each
other. My chest starts heaving with indignation. His father is
awful. He's a bully. In fact, I'm drawing breath to tell him so,
when a voice suddenly chimes in.

'Now, now.' My head jerks up in surprise: it's Dad, pushing
his way through the throng, wiping his dripping forehead.
'Leave the boy alone. All great projects have stumbling blocks
along the way. Bill Gates's first company failed completely, and
look where he is now!' Dad has reached Tarquin now and pats
him kindly on the arm. 'You had a technical hitch. It's not the
end of the world. And I think we can all see, this is going to be
a fine sight when the details are perfected. Well done to
Tarquin and all the Surge team.'

With deliberate resolve, Dad starts to applaud, and after a
few seconds, the crowd joins in. There are even a few
'Whoo-hoos!'

Tarquin is gazing at Dad with something close to adoration.

The earl has retreated, looking all cross and left out, which is no surprise, as everyone is totally ignoring him. On impulse I hurry forward and give Dad a hug, nearly spilling my wine as I do so.

'Dad, you're a star,' I say. 'And Tarkie, listen, the fountain's going to be amazing. It's just teething troubles!'

'Exactly!' echoes Suze. 'It's just teething troubles.'

'You're very kind.' Tarquin gives a heavy sigh. He still looks fairly suicidal, and I exchange anxious looks with Suze. Poor Tarkie. He's worked so hard, for months. He's lived and breathed his precious fountain. And whatever Dad says, this is a huge humiliation. I can see both TV crews still filming and I just know this is going to be the comedy 'And finally . . .' piece on the news.

'Darling, I think we need a break,' Suze says at last. 'Clear our minds and have a rest.'

'A break?' Tarquin looks uncertain. 'What sort of break?'

'A holiday! Some time away from Letherby Hall, the fountain, all the family pressure . . .' Suze flashes a mutinous glare at the earl. 'Angus says we need to make a trip to LA, to check on our investments. He recommends a trip to California as soon as we can. I think we should *definitely* go.'

PLEASEGIVEGENEROUSLY.COM

Give to the world . . . share with the world . . . enhance the world . . .

YOU HAVE REACHED THE PLEDGE PAGE OF:

DANNY KOVITZ

Personal message from Danny Kovitz

Dear Friends

I'm inspired to be writing to you in this, my year of 'giving back', of 'challenging myself', of 'taking myself to a whole new place'.

This year I will undergo a series of endeavors designed to test myself to the limit and raise funds for a number of very deserving causes. (See Danny's Charities.)

I will undertake the feat of completing all the following challenges **in the space of one year**. I know!! It's quite an undertaking. But it means the world to me to achieve this. Please follow the links and pledge generously, my darling, wonderful friends.

    Greenland Ice Sheet Expedition
    IRONMAN (Lake Tahoe)
    IRONMAN (Florida)
    Marathon des Sables (Sahara Desert)
    Yak Attack (mountain bike race in Himalayas)

Training is going well so far, and my trainer, Diederik, is SO pleased with my progress. (In case you're interested, you can look at Diederik on his site Diederiknyctrainer.com. The pictures of him doing bench presses in the tight blue shorts are to DIE for . . .)

I'll keep you up to date with my journey. Next stop Greenland!!! Love you all.

Danny xxx

SIX

It's two weeks later. And I live in Hollywood. I, Becky Brandon, née Bloomwood, live in Hollywood. *I live in Hollywood!* I keep saying it out loud to myself, to see if it feels any more real. But it still feels like I'm saying, 'I live in fairyland.'

The house that we're renting in the Hollywood Hills is made mostly of glass, and has so many bathrooms, I'm not sure what we're supposed to do with all of them. *And* there's a walk-in wardrobe, *and* an outdoor kitchen. And a pool! And a pool guy! (He comes with the house and he's fifty-three with a paunch, sadly.)

The most amazing thing is the views. Every night we sit on our balcony and look at all the twinkling lights of Hollywood, and I feel as if we're in a dream. It's a weird place, LA. I can't quite get a grip on it. It's not like European cities, where you get to the centre and think, Ah yes, *here* I am in Milan/Amsterdam/Rome. In LA you drive around endless great big roads and you peer out of the windows and think, 'Are we there yet?'

Also, the neighbours are not very neighbourly. You don't *see* anyone. People don't peep over their fences and chat. They just drive in and out of their electronic gates, and by the time

76

you've chased after them, shouting, 'Hi! My name's Becky! D'you want a cup of—' they've gone.

We have met one neighbour, who's a plastic surgeon called Eli. He seemed very friendly, and we had a nice chat about rental prices and how he specializes in 'micro-lifts'. But all the while, he was eyeing me up with this critical stare. I'm sure he was working out what he'd do to me if he had me on the operating table. And apart from him, I haven't met anyone else in the street yet.

Anyway. Never mind. I *will* meet people. Of course I will.

I step into a pair of raffia wedges, toss my hair back and survey my reflection in our massive hall mirror. It rests on top of a huge carved chest, and there are two monster armchairs opposite on the Mexican-tiled floor. Everything in this house is massive: the squashy L-shaped sofa in the living room, which seats about ten; the four-poster bed in the master bedroom which Luke and I practically get lost in; the vast, separate kitchen with its three ovens and vaulted brick ceiling. Even all the doors are huge, studded, Mediterranean-looking affairs, made of reclaimed wood and with working locks. I've removed all the keys, though they're picturesque. (Minnie and keys *really* don't mix.) It is a gorgeous house, I have to say.

But today my priority is not the house, it's my outfit. I focus on it intently, searching for flaws. I haven't felt so jittery about my look for ages. OK, let's do a rundown. Top: Alice + Olivia. Jeans: J Brand. Tassled bag: Danny Kovitz. Cool hair-slidey thing: found at vintage market. I try a few poses, walking back and forth. I think I look good, but do I *look good for LA*? I reach for a pair of Oakleys and try them on. Then I try a pair of over-sized Tom Ford sunglasses instead. Hmm. Not sure. Fabulous statement . . . or too much?

My stomach is swooping with nerves, and the reason is, today is a huge day: I'm taking Minnie to her pre-school. It's called the Little Leaf Pre-School, and we're very lucky to have got a place. Apparently several celebrity kids go there, so I'm *definitely* volunteering for the PTA. Imagine if I got in with the in-crowd. Imagine if I got to organize the school fête with

Courtney Cox or someone! I mean, it's possible, isn't it? And then she'd introduce me to all the *Friends* cast . . . maybe we'd go out on a boat or something amazing—

'Becky?' Luke's voice breaks into my thoughts and he comes striding into the hall. 'I was just looking under the bed—'

'Oh, hi,' I interrupt him urgently. 'Which sunglasses shall I wear?'

Luke looks blank as I demonstrate first the Oakleys, then the Tom Fords, and then a pair of tortoiseshell Top Shop ones which are totally fab and only cost £15, so I bought three pairs.

'It hardly matters,' he says. 'It's just the school run.'

I blink at him in astonishment. Just the school run? *Just the school run?* Doesn't he read *US Weekly*? Everyone knows the school run is the thing! It's where the paparazzi snap celebrities acting like normal parents. It's where people rock their casual looks. Even in London, all the mothers look one another up and down and dandle their bags on their arms in a showy-offy way. So how much more pressured will it be in LA, where they all have perfect teeth and abs, and half of them are genuine celebs?

I'm going for the Oakleys, I decide, and slide them on. Minnie comes running into the hall, and I take her hand to survey our reflection in the mirror. She's in a cute little yellow sundress and white sunglasses and her ponytail is held back with an adorable bumble-bee. I think we'll pass. We *look* like an LA mother and daughter.

'All set?' I say to Minnie. 'You're going to have such a lovely time at pre-school! You'll play games, and maybe make lovely cupcakes with sprinkles on . . .'

'Becky.' Luke tries again. 'I was just looking under the bed and I found this.' He holds up a garment carrier. 'Is it yours? What's it doing there?'

'Oh.'

I adjust Minnie's ponytail, playing for time. Damn. Why is he looking under the bed? He's a busy LA mover and shaker. How does he have time to look under beds?

'It's for Sage,' I say at last.

'For *Sage*? You've bought Sage a full-length fake-fur coat?' He stares at me in astonishment.

Honestly, he hasn't even looked at it properly. It's not full-length, it's to mid-thigh.

'I think it'll suit her,' I explain. 'It'll go with her hair colour. It's a really different look for her.'

Luke appears absolutely baffled. 'But why are you buying her clothes? You don't even know her.'

'I don't know her *yet*,' I correct him. 'But you are going to introduce us, aren't you?'

'Well, yes, at some point.'

'So! You know I want to get into styling, and Sage would be the perfect client. So I've been putting some looks together for her. That's all.'

'Wait a minute.' Luke's face changes. 'There were some other bags under the bed, too. Don't tell me—'

I curse myself silently. I should never, ever put anything under the bed.

'Is that all shopping for Sage?'

He looks so aghast, I feel defensive. First Suze, now Luke. Don't they understand anything about setting up a business? Don't they understand that to be a clothes stylist you need clothes? They wouldn't expect me to be a tennis player and not have a tennis racket.

'It's not "shopping"! It's essential business expenses. It's like you buying paperclips. Or photocopiers. Anyway, I've used all those clothes for my portfolio, too,' I add robustly. 'I took some brilliant pictures of Suze. So actually, I've saved money.'

Luke doesn't seem convinced. 'How much have you spent?' he demands.

'I don't think we should talk about money in front of Minnie,' I say primly, and take her hand.

'Becky . . .' Luke gives me a long, sort of sighing look. His mouth is tucked in at one side and his eyebrows are in a 'V' shape. This is another of Luke's expressions I'm familiar with. It means: 'How am I going to break this to Becky without her overreacting?'

(Which is very unfair, because I *never* overreact.)

'What?' I say. 'What is it?'

Luke doesn't answer straight away. He walks over to one of the monster armchairs and fiddles with a striped Mexican throw. You might *almost* say that he's putting the armchair between himself and me.

'Becky, don't get offended.'

OK, this is a rubbish way to start any conversation. I'm already offended that he thinks I'm someone who *could* get offended. And anyway, why would I be offended? What's he going to say?

'I won't,' I say. 'Of course I won't.'

'It's just that I've been hearing some really good stuff about a place called . . .' He hesitates. 'Golden Peace. Have you heard of it?'

Have I heard of it? Anyone who's ever read *People* magazine has heard of Golden Peace. It's the place where they wear bracelets and do yoga, and where celebrities dry out and then pretend they were just a little tired.

'Of course I have. The rehab place.'

'Not just rehab,' says Luke. 'They do a lot of programmes and deal with all kinds of . . . disorders. The guy I was talking to has a girlfriend who was a terrible hoarder. It was ruining her life. She went to Golden Peace and they really sorted out her issues. And I wondered if somewhere like that could be helpful. For you.'

It takes me a moment to realize what he's saying.

'*Me?* But I'm not a hoarder. Or an alcoholic.'

'No, but you do . . .' He rubs his nose. 'You have had a history of spending issues, wouldn't you agree?'

I inhale sharply. That's below the belt. Waaay below the belt. So I've had a few minor problems in my time. So I've had a couple of teeny financial blips. If I were a FTSE company you'd call them 'corrections' and just shove them at the back of the annual report and forget about them. Not drag them up at every opportunity. Not suggest *rehab*.

'So, what, I'm an addict now? Thanks a lot, Luke!'

'No! But—'

'I can't believe you're making these accusations in front of our child.' I clasp Minnie to me dramatically. 'What, you think I'm an unfit mother?'

'No!' Luke rubs his head. 'It was just an idea. Nanny Sue suggested the same, remember?'

I glare at him balefully. I don't want to be reminded of Nanny Sue. I'm never hiring a so-called 'expert' again. Her brief was to help us with Minnie's behaviour, and what did she do? Turn the spotlight on *me*. Start talking about *my* behaviour, as if that's got anything to do with anything.

'Anyway, Golden Peace is an American place.' I suddenly think of a winning argument. 'I'm British. So.'

Luke looks perplexed. 'So what?'

'So, it wouldn't work,' I say patiently. 'If I had issues, which I don't, they'd be *British* issues. Totally different.'

'But—'

'Want Grana,' chimes in Minnie. 'Want Grana make cupcakes. Please. Pleeease.'

Both Luke and I stop mid-flow and turn in surprise. Minnie has sunk down cross-legged on to the floor and looks up, her bottom lip trembling. 'Want *Grana* make cupcakes,' she insists, and a tear balances on her lashes.

Grana is what Minnie calls my mum. Oh God, she's homesick.

'Darling!' I put my arms around Minnie and hug her tight. 'Sweetheart, lovely girl. We all want to see Grana, and we'll see her very soon, but right now we're in a different place and we're going to make lots of new friends. *Lots* of new friends,' I repeat, almost to convince myself.

'Where's this come from?' murmurs Luke above Minnie's head.

'Dunno.' I shrug. 'I suppose because I mentioned making cupcakes with sprinkles, and she often makes cupcakes with Mum . . .'

'Minnie, my love.' Luke comes down on to the floor too, and sits Minnie on his knee. 'Let's look at Grana and say hello, shall we?' He's taken my phone from the carved chest, and summons up my photos. 'Let's see . . . there she is! Grana *and* Grandpa!' He shows Minnie a picture of Mum and Dad dressed up for a Flamenco night at their bridge club. 'And there's Wilfie . . .' He scrolls to another picture. 'And Auntie Suze . . .'

At the sight of Suze's cheerful face beaming out of my phone, I feel a tiny pang myself. The truth is, although I keep denying it to Luke, I am feeling a bit lonely here in LA. Everyone seems so far away, there aren't any neighbours to speak of, and I don't have a job . . .

'Say, "Hello, Grana!"' Luke is cajoling Minnie, and after a moment she gives a little wave at the phone, her tears gone. 'And you know what, darling? It may seem a bit scary here to begin with. But soon we'll know lots of people in Los Angeles.' He taps the screen. 'Soon this phone will be full of pictures of all our *new* friends. It's always hard at first, but we'll settle in, I'm sure we will.'

Is he talking to me or Minnie?

'We'd better go.' I smile gratefully at him. 'Minnie has toys to play with and I have new friends to make.'

'Attagirls.' He hugs Minnie, then stands up to kiss me. 'You knock 'em dead.'

Minnie's pre-school is somewhere off Franklin Avenue, and although I've driven there before, I arrive a bit flustered. God, driving in LA is stressy. I haven't got used to our rental car yet, at all. All the controls seem to be in weird places and I keep hooting the horn by mistake. And as for driving on the right-hand side, well, that's just wrong. It's unnatural. Plus, the roads in LA are far too big. They have too many lanes. London is far cosier. You know where you *are*.

At last I manage to park the car, which is a Chrysler and also far too big. Why couldn't we have rented a Mini? I exhale, my heart still thumping, and turn to face Minnie, strapped into her car seat.

'We're here! Pre-school time! Are you excited, darling?'

'Idiot American driver,' replies Minnie equably.

I stare at her, aghast. Where did she get that from? I did *not* say that. Did I?

'Minnie, don't say that! That's not a nice word. Mummy didn't mean to say it. Mummy meant to say ... lovely American cars!'

'Idiot,' says Minnie ignoring me. 'Idiot American driver, Idiot American driver ...' She's singing it to the tune of *'Twinkle, Twinkle, Little Star'*. 'Idiot American dri-ver ...'

I cannot arrive at our first day at LA pre-school with Minnie singing 'Idiot American driver'.

'Idiot American dri-ver ...' She's getting louder and louder. 'Idiot American driiiiii-ver ...'

Could I pretend it's a quaint old British nursery rhyme?

No.

But I can't sit here all day, either. Other mothers with small children are getting out of their massive SUVs, all along the street. And we were supposed to arrive early today.

'Minnie, while we're walking to pre-school, you can have a biscuit!' I say, raising my voice. 'But we have to be very, very quiet, like mice. No singing,' I add for emphasis.

Minnie stops singing and eyes me suspiciously. 'Biscuit?'

Result. Phew.

(And OK, I *know* it's bad to bribe your children, so I'll just feed her some extra green beans later, which will cancel it out.)

Hastily I jump out of the car and unstrap her. I hand her a chocolate-chip cookie from my emergency stash and we start walking along the pavement.

I mean, sidewalk. I *must* get used to that.

As we near the pre-school, I'm looking all around for paparazzi, but I can't see any. But then, they're probably all hiding in bushes. There are a few mothers leading small children in through the gates, and I subtly scan their faces as we walk in with them.

Hmm. I don't *think* any of them are celebs, although they're all toned and tanned with shiny hair. Most of them are in workout gear, and I make a mental note to wear that tomorrow.

I *so* want to fit in. I want Minnie to fit in, and for both of us to make lots of friends.

'Rebecca!'

Erica is greeting us and I smile in relief to see a familiar face. Erica is about fifty, with straight red hair and very colourful clothes, like a character from a children's film. She's leader of the Toddler Program and has already sent me lots of emails about Transition and Separation, and the Joy of Learning and Self-Discovery, which I think means dressing up, only I don't quite dare ask.

'Welcome to your first day at Little Leaf, Minnie!' she adds, and escorts us into the Toddlers' Learning Center, which is basically a room full of toys like any playgroup in England, only here they call them 'developmental aids'. 'Did you manage to park all right?' she adds, as she hangs Minnie's water bottle on her peg. 'I know some folks have had issues this morning.'

'Oh, we were fine, thanks,' I say. 'No problems.'

'Where's the brake?' says Minnie suddenly, and beams at Erica. 'Where's the bloody brake in this bloody stupid car?'

My face flushes bright red.

'Minnie!' I say sharply. 'Stop that! Where on earth did you— Gosh, I've got no idea—'

'Idiot American dri-vers,' Minnie starts singing to '*Twinkle Twinkle*' again. 'Idiot American dri-vers . . .'

'Minnie!' I practically yell. 'Stop! No singing!'

I want to die. I can see Erica hiding a smile, and a couple of assistants looking over. Great.

'Minnie's obviously a very *receptive* child,' says Erica politely.

Yes. Far too bloody receptive. I am never saying anything in front of Minnie, ever again.

'Absolutely.' I try to regain my cool. 'Gosh, what a lovely sandpit. Go on, Minnie! Play with the sand!'

'Now, as I explained to you, we at Little Leaf follow a transitional separation programme,' says Erica, watching as Minnie plunges her hands joyfully into the sandpit. 'This is the start of Minnie's great journey of independence as a human in this world. These are her first steps away from you. They need to be at her own pace.'

'Absolutely.' I'm slightly mesmerized by Erica. She sounds like she's describing an epic trip around the world, not just a toddler going to playgroup.

'So I ask you, Rebecca, to stay by Minnie's side this first morning. Shadow her. Reassure her. Identify the exciting new discoveries she's making; see the world at her level. Minnie will be wary to begin with. Introduce her slowly to the concept of life away from Mommy. Watch her gradually blossom. You'll be amazed by her progress!'

'Right. Fantastic.' I nod earnestly.

I can see another mother nearby, sitting with her blond, curly-headed boy. The mother is pin-thin and dressed in several layers of T-shirts (I happen to know that each one of those T-shirts costs a hundred dollars, something that Mum would never understand in a million years) and she's watching intently as the little boy daubs paint on a sheet of paper.

'Interesting colours, Isaac,' she's saying seriously. 'I like the world you've made.' As he smears paint on his face, she doesn't flicker. 'You're expressing yourself on your own body,' she says. 'You made that choice, Isaac. We can make *choices*.'

Blimey. They do take everything seriously here. But if I'm going to fit in, I'll have to be like that too.

'I'll be around if you need me.' Erica smiles. 'Enjoy this first morning of simultaneous discovery!'

As she heads over to another child, I turn my phone off. I'm feeling quite inspired by Erica. I'm going to be totally focused on Minnie and her morning.

OK. Here's the thing. It's all very well Erica saying 'stay with Minnie'. I honestly want to. I want to be like a mother dolphin and its young, gliding along together in a beautiful duo, simultaneously discovering the world.

But the thing about mother dolphins is, they don't have Lego to trip over, or playhouses to get in their way, or toddlers who can't make up their mind which direction to go in. It took about three seconds for Minnie to get bored with the sandpit and rush outside to the yard, to play on a trike. I'd just about got outside, stumbling over a box of blocks, when she changed her mind, dashed back in and grabbed a dolly. Then she ran outside to hurl the dolly down the slide. She's been in and out about ten times. I'm puffed out, just keeping up with her.

All the time, I've tried to keep up a stream of encouraging, reassuring chatter, but Minnie could not be less interested. All her anxiety from this morning seems to have disappeared, and when I tried to hug her tight just now, she wriggled away, exclaiming, 'No hug, Mummy! *Toys!*'

'So, you're discovering . . . er . . . gravity!' I say, as she drops a toy bear on the floor. 'Brilliant, darling! Now, are you going to express yourself through water?' Minnie has headed over to the water tray and is swishing it around with abandon. 'You've made the choice to splash yourself . . . Argh!' I cry out as Minnie sloshes water into my face. 'You've made the choice to get me wet, too. Wow. That was an . . . interesting choice.'

Minnie isn't even listening. She's run over to the playhouse, which is quite adorable, like a little gingerbread cottage. Hastily I follow her, almost tripping on the squidgy colourful alphabet matting.

'Now you're in the house!' I say, racking my brains for something to say. 'You're discovering . . . er . . . windows. Shall I come in, too?'

'No,' says Minnie, and slams the door in my face. She looks out of the window and scowls. 'No Mummy! *Minnie* house!' She bangs the shutters closed, and I sink on to my heels. I'm exhausted. I can't think of any other discoveries to identify to Minnie. I want a cup of coffee.

I pick up a toy with wooden beads strung along coloured wires and idly start to fiddle with it. It's quite a good game, actually. You have to get the different coloured beads into the four corners, which is harder than it sounds . . .

'Rebecca?'

Guiltily I jump up, dropping the game on to the playmat. 'Oh, hi, Erica!'

'How's Minnie doing?' Erica beams. 'Is she learning to take those gradual steps away from you?'

'She's playing in the house,' I say with a smile, and open the shutters – but the house is empty. Shit. 'Well, she *was* in the house . . .' I cast my eyes around wildly. 'Oh, there she is.'

Minnie has linked arms with another little girl and is marching her round the room, singing *'My Old Man's A Dustman'*, which my dad taught her. I try to follow them, but it's not easy, what with toddler trucks and jumbo foam blocks all over the place.

'Well done, darling!' I call. 'You're expressing yourself through song! Er . . . do you want to tell Mummy how you feel about that?'

'No,' says Minnie, and before I can catch her, she runs out into the yard, climbs to the top of the slide and gazes down triumphantly.

I glance at Erica, who looks lost for words.

'Minnie's a very . . . self-assured child,' she says at last. 'Very independent.'

'Er . . . yes.'

We both watch as Minnie whirls a skipping rope around her head like a lasso. Soon all the other children on the slide are copying her, and shouting, 'My old man's a dustman! My old man's a dustman!' even though they probably don't even know what a dustman is. They probably call it a 'garbage collector' or 'refuse sanitator' or something.

'Minnie seems to be transitioning with great confidence,' says Erica at last. 'Maybe you'd like to sit in the parents' lounge, Rebecca. This is a facility for our parents of children who are at the latter stages of the transition programme. It provides proximity yet independence, and helps the child attain a sense of self, while feeling secure.'

I didn't follow a word of that. All I heard was 'sit in the parents' lounge', which has got to be better than 'chase after my daughter, tripping over toy trucks and feeling like a moron'.

'I'd love to.'

'We also find it a useful forum for parents to exchange views on parenting issues. I'm sure you're burning with questions on curriculum . . . socialization . . .'

'Yes!' I perk up. 'Actually, I *was* wondering, do the mothers have lots of coffee mornings, parties, that kind of thing?'

Erica shoots me an odd look. 'I meant socialization of the children.'

'Right.' I clear my throat. 'The children. Of course.'

As we near the pale wooden door marked *Parents' Lounge*, I feel suddenly excited. At last! A chance to make some friends. What I need to do is launch myself whole-heartedly into school life and volunteer for everything and then I'm bound to meet some nice people.

'Here we are.' Erica swings open the door to reveal a room furnished with brightly coloured foam chairs, on which are sitting three women, all dressed in workout gear. They're chatting avidly, but stop and turn with friendly smiles. I beam back, noticing already that one of them has that cool embroidered bag I was looking at in Fred Segal.

'Let me introduce Rebecca,' Erica is saying. 'Rebecca is new to LA, and her daughter Minnie is joining our Toddler Program.'

'Hi!' I wave around the room. 'Lovely to meet you all.'

'I'm Erin.'

'Sydney.'

'Carola. Welcome to LA!' Carola, who has dark curly hair and lots of interesting-looking silver jewellery, leans forward as Erica leaves the room. 'How long have you been living here?'

'Not long. We're here temporarily for my husband's work.'

'And you got a place at Little Leaf?'

'I know!' I say brightly. 'We were so lucky!'

Carola stares at me blankly for a moment, then starts shaking her head. 'No. You don't understand. No one just gets a place at Little Leaf. No one.'

The others are nodding their heads emphatically. 'No one,' echoes Erin.

'It just doesn't happen,' chimes in Sydney.

I want to point out that if no one gets a place at Little Leaf, what are all their children doing here? But they all look too intense. Clearly this is a serious subject.

'We didn't just "get a place",' I explain. 'Minnie had to do a pre-test. And I think my husband made a donation,' I add a little awkwardly.

Carola is staring at me as though I understand nothing.

'We all do the *pre-test*,' she says. 'We all make *donations*. What *else* did you do?'

'We wrote five letters,' says Erin with grim satisfaction. '*Five.*'

'We've pledged to build a rooftop garden for the school,' says Sydney. 'My husband and I have already engaged the architect.'

'We coached Alexa in Karate,' adds Carola. 'She's here on a sports scholarship.'

I stare at them all, open-mouthed. Are these people *nuts*? I mean, I'm sure it's a good pre-school and everything. But at the end of the day, it's still just children hitting each other with Play-Doh.

'Well, we just turned up,' I say apologetically. 'Sorry.'

The door swings open and a woman with chestnut hair bounces in. She has merry dark eyes and is wearing a stylish blue swingy top over jeans, covering the teeniest little pregnancy bump.

'Hi!' she says, coming straight up to me. 'I'm Faith. You're Rebecca, right? Erica just told me we had a newcomer in our midst.'

She has a gorgeous lilting Southern accent which to my ear sounds as though it's from Charleston. Or Texas. Or maybe . . . Wyoming? Is that Southern?

Do I mean Wisconsin?

No. *No*. That's the cheese state. Whereas Wyoming is . . .

OK, the truth is, I have no idea where Wyoming is. I must do

Minnie's United States jigsaw puzzle and actually look at the names.

'Hi, Faith.' I smile back and shake her hand. 'Lovely to meet you.'

'Are these girls looking after y'all?'

Y'all. I just love that. *Y'all*. Maybe I'll start saying 'y'all'.

'They sure are!' I say, putting a little twang in my voice. 'They surely are!'

'What *we* want to know is, how did she get a place?' Carola appeals to Faith. 'She walks in here off the street, writes the cheque and she's in. I mean, who *does* that?'

'Didn't Queenie put in a good word for her?' says Faith. 'Because she was British? I think Erica said something about it.'

'Ohhhh.' Carola exhales like a deflating balloon. '*That's* it. OK, now I understand. You were lucky.' She turns to me. 'That wouldn't happen to everybody. You need to thank Queenie. She did you a big favour.'

'Sorry, who's Queenie?' I say, trying to keep up.

'Our President of the PTA,' explains Sydney. 'She has a daughter in the Toddler Program, too. You'll love her. She's so sweet.'

'She's super-fun,' agrees Faith. 'She's British, too! We call her Queenie because she talks like the Queen of England.'

'She organizes awesome social events,' says Carola.

'And she runs a moms' yoga class on Wednesday mornings. Knocks us all into shape.'

'It sounds amazing!' I say enthusiastically. 'I'll definitely come!'

My spirits are higher than they've been since we arrived in LA. At last I've found some friends! They're all so welcoming and fun. And this Queenie sounds fab. Maybe she and I will really hit it off. We can compare notes on living in LA and share pots of Marmite.

'How long has Queenie lived in LA?' I ask.

'Not too long. A couple of years, maybe?'

'She had quite the whirlwind romance,' puts in Faith. 'She

90

and her husband met on a Tuesday and were married by the Friday.'

'No way!'

'Oh yes.' Faith laughs. 'It's a great story. You'll have to ask her about it.' She glances out of the window into the car park. 'Oh, here she comes now.' She waves and beckons at someone, and I sit up expectantly.

'Queenie!' exclaims Carola as the door opens. 'Come meet Rebecca.'

'Thank you *so* much for helping us—' I begin, as the door swings further open. And then my words dry up on my lips and I feel my entire body shrivel. No. *No.*

A little whimper escapes my lips before I can stop it and Carola shoots me an odd glance. 'Rebecca, meet Queenie. Alicia, I should say.'

It's Alicia Bitch Long-legs.

Here. In LA. In Minnie's school.

I feel pinioned with shock. If I weren't sitting down I think my legs would collapse.

'Hello, Rebecca,' she says softly, and I give a little shudder. I haven't heard that voice for years.

She's as tall and skinny and blonde as ever, but her style has changed. She's wearing drapey yoga pants and a grey top and Keds. I've never seen Alicia in anything other than heels. And her hair is caught in a low ponytail, which is also very different. As I run my eyes over her, I notice a white and gold twisted bracelet on one wrist. Isn't that the bracelet they wear at Golden Peace?

'Do you two know each other?' says Sydney, with interest.

I want to break into hysterical laughter. Do we *know* each other? Well, let's just see now. Over the last few years, Alicia has tried to ruin my career, my reputation, my husband's business and my wedding. She's undermined me and looked down on me at every turn. Just seeing her is making my heart race with stress.

'Yes,' I manage. 'Yes, we do.'

91

'So *that's* why you recommended Rebecca!' Carola still seems obsessed by this. 'I was just saying, how on earth did she get a place at such short notice?'

'I had a word with Erica,' says Alicia.

Her voice is different, I realize. It's lower and calmer. In fact, her whole demeanour is calmer. It's creepy. It's like she's had Botox of the soul.

'Well, aren't you a sweetie-pie?' Faith puts an arm fondly around Alicia's shoulders. 'Lucky Rebecca to have such a pal!'

'We were telling Rebecca all about you,' puts in Carola. 'Turns out we didn't need to!'

'I've changed a lot since I saw you last, Rebecca.' Alicia gives a soft laugh. 'When was that?'

I'm so shocked, I actually gasp. When *was* that? How can she ask that? Isn't it etched into her brain for ever like it is into mine?

'At my wedding,' I manage to gulp. *When you were being escorted out, kicking and screaming, having tried to ruin the whole thing.*

I'm waiting for a flash of understanding, remorse, acknow-ledgement, *something*. But her eyes have a weird, bland quality to them.

'Yes,' she says thoughtfully. 'Rebecca, I know we have some issues which we should try to put behind us.' She puts a hand gently on my shoulder and I immediately recoil. 'Maybe we could have a cup of mint tea together and talk it through, just the two of us?'

What? All those terrible things she did boil down to 'issues'?

'I don't . . . You can't just—' I break off, my throat dry, my heart thumping, my thoughts all over the place. I don't know what to say.

No, is what I want to say. *You must be joking*, is what I want to say. *We can't just put all that behind us.*

But I can't. I'm not on home turf. I'm standing in the parents' lounge at a pre-school in LA, surrounded by strangers who think that Alicia is a sweetie-pie who's just done me the most massive favour in the world. And now a new feeling creeps over me. A horrible, cold realization. These women are all Alicia's friends. Not my friends, Alicia's friends. It's her crowd.

The thing about Alicia is, she's always managed to make me feel about three inches tall. And even now, even though I know I'm in the right and she's in the wrong, I feel like I'm diminishing by the second. She's in the cool gang. And if I want to join it I'm going to have to be friendly to her. But I can't. I just can't. I can barely even look at her, let alone go to her 'moms' yoga class'.

How can they all be fooled by her? How can they call her 'sweet' and 'super-fun'? An overwhelming feeling of disappointment engulfs me. For a moment I was so excited. I thought I'd found a way in. And now I find Alicia Bitch Longlegs is standing at the entrance, barring the way.

The door swings open and Erica comes in, her colourful shawl trailing behind her like a sail.

'Rebecca!' she exclaims. 'I'm glad to say that Minnie is doing extremely well. She's acclimatized remarkably quickly and seems to be making friends already. In fact, she's a natural leader.' Erica beams at me. 'I'm sure she'll have a little tribe following her in no time.'

'Brilliant.' I manage a wide smile. 'Thank you so much. That's fantastic news.'

And it is. It's a massive relief to think that Minnie feels at home in LA already and is happy and is making friends. I mean, I'm not surprised. Minnie's so confident and charms everyone she meets, it's no wonder she's fallen on her feet.

But as I look around at Alicia and all her disciples, I can't help thinking . . . what about me?

SEVEN

For the next few days I'm in a total state of shock that Alicia Billington has turned up in LA. Except she's not Alicia Billington any more, she's Alicia Merrelle. It all gets worse, as I found out when I Googled her yesterday. She's filthy rich and well known all over LA, because she's married to the founder of Golden Peace. The actual founder himself. He's called Wilton Merrelle and he's seventy-three with a goaty grey beard and those fixed, stretched eyes you get when you have too much plastic surgery, and they met on a beach in Hawaii. A *beach*. Who meets their husband on a beach? They have a daughter called Ora who is a month younger than Minnie and they are, according to one interview, 'hoping to expand their family'.

As soon as I started Googling, I found all these articles about the 'super-stylish home-maker' with her 'British wit and charm'. I sent them to Suze and she sent back a one-word email: *'WHAT?????'*, which made me feel better. Suze has no time for Alicia. And neither does Luke (which is no surprise, bearing in mind she once tried to steal all his clients and ruin his company. Oh yes, whilst trashing my reputation in the newspapers at the same time. Luke and I actually split up because of it. It was *awful*). When I told him, he just grunted, and said, 'Might have known she'd land on her Manolos.'

But the trouble is, everyone else here thinks she's adorable. I haven't seen her again at Little Leaf, thank goodness, but I've had to have about six conversations with other mothers about how great it is that Queenie and I are old friends (friends!) and isn't she divine and am I coming to her spa party?

I can't cope with an Alicia Bitch Long-legs spa party. I just can't.

Anyway. Never mind. I don't care. I'll make friends another way. There are lots of other ways. And in the meantime, I'm going to focus on my new career.

I have a plan at the ready, and it starts today. I've been totally inspired by the story of Nenita Dietz marching into a wardrobe department and landing herself a job. So today I'm going to do the tour at Sedgewood Studios, which is where Nenita Dietz works, and I'm going to sneak away and find her. Luke has even got me a free VIP ticket through some contact of his, although I haven't mentioned my plan to him. I'll wait till I have success first. *Then* he'll see.

I've put together a collection of my work as a personal shopper: look books, photos of clients, even a couple of sketches, all zipped up in a leather portfolio. I've also put together a critique of some recent Sedgewood Studios films, to show that I'm movie-minded. (Like, for example, that alien film they made, *Darkest Force*. They really could have had better costumes in that. The space uniforms were so *clunky*. By the year 2154, surely we'll be going into space in skinny jeans, with tiny little helmets designed by Prada or someone?)

I've also done extensive research on Nenita Dietz, because I want to make sure we hit it off straight away. I'm wearing a really cool dress by Rick Owens, which is a label she likes, and I'm wearing Chanel N° 5, which is apparently her favourite scent, and I've Googled Martinique which is where she goes on holiday. All I have to do is meet her and I'm *sure* we'll get along.

As I wait to join the VIP tour, I feel a fizz of excitement. My life could turn a massive new corner today! I'm standing by the famous gates, which are huge and ornate, with Sedgewood Studios in big iron letters at the top. Apparently if you kiss them, your deepest wish will come true, and lots of tourists are kissing them and filming each other. Honestly, what a load of rubbish. Like a *gate* could help. Like a *gate* could really have any secret powers. Like a *gate* could—

Oh, come on. I might as well. Just to be on the safe side. I'm kissing it and whispering, 'Get me a job, please, please, lovely gate,' when a side entrance opens.

'Come forward for the VIP tour!' A girl in a headset starts ushering us through and scanning our passes. I follow the crowd of tourists and soon find myself on the other side of the gates, in the studio lot. I'm here! I'm at Sedgewood Studios!

I quickly look around, trying to get my bearings. There's an endless road stretching ahead, lined with pretty Art Deco buildings. Beyond that is a lawned area, and I can see more buildings in the distance. I couldn't track down a map of the studio lot online so I'm just going to have to find my own way.

'This way, ma'am.' A young man with blond hair, a dark jacket and a headset is approaching me. 'We have one more space on our cart.'

I turn to see that a whole fleet of golf carts have turned up, and all the tourists are getting on. The blond guy is gesturing to the back seat of a cart that seats six people and is nearly full.

I don't want to get on. I want to find the wardrobe department. But I guess I have no choice.

'Great.' I smile at him. 'Thanks.'

Reluctantly I climb on to the back of the cart and buckle up, next to an old lady in pink seersucker shorts who is filming everything with a video recorder. She even swings round to take a shot of me, and I do a little wave. The blond guy has got into the front of the cart and is handing out headphones.

'Hi!' His voice booms into my ears as soon as my headphones are on. 'My name is Shaun and I'll be your guide for today. I'm gonna take you on a fascinating tour of Sedgewood Studios, past, present and future. We'll see the places where all your favourite shows and movies have been filmed. And while we're on our tour, keep your eyes peeled, and you might just spot one of our stars at work. Yesterday I was beginning a tour just like this one, when who should we see strolling by but Matt Damon!'

'Matt Damon!'

'I love him!'

'His films are awesome!'

At once, everyone starts looking around excitedly as if he might appear again, and one man even starts snapping his camera at empty space.

This is just like being on safari. In fact, I'm amazed they don't do celebrity safaris. I wonder who the 'Big Five' would be. Brad Pitt, obviously, and Angelina. And *imagine* if you saw the whole family together. It would be like when we came across a lioness feeding her cubs in the Masai Mara.

'Now, we're gonna travel back in time, to the glory days of Sedgewood,' Shaun is saying. 'I'm gonna share with you some magical moments in film history. So sit back, and enjoy!'

The golf cart moves off, and we all look around politely at the white buildings and the lawns and the trees. After a while we stop, and Shaun shows us the fountain where Johnno proposed to Mari on *We Were So Young*, in 1963.

I never saw *We Were So Young*. In fact, I've never even heard of it, so that doesn't mean an awful lot to me. Quite a nice fountain though.

'And now on to our next highlight!' Shaun says as we all get back on the cart. He starts it up and we drive for ages past more white buildings, lawns and trees. We turn a sharp corner and we all look excitedly to see what's next . . . but it's more white buildings, lawns and trees.

I suppose I knew this is what a studio lot looked like. But I can't help feeling it's a bit . . . meh. Where are the cameras? Where's the guy shouting 'Action'? And, more importantly, where's the wardrobe department? I really wish I had a map, and I *really* wish Shaun would stop. As if reading my mind, he pulls to a halt and turns to face us, his face glowing with professional animation.

'Ever wondered where was the famous grating that Anna lost her ring down, in the movie *Fox Tales*? Right here, on the Sedgewood Studios lot! Come and take a closer look.'

Obediently we all get off the cart and have a look. Sure enough, on a nearby fence there's a framed still from some black-and-white film of a girl in fox furs dropping a ring down a grating. To my eye, it's just an old grating. But everyone else is taking pictures of it, jostling for a good view, so maybe I should, too. I take a couple of snaps, then edge away from the group while they're all engrossed. I walk to the corner and squint up the road, hoping to see a sign saying *Wardrobe* or *Costume Design*, but it's just more white buildings, lawns and trees. Nor can I see a single film star. In fact, I'm starting to doubt whether they really come here at all.

'Ma'am?' Out of nowhere, Shaun has appeared, looking like a special agent in his dark jacket and headset. 'Ma'am, I need you to stay with the group.'

'Oh right. OK.' Reluctantly, I follow him back to the cart and get on. This is useless. I'm never going to meet Nenita Dietz, stuck on a cart.

'To your right, you'll see the buildings that house some of the most famous film-production companies in the world.' Shaun is booming down the earpiece. 'They all produce films right here on the Sedgewood lot! Now, we're heading to the gift shop . . .'

I'm peering out of the cart as we trundle along, reading every sign we pass. As we pause at an intersection, I lean out, squinting, to read the signs on the buildings. *Scamper Productions . . . AJB Films . . . Too Rich Too Thin Design*! Oh my God, that's her! That's Nenita Dietz's company! Right there in front of my eyes! OK. I'm off.

With a burst of excitement, I unbuckle my belt and start clambering off the cart, just as we start moving. The momentum sends me sprawling on to the grass, and everyone on the cart screams.

'Oh my God!' one woman exclaims. 'Are these carts *safe*?'

'Is she injured?'

'I'm fine!' I call. 'Don't worry, I'm fine!' I hastily get to my feet, brush myself down and pick up my portfolio. Right. New career here I come.

'Ma'am?' Shaun has appeared by my side again. 'Are you OK?'

'Oh, hi, Shaun.' I beam at him. 'I'd like to get off here, actually. I'll make my own way back, thanks. Brilliant tour,' I add. 'I loved the grating. Have a good day!'

I start to walk away, but to my annoyance, Shaun follows me.

'Ma'am, I'm afraid I can't allow you to walk unsupervised through the lot. If you would like to leave the tour, one of our representatives will guide you back to the gate.'

'That's not necessary!' I say brightly. 'I know the way.'

'It *is* necessary, ma'am.'

'But honestly—'

'This is a working lot, and unauthorized visitors must be accompanied at all times. Ma'am.'

His tone is implacable. Honestly. They take it all so seriously. What is this, NASA?

'Could I go to the Ladies?' I say in sudden inspiration. 'I'll just pop into that building there, I'll only be a sec . . .'

'There's a ladies' room at the gift store, which is our next stop,' says Shaun. 'Could you please rejoin the cart?'

His face hasn't flickered once. He means business. If I make a run for it he'll probably rugby-tackle me to the ground. I want to scream with frustration. Nenita Dietz's design company is right there. It's *yards* away.

'Fine,' I say at last, and morosely follow him back to the cart. The other passengers are looking at me with wonder and incomprehension. I can almost see the thought bubbles above their heads: *Why would you get off the cart?*

We whizz off again, past more buildings and round corners, and Shaun starts talking about some famous director who used to sunbathe nude in the 1930s, but I don't listen. This is a total failure. Maybe I need to come again tomorrow and try a different tack. Sneak away at the start before I've even got on a cart. Yes.

The only tiny positive is, there's a shop. At least I can buy souvenirs for everyone. As I wander around the gift store, looking at tea towels and pencils with miniature clapperboards on them, I can't help sighing morosely. The old lady who was sitting next to me comes over and picks up a novelty megaphone paperweight. She glances at Shaun, who is supervising us all with a close eye. Then she moves nearer to me and says in a lowered voice, 'Don't look at me. He'll suspect something. Just listen.'

'OK,' I say in surprise. I pick up a Sedgewood Studios mug and pretend to be engrossed in it.

'Why did you get off the cart?'

'I want to break into movies,' I say, practically whispering. 'I want to meet Nenita Dietz. Her office was right there.'

'Thought it was something like that.' She nods in satisfaction. 'That's the kind of thing I would have done.'

'Really?'

'Oh, I was stage struck. But what was I going to do? I was a kid in Missouri. My parents wouldn't let me sneeze without permission.' Her eyes dim a little. 'I ran away when I was sixteen. Got as far as LA before they tracked me down. Never did it again. Should have done.'

'I'm sorry,' I say awkwardly. 'I mean ... I'm sorry you didn't make it.'

'So am I.' She seems to come to. 'But you can. I'll create a diversion.'

'Huh?' I stare at her.

'A diversion,' she repeats a little impatiently. 'Know what that means? I distract 'em, you get away. You do what you gotta do. Leave Shaun to me.'

'Oh my God.' I clasp her bony hand. 'You're amazing.'

'Get over to the door.' She nods her head. 'Go. I'm Edna, by the way.'

'Rebecca. Thank you!'

My heart beating hard, I head towards the door and linger

by a display of *We Were So Young* aprons and baseball caps. Suddenly there's an almighty *Crash!* Edna has collapsed theatrically to the floor, taking an entire display of crockery with her. There are screams and shouts and all the staff in the place, including Shaun, are rushing forward.

Thank you, Edna, I think as I creep out of the shop. I start to hurry along the street, running as fast as I can in my H&M wedges (really cool black-and-white print, you'd never think they cost only twenty-six dollars). After I've gone a little way I slow down, so as not to look suspicious, and turn a corner. There are people walking along and riding bikes and driving around in golf carts, but none of them has challenged me. Yet.

The only trouble is, I have no idea where I am. All these bloody white buildings look the same. I don't dare ask anyone where Nenita Dietz's office is – I'll draw too much attention to myself. In fact, I'm still half expecting Shaun to come whizzing up beside me in a golf cart and perform a citizen's arrest.

I round another corner and stop in the shade of a big red canopy. What do I do now? The lot is huge. I'm totally lost. A golf cart full of tourists passes by and I shrink away into the shadows, feeling like a fugitive avoiding the secret police. They've probably circulated my description to all the golf-cart drivers by this point. I'm probably on the Most Wanted list.

And then suddenly something rattles past me, and I blink at it in astonishment. It's something so shiny and colourful and wonderful, I want to whoop. It's a gift from God! It's a rail of clothes! It's a girl pushing a rail of clothes in plastic bags. She steers them expertly along the pavement, her phone in her other hand, and I hear her saying, 'On my way. OK, don't stress. I'll be there.'

I have no idea who she is or what she's doing. All I know is, where there are clothes, there's a wardrobe department. Wherever she's going, I want to go too. As discreetly as I can, I begin to follow her along the street, ducking behind pillars for cover and shielding my face with my hand. I *think* I'm being fairly unobtrusive, although a couple of people give me odd looks as they pass by.

The girl winds round two corners and through an alley, and I stay on her tail. Maybe she works for Nenita Dietz! And even if she doesn't, there might be other useful people I could meet.

At last she turns in to a set of double doors. I wait a moment, then cautiously push my way in after her. I'm standing in a wide corridor, lined with doors, and ahead of me the girl is greeting a guy in a headset. He glances at me, and I hastily duck into a short side corridor. A bit further on I peep through a glass panel, and stifle a gasp. It's the Holy Grail! It's a room filled with tables and sewing machines and, all round the walls, rails of clothes. I *have* to have a look. The place is empty, thank God, so I push the door open and tiptoe in. There are period dresses lined up against one side, and I rifle through them, fingering all the gorgeous little pin-tucks and ruffles and covered buttons. Imagine working on a period film. Imagine choosing all those stunning dresses. And look at the hats! I'm just reaching for a poke bonnet with a broad-ribbon trim, when the door opens and another girl in jeans and a headset looks in.

'Who are you?' she demands, and I start guiltily. Shit.

My mind is racing as I put the bonnet back. I can't get chucked out now, I *can't*. I'll have to wing it.

'Oh, hi there.' I try to sound pleasant and normal. 'I'm new. Just started. That's why you haven't seen me.'

'Oh.' She frowns. 'Is anyone else around?'

'Er . . . not right now. Do you know where Nenita Dietz is?' I add. 'I have a message for her.'

Ha! Neatly done. Next I can say, 'Can you just remind me where her office is?' and I'll be in.

The girl's brow wrinkles. 'Aren't they all on location still?'

Location? My heart sinks. It never occurred to me she might be on location.

'Or maybe they got back yesterday. I don't know.' The girl doesn't seem remotely interested in Nenita Dietz. 'Where *are* they all?' She's looking impatiently around the empty room and I realize she must mean whoever normally works here.

'Dunno.' I shrug. 'Haven't seen them.' I think I'm busking

this conversation pretty well. It just goes to show: all you need is a bit of confidence.

'Don't they realize we're making a *movie*?'

'I know,' I say sympathetically. 'You'd think they'd realize.'

'It's the *attitude*.'

'Terrible,' I agree.

'I really don't have time to chase people down.' She sighs. 'OK, you'll have to do it.' She produces a white cotton shirt with a frilly collar.

'What?' I say blankly, and the girl's eyes narrow.

'You *are* a seamstress?'

My whole face freezes. A *seamstress*?

'Er . . . of course,' I say after what seems like an eternity. 'Of course I'm a seamstress. What else would I be?'

I need to get out of this room. Quickly. But before I can move, the girl is handing me the shirt.

'OK. So this is for the older Mrs Bridges. I need a hem in the bottom, half an inch. You should use slipstitch for these garments,' she adds. 'I'm sure Deirdre told you that. Did she show you the attachment?'

'Absolutely.' I try to sound professional. 'Slipstitch. Actually, I'm just on my way to get a coffee, so I'll do that later.' I put the shirt down next to a sewing machine. 'Lovely to meet you—'

'Jesus Christ!' The girl erupts and I jump in fright. 'You won't do it later, you'll do it *now*! We're shooting! This is your first day and you come in with that attitude?'

She's so scary I take a step back.

'Sorry,' I gulp.

'Well, do you want to start?' The girl nods towards the sewing machines, then folds her arms. I have no way out of this. None.

'Right,' I say after a pause, and take a seat in front of one of the sewing machines. 'So.'

I've seen Mum using a sewing machine. And Danny. You just put the material under the needle and push the pedal. I can do this.

My face hot, I cautiously insert the shirt into the sewing machine.

'Aren't you going to pin it?' says the girl critically.

'Er ... I pin as I go,' I say. 'It's just the way I do it.' Experimentally I press the pedal, and thankfully the sewing machine whirrs along vigorously as though I'm an expert. I reach for a pin, shove it into the fabric, then sew a bit more. I think I look pretty convincing, as long as the girl doesn't come anywhere near me.

'Do you want to pick this up in a minute?' I say. 'I could bring it to you, maybe?'

To my relief, there's a crackling sound from her headset. She shakes her head impatiently, trying to listen, then steps outside the room. At once I stop sewing. Thank *God*. Time to make a run for it. I'm halfway out of the chair when the door swings back open and, to my horror, it's the girl again.

'They want some pin-tucks down the front as well. Did you finish the hem?'

'Um.' I swallow. 'Nearly.'

'So, finish it and put in the pin-tucks.' She claps her hands. 'Come on! They're waiting! Now!'

'Right.' I nod, and hastily start up the sewing machine again. 'Pin-tucks. Coming up.'

'And two extra sleeve tucks at the shoulder. You can do that?'

'Sleeve tucks. No problem.'

I briskly sew a seam, then turn the blouse and sew another seam. She's still watching me. Why is she still watching me? Doesn't she have anywhere else to go?

'So,' I say. 'I'll just ... put those tucks in.'

I have no idea what I'm doing. I'm pushing the shirt back and forth, criss-crossing seams all over it. I don't dare stop; I don't dare look up. I'm just willing the girl to leave. *Go, please go ... please, please go ...*

'Are you nearly done?' The girl listens to her headset. 'They're waiting for it.'

I feel like I'm in a never-ending sewing nightmare. The shirt is a mish-mash of random wavery stitches; in fact I've actually stitched the whole thing together. I'm sewing more and more feverishly, backwards and forwards, praying that something gets me out of this . . .

'Hello? Excuse me?' She raises her voice over the sound of the sewing machine. 'Can you hear me? Hey!' She bangs a hand on the table. *'Can you hear me?'*

'Oh.' I look up as though hearing her for the first time. 'Sorry. I was just sewing.'

'The shirt?' She holds out her hand.

I stare steadily back at her. The blood is pulsing in my ears. Any minute now she's going to grab the shirt from the sewing machine and it will all be over. And she won't let me leave and I'll be arrested by the studio secret police in dark jackets and my whole plan will fail before it's even begun.

'Actually . . . I think I'm going to change career,' I say in desperation.

'What?' The girl gapes at me.

'Yes. I've had a sudden realization. I don't want to be a seamstress any more, I want to work with animals.'

'Animals?' She seems absolutely pole-axed and I take advantage of this fact to get up and start edging past her to the door.

'Yes. I'm going to go to Borneo and work with gorillas. It's always been my dream. So, er, thank you for the opportunity.' I start backing out of the room. 'Say thank you to Deirdre, too. You've all been lovely to work with!'

The girl is still staring at me, open-mouthed, as I hurry out of the double doors. I can hear her calling something, but I don't stop to listen. I have to get out.

The Missouri Echo

ST LOUIS SENIOR 'DISCOVERED' IN HOLLYWOOD GIFT STORE

By: OUR MOVIE REPORTER

When 70-year-old Edna Gatterby from St Louis went on a tour of Sedgewood Studios she expected to end up with a souvenir or two. Instead, she came away with a part in a major Sedgewood production, *Fought the Day*, a World War Two weepie which begins production next month.

The Missouri senior found herself being screen-tested by director Ron Thickson after an encounter in the gift store. 'I was browsing for a gift when an old lady tumbled to the ground,' explained Thickson. 'As I ran to help her, I caught sight of her face, and she matched perfectly my vision of Vera, the hero's grandmother.' Edna was screen-tested later that day and has been offered the small role.

'I'm ecstatic beyond belief. I've always wanted to act,' commented Edna. 'I have to thank Rebecca,' she added, but would not elaborate on who 'Rebecca' is.

EIGHT

What a disaster. I never got to meet Nenita Dietz. I never got to meet anyone. When I got outside I was so flustered, I almost ran all the way to the exit, looking behind me all the time for the men in dark jackets. I didn't even buy any souvenirs, so the whole thing was a total waste. And then Luke wanted to hear all about it, and I had to pretend I'd had a brilliant time.

As I get Minnie ready for Little Leaf the next day, I'm still downcast. And my misery has been increased about a million-fold because we've had an email saying Alicia wants to address all the parents today about a fund-raiser, so could we all please stay behind after drop-off for an informal gathering.

Which means, after managing to avoid her these last few days, I'll have to face her again. I don't know how I'm going to keep my cool.

'What shall I do?' I say to Minnie as I plait her wispy little locks into a braid.

'Cup of tea,' replies Minnie seriously, and passes me a plastic cocktail glass. We're sitting on the terrace outside, which is where Minnie chooses to get dressed most mornings (I can't blame her, with this lovely sunshine), and all her teddies and dolls are sitting around, with a cocktail glass each.

As Luke steps out of the house, briefcase in hand, he looks aghast at the sight.

'Is this Alcoholics Anonymous for teddies?' he says.

'No!' I giggle. 'They're our garden cocktail glasses. Minnie found them in the outdoor kitchen. They won't break, so I let her play with them.'

'Daddy, cup of tea,' says Minnie, handing him a cocktail glass.

'OK,' says Luke. 'A quick cup of tea.' He crouches down and takes the glass from her. A moment later, his gaze focuses on the teddy in front of him. Damn. I know what he's seen. I should have hidden it.

'Becky,' he says. 'Is that bear wearing my Asprey cufflinks? The ones you gave me?'

'Er . . .' I assume an innocent expression. 'Let me see. Ah. Yes, I believe it is.'

'And my Cartier watch.'

'So it is.'

'And that doll has got my old college tie on.'

'Has it?' I'm trying not to giggle again. 'Well, Minnie wanted to dress her toys up. You should be flattered she chose your things.'

'Oh really?' Luke grabs his watch off the bear, ignoring Minnie's protests. 'I don't notice you volunteering any of *your* priceless jewellery.'

'Your cufflinks aren't priceless!'

'Maybe they're priceless to me because they came from you.' He raises his eyebrows at me and I feel a little flicker, because although I know he's teasing me, I also know he means it.

'Drink *tea*, Daddy!' says Minnie sternly, and Luke puts his cocktail glass to his lips obediently. I wonder what all his board members in London would say if they could see him now.

'Luke . . .' I bite my lip.

'Uh-huh?'

I wasn't planning on bothering him with my problems, but I can't help myself.

'What am I going to do about Alicia?'

'Alicia,' says Luke tersely, and raises his eyes to heaven. 'God help us.'

'Exactly! But here she is, and I'm going to see her today at pre-school, and everyone thinks she's marvellous, and I want to yell, "If only you knew what an evil witch she is!"'

'Well, I wouldn't do that,' says Luke, looking amused. 'Not in public.'

'It's OK for you! You're really good when you meet people you don't like. You just go all calm and stony. I get all flustered.'

'Just think dignified. That's my best advice.'

'Dignified!' I echo, despairingly, and Minnie perks up.

'Digna-dive,' she enunciates carefully, and Luke and I both laugh, whereupon she says it again, beaming back at us. 'Digna-dive. Digna-dive!'

'That's it,' says Luke. 'Digna-dive. I have to go.' He rises to his feet, swiping his Asprey cufflinks off the teddy bear as he does so. I take a pretend swig of my tea, wishing it was a real cocktail, and that Luke could take the day off, and that Alicia lived in Timbuktu. 'Sweetheart, don't fret,' says Luke, as though reading my thoughts. 'You'll be fine. Chin up, eyes flinty.'

I can't help giggling, as that's *exactly* how he looks when he's angry with someone but isn't about to make a scene.

'Thanks.' I put an arm around him and kiss him. 'You're the most digna-dive person I know.'

Luke clicks his heels and bows like an Austrian prince, and I laugh again. I truly do have the best husband in the world. And I'm not biased at all.

As I arrive at Little Leaf, I'm resolved. Luke has inspired me. I'm going to be totally serene and *not* let Alicia get to me. Minnie prances off straight away to play with her friends, and I head for the parents' lounge, which is where Alicia is apparently giving her talk. I can hear a vacuum cleaner operating inside, so I assume the room isn't ready yet, and lean against the wall to wait. A few moments later I hear footsteps, and Alicia appears round the corner, immaculately dressed as ever in yoga wear, and holding what looks like a brand-new Hermès bag.

OK, here I go. Chin up. Eyes flinty. Stay calm.

'Hello,' I say, trying to sound detached, yet engaged, yet unflustered, while maintaining the moral high ground. All in two syllables.

'Becky.' Alicia gives a nod and leans against the wall directly opposite me. I feel as though we're in some weird game of chess, only I don't know what the next move is.

Anyway. It's not chess, I tell myself. This isn't a battle. I'm not even going to *think* about Alicia. I'm going to ... check my phone. Yes. As I start to read through a bunch of messages I've read before, I see that Alicia is doing the same thing, opposite. Only she keeps laughing softly, and shaking her head and exclaiming, 'You're kidding! Oh, hilarious,' as though to demonstrate what an entertaining life she leads.

I'm furiously telling myself not to notice her, not to think about her ... but I can't help it. Our mutual past keeps flashing through my head like a film. All the times she's undermined me, all her scheming, all her bitchiness ...

My chest is starting to rise and fall in indignation, my fingers are clenching, my jaw is tightening. After a few moments, Alicia clearly notices, because she puts down her phone and surveys me as though I'm an interesting curiosity.

'Rebecca,' she says, in that new-agey, softly-softly way she has that makes me want to slap her. 'I know you're hostile towards me.'

She pronounces it 'hostel' now. Of course she does.

'Hostile?' I stare at her incredulously. 'Of course I'm hostile!'

Alicia says nothing but just sighs, as though to say, *How sad that you feel this way, but I have no idea why.*

'Alicia,' I say evenly. 'Do you actually remember the way you've behaved towards me over the years? Or have you blanked it all out?'

'Let me tell you a little about my journey,' says Alicia

seriously. 'When I met Wilton I was in a very unhappy place. I believed I was deficient in every possible way. He helped me to self-actualize.'

Argh. *Self-actualize*. What does that mean, even? Self-obsess, more like.

'The old Alicia was in a very toxic cycle.' She looks wistful. 'The old Alicia was still a child in many ways.' She's talking as though 'the old Alicia' has nothing to do with her.

'That was you,' I remind her.

'I know our relationship in the past was maybe . . .' She pauses as though to select the right word. 'Unbalanced. But now I've righted the scales, we should move on, no?'

'Righted the scales?' I stare at her. 'What scales?'

'Why else did I recommend your daughter to Little Leaf?' she says, looking supremely pleased with herself.

The pieces suddenly fall into place in my head.

'You recommended Minnie . . . what, to make amends?'

Alicia simply bows her head with a faint smile, as though she's Mother Theresa giving me benediction.

'You're welcome,' she says.

Welcome? I'm prickling all over in horror. I feel like striding into the toddler playground, plucking Minnie out and leaving Little Leaf for ever. Except that would be unfair to Minnie.

'So you think we're quits now?' I say, just to make sure I've got this right. 'You think everything's square?'

'If that's the way you see it, then that works.' She shrugs easily. 'For me, the world isn't so linear.' She gives me a patronizing smile, just like she used to when she was in financial PR and I was a journalist and her suit was more expensive than mine and we both knew it.

'Forget linear!' My thoughts are so scattered and furious, I'm finding it hard to articulate them. Let alone stay digna-dive. 'Just answer me one question, Alicia. Are you actually sorry for anything you did to me? Are you *sorry*?'

The words hang in the air like a challenge. And as I stare at her, my heart is suddenly pounding in expectation. My cheeks are hot and I feel like a ten-year-old in the playground. After all the damage she caused Luke and me, if she really wants to make amends, she has to say sorry. She has to say it and *mean* it. I'm holding my breath, I realize. I've been waiting to hear this for a long time. An apology from Alicia Bitch Long-legs.

But there's silence. And as I look up to meet her blue eyes, I know she's not going to do it. Of course she isn't. All this talk of amends. She isn't sorry a bit.

'Rebecca . . .' she says thoughtfully. 'I think you're obsessed.'

'Well, I think you're still an evil *witch*!' The words burst from me before I can stop them, and I hear a loud gasp from behind me. I wheel round to see a cluster of mothers standing behind us in the corridor, all with eyes wide and some with hands to their mouths.

My heart plummets. They all heard me. And they all love Alicia. They would never understand in a million years.

'Rebecca, I know you didn't mean that,' says Alicia at once, in her most syrupy, new-agey voice. 'You're at a stressed time in your life, it's understandable, we're all here for you . . .' She reaches for my hand, and in a slight daze, I let her hold it.

'Queenie, sweetheart, you're so understanding!' exclaims Carola, shooting me daggers.

'Queenie, are you OK?' chimes in Sydney as she walks into the parents' lounge. As the other mothers file past, everyone has a kind word for Alicia and everyone avoids looking at me. It's like I've got an infectious disease.

'I'm going,' I mutter, and pull my hand away from Alicia's cool grasp.

'Not coming to the talk, Rebecca?' says Alicia sweetly. 'You're very welcome.'

'Not this time,' I say, and turn on my heel. 'Thanks anyway.' As I stride away down the corridor, my head is high but my face is puce and I'm dangerously near tears. I failed and Alicia won again. How come she won again? How is this fair?

As I get back home, I feel at my lowest ebb since we've arrived in LA. It's all going wrong, in every direction. I've failed on my mission to meet Nenita Dietz. I've failed on my mission to make lots of new friends. Everyone at Little Leaf will think I'm some awful psycho.

I'm just going into the kitchen and wondering whether to pour myself a glass of wine, when my phone rings. To my surprise, it's Luke. He doesn't usually phone in the middle of the day.

'Becky! How's it going?'

He sounds so warm and kind and familiar that for an awful moment I think I might burst into tears.

'I just saw Alicia,' I say, slumping into a chair. 'Tried to be digna-dive.'

'How'd that work out?'

'Well, you know how you said not to call her an evil witch? I called her an evil witch.'

Luke's laugh is so hearty and reassuring, I feel better at once.

'Never mind,' he says. 'Just ignore her. You're so much bigger than her, Becky.'

'I know, but she's at school every day, and everyone thinks she's lovely . . .' I trail off feebly. Luke doesn't really *get* the whole school-gate thing. Whenever he picks Minnie up he strides straight to the door and leads her away and doesn't even seem to notice that there are any other parents. Let alone what they're wearing or gossiping about, or what sidelong looks they're shooting at whom.

'Are you at home?' he says now.

'Yes, just got back. Why, have you forgotten something? D'you want me to bring it in?'

'No.' Luke pauses. 'Now, Becky, I want you to relax.'

'OK,' I say, puzzled.

'Please stay relaxed.'

'I *am* relaxed!' I say impatiently. 'Why do you keep telling me to relax?'

'Because there's been a change of plan. I'm coming back home to hold a meeting at the house. With . . .' He hesitates. 'With Sage.'

It's as if lightning zings through me. I sit bolt upright, every nerve alive. My misery has vanished. Alicia suddenly seems irrelevant to my life. Sage Seymour? Here? What shall I wear? Have I got time to wash my hair?

'We probably won't see you,' Luke's saying. 'We'll probably just go into the library. But I wanted to warn you.'

'Right,' I say breathlessly. 'Do you want me to sort out some snacks? I could make some cupcakes. Quinoa ones,' I add hastily. 'I know she likes quinoa.'

'Darling, you don't need to make any special effort.' Luke seems to think for a moment. 'In fact, maybe you should go out.'

Go out? Go *out*? Is he mad?

'I'm staying here,' I say firmly.

'OK,' says Luke. 'Well . . . I'll see you in about half an hour.'

Half an hour! I put the phone down and look around the house in sudden dissatisfaction. It doesn't look nearly cool enough. I should rearrange the furniture. I have to choose the right outfit, too, and do my make-up again . . . But first things first. I grab my phone and text Suze and Mum, my fingers clumsy with excitement: **Guess what? Sage is coming to our house!!!**

Somehow, half an hour later I'm almost ready. I've washed my hair and blasted it with the hairdryer, and I've got Velcro rollers in (I'll quickly take them out when I hear the car). I've moved the sofas around in the living room and plumped up the cushions. I'm wearing my new slip dress from Anthropologie and I've memorized the storylines of all Sage's forthcoming films, which I Googled.

I have a couple of complete outfits ready for Sage, but I won't show them to her at once. I don't want her to feel bombarded. In fact, I'm going to have to do this subtly, as I know Luke won't appreciate me hijacking his meeting. I'll just be very casual about it, I decide. I'll have the brocade coat lying about and she'll admire it and try it on and it will all snowball from there.

The sound of an engine comes distantly from the front of the house, followed by that of car doors. They're here! I put up a hand to smooth down my hair – then suddenly remember my Velcro rollers. Quickly I start pulling them out and hurling them one by one behind a big potted plant. I shake out my hair, casually recline on the sofa and grab *Variety*, which is a brilliant accessory as it instantly makes you look like a cool movie person.

I can hear the front door opening. They're coming in. Stay calm, Becky . . . stay cool . . .

'. . . go into the library, I thought.' Luke is speaking. 'Sage, meet my wife, Becky.'

My face starts prickling as three figures appear round the door. Oh my God. It's her. It's her! Right here in this room! She's smaller than I expected, with tiny bronzed arms and that familiar treacly hair. Clothes: teeny white jeans, orange flats, a little grey vest and The Jacket. *The Jacket*. I can't believe she's wearing it! It's pale, buttery suede and she was wearing it in *US Weekly* last week. It was in 'Who Wore It Best?' and she won. Of course she did.

I've met Aran before: he's Sage's manager. He's tall and buff and blond, with blue eyes and slanty eyebrows, and kisses me politely in greeting.

'Hi, Becky,' Sage says pleasantly. 'We spoke on the phone, right? For Luke's party.'

She's got the most amazing accent. It's mostly American, but with a hint of French, because her mother's half-French and she spent her early childhood in Switzerland. *People* magazine once called it 'the sexiest accent alive' and I kind of agree.

'We did,' I gulp. 'Yes. Hi.'

I try to think of something else to say . . . something witty . . . come on, Becky . . . but something's wrong with my head. It's gone blank. All I can think is, *It's Sage Seymour! In my living room!*

'You have a nice yard,' says Sage, as though she's making a really deep pronouncement.

'Thank you. We like it.' Luke strides ahead and pushes open

the glass doors to the garden. Sage and Aran follow him out and I follow behind. We all look at the inviting blue of the pool, and I urgently try to think of something to say. But it's like my brain has been replaced by cotton wool.

'Shall we sit out here?' says Luke, gesturing to our outdoor dining table. It has a massive parasol above it and the pool guy hoses it every day to keep it clean.

'Sure.' Sage slides gracefully into a chair, followed by Aran.

'There's water in the chiller . . .' Luke hands bottles around.

'Can I get anyone coffee?' Finally I manage to string two words together.

'No thanks,' says Aran politely.

'I think we're fine, Becky,' says Luke.. 'Thanks.' He gives me a nod which I understand. It means, *Leave us alone now*. I'll just pretend I didn't see it.

As the three start getting out folders and papers, I hurry back into the house, grab the brocade coat, a belt and a pair of shoes, and zoom back out into the garden. I arrive breathlessly next to Sage and hold the coat out on one arm.

'I just bought this,' I say chattily. 'It's nice, isn't it?'

Sage surveys the coat. 'Cute,' she says with a nod, and turns back to a page of photocopied press clippings.

'D'you want to try it on?' I say casually. 'I'm sure it's your size. It would really suit you.'

Sage gives me an absent smile. 'No, that's OK,' she says.

I stare at her in slight shock. It's so beautiful, I was sure she'd want to try it on. Well, maybe she's just not into coats.

'I bought this belt, too.' I quickly proffer the belt. 'Isn't it amazing?'

The belt is from Danny's new collection. It's black suede, with three chunky buckles in green resin. You'd put it on over a simple dress and the whole outfit would pop.

'It's by Danny Kovitz,' I tell her. 'He's a friend of mine, actually.'

'Great,' says Sage, but she makes no move to stroke it or touch it, let alone ask to try it on. This is really not going as I planned.

'You're size 6½, aren't you?' I say in desperation. 'I bought these shoes by mistake. Why don't you have them?'

'Really?' She looks at me in surprise, eyeing my bigger feet.

'Yes! Absolutely! Have them.' I put them on the table. They're pale coral-coloured sandals by Sergio Rossi, just very simple and gorgeous. In fact, I covet them myself, and it was really hard buying them in Sage's size, not mine.

'Nice.' At last! Sage is finally showing some interest. She picks up a sandal and turns it this way and that. 'My sister would love these. We're the same size. I give her all my cast-offs. Thanks!'

I stare at her, dismayed. Her sister? *Cast-offs?*

A thought suddenly occurs to Sage. 'How come you bought them in the wrong size? Isn't that weird?'

I'm aware of Luke's sardonic gaze from across the table.

'Oh. Right.' I can feel myself flushing. 'Well ... I got confused between British and American sizing. And I never tried them on. And I can't take them back.'

'That's a shame. Well, thanks!' She hands the shoes to Aran, who places them in a tote bag at his feet. Feeling crestfallen, I watch them disappear.

She didn't admire a single thing I'd bought. She didn't suggest shopping together, or ask for advice on her next red-carpet appearance, or any of my fantasies. I can't help feeling dispirited. But I'm not going to give up. Maybe I just need to get to know her a bit better.

Luke is circulating a sheet headed *Agenda*. Everyone's ignoring me. I can't hover near the table any more. But I *can't* just go tamely back inside the house. Maybe ... I'll sunbathe. Yes, good idea. I hurry into the house and collect *Variety* from the living room, then nonchalantly walk to a sunbed about ten feet away from the table and sit down on it. Luke glances up with a slight frown, but I ignore him. I'm allowed to sunbathe in my own garden, aren't I?

I open *Variety* and read some piece about the future of 3D franchises, while trying to listen in on the conversation at the table. The trouble is, they're all talking so *quietly*. Mum always complains that modern movie stars mumble, and I have to agree. I can't hear anything Sage is saying. She should have some proper speech and drama lessons. She should project!

Luke is being equally discreet, and the only one whose voice is resonating through the garden is Aran. Even so, I'm only catching the odd intriguing word.

'... brand ... positioning ... Cannes ... next year ... Europe...'

'I agree,' chimes in Luke. 'But ... *mumble mumble* ... big budget ... Academy Awards...'

Academy Awards? My ears prick up. What about the Academy Awards? God, I wish there were subtitles.

'You know what?' says Sage with sudden animation. 'Fuck them. They're a ... *mumble mumble* ... Pippi Taylor ... well, their choice...'

I'm nearly falling off my sunbed, trying to hear. It said in the *Hollywood Reporter* last week that Sage Seymour had lost out to Pippi Taylor in the last three roles she'd gone for. It also said that Sage was on a 'downward slide', not that I would mention this. I think that's why she's hired Luke – to help turn things round for her.

'... Lois Kellerton situation...'

'... have to ignore Lois Kellerton, Sage.'

Lois Kellerton. I sit up straighter, my mind working frantically. Now I remember. There's some old feud between Sage and Lois Kellerton. Isn't there a clip of them on YouTube, yelling at each other backstage at an awards ceremony? But I can't remember what it's all about.

'Ignore that bitch?' Sage's voice rises indignantly. 'After everything she did to me? Are you kidding? She's a ... *mumble mumble...*'

'... not relevant...'

'... totally relevant!'

Oh, I can't bear it. For once, I have something to contribute to the conversation! I *can't* keep quiet any longer.

'I met Lois Kellerton!' I blurt out. 'I met her when we were out here house-hunting.'

'Oh, really?' Sage glances briefly up towards me. 'Poor you.'

'I didn't know that, Becky.' Luke looks surprised.

'Yes, well. It was quite bizarre. You'll never *guess* what she was doing.' I feel a flash of triumph as Sage finally gives me her full attention.

'What was that maniac doing?'

'She was . . .'

I hesitate for a moment as Lois's pale, tense face flashes through my mind. Her pleading voice. Her hand on mine. I did promise to keep her secret, I think uncomfortably. And I've kept that promise until now. (Except telling Suze. That doesn't count.)

But on the other hand, why should I protect her? She was breaking the law. Exactly. Exactly! I should really have marched her to the nearest police station. And then she tried to bribe me. Well, I'm not someone who can be bribed. No way. Not Becky Brandon. Besides which . . .

I mean, the point is . . .

OK. The real, honest truth is, I'm desperate to keep Sage's attention.

'She was shoplifting!' The words pop out of my mouth before I can think about it any more. And if I wanted a reaction, I'm not disappointed.

'No way.' Sage's eyes flash, and she bangs the table with her hand. 'No *way*.'

'*Shoplifting?*' says Aran, in astonishment.

'Come here. Come!' Sage pats the chair beside her. 'Tell us all about it.'

Trying to hide my delight, I hurry over to the table and sink down in the chair next to Sage.

Oh God, my thighs are about *twice* the size of hers. Never mind. I'll just keep my gaze away from the general thigh direction.

'What happened?' Sage is demanding eagerly. 'Where were you?'

'She was in a sports shop on Rodeo Drive. She pinched three pairs of socks. I mean, she gave them back,' I add hurriedly. 'I think it was just . . . you know. A moment of madness.'

'And you caught her?'

'I chased her down the street,' I admit. 'I didn't know who she was at first.'

'You're a hero!' Sage lifts a hand and high-fives me with her tiny, beringed hand. 'Go Becky!'

'I had no idea.' Luke looks gobsmacked.

'Well, I promised I wouldn't tell anyone.'

'But you've just told us.' Luke raises his eyebrows at me and I feel an uneasy pang, which I squash down. Come on. It's no big deal. It's not like I've blabbed to the whole world.

'Don't tell anyone else, will you?' I look around the table. 'It was only three pairs of socks.'

'Sure.' Sage pats my hand. 'Your secret's safe with us.'

'She was lucky it was you that caught her and not store security,' says Aran dryly.

'Typical. That witch always lands on her feet.' Sage rolls her eyes. 'Now, if it had been *me* who caught her . . .'

'Don't even go there.' Aran gives a short laugh.

'What happened between you two?' I venture timidly. 'I know there was some kind of . . . argument?'

'Argument?' Sage gives a snort. 'More like a completely unprovoked attack. She's, like, a total psycho. She has a screw loose, if you ask me.'

'Sage.' Aran sighs. 'This is old ground.' He glances at Luke. 'Maybe we could move on.'

'Absolutely.' Luke nods. 'Let's—'

'No! Becky wants to hear about it!' Sage turns to me, ignoring both Aran and Luke. 'It started at the SAG Awards. She said she should have won Best Actress because she looked better than me in her movie. Hello? I was playing a *cancer victim.*'

'No way,' I stare at her, shocked. 'That's awful.'

'You know what she said? "You don't get any acting awards for shaving off your hair."' Sage's eyes open wide. 'D'you know how much research I put into that role?'

'Anyway—'

'Well, she's getting what she deserves now.' Sage's eyes narrow. 'D'you hear about this athletics film she's doing? Nightmare. Ten million over budget and the director just walked out. Everyone hates her. She's gonna go *down*.' Her phone bleeps and she squints at it. 'Oh. I gotta go. You guys finish up without me.'

'You have to *go*?' Luke stares at her. 'We've only just started!'

'Sage, hon.' Aran sighs again. 'We cleared your schedule for this. We want to hear what Luke has to say.'

'I have to go,' she repeats, shrugging. 'I forgot I have a class at Golden Peace.'

'Well, cancel it.'

'I'm not going to cancel it!' she retorts, as though he's crazy. 'I'll catch up with you guys later.' I can see Aran and Luke exchanging frustrated looks, as she picks up her bag, but I'm more interested in the fact that she's going to Golden Peace.

'So, do you go to Golden Peace a lot?' I ask casually.

'Oh, all the time. It's amazing. You should go.'

'Actually, I'm planning to,' I hear myself saying. 'So I'll see you there!'

'You're going to Golden Peace, Becky?' says Luke, deadpan. 'I didn't know that.'

'Yes, actually.' I avoid his quizzical gaze. 'I'm going to sign up for some classes.'

'Oh, do it!' says Sage earnestly. 'That place is great. I have, like, huge self-esteem issues, and they've really worked on them. I have self-assertion issues, too, self-acceptance issues . . . I'm battling some pretty big stuff.' She flicks back her hair. 'How about you?'

'Me too,' I say hastily. 'I'm battling some big stuff too. I have . . . er . . . spending issues. I want to work on those.'

I hear a snort from Luke's direction, which I choose to ignore.

Sage nods. 'They have a good programme for that. It's just a great place for getting your shit together. I mean, what good is all of this if we don't love ourselves, right?' She spreads her arms wide. 'And how can we love ourselves if we don't *get* ourselves?'

'Exactly.' I nod too. 'That's exactly what I've always thought.'

'Great. Well, see you there. We could have coffee?'

'Love to,' I say as carelessly as possible.

'This is my new cell number . . .' She reaches for my phone and punches in a number. 'Text me back, then I'll have yours.'

Oh my God! I want to pinch myself. I'm making a date for coffee with Sage! *Finally* I have something to tell Mum and Suze!

As soon as Sage has left I hurry into the house and call Suze.

'Hey, Suze!' I blurt out as soon as she answers. 'Guess what?'

'No, *you* guess what!' she replies, her voice bubbling over with excitement. 'We're coming to LA! I've swung it with Tarkie. He's going to have a meeting with his investment people out there. I said to him, "It's irresponsible to have investments in the States and not even know what they are." So at last he agreed. And he really needs a break.' She sighs. 'He's still devastated about The Surge. Did you see the newspaper write-ups?'

I wince. 'A couple.'

'His father keeps sending him newspaper clippings and saying he's disgraced the Cleath-Stuart name.'

'No!' I say in horror.

'Poor Tarkie feels like such a failure. And the stupid thing is, the fountain *works* now. It's a brilliant tourist attraction. But everyone just remembers the launch going wrong.'

'Well, come out to LA as soon as you can,' I say firmly. 'We'll walk on the beach and forget all about it and Tarkie will cheer up.'

'Exactly. I'm looking into flights right now. I've told the school we're taking the children on an educational sabbatical. LA is educational, right?'

'Definitely! So how long are you coming for?'

'I don't know,' says Suze. 'At least a month, maybe more.

Tarkie needs some serious time off. A week won't do it. Oh, what was your news?' she adds as an afterthought.

'Nothing much,' I say casually. 'Just that I met Sage Seymour and we really got on and we're going to have coffee at Golden Peace.'

Ha!

'Oh my God!' Suze's voice blasts me away. 'Come on, spill! What was she like? What was she wearing? What did— Hang on,' she interrupts herself. 'Did you say Golden Peace?'

'Yes.' I try to sound nonchalant.

'The rehab place?'

'Yes.'

'Started by Alicia Bitch Long-legs' husband?'

'Yes.'

'Bex, are you insane? Why are you going there?'

'To . . . um . . . to go on the spending-addiction programme.'

'*What?*' She actually splutters down the phone.

'I want to work on my issues.' I clear my throat. 'I have some big stuff to sort out.'

Somehow when I say it to Suze it doesn't sound as convincing as it did before.

'No you don't!' she says in derision. 'You just want to hang out with Sage Seymour and all the celebrities!'

'Well, so what if I do?' I say defensively.

'But they're all *weird*,' she says, sounding unhappy. 'Bex, don't get weird on me, please.'

I'm momentarily silenced. She's right. They are a bit weird. Alicia's *totally* weird. But then, if I don't go to Golden Peace, how will I get to have coffee with Sage?

'I'll be fine. I'll only listen with one ear.'

'Well . . . all right.' Suze sighs. 'But don't get sucked in. Please.'

'I promise.' I cross my fingers.

I'm not going to admit the truth: I quite *want* to get sucked in. Because it's occurred to me that if Sage goes to Golden Peace, who else might go? What career opportunities might there be? What if I meet some famous director and we get talking about the costumes for his next film over herbal tea, or whatever they drink. (Probably coconut water or yam water. Or banana water. Something gross like that.)

'Bex?'

'Oh.' I come to. 'Sorry, Suze.'

'So, come on,' she demands. 'What was Sage wearing? And don't leave anything out.'

'*Well* . . .' I sit back happily, settling in for a proper long chat. LA is fab and exciting and everything . . . but I do miss my best friend.

From: Kovitz, Danny
To: Kovitz, Danny
Subject: I'm alive!!!!!!

_____

dearest friends

i write this from training camp on the island of kulusuk. i have been
here one day and already i know this will be a transformating
experience for me. i've never felt so alive. i have taken shots of the
snow ice and the cute inuit people with their darling clothes. i am
ready for the challenge. i am ready to push myself. i am ready to be
at one with the soaring powerful nature that is around me. it is a
mystical experience. i feel proud and humbled and enlivened and
excited. i will see landscapes few people have ever seen. i will push
myself to the brink. my new collection will be based on the
experience.

all my love and wish me luck. i will email again from the next camp.

danny xxxxx

NINE

All I can say is . . . wow. I mean, *Namaste*. Or maybe *Satnam*? (I've been learning lots of spiritual, yoga-ish words and trying to use them in conversation. Except that 'Satnam' always makes me think of 'sat nav'.)

Why have I never got into Mind Body Spirit before? Why did I never do wellbeing classes in England? Or Navigate Your Inner Terrain? Or Sound Healing for Childhood Damage? I've been attending Golden Peace for two weeks now, and it's transformed my life. It's just amazing!

For a start, the place is fantastic. It's a huge site on the coast, just south of LA. It used to be a golf club, but now it's all low sandy-coloured buildings and koi lakes and a running track, which I'm totally intending to use sometime. Plus they sell fresh juices, and healthy meals, and there's free yoga at lunchtime on the beach, and in the evenings they show inspirational movies outside while everyone lolls on beanbags. Basically, you don't ever want to leave.

I'm sitting in a room with a dark wooden floor and billowing white curtains at the windows and a softly fragranced air. All the rooms at Golden Peace smell the same – it's their signature scent of ylang ylang and cedar and . . . some other really healthy thing. You can buy the scented candles at the gift shop. I've already bought eight, because they'll make *perfect* Christmas presents.

All the spending-addiction programmes were full when I phoned up, but that doesn't matter, because this really nice girl, Izola, recommended a whole programme of general well-being classes for me. The point is, everyone can work on their soul and inner being, because the spiritual muscle needs exercise like any other. (I read that in the brochure.)

I do self-esteem group on Mondays, Compassionate Communication on Tuesdays, The Transitive Self on Wednesdays, and this brilliant class called Tapping for Wellbeing on Fridays. Right now it's a Thursday morning, and I'm in Mindfulness for a Positive Life. At the start of the class, the teacher always says how hard mindfulness is and how it will take time to let go of the outside world, and we mustn't be impatient with ourselves. But actually, I find it really easy. I think I must be a natural.

The group is quiet, and we're all meditating on something in the room, which is what we do every week. Luckily, the people at Golden Peace are all really stylish, so there's always something interesting to meditate on. Today I'm focusing on a gorgeous leather backpack in teal, which the dark-haired girl opposite me has slung below her chair. I want to ask her if they come in slate grey, but perhaps I'll do that after the class.

'Brian,' says our teacher Mona, in a soft voice. 'Could you please vocalize for us your mindfulness journey today? What are you meditating on?'

I've seen Brian before. He's tall and buff with quite a prominent nose, which is unusual in LA, and he brings in a Starbucks, although I'm sure that's not allowed.

'I'm focusing on the grain in the wooden floor,' says Brian, in a stilted voice. 'I'm looking at the way the wood swirls around and ebbs and flows. I want to think about my ex-wife, but I'm going to push those thoughts away.' He sounds suddenly fierce. 'I'm not going to think about her *or* her lawyer—'

'Brian, don't judge yourself,' says Mona gently. 'Simply allow your thoughts to return to the floor. Absorb every detail.

127

Every line, every speck, every curve. Be in the moment. Try to reach a heightened sense of awareness.'

Brian exhales. 'I'm in the moment,' he says shakily, his eyes riveted on the floor.

'Good!' Mona smiles. 'Now, Rebecca?' She turns to me. 'We haven't heard much from you. How is your meditation going today?'

'Great, thanks!' I beam at her.

'What are you meditating on today?'

'That bag.' I point. 'It's really nice.'

'Thanks.' The dark-haired girl smiles.

'A bag.' Mona blinks. 'That's different. Are you focusing on the texture of the bag . . . the buckles . . . the colour?'

'The straps,' I say.

'The straps. Good. Perhaps you could share your meditation with us. Just . . . give us a stream of consciousness. Take us where your thoughts are going.'

'OK.' I take a deep breath. 'Well, I'm thinking that those straps look really comfortable but it depends how wide your shoulders are, doesn't it? So then I'm wondering if I could try it after the class. And I'd prefer it in slate grey because I've already got a teal leather bag, but actually, I might give that to my friend Suze because she's always liked it, and she's coming out to visit me. In fact, she's arriving today! And then I'm wondering if they stock them in Barneys because I've got a gift voucher for there, although I have also seen this *really* nice jacket for my daughter Minnie in the children's department which I also want to get—'

'Rebecca, stop!' Mona holds up a hand, and I come to a halt in surprise. 'Stop there!'

What's wrong? I thought I was doing really well. I was much more interesting than Brian with his boring old grainy wood.

'Yes?' I say politely.

'Rebecca . . . Let's remind ourselves of what mindfulness means. It means we bring our attention to the present experience on a moment-to-moment basis.'

'I know.' I nod. 'My present experience is thinking about that bag,' I explain. 'Is it by Alexander Wang?'

'No, it's 3.1 Phillip Lim,' says the girl. 'I got it online.'

'Oh, right!' I say eagerly. 'Which site?'

'I don't think you understand.' Mona cuts across me. 'Rebecca, try to focus on just one aspect of the bag. As soon as you notice your mind wandering off, gently bring it back to the object of attention. OK?'

'But my mind didn't wander off,' I protest. 'I was thinking about the bag the whole time.'

'I can send you the link,' chimes in the dark-haired girl. 'It's a really great backpack. You can fit an iPad in it.'

'Oh, can I try it on?'

'Sure.' The girl reaches for the bag.

'People!' Mona's voice sounds a little sharp, and she immediately smiles as though to compensate. 'Put the bag down! OK! Let's . . . focus. Rebecca, I'm going to recommend that you leave the bag meditation for now. Instead, try to concentrate on your breathing. Just become aware of your breath, going in and out of your body. Don't judge it . . . don't judge yourself . . . just observe your breath. Can you do that?'

I shrug. 'OK.'

'Great! We'll take five minutes' meditation, all of us. Close your eyes if you'd like.'

The room lapses into silence, and I dutifully try to focus on my breath. In. Out. In. Out. In.

God, this is boring. What is there to think about breathing?

I know I'm not an expert on mindfulness, but surely meditation is supposed to make you feel good? Well, I'd feel *much* better if I was meditating on a lovely bag than on my breathing.

My eyes open and drift to the backpack. No one can tell what I'm meditating on. I'll say it was my breath. They'll never know.

Oh, I really do love it. The zips are so cool. And the point is, I should get it because backpacks are good for your posture. Suze will be delighted if I give her my Marc Jacobs.

Surreptitiously I glance at my watch. I wonder where she is. At the airport, hopefully. Her plane should have landed by now and I've told her to come straight here for lunch. Thank God it isn't all coconut water; they serve a decent decaf cappuccino and some really quite yummy carob brownies, and Suze said she'd bring me out some Lion bars . . .

'And gradually bring your thoughts back to the group.' Mona's voice interrupts my meditation. Around the room, people open their eyes and stretch their legs and a couple yawn. Mona smiles at me. 'How was that? Did you manage to keep your mind focused, Rebecca?'

'Er . . . yes!' I say brightly.

Which is sort of true. My thoughts *were* focused, just not on my breathing.

We end with a minute's silent contemplation, and then file out of the room, into the grounds, blinking as we re-enter the bright sunlight. At once, everyone who was in the class switches their phones back on, and stares at them intently. *That's* mindfulness, if you ask me. We should meditate on our phones. In fact, I might suggest it next week—

Yessss! A text bleeps in my phone, and I nearly whoop. It's from Suze! She's here!

OK, here's the thing about Suze. She's one of the most beautiful people I know, and I'm not being biased. She's tall and slim and she has amazing clothes. She can totally shop for Britain and she once nearly modelled for *Vogue*. But she *does* tend to spend quite a lot of time in jodhpurs or jeans or some ancient old Barbour, especially now that she lives in the country all the time. So that's what I'm expecting to see as I hurry towards the entrance gates. Suze in skinny jeans and ballet pumps, with maybe a nice linen jacket, and the children in their usual bumpy corduroy pinafores and shorts, handmade by Nanny.

What I'm not expecting to see is the vision before me. I have to blink to make sure it's the Cleath-Stuarts. They look like some celebrity LA family. What's *happened*?

Suze looks so spectacular I barely recognize her. For a start, she's wearing teeny denim shorts. I mean, really, really teeny. Her legs are long and brown and her pedicured feet are in Havaianas. Her long hair is blonder than usual (has she bleached it?) and she's wearing the most amazing pair of Pucci sunglasses. The children look super-cool, too. The two boys are wearing bomber jackets and gel in their hair and Clementine is rocking teeny little skinny jeans with a vest top.

For a moment I can't do anything except blink in astonishment. Then Suze sees me and starts waving frantically, and I come to life again and rush forward.

'Suze!'

'Bex!'

'You made it!' I fling my arms around her, then hug all the children in turn. 'Suze, your *clothes*!'

'Are they OK?' Suze says at once, anxiously, and brushes at her micro-shorts. 'I wanted to fit in. Do I look all right?'

'You look phenomenal! Did you spray that tan on?' I spot an inked dolphin on her ankle and gasp. 'Suze, you *haven't* gone and got yourself a tattoo!'

'God, no!' She laughs. 'It's temporary. Everyone's got tattoos in LA, so I thought I'd better have one for the trip. And some friendship bracelets.' She waves her arm at me, and I see a stack of about twenty friendship bracelets on her wrist, where normally she has an antique Cartier watch.

'You've been very thorough!' I say, impressed. 'You look totally LA. Has Tarkie done the same? Where is he, anyway?'

'Coming. He stopped to look at some special tree variety in the grounds. And no, he hasn't done the same.' She looks suddenly disconsolate. 'He won't join in. I bought him this really cool ripped T-shirt and cut-offs, but he won't wear them. I can't get him out of his shooting coat.'

'His shooting coat? In LA?' I stifle a giggle. Tarquin's shooting coat is an institution. It's made of the family tweed and has about ninety-five pockets and smells of wet dog all year round.

'Exactly! I wanted him to wear a leather bomber jacket, but he refused. He thinks friendship bracelets are stupid and my tattoo is ghastly.' She looks indignant. 'It isn't ghastly. It's cool!'

'It's lovely,' I say reassuringly.

'I just thought it would be a chance for him to break away, you know?' Suze's indignation fades to a familiar anxiety. 'He needs to stop moping. He needs to forget about his father, and the LHA, and all of them.'

'The LHA?' I say. 'What's that?'

'Oh.' She grimaces. 'Didn't I tell you? It's the Letherby Hall Association. They're members of the public who support Letherby Hall. They've started a petition against the fountain.'

'No!' I exclaim in dismay.

'I know. And then another lot of them have started a petition *for* the fountain. They hate each other. They're all nuts.' She shudders. 'Anyway, forget about that. Are there any celebs here?' Her eyes dart all around as we walk along the path towards the leisure area. 'I can't *believe* you've started coming to Golden Peace.'

'Isn't it great?' I say enthusiastically. 'There are brilliant groups, and yoga, and they serve brownies . . .' I pause at a paved area with bronze bells set into small stone pillars all around. 'These are Paths of Serenity, by the way,' I add. 'You can ring the bells if you need clarity.'

'Clarity?' Suze raises an eyebrow.

'Yes. You know. Clarity in your life.'

'You get clarity in your life from ringing a bell?' She snorts with laughter as she pings one of the bells.

'Yes!' I say defensively. 'You need to keep an open mind, Suze. It's like, a vibration thing. The chiming of the bell changes the rhythm of your inner ear, promoting understanding and resolution and . . . er . . .' Oh God, I've forgotten the rest. 'Anyway, they sound nice,' I finish lamely.

It was Bryce, the Personal Growth Leader, who explained to me about vibrations and clarity, during my induction session, and I totally understood at the time. I'll have to ask him to explain again.

There's a sudden violent clanging all around us. Suze's children have decided to have a go at bashing the bells. Ernest, who is my godson, is actually kick-boxing his, and it's nearly coming off its pillar.

'Stop!' Suze says, dragging them away. 'Too much clarity! Can we get a cup of—' She stops herself. 'A smoothie?'

Ha. She was going to say 'cup of tea'. I know she was.

'D'you want a cup of tea, Suze?' I say, to tease her. 'And a nice digestive biscuit?'

'No thanks,' she says at once. 'I'd far rather have a fresh juice. With a wheatgrass shot.'

'No you wouldn't.'

'I would,' she says obstinately.

She so wants a cup of tea. But I won't wind her up any more. She can have one when we get home. I've bought English tea bags especially, *and* Cooper's Oxford Marmalade *and* Branston Pickle.

I lead them all to the leisure area, where there's a café and a children's playground. Nearby some guys are playing volleyball and about a hundred yards away there's a t'ai chi class going on under the trees.

'How come they have a playground?' says Suze, as the children all run off to the swings and we sit down at a café table. 'They don't have children here, do they?'

'Oh no,' I say knowledgeably. 'But the residents often have their families to visit.'

'Residents?'

'You know. The burnt-out drug-addict rehab ones. They live over there.' I gesture at a gated enclosure within the resort. 'Apparently there's some major, *major* A-list star in residence at the moment. But no one will say who.'

'Damn!'

'I know.'

'Shall we walk past and casually peek?'

'I've tried,' I say regretfully. 'The security people shoo you away.'

'But there are other celebs here, aren't there?'

'Yes! Loads!' I'm about to elaborate when I notice a staff member walking nearby. 'But of course that's all really hush-hush so I can't tell you anything,' I add hastily.

Actually the truth is, I've only seen a couple of celebs in groups, and they weren't much to speak of. One was a Victoria's Secret model, and held up our entire self-esteem group by making us sign individual confidentiality agreements. Then she'd spelled her name wrong and we all had to change 'Brandie' to 'Brandee' and initial it. And then she didn't say anything remotely interesting, anyway. I mean, honestly.

'I'm going to have coffee with Sage Seymour,' I offer, and Suze wrinkles her brow, dissatisfied.

'Weren't you going to do that two weeks ago?'

'Yes, well, she's been busy . . .' I break off as my eye catches a figure walking towards us.

'Oh my God,' I breathe. 'Tarquin looks *terrible*.'

'I know!' says Suze. 'Exactly! He could at least have worn jeans.'

But that's not what I meant. I'm not looking at his tweed shooting jacket, or his ancient brogues, or the mustard-coloured knitted tie around his neck. It's his face. He looks so wan. And there's a stooped slant to his shoulders which I don't remember.

Luke often gets hassled by his business, too, I find myself thinking. But it's different. He built his own company up himself. He drove it. He created it. Whereas Tarquin just had a massive empire plonked on his shoulders when his grandfather died. And right now it looks like it's too heavy for him.

'Tarkie!' I hurry forward to greet him. 'Welcome to Hollywood!'

'Oh. Ahm.' He raises a meagre little smile. 'Yes. Hollywood. Marvellous.'

'Tarkie, take off your shooting coat!' says Suze. 'You must be boiling. In fact, why not take your shirt off too?'

'Take my shirt off? In public?' Tarquin looks scandalized, and I hide a giggle. I'd better not take him to visit Venice Beach.

'Get some sun! It's good for you! Look, all those men there have taken their shirts off.' Suze points encouragingly to the volleyball players on the beach, who are mostly dressed in cut-offs and bandanas.

Suze can be quite bossy when she wants to, and within thirty seconds Tarkie has taken off his shooting coat, his tie, his shirt and his socks and shoes. To my amazement, he's quite tanned and muscled.

'Tarkie, have you been working out?' I say in astonishment.

'He's been helping with the fencing on the estate,' says Suze. 'You don't mind taking your shirt off for that, do you?'

'That's on my own land,' says Tarkie, as though it's obvious. 'Suze, darling, I think I'll put my shirt back on—'

'No! Now, put these on.' She hands him a pair of Ray-Bans. 'There! Brilliant.'

I'm just about to take pity on Tarquin and offer to get him some Earl Grey tea, when the volleyball bounces near us, and Suze leaps up to get it. A bronzed guy in cut-offs and a Golden Peace T-shirt comes running up, and as he draws near I see that it's Bryce.

He's quite amazing, Bryce. He's got the most piercing blue eyes you've ever seen, and he stares at you very intently before he says anything. I don't know how old he is – his hair is greying but he's incredibly lithe and energetic. He doesn't seem to take any groups, but he wanders around and gets to know people and says things like 'Your journey begins here' and really seems to *mean* it.

'Rebecca.' His eyes crinkle into a smile. 'How's your day going?'

'Really well, thanks!' I beam at him. 'Bryce, these are my friends, Suze and Tarquin.'

'Here's your ball,' says Suze, handing it to him. She flicks her hair back a little self-consciously, and I can see her sucking in her stomach, not that she needs to.

'Thank you.' Bryce turns his dazzling smile on her. 'Welcome, both of you.' His eyes fall on Tarquin's shooting coat. 'Cool jacket.'

'Oh,' says Tarquin. 'Ahm. My shooting coat.'

'*Shooting* coat.' Bryce's eyes light up. 'Now that's a great

135

idea. I guess it works in all weathers, right? And great pockets. May I?' Bryce picks up the coat and examines it admiringly.

'Useful for cartridges,' says Tarkie.

'You shoot on film?' Bryce glances up, interested. 'Old school, huh. Excuse me for asking, but . . . do I know your work?'

I hear Suze give a sudden snuffle of laughter, just as I catch on myself. Bryce thinks Tarkie's a director. Tarkie! I cannot think of anyone in my life less likely to direct a film.

'My work?' Tarquin looks slightly hunted. 'You mean . . . the work on Letherby Hall?'

'*Letherby Hall.*' Bryce frowns. 'I didn't see it, I'm afraid. Was it released worldwide?'

Tarquin seems totally baffled. I catch Suze's eye and try not to burst into giggles.

'Anyhow.' Bryce bounces the ball a couple of times. 'You want to join in?'

'Join in?'

'Volleyball.' He gestures at the guys waiting for him on the beach.

'Oh.' Tarquin looks taken aback. 'I don't think—'

'Go on!' says Suze. 'Go *on*, Tarkie. It's just what you need after the flight.'

Reluctantly, Tarquin gets to his feet and follows Bryce down on to the beach. A few moments later he's in the game, and hitting some pretty good shots, I notice.

'Tarkie's excellent at volleyball!' I exclaim.

'Oh yes, he's quite good at that kind of thing,' says Suze vaguely. 'He played Fives for Eton. That Bryce is something, isn't he?'

She's not even watching her own husband. Her eyes are fixed on Bryce. This is what he's like. Everyone gets a crush on him, male and female alike.

A waiter comes over and I order lots of different juices for us and the children, and I'm about to ask Suze what she wants to do first, like maybe the Walk of Fame or Rodeo Drive or the Hollywood sign . . . when I notice someone out of the corner of my eye. A blonde someone, wandering down towards the beach in white yoga pants and a pink racing-back top.

'She's here,' I mutter, turning my head away swiftly. 'Don't look.'

'Who?' Suze immediately swivels her head all around. 'Someone famous?'

'No. Someone hideous in every way.'

Suze suddenly spots her and gasps, 'Alicia Bitch Long-legs!'

'Sssh!' I pull at Suze. 'Turn away. Don't engage. Aloof and flinty.'

'Right,' says Suze vaguely, without moving.

I related the whole awful Alicia encounter to Suze on the phone, but she was waxing her legs at the same time, and I'm not sure she was listening properly.

'She's lost weight,' says Suze critically. 'And her hair looks really good. I like her top . . .'

'Stop complimenting her! And don't attract her attention.'

But it's too late. Alicia's heading our way. This isn't the first time I've seen her at Golden Peace, but it's the first time she's actually come over to speak to me. In Golden Peace terms, Alicia is virtually royalty. There's actually a great big picture of her and Wilton up in the lobby, and when the pair of them walked through the crowded café last week, everyone was practically bowing. Everyone except me.

'Suze.' Alicia doesn't even look at me, but greets Suze with her new soft voice, and I see Suze blink in surprise. 'It's been a long time.'

'Hi Alicia,' says Suze warily.

'You must be here visiting Rebecca. Are those your children?' She turns to look at Ernest, Wilfrid and Clementine, who are running raucously around the slide. 'They're stunning! And I love those cute little jackets.'

'Oh, thanks!' says Suze. She sounds disarmed, and I scowl inwardly. That's a typical underhand trick. Compliment the children.

'How long are you here?' adds Alicia.

'Not sure yet,' says Suze.

'Only, I was going to say, if you'd like them to go to school during your stay, I could fix it up. Our children go to a very good pre-school, don't they, Rebecca?' She manages to glance towards me without meeting my eye. 'And there's a private school nearby which might do for the older one. I should think he's quite advanced?'

'Well.' Suze blossoms. 'He is quite bright . . .'

'I could have a word with the principals. It might be fun for them to experience a US education briefly. The semester's nearly over, but then there are great summer programmes.'

'Wow.' Suze seems taken aback. 'Well, that would be great. But are you sure—'

'It's no trouble.' Alicia gives her wafty smile again, then turns serious. 'Suze, I know our friendship hasn't always been straightforward.'

Friendship? They don't have a friendship.

'But I want you to know,' Alicia continues, 'that I'm set on remoulding that path, and I'm sorry for any discomfort I may have caused you in the past. Let's carry on life's journey in a different spirit.'

'Right.' Suze seems totally flummoxed. Meanwhile, I'm just staring, rigid with shock. She said sorry? She said sorry to Suze?

'I'll let you know about the schools.' Alicia smiles and touches Suze's shoulder, as though giving a blessing. She nods gravely to me, then moves off, down towards the beach.

'Oh my God.' Suze exhales when she's out of earshot. 'What's *happened* to her? That weird voice, and that smile . . . and all that stuff about remoulding her life . . .' She looks at me, giggling, but I can't join in.

'She said sorry to you,' I say incredulously.

'I know.' Suze looks chuffed. 'That was sweet, I thought. And it was nice of her to offer to help with the schools—'

'No!' I clutch my head. 'You don't understand! She refused to say sorry to me! After everything she did to Luke and me, she wouldn't apologize. I asked her to, straight out.'

'Well . . .' Suze thinks for a moment. 'Maybe she was too embarrassed.'

'*Embarrassed?* Alicia Bitch Long-legs doesn't get embarrassed!'

'Maybe she thought she'd already apologized.'

'You're sticking up for her.' I stare at Suze in dismay. 'I can't believe you'd stick up for Alicia Bitch Long-legs.'

'I'm not sticking up for her!' ripostes Suze. 'I'm just saying, people change, and—' She breaks off as our drinks arrive, and the waitress presents us with two Golden Peace gift bags: glossy white with golden rope handles.

'Alicia asked me to give you these.' She smiles. 'A little welcome pack.'

'Ooh! Thank you!' says Suze, and starts unpacking hers straight away. 'Look, bath oil . . . and a candle . . .'

'You're accepting it?' I say, scandalized.

'Of course I am!' says Suze, rolling her eyes. 'It's an olive branch. She's changed. You should let people change, Bex.'

'She hasn't changed.' I glare at Suze. 'If she'd changed she would apologize.'

'She did apologize!'

'Not to me!' I practically yell. 'Not to *me!*'

'Look, Bex,' Suze pauses, halfway through unwrapping some herbal tea bags. 'Please don't let's argue. Especially not about Alicia, for goodness' sake! I think you should have your goodie bag and enjoy it. Go on.' She prods me with a teasing smile. 'Open it. I know you want to . . .'

Even though I'm still simmering inside, I can't argue any more with Suze. Especially on her first day here. So I make a huge effort and smile back. I'll never get her to understand about Alicia, I think dolefully. Maybe no one will ever properly understand except Luke (kind of) and me, and I'll just have to accept that. Reluctantly, I pull the gift bag towards me and open it. I've got a candle too, and some olive-oil soap and . . . Wow. A Golden Peace bikini. I've seen those in the shop, and they're $100.

I mean, it's nice. But it doesn't change Alicia.

'I really want one of those white and gold bracelets,' says Suze, eyeing mine. 'Maybe I'll take some classes. Let's have a look . . .' She opens the brochure, which was in the bag, then a moment later puts it down, her eyes wide. 'Bex, this place costs a fortune! How many times a week do you come here?'

'Er . . . every day.'

'Every day?' Suze is goggle-eyed. 'But how much does that cost?' She starts flicking through the brochure, gasping at every page. 'Have you seen how much a yoga class costs? I pay a fifth of that in London.'

She seems so flabbergasted, I feel a bit defensive.

'It's not about money, Suze. It's about mental health and spiritual wellbeing and my personal journey.'

'Oh yes?' she says sceptically. 'Well, have they stopped you shopping too much?'

I wait for a beat, then answer with a flourish: 'Yes!'

'Yes?' Suze drops the brochure and stares at me, with huge blue eyes. 'Bex, did you say, "Yes"?'

Ha. Ha-di-ha. I was *waiting* for this subject to come up.

'Yes,' I say smugly. 'I had a special one-to-one session yesterday with David, one of the therapists, and we talked through my issues, and he gave me lots of coping mechanisms. I'm a changed person, Suze!'

'Oh my God,' says Suze weakly. 'You're serious.'

'Of course I'm serious!'

'So . . . what, you walk into a shop and you don't want to buy anything?'

'That's not how it works,' I say kindly. 'It's a journey, Suze. We're all on a journey.'

'Well, how *does* it work?'

'I'll show you! Come on, we'll go to the gift shop.'

I drain my juice and leap up, by now totally cheered. I'm longing to show off all my new techniques. I haven't had a chance to practise them yet, except in the mirror at home.

'Ernie!' commands Suze. 'You're in charge. Stay in the play-ground. We'll just be in the shop, OK?'

'It's fine,' I say. 'We can see the playground from the shop. Come on!'

To be honest, I've been quite amazed at my own spectacular progress. When David came to find me at lunch one day, and suggested a one-to-one session to 'discuss my shopping issues', I wasn't that keen. In fact I said, 'Wow, that sounds fab, but actually, I'm a bit too busy.'

Then, when he set up a session anyway, I accidentally-on-purpose forgot to turn up. And then, when he came to find me in yoga, I . . . Well. I avoided him.

OK, I ran away, and hid behind a tree. Which I do appreciate was a bit childish. But he tracked me down in the café later that day and talked really sweetly to me and said if I hated what he said I could ignore it all.

So at last I had the session. And all I can say is, *why* did I never do this before? David kept saying, 'These are the first baby steps,' and, 'I know you'll find these ideas hard,' and I agreed because I sensed that was what he wanted me to say. But honestly. I found them *easy*. I must be mentally very strong, or something.

He talked about 'why people shop', and then he told me about lots of different techniques that we could work on together, and then he told me how the lessons I'm learning in my other classes, like Mindfulness for a Positive Life and Tapping for Wellbeing, all feed into the same picture. And I nodded earnestly and took notes and then we talked about how I could go into the spending addiction programme when a space becomes available.

But the truth is, I don't need to go into any spending addiction programme. I'm clearly a very fast learner, because I've totally got it. I have control over myself! I can't wait to show Suze.

'Here we are!' I push open the doors to the gift shop. I have to say, it's the most gorgeous shop. It's all pale wood and scented candles burning, and everywhere you look is some beautiful, uplifting thing to help you on your journey, like a cashmere yoga hoody, or a soft, leather-bound 'thought diary', or positive affirmations printed on canvases. There's a jewellery range, which is all made of organic crystals, and there are stacks of books and CDs, and even a range of 'healing energy' make-up.

I look at Suze, waiting for her to say, 'Wow, what an amazing shop!' But she's just staring at me expectantly.

'OK,' she says. 'What now? Do you just look around and think, "No, I don't want any of this"?'

'It's a *process*,' I say patiently, and get out my notebook. 'First of all, I have to think, "Why I am shopping?" And I have to write it down.' I look at the list of suggestions David gave me. Am I bored? No. Lonely? No. Anxious? No. For a moment I'm stumped. Why *am* I shopping?

'I'll put: "To show friend that I don't shop too much any more,"' I say at last. I write it down and underline it proudly. 'Now what?'

'Going shopping can often be a way of boosting low self-esteem,' I say knowledgeably. 'So I have to boost my self-esteem myself, with affirmations.' I get out the Positive Thought cards that David gave me, and rifle through them. 'Like this: *I approve of myself and feel great about myself.*' I beam at Suze. 'Isn't that great? I've got loads of them.'

'Let's see!' she says at once, holding out her hand.

'Here you are.' I hand her a card that says *I accept others as they are and they in turn accept me as I am.* 'You can buy them here,' I add. 'And you can get really nice T-shirts with the affirmations printed on. Shall we try some on?'

'Try on T-shirts?' Suze stares at me. 'Bex, I thought you'd given up shopping.'

'I haven't *given up shopping.*' I almost laugh at her naive, simplistic attitude. 'That's not what this is about, Suze. It's not about abstinence, it's about getting into a *healthy shopping pattern.*'

That's the lesson that really stuck with me from the session yesterday. It's *not* about giving up shopping. As soon as David said that, the whole thing made more sense to me.

'Well, wouldn't it be healthier not to shop at all?' Suze demands. 'I mean, shouldn't we leave?'

Suze really doesn't get it. But then, she isn't as tuned in to her inner mental landscape as me.

'It's actually a very bad idea to give up shopping altogether,' I explain. 'You have to learn to exercise your control muscle. Being in here is like a workout for me.'

'Right.' Suze looks dubious. 'So what happens next?'

'So, I'll just make the purchases I need to, calmly and with meaning.'

I love that phrase. David kept saying it yesterday. *You need to learn to shop calmly and with meaning.*

'But you don't need to buy anything,' objects Suze.

'Yes I do! I need a book, actually. David told me to buy it. So.' I lead my way over to the Cognitive Behavioral Therapy section, and reach for a book titled *Catching Thoughts: Your Introduction to CBT.*

'This is what I do in my group,' I say importantly, pointing at the title. 'Cognitive Behavioral Therapy. If I want to buy something and it's not appropriate, I have to restructure my thoughts. I have to identify my cognitive errors and challenge them.'

'Wow.' For the first time, Suze looks genuinely impressed. 'Is that hard?'

'No, it's quite easy,' I say, flipping through the book. 'I'll get the audio version too, so I can listen to it when I'm out jogging. And there are some other titles David said I should look at, too.'

I start scooping hardbacks into my basket. *CBT Thought Diary, CBT for Spending Addiction, The Compulsive Spender's Journal, Shopaholic: Break the Pattern* . . . As I pile the books up I feel a glow of virtue. David was right, I *can* break free of my old ways. There are some really cool pencils too, matt black with slogans like *Growth* and *Exhale*. I'll get a pack.

Suze is watching me, a bit nonplussed.

'But Bex, how is this different from normal shopping? Where's the challenging or whatever it is?'

Oh, right. I'd forgotten about that, just for a moment.

'I was *coming* to that,' I say, a little severely. 'You put the things in your basket and *then* you challenge yourself.'

I lift up the top book and stare at it intently. I'm actually a bit hazy about what I should do next, not that I'll admit that to Suze.

'I need this book,' I say at last, in a sonorous voice. 'This is my belief. The evidence for this belief is: David told me I should get it. The evidence against it is . . . none. So. I will buy it, calmly and with meaning. Amen.'

'*Amen?*' Suze gives a sudden giggle.

'That just slipped out,' I admit. 'Anyway, wasn't that cool? I've totally learned how to challenge myself.'

'Do the pencils now,' Suze says.

'OK.' I take the pencils out and focus on them. 'I need these pencils. This is my belief. The evidence for this belief is: pencils are always useful. The evidence against is . . .'

I stop dead as a thought strikes me. I've already bought a pack of these pencils, haven't I? The first day I came here. What did I do with them?

'The evidence against,' I continue triumphantly, 'is that I've already got some! So I'm going to put them back!'

With a flourish, I put the pack of pencils back on the shelf. 'You see? I'm *controlling* myself. I'm a completely different person. Impressed?'

'Well, OK. But what about all those books?' Suze nods at my basket. 'Surely you don't need so many?'

Hasn't she been listening to anything I've been saying?

'Of course I need them,' I say as patiently as I can. 'They're essential for my progress. I'm going to buy them calmly and with meaning.' I reach for a gorgeous notepad. 'I'm going to buy this calmly and with meaning, too. I can keep my dream journal in it. Everyone should keep a dream journal, did you know that?'

Suze still looks dissatisfied as I put it in my basket.

'All right, so suppose you *do* shop too much,' she says. 'What do you do then?'

'Then you use different techniques,' I explain. 'Like tapping.'

'What's tapping?'

'Oh, it's brilliant,' I say enthusiastically. 'You tap your face and chin and stuff, and you say mantras, and it frees your meridians and cures you.'

'*What?*' Suze stares at me.

'It's true!'

Tapping is almost my favourite class. Plus, I think it must be very good for toning the facial muscles, tapping your chin the whole time. I put my basket down and turn to demonstrate.

'You tap your forehead and you say, "I know I have bought too much but I deeply and completely accept myself." See?' I beam at her. 'Easy.' I tap my chest for good measure, and the top of my head.

'Bex . . .' Suze seems perplexed.

'What?'

'Are you *sure* you're doing it right?'

'Of course I'm doing it right!'

The trouble with Suze is, she hasn't had her mind opened, like I have. She hasn't been exposed to the wealth of mind–spirit enhancement that's out there.

'You'll learn the ways of Golden Peace after you've been here a bit,' I say kindly. 'Now, let's try on T-shirts!'

GOLDEN PEACE GIFT STORE

Customer invoice

Ms Rebecca Brandon
Membership No: 1658

Dept	Item	Quantity	Tot. Price
Books:	*Shopaholic: Break the Pattern*	1	$19.99
Gifts:	Coconut lip balm	5	$20.00
Gifts:	Mandarin lip balm	5	$20.00
Home:	Wind chime (large)	3	$89.97
Home:	Wind chime (small)	3	$74.97
Audio CDs:	*Never Overspend Again*	1	$24.99
Jewelry:	Earth crystal pendant	2	$68.00
Apparel:	Affirmation T-shirt: *Learn*	1	$39.99
Apparel:	Affirmation T-shirt: *Grow*	1	$39.99
Apparel:	Hiking jacket (50% discount)	1	$259.99
Books:	*The Compulsive Spender's Journal*	1	$15.99
Food:	Manuka Honey (bulk discount)	10	$66.00
Books:	*CBT for Spending Addiction*	1	$30.00
Jewelry:	Healing silver bangle	2	$154.00

TEN

I would have thought Suze would be more impressed by Golden Peace. I think she's got a mental block. She's prejudiced, that's what it is. She hasn't signed up for a single class, and she didn't even buy a T-shirt. All she keeps saying is, she thinks it's all really expensive, and what's the point?

The point? Hasn't she noticed how transformed I am?

Luckily Tarkie is on my side. He thinks Golden Peace is great, and he's really bonded with Bryce.

'We both think exactly the same way about light pollution,' he's saying now. It's breakfast time the next day, and we're all gathered in the kitchen. 'Light pollution is a modern evil, but politicians simply won't listen.'

I can see Suze rolling her eyes, and give her a little smile. Tarkie is so obsessed about light pollution, he goes around Letherby Hall all the time, switching off lights, and Suze creeps after him, switching them back on.

'Right!' I approach the table triumphantly, holding a plate. 'Here's our healthy LA breakfast. It's a steamed egg-white omelette, made with kale.'

There's silence around the table. Everyone is looking at the plate in horror.

OK, I admit it doesn't look exactly like an omelette. It's kind of white and shapeless, and the kale has turned grey-green. But it's healthy.

'A steamed omelette?' says Suze, at last.

'I did it in the microwave, in a Ziploc bag,' I explain. 'It's fat-free. Who'd like the first one?'

There's another silence.

'Ahm . . . It looks delicious, I must say.' Tarquin plunges in. 'But you don't have any kippers, do you?'

'No, I don't have any kippers!' I say, a bit rattled. 'This isn't Scotland, it's LA, and everyone eats steamed omelettes.'

Luke finally looks up from the letter he's been reading. 'What's *that*?' he says in horror, then sees my face and adjusts his expression. 'I mean . . . what's that?'

'It's a steamed omelette.' I prod it disconsolately.

They're right, it does look disgusting. And I spent *ages* separating all the eggs and chopping up all the kale. The recipe was in a book called *Power Brunch*, and I thought everyone would be really impressed. I don't dare tell them about the mushroom protein shake, which I've got waiting in the blender.

'Bex, where are the egg yolks you didn't use?' says Suze suddenly.

'In a bowl.'

'Well, why don't I make an omelette with them?'

Before I can stop her, Suze is heating up a pan, putting lashings of butter into it, and frying up the most delicious, yellow, crispy omelette I've ever seen, together with ribbons of bacon which she got from the fridge.

'There.'

She puts it on the table, and everyone falls on it. I take a forkful myself and nearly die with pleasure.

'They should do egg-*yolk* omelettes in restaurants,' says Suze, her mouth full. 'Why's everyone so obsessed by egg whites, anyway? They don't taste of anything.'

'They're healthy.'

'Crap,' says Suze robustly. 'We feed egg yolks to our lambs and they're perfectly healthy.'

Luke is pouring coffee for everyone, Suze is slathering marmalade on a slice of toast, and spirits have generally lifted.

'So.' Luke looks around the table. 'I've had an invitation today. Who fancies coming to a gala benefit at the Beverly Hilton?'

'Me!' Suze and I exclaim simultaneously.

'It's for . . .' He squints at the letter. 'Victims of discrimination. Some new charity.'

'I read about that!' says Suze in excitement. 'Salma Hayek will be there! Can we really go?'

'Sage is asking us all to sit on her table, house guests included.' Luke smiles at Suze. 'You're in.'

'Tarkie, did you hear that?' Suze leans across the table, brandishing her toast. 'We've been invited to a real Hollywood party!'

'A party.' Tarquin looks as though he's been told he has to have a tooth out. 'Wonderful.'

'It'll be *fun*,' says Suze. 'You might meet Salma Hayek.'

'Ah.' He looks vague. 'Marvellous.'

'You don't know who Salma Hayek is, do you?' says Suze accusingly.

'Of course I do.' Tarkie looks trapped. 'He's . . . an actor. Jolly talented.'

'She! *She's* jolly talented!' Suze sighs. 'I'll have to coach you before we go. Here, read this, for a start.' She passes him a copy of *US Weekly*, just as Minnie and Wilfrid run into the kitchen.

Having the Cleath-Stuarts to stay is brilliant for Minnie. I don't think she's ever had so much fun in her life. She's wearing two baseball caps, one on top of the other, holding a shoe horn like a riding crop, and 'riding' Wilfrid like a horse.

'Go, horsey!' she yells, and pulls on the 'reins', which consist of about six of Luke's belts buckled together. The next minute, Clementine appears, 'riding' Ernest.

'Let's jump, Minnie!' she squeals. 'Let's jump over the sofas!'

'No!' says Suze. 'Stop running about and come and have some breakfast. Who wants toast?'

I notice she's diplomatically not even referring to the

egg-white omelette. I think we'll all just pretend it never existed.

As all the children get settled into their seats, I suddenly notice that Minnie has reached out for my phone.

'Please phone,' she says promptly. 'Pleeeeeease. *Pleeeeeeease!*' She hugs it to her ear as though it's her newborn infant and I'm Herod.

I've given Minnie about three plastic toy phones, but they don't fool her for an instant. You have to admire her, really. So I always end up giving in and letting her hold my phone – even though I'm paranoid she's going to drop it in her milk or something.

'All right,' I say. 'Just for a minute.'

'Hello!' says Minnie into the phone, and beams at me. 'Hello, Oraaaa!'

Ora? Ora Bitch Long-legs?

'Don't talk to Ora, darling,' I say lightly. 'Talk to someone else. Talk to Page. She's a sweet little girl.'

'Talk Ora,' Minnie says stubbornly. 'Love Ora.'

'You don't love Ora!' I snap, before I can stop myself.

'Who's Ora?' says Suze.

'Alicia's daughter,' I mutter. 'Of all the children in all the world for Minnie to become friends with.'

'Honestly, Bex!' retorts Suze. 'You're ridiculous. What is this, the Montagues and the Capulets?'

Minnie looks from Suze to me, then back again. Then she screws up her face for a scream. 'Love Oraaaaaaa!'

All this time, Luke has been tapping away on his BlackBerry. He has this almost mystical power to tune out his immediate surroundings when they consist of Minnie screeching. But now he raises his head.

'Who's Ora?'

I can't believe our entire breakfast table is discussing Alicia Bitch Long-legs' daughter.

'No one,' I say. 'Minnie, come here and help me do my toast.'

'Toast!' Her eyes light up with instant excitement and I can't help giving her a little kiss. Minnie thinks spreading butter on toast is the most fun activity in the world, except I have to dissuade her from adding marmalade *and* chocolate spread *and* peanut butter. (Luke always says, 'Like mother like daughter,' which is absolute nonsense, I don't know what he means.)

As I sip my coffee and try to stop Minnie from smearing butter all over her fingers, I find myself watching Luke. He's gazing at his BlackBerry and there's a vein pulsing in his neck. He's stressed out about something. What?

'Luke?' I say cautiously. 'Is something up?'

'No,' he says at once. 'Nothing. Nothing.'

OK. That means it's something.

'Luke?' I try again.

He meets my eye and exhales. 'It's an email from my mother's lawyer. She's having some kind of surgery. He thought I should know.'

'Right,' I say warily.

Luke is glowering at the screen again. Any stranger looking at him would simply see a man in a bad temper. But I can see the special, devastated overlay that appears whenever Luke's thinking about his mother, and it makes my heart crunch. Luke just can't find happiness with his mother. He used to worship her unreasonably; now he loathes her unreasonably. Elinor abandoned him to go and live in the States when he was just a child, and I don't think he's ever quite forgiven her. Especially now he has Minnie; now he knows what it is to be a parent.

'What does she expect?' he suddenly bursts out. 'What does she expect me to do?'

'Maybe she doesn't expect anything,' I venture.

Luke doesn't reply, just sips his coffee with a murderous scowl.

'What kind of surgery is she having?' I ask. 'Is it serious?'

'Let's just forget about it,' he says abruptly and gets to his feet. 'So I'll tell Aran there are four acceptances for the benefit. It's black tie,' he adds, and kisses me. 'See you later.'

'Luke—' I grab his hand to stop him. But as he turns back, I realize I don't know what I want to say, except, 'Please make peace with your mother,' which I can't just blurt out with no build-up. 'Have a good day,' I say lamely, and he nods.

'Black tie?' Tarquin is looking dismayed as he turns to Suze. 'Darling, what will I wear? I don't have my kilt.'

His *kilt*? Oh my God. The idea of Tarkie turning up to some LA benefit in a kilt and sporran and those big woolly socks makes me want to collapse in laughter.

'You're not going to wear a kilt!' expostulates Suze. 'You're going to wear . . .' She thinks for a moment. 'An Armani tuxedo. And a black shirt and a black tie. That's what all these Hollywood types wear.'

'A black shirt?' Now it's Tarquin's turn to expostulate. 'Suze, darling, only spivs wear black shirts.'

'Well, OK, a white shirt,' Suze relents. 'But *not* a wing collar. You need to look cool. And I'm going to test you on celebrities later.'

Poor Tarkie. As he leaves the kitchen he looks like a man sentenced to prison, not a man who's got a ticket to the coolest party in town.

'He's hopeless,' sighs Suze. 'You know, he can name about a hundred breeds of sheep, but not *one* of Madonna's husbands.'

'I've never seen anyone so out of place.' I bite my lip, trying not to laugh. 'Tarkie's really not suited to LA, is he?'

'Well, we've been on enough holidays to grouse moors,' says Suze. 'It's my turn. And I *love* it here.' She pours herself some more orange juice, then lowers her voice. 'What do you think's up with Elinor?'

'I don't know.' I lower my voice even further. 'What if she's really ill?'

We look at each other anxiously. I can tell our thoughts are heading in the same direction, then sheering away.

'He has to know the truth about the party,' says Suze at length. 'He has to know how generous she was. Just in case . . . anything happens.'

'But how do I tell him? He'll just fly off the handle. He won't even listen!'

'Could you write it down?'

I consider this for a moment. I *am* quite good at letter-writing, and I could make Luke promise to read to the end before shouting. But even as I'm considering it, I know what I truly want to do.

'I'm going to invite her over,' I say with resolve. 'Either before her surgery or afterwards, depending.'

'Invite her where? *Here?*' Suze's eyes widen. 'Are you sure, Bex?'

'If I write a letter, he'll just ignore it. I need the two of them together. I'm going to stage an intervention,' I say with a flourish.

We were talking about interventions at Golden Peace the other day, and I was the only one who hadn't been in one. I felt quite left out.

Suze looks doubtful. 'Aren't they for drug addicts?'

'And family disputes,' I say authoritatively.

I don't actually know if this is true. But I can always start my own kind of intervention, can't I? I have a vision of myself, dressed in flowing white clothes, talking in a low melodious voice and bringing harmony to the fractured souls of Luke and Elinor.

Maybe I'll buy some healing crystals for the occasion. And some scented candles, and a CD of soothing chants. I'll come up with my own special cocktail of techniques, and I won't let Luke or Elinor leave until they've achieved some sort of resolution.

'Shouldn't you get someone specially trained?' Suze is still looking dubious. 'I mean, what do you know about it?'

'Loads,' I say, a bit offended. 'I've picked up a lot from Golden Peace, you know, Suze. I've done conflict resolution, and everything. "To understand everything is to forgive everything,"' I can't resist quoting. 'Buddha.'

'OK, if you're such an expert, sort out this conflict.' Suze points at Wilfie and Clemmie, who are fighting desperately over some tiny plastic animal.

'Er ... hey, Wilfie! Clemmie!' I call out. 'Who wants a sweetie?'

Both children instantly stop tussling and hold out their hands.

'There!' I say smugly.

'Is that how you're going to sort out Luke and Elinor?' scoffs Suze. 'Offer them sweeties?'

'Of course not,' I say with dignity. 'I'll use a variety of techniques.'

'Well, I still think it's risky.' She shakes her head. '*Very* risky.'

' "One cannot refuse to eat simply because there is a risk of being choked," ' I say wisely. 'Chinese proverb.'

'Bex, stop talking like a bloody T-shirt!' Suze suddenly flips out. 'I hate this stupid Golden Peace place! Talk about something *normal*. What are you going to wear for the benefit? And *don't* say something stupid like, "*Clothes are a metaphor for the soul.*" '

'I wasn't going to!' I retort.

Actually, that's quite good. I might drop that into a class at Golden Peace. *Clothes are a metaphor for the soul.*

Maybe I'll get it printed on canvas and give it to Suze for Christmas.

'Why are you smiling?' says Suze suspiciously.

'No reason!' I force my mouth straight. 'So. What are *you* going to wear to the benefit?'

ELEVEN

Suze can talk about shopping. She can talk about shopping!

Not only has she bought a new dress for the benefit, she's bought new shoes, a new necklace and new hair. New *hair*. She didn't even tell me she was doing it. One moment she was 'popping out to the hairdresser', and the next she was walking back in the door with the most luscious, glossy extensions I've ever seen. They stream down to her waist in a blonde river, and what with that and the tanned legs she looks like a movie star herself.

'You look fantastic,' I say honestly, as we stand in front of my mirror. She's in a beaded shift, the colour of a glassy sea, and her necklace has a mermaid on it. I've never seen a mermaid necklace before, but now I'm desperate for one, too.

'Well, so do you!' says Suze at once.

'Really?' I pluck at my dress, which is Zac Posen and very flattering around the waist, though I say so myself. I've styled it with my Alexis Bittar necklace and my hair is in a really complicated up-do, all little plaits and waves. Plus, I've been practising how to stand on the red carpet. I found a guide on the internet, and printed it out for both of us. Legs crossed, elbow out, chin tucked in. I take up my pose, and Suze copies me.

'I look like I've got a double chin,' she says fretfully. 'Are you sure this is right?'

'Maybe we're tucking our chins in *too* much.'

I lift my chin, and immediately look like a soldier. Suze, meanwhile, is doing a perfect Posh Spice pose. She has the expression and everything.

'That's it!' I say excitedly. 'Only, smile.'

'I can't stand like this *and* smile,' says Suze, sounding strained. 'I think you have to be double-jointed to get it right. Tarkie!' she calls as he passes the open door. 'Come and practise being photographed!'

Tarquin has looked shell-shocked ever since Suze appeared with extensions. Now he looks like a condemned man. Suze has forced him into a tailored Prada DJ, complete with narrow black tie and dapper shoes. I mean, he looks very good, for Tarkie. He's tall and strapping, and his hair has been artfully mussed by Suze. He just looks so . . . different.

'You should wear Prada all the time, Tarkie!' I say, and he blanches.

'Stand here,' Suze is saying. 'Now, when you have your picture taken, you need to tilt your face at an angle. And look kind of moody.'

'Darling, I don't think I'll be in the photos,' says Tarkie, backing away. 'If it's all right.'

'You have to be! They photograph everyone.' She glances uncertainly at me. 'They do photograph everyone, don't they?'

'Of course they do,' I say confidently. 'We're guests, aren't we? So we'll be photographed.'

I feel a fizz of excitement. I can't wait! I've always wanted to be photographed on a red carpet in Hollywood. My phone bleeps with a text and I pull it out of my clutch bag.

'The car's here! Let's go!'

'What about Luke?' says Tarquin, who is obviously desperate for some moral support.

'We're meeting him there.' I spray a final cloud of scent over me and grin at Suze. 'Ready for your close-up, Lady Cleath-Stuart?'

'Don't call me that!' she says at once. 'It makes me sound ancient!'

I head into the children's bedroom, where our babysitter, Teri, is presiding over a massive game of Twister. Minnie doesn't understand Twister, but she understands rolling around on the mat, getting in everyone's way, so that's what she's doing.

'Night night!' I plant a kiss on her little cheek. 'See you later!'

'Mummy.' Wilfrid stares at Suze in awe. 'You look like a fish.'

'Thank you, darling!' Suze hugs him. 'That's *exactly* what I wanted to look like.'

Tarquin has edged over and is fiddling with Wilfrid's toy train.

'Maybe I'll stay here and help look after the children,' he says. 'I'd be very happy to—'

'No!' Suze and I shout in unison.

'You'll love it,' says Suze, chivvying him out of the room.

'You might meet Angelina Jolie,' I chime in.

'Or Renée Zellweger.'

'Or Nick Park,' I say craftily. 'You know? The *Wallace and Gromit* man?'

'Ah!' says Tarkie, suddenly perking up. '*The Wrong Trousers*. Now, *that* was a jolly good film.'

The Beverly Hilton is where they hold the Golden Globes. We're going to the same place they hold the Golden Globes! As our car edges along in early evening traffic, I can barely keep still.

'Hey, Suze!' I say suddenly. 'D'you think it'll be the exact same red carpet as at the Golden Globes?'

'Maybe!'

I can tell Suze is as gripped by this idea as I am. She starts rearranging her hair extensions on her shoulders, and I check my lipstick for the millionth time.

I'm not going to waste this opportunity. There are going to be some A-list celebrities at this party, and if I keep my wits about me I can do some major networking. I've got my cards in my bag, printed with *Rebecca Brandon, Stylist*, and I'm planning to work every single conversation I can round to fashion. I just need one influential person to hire me, and then word will spread, and my reputation will grow, and . . . well, the sky's the limit.

It's just finding that one influential person which is the tricky bit.

The car pulls up outside the hotel and I give a little squeak of excitement. There aren't crowds, like at the Golden Globes, but there are barricades, and banks of photographers, and a red carpet! An actual red carpet! There are big screens with *E.Q.U.A.L.* printed all over, which is the name of the charity. (It stands for something, but I have no idea what. I don't think anyone does.) In front of them, an elegant blonde woman in a nude dress is posing for the cameras, along with a bearded man in black tie.

'Who's that?' I say, nudging Suze. 'Is that Glenn Close?'

'No, it's the one out of . . . you know. That show.' Suze wrinkles her nose. 'Oh God, what's her name . . .'

'Look!' I point ahead at a young guy with spiky hair and a DJ getting out of his limo. Photographers are clustered around the car, clicking away and calling out, but he's ignoring them, in a totally cool way.

'Are you ladies ready?' The limo driver turns to face us.

'Right. Yes.' I take a deep breath, calming my nerves.

Suze and I practised all afternoon in her hire car, getting out and taking pictures of each other, and we've totally nailed it. We won't be flashing our underwear, or tripping over our heels. Nor will we wave at the camera, which Suze always wants to do.

'Ready?' Suze is grinning tremulously.

'Ready!'

The limo driver has opened the door on my side. I give my hair a last-minute pat and take my most elegant step out, waiting for the flash of bulbs, the shouts, the clamour . . .

Oh. What?

Where did all the cameras go? They were here a minute ago. I turn round, discomfited, and see them all clustered around another limo, behind us. Some red-haired girl in blue is getting out of it and smiling prettily around. I don't even recognize her. Is she a real celebrity?

Suze emerges from the limo beside me, and looks around, bewildered.

'Where are the photographers?'

'There.' I point. 'With her.'

'Oh.' She looks as disconsolate as me. 'What about us?'

'I suppose we're not celebrities,' I say reluctantly.

'Well, never mind.' Suze brightens. 'We've still got the red carpet. Come on!' Tarquin has got out of the limo too, and she grabs him by the arm. 'Red-carpet time!'

As we get close to the hotel, there are loads of people milling about in black tie, but we manage to push our way through to the entrance to the red carpet. I'm fizzing with anticipation. This is it!

'Hi!' I beam at the security guard. 'We're guests.' I proffer our invitations, and he scans them dispassionately.

'This way, ma'am.' He points away from the celebs, to some kind of side route which a crowd of people in evening dress are filing down.

'No, we're going to the benefit,' I explain.

'That's the way to the benefit.' He nods, and opens a rope barrier. 'Have a good evening.'

He doesn't get it. Maybe he's a bit slow.

'We need to go *this way*.' I gesture clearly to the bank of photographers.

'On the red carpet,' puts in Suze. She points at our invitation. 'It says, "Red Carpet Entrance".'

'This is the red carpet, ma'am.' He points at the side route again, and Suze and I exchange looks of dismay.

OK, I suppose strictly speaking there is a carpet. And it is a kind of dull red. But *don't* tell me that's where we're supposed to go.

'It's not red,' objects Suze. 'It's maroon.'

'And there aren't any photographers or anything. We want to walk on *that* red carpet.' I point behind him.

'Only Gold List Guests will be walking that red carpet, ma'am.'

Gold List Guests? Why aren't we Gold List Guests?

'Come on,' says Tarkie, clearly bored. 'Shall we go in, have a titchy?'

'But the red carpet's the whole point! Hey, look, there's Sage Seymour!' Sage is talking earnestly to a TV camera. 'She's my friend,' I say to the security guard. 'She wants to say hello.'

'There'll be a chance to greet her inside the benefit,' says the security guard implacably. 'Could you move along, ma'am? People are waiting behind you.'

We don't have any choice. Morosely, we all move through the barrier and start down the Non-Gold List, Totally Inferior Sub-Red Carpet. I don't believe it. I thought we'd be on the red carpet with Sage and all the famous people. Not filing along like cattle down some dimly lit *maroon* carpet that has stains on it.

'Hey, Suze,' I whisper suddenly. 'Let's go round again. See if we can get on the proper red carpet.'

'*Definitely*,' says Suze. 'Hey, Tarkie,' she says more loudly. 'I need to adjust my bra. I'll see you in there, OK? Get us a titchy.'

She hands him his invitation, then we swing round and begin to hurry back up the non-red carpet. There are so many people piling down by now, in evening dress and jewels and clouds of scent, it feels as if we're like fish swimming against a very sparkly, glamorous tide.

'Sorry,' I keep saying. 'Just forgot something . . . Excuse me . . .'

At last we reach the top of the carpet, and pause for a breather. The security guard is still standing at his post, directing people down the maroon carpet. He hasn't spotted us yet, but that's because we're hidden behind a screen.

'What now?' says Suze.

'We cause a diversion.' I think for a moment, then squeal, 'Oh my God! My Harry Winston earring! Please, everyone! I lost my Harry Winston earring!'

Every woman in the vicinity stops dead in shock. I can see blood draining from faces. You don't joke about Harry Winston in LA.

'Oh my *God.*'

'Harry *Winston?*'

'How many carats?'

'Please!' I say, almost tearfully. 'Help me look!'

About ten women bend down and start patting the carpet.

'What does it look like?'

'Frank, help! She lost her earring!'

'I lost my Harry Winston ring once, we had to empty the whole pool . . .'

It's complete mayhem. There are women on their hands and knees, and people trying to get on to the maroon carpet, and men trying to chivvy their wives along, and the security guard keeps calling, 'Move along, folks! Please move along!'

At last he drops his rope barrier and comes striding on to the carpet.

'Folks, we need to keep moving along.'

'Ow! You trod on my hand!' cries out a woman.

'Don't step on the earring!' exclaims another.

'Did someone find the earring?'

'What earring?' He looks at the end of his tether. 'What the hell is going on?'

'Now,' I whisper in Suze's ear. '*Run!*'

Before I can think twice, we're both careering up the maroon carpet, past the unattended velvet-rope check-point and on to the red carpet . . . I can't help laughing out loud with glee. We're there! On the actual, proper, red carpet! Suze looks pretty exhilarated, too.

'We did it!' she says. 'Now, *that's* what I call red.'

I look around, getting my bearings, whilst trying to stand properly and smile. The carpet's definitely red. It also feels quite big and empty, which is maybe because all the photographers have turned away. As Suze and I move slowly along we're doing our best Hollywood poses, elbows out and everything. But not one cameraman is taking a picture. Some of them are still clustered around the young guy with spiky hair, and the others are chatting or on the phone.

I mean, I know we're not *exactly* famous, but still. I feel quite aggrieved on behalf of Suze, who looks absolutely gorgeous.

'Suze, do that bendy-back pose where you look over your shoulder,' I say, and then hurry over to a photographer with dark hair and a denim jacket who's leaning on the barrier, yawning. Yawning!

'Hey, take her photo,' I say, pointing at Suze. 'She looks gorgeous!'

'Who is she?' he retorts.

'Don't you recognize her?' I try to sound incredulous. 'You're going to lose your job! She's the latest thing.'

'The photographer seems unimpressed. 'Who is she?' he repeats.

'Suze Cleath-Stuart. She's British. Really, really hot.'

'Who?' He leafs through a printed crib sheet, with faces and names of celebrities. 'Nope. Don't think so.' He puts the crib sheet away, then takes out his phone and starts sending a text.

'Oh, take her photo,' I beg, all pretence gone. 'Go on! Just for fun.'

The photographer looks at me as though for the first time. 'How did you get on the red carpet?'

'We sneaked on,' I admit. 'We're visitors to LA. And if *I* was a Hollywood photographer, I'd take pictures of normal people as well as celebrities.'

A tiny, reluctant smile tweaks at the photographer's mouth.

'Oh, you would?'

'Yes!'

He sighs and rolls his eyes. 'Go on then.' He lifts his camera and focuses it on Suze. Yessss!

'Me too!' I squeak, and skitter over the red carpet to join her. OK, quick. Elbow out. Legs crossed. It's actually happening! We're actually having our photo taken, in Hollywood, on the red carpet! I smile at the lens, trying to look natural, waiting for the flash . . .

'Meryl! Meryl! MERYL!'

In a blink, the lens vanishes from sight. Like stampeding wildebeest, every single photographer, including our guy in the denim jacket, has charged to the far side of the red carpet. I don't think he took a single shot of us, and now he's in the thick of the paparazzi, yelling and screaming.

'OVER HERE, MERYL! MERYL! HERE!'

The flashes are like strobe lighting. The clamour is extra-ordinary. And all because Meryl Streep has arrived.

Well, OK. Fair enough. No one can compete with Meryl Streep.

We both watch in awe and fascination as she makes her way graciously along the red carpet, surrounded by several flunkeys.

'Meryl!' calls Suze boldly as she comes near. 'Love your work!'

'Me too!' I chime in.

Meryl Streep turns her head and gives us a slightly bewildered smile.

Yes! We networked with Meryl Streep on the red carpet! *Wait* till I tell Mum.

As we enter the ballroom where the benefit is happening, I'm still on a high. Never mind if no one took our picture, this is *exactly* what I imagined Hollywood would be like. Lots of people in amazing dresses, and Meryl Streep, and a band play-ing smooth jazz, and delicious citrussy cocktails.

The whole place is decorated in pale grey and pink, and there's a stage on which some dancers are already performing, and a dance floor and loads of circular tables. And I can already see a goodie bag on each chair! My head is swivelling around as I try to catch sight of all the celebs, and Suze is doing the same.

I notice Luke by the bar, and Suze, Tarkie and I hurry over. He's standing with Aran and a couple I don't recognize. He introduces them as Ken and Davina Kerrow, and I remember him telling me about them last week. They're both producers, and they're making a film about the Crimean War. Luke and Aran are jockeying to get Sage considered for the part of Florence Nightingale. Apparently, Sage needs a 'change of direction' and 'rebranding' and being Florence Nightingale will achieve that.

Personally, I don't think she's at all suited to being Florence Nightingale, but I'm not going to say that to Luke.

'Sage is very interested in the role,' he's saying now to Ken, who is bearded and intense and frowns a lot. 'I would say she's passionate about it.'

Davina is also fairly intense. She's dressed in a black tuxedo suit and keeps checking her BlackBerry and saying 'Uh-huh?' when Luke is in the middle of a sentence.

'Sage feels this is a story that must be told,' Luke presses on. 'She really felt the role spoke to her . . . Ah, here she is! Just talking about you, Sage.'

Ooh! There's Sage, approaching in a swishy red dress that sets off her treacly hair perfectly. I feel a small thrill of excitement at the idea of introducing her to Suze and Tarkie.

'I'd hope you *are* talking about me,' says Sage to Luke. 'Why else do I pay you?' She gives a roar of laughter and Luke smiles politely.

'Just talking about Florence,' he says. 'I was saying how passionate you are about the role.'

'Oh totally.' Sage nods. 'Did you see my new tattoo?' She holds out her wrist, waving her fingers playfully, and Luke flinches.

'Sage, sweetie,' says Aran evenly. 'I thought we said no more tattoos.'

'I had to have it,' says Sage, looking hurt. 'It's a swallow. It means peace.'

'That would be a dove,' says Aran, and I see him exchange a look with Luke.

'Hi Sage,' I say casually. 'You look lovely.'

'You're so kind.' Sage sweeps a dazzling smile over me, Suze and Tarkie. 'Welcome to the benefit. Would you like a photo? Aran, these people would like a photo, could you . . . ?'

I stare at her, confused. She thinks I'm some random fan.

'It's me, Becky,' I say, turning red with embarrassment. 'Luke's wife? We met at the house?'

'Oh, *Becky*!' She bursts into laughter again, and presses a hand on my arm. 'Of course. My bad.'

'Sage, I'd like you to meet my friends, Suze and Tarquin Cleath-Stuart. Suze and Tarkie, may I present Sage . . .' I trail off mid-introduction. Sage has turned away from us and is enthusiastically greeting some guy in a midnight-blue tuxedo.

There's a moment of awkward silence. I can't believe Sage has been so rude.

'Sorry,' I mumble at last.

'Bex, it's not your fault!' says Suze. 'She's quite . . . um . . .' She stops, and I can tell she's trying to be diplomatic.

'I know.'

Sage looks hyper to me. Is she *high*? Now she's talking loudly about Ben Galligan, who is her ex-boyfriend from about three years ago. He cheated on her while he was making *Hour of Terror 5*, and he dumped Sage at the premiere, and now his new girlfriend is pregnant. And Sage has never got over it.

It was all in *People* magazine and Luke says most of it is true. But then, annoyingly, when I asked him to tell me exactly which bits were true and which bits weren't, he said I should stop reading that trash and remember that celebrities are human beings.

'Is the rat here?' Sage is looking wildly around. 'Because I swear, I will tear his eyes out.'

'Sage, we talked about this!' says Aran in a low voice. 'Tonight you're an ambassador for world equality and justice, OK? You can be a pissed-off ex-girlfriend in your own time.'

Sage doesn't seem to be listening. Her eyes are darting wildly about. 'Suppose I throw a bottle of wine over him. Think of the exposure. It'll go viral.'

'That's not the kind of viral we want. Sage, we have a strategy, remember?'

'I really couldn't tell you who else is in the running,' I can hear Davina Kerrow saying to Luke. 'Although you can probably guess . . .'

'It's Lois,' says Sage, who has overheard this, too, and is scowling. 'She's up for Florence, I know she is. Can you see Lois as a nurse? A *nurse*? This is the girl who said, "You don't get any acting awards for shaving off your hair," remember?'

'Not this again.' Aran closes his eyes.

'She could play a psycho-freak nurse. That would work. Or maybe a kleptomaniac nurse, right, Becky?' she says, flashing me a wild grin.

I feel a thud of alarm at the word *kleptomaniac*. Sage is talking really loudly, and the place is crowded. Anyone could overhear.

'Um, Sage.' I move close to her and drop my voice right down. 'I told you that about Lois in confidence.'

'Sure, sure,' says Sage. 'I'm only having some fun, right? Right?' She flashes me her smile again.

God, Sage is exhausting. She flips this way and that like an eel. I don't know how Luke does business with her.

I turn to make sure that Suze and Tarkie are OK, and see that Tarkie is in conversation with Ken Kerrow. OK, this could be interesting.

'We're calling the movie *Florence in Love*,' Ken Kerrow is saying animatedly. 'Like *Shakespeare in Love*, only more authentic. We're recasting Florence as an American but we're keeping the *essence* of Florence. Her conflict. Her growth. Her sexual awakening. We think she would have dressed as a boy to get on to the battlefield. We think she would have been in a passionate love triangle. Think *The Age of Innocence* meets *Saving Private Ryan* meets *Yentl*.'

'Right.' Tarkie looks none the wiser. 'Well, I'm afraid I haven't seen any of those films, but I'm sure they're jolly good.'

Ken Kerrow looks profoundly shocked. 'You haven't seen *Yentl*?'

'Ahm . . .' Tarkie looks trapped. 'Sorry . . . did you say "Lentil"?'

'*Yentl!*' Ken Kerrow almost shouts. 'Streisand!'

Poor Tarkie. He clearly doesn't understand a word Ken is saying.

'I watch a lot of wildlife documentaries,' he says desperately. 'David Attenborough. Marvellous man.'

Ken Kerrow just shakes his head pityingly, but before he can say anything else, Suze swoops in.

'Darling, let's go and watch the dancers.' She gives Ken Kerrow a charming smile. 'I'm so sorry to drag my husband away. Bex, shall we go and watch the dancers?'

As we're heading towards the stage, I'm distracted by a sign on one of the tables: *Silent Auction Prizes*.

'I'm just going to have a quick look,' I say to Suze. 'I'll catch up with you in a sec.'

There's an amazing necklace on a stand, which is up for auction, and as I draw near I feel the tugging of lust. God, it's beautiful, all pale-pink crystals and a hammered-silver heart, I wonder how much . . .

Oh my God. I've suddenly seen the printed label below it: *Reserve price $10,000*. I hastily back away, in case anyone thinks I'm bidding for it. Ten thousand? Seriously? I mean, it's a nice necklace and everything, but . . . $10,000? Just for some pink crystals? I don't even *dare* go near the pair of watches at the end of the table. Or that voucher for a Malibu villa. Maybe I'll go and watch the dancers with Suze instead. I'm about to turn away, when I see a doddery old man making his way slowly along the prizes. He looks quite frail, and is keeping his balance by clutching at the table.

Not a single person has noticed him, which makes me feel quite incensed. I mean, what's the point of coming to a benefit to help people, and then ignoring a poor old man who needs help right in front of your eyes?

'Are you all right, sir?' I hurry forward, but he bats me away. 'Fine, fine!'

He's very tanned, with perfect teeth and what looks suspiciously like a white toupee, but his hands are gnarled and his eyes are a bit rheumy. Honestly, someone should be looking after him.

'It's a lovely event,' I say politely.

'Oh yes.' He nods. 'Wonderful cause. Discrimination is the blight of our lives. I myself am gay, and let me tell you, the world is not an open place. Not yet.'

'No,' I agree.

'Don't tell me you haven't encountered discrimination yourself. As a woman. And in other ways. Because in my opinion, no human on this earth is free from discrimination in some way or other.'

He's so full of fervour, I don't like to contradict him.

'Definitely,' I nod. 'I've been discriminated against in lots of ways. *Heaps*. All the time.'

'Tell me some examples of this shocking behaviour.' His rheumy eyes fix eagerly on me.

My mind is blank. Come on, quick. Discrimination.

'Well, obviously as a woman . . . and . . .' I cast my mind around. 'I once had to take out my earrings to work in a café, so that was discriminating against jewellery . . . and . . . er . . . hobbies can be discriminated against and . . . pets . . .' I have no idea what I'm saying. 'It's terrible,' I end lamely. 'We need to fight it.'

'And we will.' He clutches my hand. 'Together.'

'I'm Rebecca, by the way,' I add. 'Rebecca Brandon.'

'And I'm Dix.' He flashes me a white smile. 'Dix Donahue.'

Hang on. Dix Donahue. That sounds familiar. I glance at a nearby poster and sure enough, it's printed in big grey letters: HOST: DIX DONAHUE.

This is the *host*? He looks about a hundred.

'Dix!' A plump man with a neat black moustache bears down on us and pumps his hand. 'Victor Jamison from E.Q.U.A.L. I'm a big fan. All set for your introductory speech?'

'Gathering inspiration all the time.' Dix flashes his smile at me, and I beam back. He must be famous in some sort of way. I wonder how. Luke will know.

The two men head off, and I drain my glass. I really must find Luke and Suze, but the trouble is, everyone's started clustering around the stage area and it's hard to see. The dancers have stopped their routine and the band has fallen silent and there's an expectant air. Then suddenly, the band strikes up again with some tune that everyone seems to recognize, going by their nods and smiles at each other. Dix Donahue mounts the steps with a hop and a jump – and it's obvious he's an entertainer. He seems to sparkle under the lights, even if he is a zillion years old.

As he starts to tell jokes, I edge my way round the corner of the throng, and suddenly see Luke. I'm about to join him, when the room goes dark and a spotlight moves around the crowd, and Dix Donahue takes on a grave manner.

'But seriously, folks,' he says. 'We're here for a very fine cause tonight. Discrimination is an evil and it takes place in all shapes and forms, often in the place you'd expect the least. Later we'll be hearing from Pia Stafford, who battled workplace discrimination regarding her disability after a car accident.'

The spotlight falls on a lady in black, who lifts a hand and nods soberly.

'But you know, I was talking to a young lady just now, who had maybe the most unusual tale of discrimination I've heard . . .' Dix Donahue shades his eyes and squints into the audience. 'Rebecca, where are you? Ah, there!'

Does he mean *me*? I stare up at him in horror. A moment later the spotlight is glaring into my face.

'Rebecca was discriminated against because of – of all things' – he shakes his head sombrely – 'her pet.'

My eyes nearly pop out of my head. He can't have taken me seriously. I only said 'pets' because I ran out of other things to say.

They should never have hired a hundred-year-old host. He's batty.

'Rebecca, let's hear your story,' says Dix Donahue in a soft, coaxing voice. 'What was your pet?'

I stare at him, transfixed.

'A . . . a hamster,' I hear myself saying.

'A hamster, ladies and gentlemen.' Dix Donahue starts

clapping, and a half-hearted round of applause breaks out. I can see people whispering to each other, looking puzzled, as well they might.

'And what form did the discrimination take?'

'Um . . . well . . . People wouldn't accept it,' I say cautiously. 'I was ostracized by my community. Friends turned against me and my career suffered. My health, too. I think it's up to the government and society to change attitudes. Because all humans are the same.' I'm rather warming to my speech now. 'All of us, whatever religion we practise or colour skin we have, or, you know, whether we have a hamster or not . . . we're the same!'

I make a sweeping gesture and catch Luke's eye. He's staring at me from a few yards away, his mouth open.

'That's it,' I finish hastily.

'Wonderful!' Dix Donahue leads another round of applause, and this time it feels really genuine. A lady even pats me on the back.

'One more question before we move on.' Dix Donahue twinkles at me. 'What was your hamster's name, Rebecca?'

'Er . . .' Shit. My mind has gone totally blank. 'It was . . . er . . . called . . .'

'Ermintrude,' comes Luke's deep voice. 'She was like family.'

Oh, ha, ha. Very funny.

'Yes, Ermintrude.' I muster a smile. 'Ermintrude the hamster.'

The spotlight finally moves off me and Dix Donahue comes to the end of his speech, and I look up to see Luke giving me a little wink as he approaches through the crowd.

'I'll get you a new hamster this Christmas, darling,' he says over the sound of applause. 'We'll fight the discrimination together. If you can be brave enough, so can I.'

'Shhh!' I can't help giggling. 'Come on, it's time to eat.'

That's the last time I make conversation with some random old man just to be kind. As we move back to our table, I'm totally mortified, especially as people keep stopping me to congratulate me and ask about the hamster and tell me about how their kids have a rabbit and they wouldn't stand for discrimination, it's *shocking* in this day and age.

But at last we're able to sit down, and on the plus side, the food is delicious. I'm so engrossed in my fillet of beef that I don't pay much attention to the conversation, which doesn't matter, because it only consists of both Kerrows droning on to the entire table about this Florence Nightingale film they want to make. They talk like some sort of song duet, overlapping every phrase, and no one else can get a word in. This is another lesson I'm learning in Hollywood. You'd think hearing about a film would be exciting – but it's deathly. I can tell Suze is just as fed up as me, because her eyes are glassy, and also she keeps mouthing 'Booooriiiing' at me.

'. . . locations are the challenge . . .'

'. . . wonderful director . . .'

'. . . problems with the third act . . .'

'. . . he really *gets* Florence's arc . . .'

'. . . talked to the studio about budget . . .'

'. . . finances lined up. We're waiting on the last investor, but it depends on some British guy with a crazy name. John John Saint John. Kind of a name is that?' Kerrow spears a mangetout and eats it ferociously.

'D'you mean John St John John?' says Suze, suddenly tuning into the conversation. 'How on earth do you know him? That's Pucky,' she adds to me. 'Have you met Pucky?'

God knows if I've met Pucky. All Suze's childhood friends are called things like Pucky and Binky and Minky. They basically blend into one braying, cheery human Labrador.

'Er . . . maybe.'

'*You've* met Pucky.' She turns to Luke. 'I know you've met him.'

'Tarquin's investment manager,' says Luke thoughtfully. 'Yes, I did. Runs the media arm of your business interests?'

'Something like that,' says Suze vaguely, then beams at

Tarkie, who's returning from the Gents. 'Darling, they know Pucky.'

'Good Lord.' Tarkie's face brightens. 'Extraordinary coincidence.'

'Pucky?' Ken Kerrow looks perplexed.

'Called him that ever since prep school,' Tarkie explains. 'Marvellous chap. He's worked with me, what, ten years now?'

'*Worked* with you?' Ken Kerrow's eyes focus on Tarquin anew. 'You in film?'

'Film?' Tarkie looks horrified at the idea. 'Good Lord, no. I'm a farmer. You were saying something earlier about an "ark"? Do you mean Noah's Ark?'

'Tarquin, can I ask you a question?' says Luke. His mouth is twitching and he looks highly amused at something. 'I know you have a few media interests among your investments. Has Pucky ever backed any films for you?'

'Oh!' Tarquin's expression clears. '*Ahm*. Well. As a matter of fact, yes, he has. Perhaps that's the connection.'

'Films?' Suze stares at him. 'You never told me!'

'This is your investor,' says Luke to Ken Kerrow, and jerks a thumb at Tarquin. 'Lord Cleath-Stuart.'

'Please,' says Tarkie, flushing red. 'Tarquin.'

Ken Kerrow looks as though he's choked on his fillet steak. 'That's *you*?'

'*Lord?*' Sage looks up from her phone for the first time.

'Lord Cleath-Stuart.' Ken Kerrow is gesticulating at his wife. 'This is the Brit backer. You backed *Fiddler's Game*,' he adds to Tarquin, in sudden realization. 'Didn't you?'

'Ahm . . . yes.' Tarquin looks a little hunted. 'That sounds right.'

'It made thirty million its opening weekend. You picked a winner.'

'Well, it was Pucky,' says Tarkie modestly. 'I mean, I wouldn't know one film from another.'

'Excuse me,' says Ken Kerrow. 'I'm going to find my coproducer. I'd love for you to meet him.' He leaps up and practically sprints to a nearby table, where I can see him whispering frantically to another guy in a tux.

'Tarkie!' exclaims Suze, and bangs the table. 'Since when do we invest in films? You should have told me!'

'But, darling,' says Tarkie anxiously. 'You said you weren't interested in our investments.'

'I meant boring things like stocks and shares! Not films—' Suze breaks off and fixes Tarkie with an accusing gaze. 'Tell me the truth. Have we been invited to premieres?'

'Ahm . . .' Tarkie's eyes slide around nervously. 'You'd have to ask Pucky. I probably told him we weren't interested.'

'Weren't *interested*?' Suze's voice rises to a screech.

'Your Lordship!' Ken Kerrow is back at the table. 'It is my honour to present my co-producer, Alvie Hill.'

A broad man pumps Tarkie's hand with a meaty handshake. 'Your Lordship. What a pleasure to welcome you to Los Angeles. If there is *anything* we can do to make your stay more pleasant . . .'

He continues talking for about five minutes, complimenting Tarkie, complimenting Suze, suggesting restaurants and offering to drive them out to the canyons for a hike.

'Ahm, thank you.' Tarkie gives him an embarrassed smile. 'You're very kind. I'm so sorry,' he says to the table, as Alvie finally leaves. 'What a fuss. Let's get back to our dinner.'

But that's just the beginning. An hour later, it seems as if every single person in the room has dropped by our table to introduce themselves to Tarkie. Several have pitched movies, several have invited him to screenings, several have tried to set up meetings, and one has suggested flying the whole family to his ranch in Texas. Tarkie is totally an LA player. I can't quite believe it.

In fact, no one can believe it. Luke has been bursting into laughter a lot – especially when some studio executive asked Tarkie what was his view of the *American Pie* franchise and Tarkie said, Gosh, he wasn't sure – was it similar to Starbucks? Meanwhile Tarkie himself looks rather shell-shocked again. I feel a bit sorry for him, actually. He came here to get away from everything, not to be besieged by people after his money.

I can understand why he spends so much time wandering around moors on his own. At least the deer don't keep running up saying they've got a fabulous concept which they'd love to share with him over breakfast. Now, some guy in a shiny grey suit is asking Tarkie if he wants to visit a film set.

'We're shooting this great drama; it's set on the high seas. Bring your kids, they'll love it . . .'

'You're very kind.' Tarkie is starting to sound robotic. 'But I'm here for a holiday . . .'

'I'll come!' Suze interrupts.

'Terrific!' The grey-suited guy smiles at her. 'We'd be delighted to welcome you, give you the tour, you can watch some scenes being shot—'

'Can I be an extra?' Suze says boldly.

The grey-suited man stares at her, apparently baffled.

'You want to—'

'Be an extra in the film. And so does my friend Bex.' She grabs my arm. 'Don't you?'

'Yes! Definitely!'

I have *always* wanted to be an extra on a film! I beam delightedly at Suze and she grins back.

'Your Ladyship.' The grey-suited man seems totally perplexed. 'You won't be comfortable being an extra. The day is long, it's tiring, the scenes are shot again and again . . . Why don't you *watch* the scene, and then you can meet the cast, we'll have lunch someplace nice . . .'

'I want to be an extra,' says Suze obstinately. 'And so does Bex.'

'But—'

'We don't want to watch it, we want to be *in* it.'

'We want to be *in* it,' I echo emphatically.

'Well.' The man seems to admit defeat. 'OK. No problem at all. My people will fix it up for you.'

'Bex, we're going to be extras!' Suze clutches me in excitement.

174

'We're going to be in a film!'

'We can go and watch ourselves at the cinema! Everyone will see us— Ooh, what's the film about?' says Suze as an after-thought, and the man looks up from where he's writing his mobile number on a card.

'Pirates.'

Pirates? I look at Suze with renewed glee. We're going to be in a film about pirates!

c/o 6389 Kester Avenue ❑ Van Nuys CA 91411

Dear Mrs Brandon

I was given your name by Andy Wyke, who was at the recent E.Q.U.A.L. benefit and heard your inspiring story.

I am president of the charity DiscriminHate LA, a lobby group set up to combat discrimination in all its forms. We consider that current definitions of discrimination are far too narrow. We have identified no fewer than 56 common grounds for discrimination and the list grows longer every day.

However, you are the first case of 'pet-ism' we have come across, and we would like to talk to you about your experience. Many of our members have spearheaded campaigns and we hoped you could do the same. For example you could:

- ❑ Write an account of your discrimination story for our website.

- ❑ Develop an outreach program for high school students who may suffer the same type of discrimination.

- ❑ Lobby your local government representative for 'Ermintrude's Law'.

May I, at this point, offer you my sincere solidarity and sympathy. I am not familiar with the exact details of your case, but I gather it was a moving story and must have been painful for you to share.

I look forward to hearing from you and welcoming you to our fight.

All my best

Gerard R. Oss
President DiscriminHate LA
Survivor and Fighter: size-ism, name-ism, odor-ism, and sexual-practice-ism.
Author of *I'm Different, You're Different, S/He's Different*

Dear Mrs Ermintrude Endwich

Thank you for your recent letter.

It is always interesting to hear from an 'unbiased member of the public' as you describe yourself. However, I must take issue with your various points. The LHA is not a 'bunch of Nazis with nothing better to do than complain about fountains'. We do not 'meet every night in some grim little cavern'; nor 'plot like the witches in *Macbeth*'. Our dress sense is, I would suggest, irrelevant.

I also rebut your assertion that The Surge is 'one of the wonders of the world'. It is not. Nor will we 'all be sorry when the brilliant Tarquin Cleath-Stuart is given a medal for it by the Queen'. I cannot quite imagine which medal this would be.

May I have your address in the UK? I cannot find any record of you on the electoral roll.

Maureen Greywell

President
LHA

TWELVE

I've done my research. I'm taking this seriously. I'm going to be the best extra ever.

No, not 'extra'. The proper term is 'background actor'. I've found out so much on the internet about being an extra, I feel really well prepared. For example, you should always bring playing cards or a book in case you get bored. And you shouldn't wear green, in case they're using a green screen for CGI. And you should bring a variety of outfits. Although that doesn't apply in this case, as apparently our costumes will be provided. A limo has also been provided to take us to the film set, which is definitely not standard practice. They're being super-nice to us because of Suze being married to Tarkie.

In fact, I'm secretly hoping they might be so nice that they give us each a little line to say. I mean, why not? Obviously not *big* lines or speeches or anything. Just something small. I could say, ''Tis true, cap'n,' after the Pirate Captain makes a speech. And Suze could say, 'Land ahoy!' or 'Ship ahoy!' or 'Pirate ahoy!' Anything ahoy, really. I've been practising a special growly, piratess voice in the mirror, and I've read an article on acting for film. It says the most common mistake, even for trained actors, is to over-act, and that the camera picks up the most infinitesimal movements and magnifies them, so you need to make everything tiny.

I'm not sure Suze realizes this, because she's spent the whole of breakfast doing all these loud warm-up exercises and shaking her hands out to 'loosen herself up' and saying 'Wibble-wobble' over and over again. But I can't tell her anything about acting, because she just says, 'Bex, I went to *drama school*, remember.'

The film is being shot at a soundstage in Burbank, and that's where we're heading right now. Luke is dropping off Minnie at pre-school today, as well as Suze's children. (As soon as the headmistress found out who Tarkie was, she fell over herself to offer the Cleath-Stuarts temporary places, and the principal of a nearby school immediately found space for Ernest too.) We're sitting in the limo, watching the billboards speed by and grinning madly at each other. This is the most exciting thing I have done in my life, *ever*.

I don't know what the scene's about – in fact, I don't really know what the film's about because all it says online is 'Drama set on the high seas'. But I've done a bit of practice at swinging a cutlass (I used a kitchen knife) because you never know, it might be a fight scene.

'Hey, Suze, if I have to fight someone, bagsy it's you,' I say.

'Me too,' agrees Suze at once. 'Except, will the womenfolk fight? They might just look on and jeer.'

'There are female pirates,' I say knowledgeably. 'We can be one of those. Look at Elizabeth Swann.'

'I want to fight Captain Jack Sparrow,' says Suze longingly.

'He's not in it!' I say for the millionth time. Suze is a bit hung up on Johnny Depp, and I think she was hoping that we were going to be in a new *Pirates of the Caribbean*. But it's not that. It's called *The Black Flag*, and I don't recognize the names of any of the stars except April Tremont, who is playing 'Gwennie'.

'I know he's not. But still. Wouldn't it be amazing?' She sighs.

'There'll probably be an even hotter pirate king in this one,'

I point out, as my phone rings. It's Dad calling, which surprises me. Normally it's Mum who rings, and then passes me over to Dad, and then instantly grabs the phone back as there's something she's forgotten to tell me about Janice's new sofa covers or the geraniums.

'Dad!' I exclaim. 'Guess what Suze and I are doing right now?'

'Drinking orange juice in the sunshine,' says Dad with a laugh. 'I hope you are.'

'Wrong! We're in a limo, going to the film set!'

Mum and Dad already know we're going to be extras in a movie, because I phoned them up to tell them, straight away. And Janice and Martin. And Jess and Tom, and my old bank manager Derek Smeath . . .

I suppose I did phone quite a few people, now I think about it.

'Wonderful, darling!' says Dad. 'Make sure you hobnob with the movie stars.'

'We will!'

'I was just wondering, did you ever manage to look up my old friend Brent?'

Oh. Damn. What with Golden Peace, and Suze arriving, it completely slipped my mind.

'Not yet,' I say guiltily. 'I haven't quite had time. But I will, I promise.'

'Well, that would be marvellous.'

'I'll go and see him really soon, and I'll give him all your details.'

We've arrived at a barricaded entrance to a large complex with buildings and courtyards, and as the driver slows down, I see a row of trailers out of the window. Real film trailers!

'We're here! There are trailers!' I say in excitement. 'Oh Dad, you should see it!'

'Sounds fantastic,' says Dad. 'Well, you let me know about Brent.'

'I will,' I say, only half paying attention. 'See you, Dad.'

The driver is giving our names to the gate man. As Suze

and I stare out of the window, agog, I see a man in a pirate costume walk to one of the trailers, knock on the door and go inside.

'Oh my *God*,' says Suze.

'I know!' I can't help giggling.

As we're whisked into the complex, my head is swivelling this way and that, trying to take in every detail. It's all just as I imagined. There are girls with earpieces and clipboards. There's a guy carrying what looks like a marble statue under his arm. There's a woman in a crinoline, talking to a man in a leather jacket.

'I'm nervous,' says Suze suddenly. 'What if I'm crap?'

'Nervous?' I say in astonishment. 'Suze, you'll be great!' The car stops and I squeeze her arm encouragingly. 'Come on, let's go and find some coffee. You know, the *main* thing about being in a film is the catering.'

I'm so right about the catering. After wandering about for a few minutes we find this great big table called Craft Service, covered with a fabulous array of coffee, tea, biscuits, cupcakes and even little sushi rolls. As I'm eating my third cherry-almond cookie, a guy in a headset comes up, looking a little hassled.

'Are you Lady Cleath-Stuart?'

'Here,' says Suze, her mouth full of muffin.

'I'm Dino, the second AD. You were supposed to meet me out front.'

'Oh, sorry. We wanted some coffee.' Suze beams at him. 'This hazelnut latte is delicious!'

'Oh. Great.' He mutters something into a tiny walkie-talkie, then looks up again. 'Well, let me take you to meet Don. He's our publicist and he'll be looking after you today.'

Don is very dapper and has the strangest cheekbones I've ever seen. *What* has gone on with those? Has he had them filled? Or has he had his cheek fat sucked out? Either way, it hasn't been a success, *not* that I'm going to mention this or stare at his face. Much. He ushers us into a massive warehouse-like space, and lowers his voice as we pick our way over wires and cables.

'Lady Cleath-Stuart,' he says with reverence, 'we're delighted to welcome you to the set of *The Black Flag*. We want today to be as enjoyable and interesting for you as possible. Please, follow me. We thought you'd like to see the set before we take you to Wardrobe.'

Suze is totally a VIP! This is so great! We both hurry after him, dodging past some guys carrying a fake stone wall made out of wood. We head towards a cluster of directors' chairs and a monitor, and lots of people with headphones and serious expressions.

'That's what we call "video village",' Don says in an undertone. 'This is where the director watches the action. Please make sure your phones are switched off. I think we're about to have a take.'

We edge round until we can see the set properly. It's the interior of a library, and two actors are sitting on armchairs. The lady is all dressed up in a velvet crinoline and the man is in a tailcoat. Bending down, talking to them intently, is a skinny guy in jeans with bright-red hair.

'That's Ant, the director,' murmurs Don. As we're watching, Ant leaps back to his chair, puts on his headphones and stares intently into his monitor.

'Rolling!' yells someone from the set.

'Rolling!' several other people echo at once. 'Rolling! Rolling!' Even behind us, by the door, two girls are yelling, 'Rolling!'

'Rolling!' I join in helpfully. 'ROLLING!'

This is so cool. I feel like a member of the film crew already!

'Action!' calls Ant, and, like magic, the whole place becomes totally still. Anyone who was walking has stopped dead, and all conversations have ceased, mid-sentence.

'Kidnapped,' says the lady in velvet. 'Kidnapped!' The man takes hold of her hand and she gazes at him mournfully.

'Cut!' shouts Ant, and leaps down on to the set again.

'This scene is set in the home of Lady Violet,' whispers Don.

'She's just learned that their daughter Katriona has been kidnapped by pirates. Would you like to go closer?'

We tiptoe forward, till we're at 'video village'. There are several directors' chairs with names printed on the backs of them and I look at them lustfully. I would *die* to have a chair with my name on it. My mind is suddenly seized with an image of a chair reading: *Becky Brandon, Wardrobe Designer.* Just imagine if I started working in movies and I got my name on the back of a chair! I wouldn't ever want to stand up. I'd walk around with my chair stapled to me.

The wardrobe designer on this movie is called Renée Slattery. I've already Googled her and planned what I'll say if we meet. I'll compliment the costumes in *Saw Her Too Soon*, which is another movie she worked on, and then I'll talk about the challenges of working with period dress. (I don't know much about that, but I can busk it.) And then I'll ask casually if she needs any help, maybe with shopping for grosgrain ribbon, or button boots, or whatever.

I mean, she's *bound* to need help, surely? And then we can start working together and bouncing ideas around, and I'll edge myself in that way.

Both Suze and I are given directors' chairs with *Visitor* written on the back, and we perch self-consciously on them, watching as they shoot the scene twice more. I can't actually tell the difference between the takes, not that I'll admit that. Ant keeps swigging coffee and staring into the monitor and shouting instructions to some guy with a high-up camera to the left.

Suddenly he swivels round and stares at me and Suze, then says, almost aggressively, to Don, 'Who are they? What are they doing on my set?'

Don ducks his head down and I can hear him murmuring, 'Lord Cleath-Stuart ... financier ... special guests ... studio . . .'

'Well, keep them out of the way,' says Ant brusquely.

Honestly! We're not in the way! I roll my eyes at Suze, but she has found a script from somewhere and is reading through it, mouthing lines to herself. Suze would really have loved to be an actress. (Or an eventer. Or an artist. Or a newsreader. She's had lots of career ideas, to be honest.)

'Dylan!' The director suddenly raises his voice. 'Where's Dylan?'

'Here!' A mousy guy in a grey T-shirt hurries forward.

'This is the writer,' Don explains to me and Suze. 'He stays on set in case we need extra dialogue.'

'We need another line here for Lady Violet,' Ant is saying. 'We need to convey the gravitas of what's happened, but also, like, the *dignity* of Lady Violet. She's not going to buckle. She's going to fight.' He pauses. 'Only in, like, three or four words.'

'Right.' Dylan is nodding anxiously. 'Right.'

As Ant strides away, he starts scribbling on a yellow legal pad and I watch him in fascination. He's creating a film, right here. We're watching film history being made! Then suddenly an idea comes to me. It's so good, I almost gasp out loud.

'Sorry,' I say, waving to get Dylan's attention. 'Excuse me. I don't mean to interrupt, but a line came to me, and I thought you could use it. It just popped into my head,' I add modestly.

'Well done, Bex!' exclaims Suze.

Dylan sighs. 'What is it?'

'With great power comes great responsibility.' As I say it out loud, I can't help feeling proud of myself.

'That's brilliant!' says Suze. 'Only you should say it with more passion. "With great power comes great responsibility,"' she repeats in a low, throbbing voice. '"With great *power* comes great *responsibility*."'

'Perfect!' I add to Dylan, 'She went to drama school, you know.'

Dylan is looking at us as though we're both insane.

'That line is from *Spider-Man*,' he says shortly.

Spider-Man?

'Really?' I wrinkle my brow. 'Are you sure? Because I don't remember it—'

'Of course I'm sure! Jeez!' He crosses out the line he's writing and scribbles something else.

'Oh,' I say, discomfited. 'Right. Sorry.'

'Well then, what about, "With great grief comes great challenge"?' suggests Suze.

'Or, "With great trouble comes great fortune,"' I chime in eagerly. 'Or, "With great sadness comes great light."' I'm quite proud of this one, but Dylan is looking more and more rattled.

'Could you let me concentrate, please?' he snaps.

'Oh, OK. Sorry.' Suze and I subside, making faces at each other. We watch, fascinated, as he covers his page with writing, then abruptly heads over to Ant.

'How about this?'

'OK. We'll try it.' Ant walks on to the set and I can see him showing the page to the actress in the velvet dress.

'Why don't you just take the line to the actors yourself?' I say as Dylan sits down.

'I don't approach the set.' He sounds shocked at the idea. 'The *director* approaches the set.'

He sounds like he's saying, 'I don't approach the throne.' Blimey, film sets are complicated places. 'So, I hope you enjoyed your visit,' he adds, clearly forcing himself to be polite. 'It was nice to meet you.'

'Oh, we haven't finished our visit yet,' I explain.

'We're going to be in the film!' adds Suze.

'We're extras!'

'You?' He looks from me to Suze and back again.

I'm about to say he needn't look so dubious, when Ant appears, scowling at Dylan, and chucks the legal pad at him.

'Yolanda says this is flaccid, and I agree. Can't you do better than that?'

Honestly. What a bully. I bet Dylan's written a brilliant line. (Although not as good as 'With great power comes great responsibility.')

'I was distracted by these two,' says Dylan meanly, gesturing at us, and my sympathy instantly evaporates. He didn't have to blame us! We were trying to help! Ant glowers at us, then glowers even more at Dylan.

'Well, give me some more options. We're taking five.' Ant strides away, and Dylan frowns over his legal pad again, chewing his pen. The atmosphere is quite tense, and I'm relieved when Don appears and beckons us away from the chairs.

'The actors are having a break,' he says. 'So I thought you'd like to look over the set before we head to Wardrobe.'

We follow him to the set, and step cautiously on to the carpet. We're standing on a real movie set! It's quite small, but really well designed, with shelves of books and a table with ornaments and a fake window with a velvet curtain.

'Excuse me,' says Don as his phone buzzes, 'I must take this call.'

He steps off the set, and Suze sits on Lady Violet's chair. 'Kidnapped,' she says in a mournful voice. 'Kidnapped!'

'Really good!' I say. 'D'you think Lady Violet's dress is a bit bunchy? I think it could be more flattering. I might tell the wardrobe person.'

'Kidnapped!' says Suze again, and stares out to the camera, extending her hands as though she's on a massive London stage and that's the audience. 'Oh my God. Kidnapped! Will our nightmare never end?'

'Everything looks so realistic,' I say, trailing my hand over a row of fake book spines. 'Look at this cupboard.' I rattle the door but it's stuck fast. 'It looks so real, but it's fake, like everything.' I wander over to the little table. 'I mean, look at these cakes. They look totally real. They even smell real. It's so clever.'

'They might *be* real,' points out Suze.

'Of course they're not real. Nothing on a film set is real. Look.' I lift one up confidently and take a bite out of it.

Shit. It was real. I have a mouthful of sponge and cream.

'Bex!' Suze is staring at me in consternation. 'That cake is in the film! You can't *eat* it!'

'I didn't mean to!' I say defensively.

I feel slightly outraged. They shouldn't have real cakes on a movie set. It goes against the whole spirit of the thing.

I look around, but no one seems to have seen me. What shall I do now? I can't put half a cake back on the table.

'OK, we're going again,' comes a booming voice. 'Clear the set!'

Oh God. The actors are returning and I still have half a cake in my hands.

Maybe they won't notice.

I hastily leave the set, my hands hidden my back, and find a place where I'm almost hidden behind a stone pillar. The two actors are sitting back down on the chairs and everyone is gathering for a new take.

'Wait a minute.' A girl dressed all in black comes running on to the set. She squints into the screen of a little camera, then peers at the table. 'What happened to the other cake?'

Damn.

The actors are looking around blankly, as though they hadn't even realized there were any cakes in the shot.

'Cake?' says the man at last.

'Yes, cake! There should be six!' She jabs at her camera screen. 'What happened to it?'

'Well, don't look at me!' says the man, sounding affronted. 'I never saw the cake.'

'Yes you did!'

'I think there were five,' says the actress playing Lady Violet.

'Excuse me,' says the girl in black tightly. 'If I say there were six, then there were six, and unless you want to reshoot everything we've done this morning I suggest you don't move the props around.'

'I didn't move anything around!' retorts Lady Violet.

I have to confess. Go *on*, Becky. I force myself to step forward on to the edge of the set and clear my throat.

'Um, excuse me?' I say awkwardly. 'It's here. Sorry.'

I proffer my hand and everyone stares at the half-eaten, crumby cake. My cheeks are flaming with embarrassment, especially when a chunk falls on the floor. I quickly bend to get it, feeling worse than ever.

'Shall I put it back on the table?' I venture. 'We could hide the eaten side . . .'

The girl in black raises her eyes to mine disbelievingly.

'You *ate* a prop?'

'I didn't mean to!' I say hurriedly. 'I thought it was fake, and I was just biting it to prove it—'

'I knew it wasn't fake,' puts in Suze. 'I told her. I said, no fake cake could be that good—'

'Yes it could!' I object. 'They have amazing modern technology.'

'Not *that* amazing—'

'Anyway.' A thought suddenly occurs to me. 'Maybe it's a good thing. Because would they actually have that many cakes?' I appeal to Ant. 'Six is a lot for two people. You don't want them to look greedy, do you? You don't want the audience thinking, "No wonder Lady Violet needs a corset if she's eating all these cakes—"'

'Enough!' Ant suddenly flips out. 'Get these girls off my set!' He glares at Don. 'I don't care who they are, they're banned.'

Banned? Suze and I exchange shocked looks.

'But we're going to be extras!' says Suze in dismay.

'I'm really sorry we disturbed you,' I say hastily. 'I didn't mean to eat the cake. I won't eat anything else.'

'Ant, listen a moment,' Don says soothingly. He hurries over and starts murmuring in Ant's ear.

I can see Ant shooting us baleful looks, but at last he puffs angrily and says, 'Fine. Whatever. I need to get *going*.'

I'm holding my breath as Don returns to us and firmly ushers us away from the set.

'Can we still be extras?' demands Suze anxiously.

'Of course!' he says, smiling tensely. 'No problem. Let's just get you to Wardrobe and then . . . well. What I would recommend is that in the upcoming scene you take more of a *backseat* role.'

'You mean, don't talk to the director,' says Suze. 'And don't eat the props.'

He nods. 'That kind of thing.'

'Hear that, Bex?' Suze nudges me. 'No scoffing the set.'

OK, I'm going to make amends. I'm going to be really quiet and unobtrusive on set. Or at least, as unobtrusive as I can be, bearing in mind I'm now in a curly red wig, blackened teeth, hoop skirt and a laced bodice which makes my boobs look . . . Well. *Prominent* would be one word. *Ridiculous* would be another.

My make-up was slapped on in about five seconds by a girl listening to an iPod, but still, I'm transformed! I look dirty, grimy, wrinkled and kind of scary. As for Suze, she looks like an old crone. She's got a black matted wig and some kind of tooth plate which changes the shape of her mouth, and warts all over her hands. She's walking around with a limp and, honestly, she looks just like a pirate. I'm not doing a limp, but I think I might do a little palsied shake in my hands. Or a twitch. Just a very subtle one.

We've been put in a side room and all the other extras are sitting around reading books and looking bored, but I'm roaming about, staying alert. The only slight downside is I haven't yet managed to speak to anyone about job opportunities in Wardrobe. Renée Slattery is nowhere to be seen, and all the wardrobe staff are quite harassed. I asked a question about my petticoat length, and the girl in charge said, 'Doesn't matter. Next?'

Doesn't matter? How can a petticoat not matter?

Then I asked her how she got into her job, and she said, 'I was idiot enough to want to get up at five a.m. my whole life,' which is *not* an answer, and shooshed me along.

'Background actors!' The second AD, Dino, is standing at the door. 'Background actors to set, please!'

Ooh! That's us!

As we file through the soundstage and on to the set, I feel a sizzle of excitement. It's really happening! I'm going to be in a film! This set is far bigger than the last one and is the inside of a ship's cabin. There are about ten extras, including me and

Suze – all women – and according to a conversation I over-heard just now, this is a really key, important scene.

A key, important scene! What if it becomes one of those really famous movie scenes that gets shown on the telly all the time and I'm in it! What if I get discovered! I feel a ridiculous flicker of hope. I mean, I know I've never really considered acting as a career, but what if I have the right face for film and I never realized it before?

I'm gripped by a vivid fantasy in which Ant suddenly stops the shooting and focuses the camera on me, and then turns to his assistant and says, simply, 'My God. Look at her cheek-bones.'

I mean, OK, I know it's not *that* likely. But I do have quite good cheekbones, and everything's different when you look at it through a camera and—

'Bex!' Suze prods me. 'Dino's calling you!'

I hurry over to Dino and look expectantly at him, hoping he might say something like, 'I'd like to audition you for the small part of Pirate Princess.'

'OK, you. Cake-eater girl.' He looks up from a list.

Cake-eater girl?

'I'm called Becky,' I tell him.

'Nice.' He's clearly not listening. 'Now, I'm placing you where Ant can't see you. We don't want him wound up any further. You'll be polishing Gwennie's shoes with this rag, and you stay in this position the whole scene. Keep your face down, away from the camera. Got it? *Away* from the camera.' He turns away, summoning the next girl and I stare at him, crestfallen.

Away from the camera? But no one will see me. What about my family? I want to wail. How will they know it's me?

I feel totally crushed as I get into position, grovelling on the floor and clutching a manky old rag. This isn't what I imagined at all. A girl who looks a bit like April Tremont has sat down on the chair and shoots me an uninterested glance. I guess she's the stand-in.

'People!' Dino is clapping his hands. 'A little background to the scene we'll be playing. The pirates' womenfolk are preparing for the marriage ceremony. Gwennie, played by April Tremont . . .' There's a burst of applause from some of the extras, and Dino smiles in acknowledgement. 'Gwennie is being given to the pirate bandit, Eduardo, played by Curt Millson. However, she's in love with the rival pirate Captain Arthur, aka captain of the *Black Flag*, and in this scene we'll see this fact being discovered by Eduardo.'

'Hi,' I say miserably to the stand-in. 'I have to polish your shoes.'

'Fine.' She lifts up her skirt and I rub her shoe dispiritedly.

'OK, we're going to rehearse!' comes Dino's voice. 'Action!'

'Marriage to Eduardo,' says the stand-in, in a monotone. 'Never while I'm alive.' She takes out a scarf and fondles it. 'Oh, Arthur.'

'Background actors,' instructs Dino. 'I want you to look at the scarf. You're interested in it.'

Obediently I crick my head to look at the scarf, but Dino immediately says, 'Not you, cake-eater girl.'

Great. Everyone else gets to look at the scarf while I get to grovel on the floorboards. The door swings open with a creak and I hear the tramp of heavy boots.

'What is that pretty thing?' comes a deep, masculine voice. 'Show me.'

'Never!' says the stand-in.

Then there's some sort of tussle, but I can't see because I don't dare lift my head. This is so frustrating. I'm *longing* to see what it's all about, but I can't see a bloody thing, stuck down here. I'll never get to do my twitch, let alone say, ''Tis true, cap'n.' It's so depressing.

'Cut!'

I sit back on my heels and wave at Suze, trying not to feel envious. It's OK for her, she's on a step, where everyone can see her. She's even been given a proper prop – an old broken comb – and she's combing her tangled hair with a theatrical flourish.

'Excuse me.' A mellifluous voice hits my ear, and a tiny button boot appears in front of my eyes. I look up and feel a jolt of awe. It's April Tremont! Herself! She's stepping into the chair, and lifting up her skirts so I can rub at her boots.

'I guess you're polishing these,' she says with a nod. 'Poor you.'

'Oh it's fine!' I say at once. 'It's fun. You know. I love polishing boots. I mean, not just on film sets, I love polishing them at home, and in the garden and . . . er . . .'

Argh. Stop babbling, Becky.

'I'm April,' she says pleasantly.

Like I didn't know that. Like she's not really, really famous.

'I'm Becky.'

'You're the one who ate the cake?'

'It was a mistake,' I say hastily.

'That made me laugh.' She smiles, that amazing smile which I've seen in loads of movies. Well, not loads of movies exactly. Two movies and one sitcom and an ad campaign for moisturizer. But still.

'April. Curt. A word with you both?' Ant is heading over this way and I hurriedly bury my face in April's skirt, so he won't notice me. Not that he seems to notice any of the extras, anyway.

'I want some real violence in this scene,' I hear him saying above my head. 'Curt, when you see the insignia of your enemy on Gwennie's scarf, everything changes. You know she's in love with Arthur, and it infuriates you. Remember, this scene is the pivot; it's what drives you to attack the Fleet of Foes; it's what starts the whole chain of events. OK, guys? Passion. *Intensity*. Let's go for a take.'

Despite everything I can't help feeling a jolt of excitement. A take! We're going for a take! It's happening!

An hour later, I'm feeling a *teeny* bit less excited. We've done the scene over and over, and every time I have to keep my head down while all the action goes on above, and I'm getting achy knees from being in this position.

Plus, the more we do the scene, the less I understand it.

'Are you OK?' April Tremont smiles down from where she's having her make-up touched up. 'Pretty tough down there.'

'Oh, it's fine!' I say at once. 'Fine! Really fab!'

'Enjoying the scene?'

'Er . . .' I hesitate. I know I should say, 'Yes, it's brilliant!' But the truth is, I just can't relate to it.

'I don't get it,' I say at last. 'But *you're* really good,' I add quickly.

'Which part don't you get?' says April, looking interested.

'Well, why are you playing with your scarf?'

'It's a memento from my lover, Arthur,' explains April. 'It has his distinctive insignia on it. See?' She holds the scarf out so I can see.

'I know that.' I nod. 'But you're on Eduardo's ship. He's really violent and he hates Arthur. So wouldn't you keep it hidden? If you really loved Arthur you'd protect him, surely.'

April Tremont stares at me silently for a few moments. 'That's a good point,' she says. 'Why *am* I playing with it?'

'Maybe you're supposed to be quite stupid?' I suggest.

'No!' says April sharply. 'I'm not. Ant!' She raises her voice. 'Ant, come over here!'

Oh God. I tuck my face down into her skirt and try to look as inconspicuous as possible.

'Ant, I have a problem with my motivation,' says April. 'Why does Gwennie get out the scarf?'

I sneak a quick glance upwards – and Ant is staring at April as though suspecting a trick question.

'We went through this already,' he says. 'It's sentimental. She's thinking of her lover.'

'But why get the scarf out now, when it's so dangerous? She's on an enemy ship. Why would she be so foolhardy?'

There's silence for a few moments, then Ant yells, 'Dylan! Get over here. Please explain to April the motivation of her character.'

At once Dylan comes hurrying over, his sneakers squeaking on the floor of the soundstage.

'Oh, OK,' he says, sounding a bit nervous. 'Well, Gwennie is thinking of her lover Arthur. She's remembering the times they had together. So she gets out the scarf—'

'Why?' interrupts April.

'To remember him by.' Dylan sounds a bit flummoxed. 'That's her motivation.'

'But she can remember him without a scarf. Why would she risk his life for the sake of a scarf?'

'She's a woman,' says Dylan feebly. 'She's sentimental.'

'She's a *woman*?' retorts April, sounding suddenly livid. 'She's a *woman*? That's no kind of answer! Just because she's a woman, it doesn't mean she's an imbecile! I'm not doing it,' she says firmly. 'I'm not taking out the scarf. Gwennie isn't a moron. She wouldn't do it.'

'But you have to take out the scarf!' says Dylan in consternation. 'That's the point of the scene!'

'Well, you'll have to find a different point for the scene.'

'April, sweetie,' says Ant, breathing hard. 'You have to take out the scarf. If Eduardo doesn't see the scarf, then he won't launch the attack on the Fleet of Foes. That's the whole second act. That's the whole fucking *movie*.'

'Well, it doesn't make any sense,' says April obstinately. 'Becky's right.'

'*Becky?*' Ant sounds at the end of his tether. 'Who's Becky?'

Reluctantly I raise my head from April's skirts to see Ant staring at me with a thunderous disbelief.

'Oh, hi,' I say nervously, and risk a little smile. 'Fab directing,' I quickly add. 'Really inspired.'

'You again?' says Dylan incredulously.

'Who the fuck *are* you?' Ant expostulates. 'You're derailing my movie!' He almost looks like he might hit me.

'No I'm not!' I say in horror. 'I mean – I didn't mean to!'

'You should be thanking her!' says April. 'The scene has a big hole in it and she's the only one who noticed.' She stands up. 'Sort out your scene, gentlemen. I'll be in my trailer. Gilly, Uggs?'

One of the wardrobe girls hurries forward and unlaces April's button boots.

'April!' says Ant. 'Don't be ridiculous!'

'If you don't pick it up, the critics will,' she snaps. She steps into a pair of Uggs and strides across the soundstage. She's leaving. Oh my God.

'Come back here!' says Ant furiously.

'Fix the scene!' she retorts over her shoulder.

I can see Ant and Dylan exchanging perturbed looks.

'April, be reasonable.' Ant hurries after her. 'Look, we'll discuss it.'

As I glance around, all the extras and crew are watching, riveted. What do we do now?

There's a hurried confab going on between Dino and some other guy in a headset, then Dino strides towards the set.

'OK, lunch. Lunch, everybody.'

At once, the extras all start to head off, and Suze bounds across the set to me, as fast as she can in her big skirt.

'What did you do?' she demands.

'I didn't do anything!'

'Well, everyone's blaming you.'

'Really?' I stare at her in dismay. 'That is so unfair!'

'No, they're *pleased*. They might get overtime. Shall we go and get some lunch? They might have some more of that sushi. You know, I might become a full-time extra,' she adds as we walk along. 'I've learned such a lot. There's a special agency you join, and there's plenty of work if you have the right look. You can make good money!'

Good money? I want to point out to Suze that she already *has* good money, what with her husband being a squillionaire, only she looks so animated, I don't like to.

'And if you can ride a horse that counts as a special skill,' she's saying, when a fresh-faced girl hurries up to us.

'Becky? Is one of you Becky?'

'That's me,' I say, a bit nervously.

'Miss Tremont would like to see you in her trailer.'

Suze and I look at each other, agog. A trailer! A proper movie star wants to see me in her trailer!

'Can my friend come too?' I say.

'Sure. This way.'

I'm *slightly* disappointed in the trailer, to be honest. I was expecting it to be full of roses and champagne buckets and cards from the producers and maybe some signed photos from George Clooney, not just look like a mini-caravan with magazines and bottles of Evian and energy bars scattered around. April is on the phone as we enter, and I sit down cautiously on a bench-thing next to Suze.

I wouldn't mind having a trailer, I find myself thinking idly. Imagine if, everywhere you went in life, there was a little trailer waiting for you to go and relax in whenever you felt like it.

Imagine taking a trailer *shopping*. God, yes! You could put all your bags in it, and have a little rest, and make yourself a cup of tea and—

'Becky.' April puts down her phone and smiles at me. 'How are you?'

'Er, fine!' I say. 'Thank you. This is my friend Suze.'

'Hi, Suze.' April bestows her radiant smile on Suze, then turns back to me. 'I just wanted to make sure you were OK. I don't want you getting any backlash from Ant. You have any trouble with him, you let me know.'

'Thank you!' I say, touched.

'Well, I owe you.' She sighs. 'I should have picked up that issue at the read-through. Or someone should have. Those guys are idiots.'

'What will they do now?' I say, in slight trepidation. 'Have I really derailed the whole movie?'

'Sheesh, no!' She laughs. 'They'll write another scene. They'll fix it. That's their job. But I'd like to do you a favour in return, if I can.' She looks earnestly at me. 'Do you have an agent? Do you need a better one? Would you like a contact? I know how tough it is out there, anything can help.'

'Actually, I don't have an agent,' I start to explain. 'This isn't *really* what I do—'

'I'd love an agent!' chimes in Suze. 'I want to be an extra. I really think it could be my new career.'

April Tremont surveys us both curiously. 'You're not actors?'

'I went to drama school,' says Suze quickly. 'I've got a diploma. I was highly commended in my modern speech.'

'I'm in fashion.'

'We got on the film because of Tarkie.'

'Tarkie's her husband,' I explain. 'He finances films.'

'*Now* I find out,' says Suze bitterly.

'So everyone was like, Do you want to watch a film being made, and we said, No, we want to be in it.'

'So here we are!'

We both come to a halt and look expectantly at April. It seems as though she's having slight trouble following.

'So *you* need an agent,' she says to Suze.

'Yes please!' says Suze.

'And *you* need . . .' She turns to me. 'Do you need anything?'

'I'd love a job in styling,' I say. 'That's what I do. I used to work in Barneys, and I'm trying to make it in Hollywood, but it's really hard to get a foot in the door.'

'Bex is brilliant,' says Suze loyally. 'She makes *anyone* look good. Even my sister-in-law Fenella, who believe me . . .' She makes a face.

'She's got good shoulders,' I say. 'You just have to focus on the shoulders.'

'OK,' says April thoughtfully. 'Well, how about this? I have a friend who's a stylist and she's run ragged. I know she's always looking for talented people to work with her. How about I fix up a meeting for you?'

'That would be *amazing*!' I gasp. 'Really?'

'We'll both be at the Actors' Society Awards, Friday night. How about I get you a ticket? I'll get you both double tickets. It's a fun evening.'

'Thank you!' I grin delightedly at Suze. 'Thank you so much!'

'My friend's name is Cyndi.' April scribbles the name on a piece of paper. 'She'll be there with her new client. You can meet her too. Maybe you guys will all end up working together!'

'Wow!' I take the piece of paper. 'Thanks. Who's her new client?'

'Lois Kellerton,' says April, and I freeze. I'm aware of Suze opening her eyes wide and I try desperately to ignore her.

'What's up?' says April, sensing the tension. 'Do you know Lois?'

'No,' I say quickly. 'Not at all. No. Never met. Why would I have met Lois Kellerton?' I give a shrill, unnatural laugh.

'OK. Well, Lois's lovely,' says April. 'We're friends too, in fact we're neighbours. We've both lived on Doheny Road for ever. You'll get along great.'

This is the first time I've heard anyone describe Lois as 'lovely' and April clearly notices my surprise.

'What is it?' she says.

I know I should keep my mouth shut, but I can't resist it.

'It's just I heard Lois was . . . tricky to deal with?' I venture. 'Isn't her new film running into problems?'

April sighs. 'I wish Lois didn't have this reputation. She's a wonderful girl. And the film will be wonderful. It's the story of the early female athletes, you know, using some original footage from the Olympics. So smart. And yes, there have been glitches, but every movie has glitches.'

'Sorry,' I say awkwardly. 'I didn't mean to . . . I just heard . . .'

'I know.' April drops her hands as though in exasperation. 'Everyone says the same. The thing is, Lois's bright, she expects high standards, and she doesn't necessarily win herself friends. But you'll like her. I'm sure you will.'

A text bleeps in her phone and she reaches for it. 'Sorry, I have to go. Give your address to my assistant and I'll messenger the tickets over. Let yourselves out when you're ready.'

She heads out of the trailer, clumping down the steps in her Uggs, and Suze and I just stare at each other.

'Lois Kellerton,' says Suze at last. 'Oh my God, Bex.'

'I know.' I rub my head. 'Freaky.'

'What will you *say* to her? I mean, about . . . you know.'

'I'll say nothing. It never happened, OK? And I never told you, either.'

'All right.' Suze nods fervently, then looks up. 'Hey, what will Luke say about you meeting Lois? Isn't Lois Sage's big nemesis? Aren't you supposed to be on Team Sage?'

Oh God. In the heat of the moment, I'd forgotten all about that. Damn. I reach for an energy bar, thinking hard. OK, so it's not ideal. If I could have chosen any other celebrity, I would have. But I can't turn down this amazing chance. I *can't*.

'Luke will be completely supportive of my career,' I say at last, a bit more firmly than I feel. 'I mean, we don't both have to be on Team Sage, do we? We can have Chinese whatsits.'

'What?' Suze looks blank. 'Fortune cookies?'

'No!' I can't help giggling. '*Walls*. Where you're on different sides but it's OK because you don't pass on any secrets.'

'Walls?' says Suze mistrustfully. 'I don't like the idea of walls. You shouldn't have walls in a marriage.'

'Not real walls, *Chinese* walls.'

Suze doesn't look convinced. 'I still don't like it. I think you should be on the same side.'

'Well, so do I,' I say defensively. 'But what am I supposed to do? I tried styling Sage and she wasn't interested.'

'Style a different celebrity, then.'

'Who? They're not exactly queuing up for my services, are they?' I feel a bit ratty with Suze, partly because I know she's got a point. 'Look, it'll be fine. It'll be like that film where the husband and wife are opposing lawyers in the courtroom, but when they're at home everything's fine and lovely.'

'What film?' says Suze suspiciously.

'Er . . . you know. That one.'

I'm making this up as I go along, but I won't admit it.

'What's it called?' demands Suze.

'It doesn't matter what it's called. Look, I'm only in Hollywood once, Suze. I have to at least *see* if I can make it as a stylist.' As I say the words, I realize how much I've been wanting this opportunity; how disappointed I've been at all my failures. And now a real, proper chance is within my grasp. 'Luke will understand,' I add. 'I'll work it out with him somehow. It'll all be OK.'

BACKGROUND ARTISTS UNLIMITED AGENCY
APPLICATION FORM FOR ARTISTS

Title (delete as appropriate): ~~Mr/Mrs/Ms~~ Lady

Forename (s): Susan deLaney Margaret

Surname: Cleath-Stuart

Date of Birth: Didn't you know that it's not done to ask someone's age?

Place of Birth: Sandringham, in the riding stables (Mummy had just been out hunting).

Previous Acting Experience: I played a bumble-bee at Mrs Darlington's Academy and then I was a rabbit, and then I was that Blanche Dubois, my most brilliant role, and then that girl in The Merchant of Venice. Oh, and Juliet. Except we only did three scenes, because Shakespeare IS a bit long.

Special Skills (e.g. riding, juggling): Oh, loads! Riding, tennis, fly-fishing, yoga, making photo frames, flower arranging, folding napkins into shapes, icing cakes (I did a course, Daddy thought I might go into catering). I'm not much good at typing but I could always pretend. And if you're filming a movie set in an old English house, I can tell you where the knives and forks go, because you always get it wrong. And the English don't all wear tweed the whole time. Oh, and WHY are the villains always British??

Accents: I can do a brilliant American accent. And French. I can do Welsh but it starts to sound Indian.

Are you willing to appear nude? Are you mad? What would Daddy say? And my husband? Anyway, why do you need anyone to appear nude? When anyone strips off on the screen I start squirming with embarrassment and my husband gets up and says, 'Who's for a titchy?' People in films should keep their clothes on. Apart from Captain Jack Sparrow, he can take his off!! (Don't tell Tarkie I said that.)

Page 1 of 3

THIRTEEN

It'll be fine. I've dealt with many awkward social encounters in my time; it'll be fine. I mean, OK, so I've never met a movie star who: 1. I've caught shoplifting; 2. has a tricky reputation (perhaps undeserved); 3. I know the entire life history of, having Googled her solidly for about three days.

But still. I expect it'll go really well. We'll probably really hit it off, and meet up for coffee, go shopping together . . .

No. I pull myself up short. *Not* shopping. I mean, what if she pinches something? What if she asks me to be her accomplice and I don't know how to say no? I have a sudden hideous vision of the headlines:

Stylist and movie star arrested in Barneys stuffing designer socks in bags. See pictures pages 8 to 10.

Argh. Stop it, Becky. That's not going to happen. Decision one: If I get to work on Lois's styling team, then I'll tell her I never shop with my clients. And if by any chance we *do* go shopping and she asks me to shoplift something, I'll . . . I'll pretend I don't understand and back away. And then run. Yes. Good plan.

At least I've done my research. I know so much about Lois Kellerton, I could write a book about her. I know she started her career aged two in an infomercial about road safety, and she had an agent at age three, and her parents gave up their jobs to focus on her career. Her mother is the driven one and her father is the had-lots-of-affairs-and-ran-off one, so I won't mention him.

Nor will I mention Sage. I hadn't quite realized what a feud they've been having. It's not just the cancer-victim-shaving-head remark which Sage keeps going on about. It started ages ago, when they both arrived at an event in the same vivid-green dress, and Sage accused Lois of doing it on purpose. Then Sage didn't turn up to an AIDS event organized by Lois. She was supposed to be presenting the whole evening, apparently, and Lois said she felt 'snubbed and let down' but that she wasn't surprised that Sage had 'once again displayed her innate selfishness'.

Then last year, Lois did the Hollywood Walk of Fame and said in her speech, 'Hollywood is in my DNA.' Whereupon Sage immediately commented on Facebook, 'God help Hollywood.'

What's really sad is that they used to be friends, years ago. They even appeared in a TV show together as children. But Hollywood is a tough place for the twenty-first-century actress, and she learns to look on every other star as an enemy (according to *Hollywouldn't.com*, this brilliant blog I found). Apparently actresses compete over roles, men, ad campaigns and even plastic surgeons. They set up camps like royal courts and become paranoid about their competitors, even those they're 'friends' with.

It all sounds super-stressy. I can't imagine competing with Suze over a plastic surgeon. Although, to be fair, we *did* once clash over an Orla Kiely coat which we both wanted to buy on eBay. (Suze got it. But she lends it to me.)

Anyway, so there are quite a few possible conversational pitfalls, if and when I meet Lois tonight. I won't mention Sage, or shoplifting (or shopping) or Lois's dad, or Lois's latest film, *The Spiked Bed* (it got bad reviews), or white sugar (she thinks it's evil). Not that I was planning to mention white sugar, but still. Worth remembering. Topics I *can* safely mention: Lois's Golden Globe, kettlebells, macadamia nuts. I've written them down in case I get tongue-tied.

'Why macadamia nuts?' says Suze, who has been reading the list with interest.

'Because Lois loves them,' I say. 'It said so in *Health and Fitness*. So I'll pretend to love them too and we'll connect.'

'But what can you say about macadamia nuts?' objects Suze.

'I don't know!' I say defensively. 'I'll say, "They're really nutty, aren't they?"'

'And what will you say about kettlebells? Have you ever even *seen* a kettlebell?'

'That's not the point. Lois's done a kettlebell DVD, so it's a good conversational topic.'

We're in my room getting ready for the Actors' Society Awards or 'ASAs', as everyone calls them. And I can't help feeling a little bit hyper. I have to get it right tonight. I have to make a good impression. I've analysed Lois's style endlessly over the last few days and I've got loads of ideas for her. I think she could go far more young and glam. She wears dresses that are too old for her. And *who* does her hair?

'I read another piece in *Variety* today saying Lois's career is on the skids,' says Suze conversationally. 'Hair up or down?' She grabs her hair extensions in one hand and piles them in a knot on her head. I look at it critically.

'Up. That looks amazing. And it *isn't* on the skids.'

'Well, her price has fallen. Apparently she's really moody. Shannon's worked with her. Shannon says she's permanently on the edge.'

'Shannon's just jealous,' I snap.

I'm getting a bit sick of this Shannon. After our departure from *The Black Flag*, Suze got herself a day's work as an extra on a TV show called *Cyberville* and made a new friend called Shannon, who's been a professional extra for over twenty years. Shannon considers herself an expert on Hollywood and Suze treats all her views with total reverence and keeps spouting them back to me. I mean, honestly. Just because you've been in *The Matrix*, it doesn't mean you know everything.

'Lois just needs an exciting new look,' I say firmly. 'Which I will give her.'

'What did Luke say about it?' Suze turns, her voice muffled by hairpins in her mouth. 'You never told me.'

'Oh. Um.' I play for time by lining my lips carefully, even though I've already lined them.

'He is OK with it, isn't he?' Suze gives me a sharp look. 'Bex, you did tell him, didn't you?'

'Look.' I cast around for the best answer. 'There's no point telling him yet.'

'You have to tell him!' Suze shoves a sparkly hair clip into her hair. 'You can't just join Team Lois and he has no idea!'

'I haven't even met Lois properly yet,' I retort. 'What if we don't get on? Then I'll have told Luke for no reason. I'll wait till I get hired and *then* I'll tell him.'

I don't want to tell Luke yet about meeting Lois. First, because I secretly know that Suze is right – Luke might raise objections. And secondly, I want to tell him when I'm already a success. I want to prove that I *can* make it here on my own.

'What if he sees you making conversation with Lois tonight?'

'Suze, this isn't the Cold War! I'm allowed to talk to people! I'll just say we were chatting. Can you hook me up?'

As Suze starts pulling at the fabric of my corset dress, my phone bleeps with three new texts, all in a row, and I reach for it on a nearby chair.

'Stop it!' Suze scolds me. 'I can't hook you if you move around. It's only a text.'

'It might be an emergency.'

'It's probably just Luke.'

'What do you mean, *just* Luke?' I say, punching in my code. 'I wouldn't say it's "*just*" Tarquin.'

'Yes you would, you say it all the time.' Suze wrenches at my dress. 'Are you sure this is the right size?'

I can't answer. I'm staring at my phone in a state of shock.

'Bex?' Suze pokes me. 'Hello?'

'She's coming,' I say at last.

'Who's coming?'

'Elinor. Here.'

'*Now?*' says Suze in alarm.

'No, not now, but soon. In a week or so. I sent her a text, asking her to come, but I never thought she would—' I turn to face Suze, suddenly petrified. 'Oh God. What shall I do?'

'You'll stage an intervention, remember?' says Suze. 'Because you're so brilliant at conflict resolution, *remember*?'

'Right.' I swallow. 'Yes.'

Somehow it all sounded better in theory. But the idea that Elinor is actually going to get on a plane to LA, and Luke has no idea, and I'll have the two of them to manage . . .

'Suze, you have to help me,' I say plaintively.

'I'm not helping you!' she says at once. 'Count me out. I always thought it was a bad idea.'

'It isn't a bad idea! It's just . . . it might be more difficult than I thought.'

'I thought you were an expert,' says Suze, rather unfeelingly. 'I thought you had a variety of techniques up your sleeve and Buddha would guide you with his infinite wisdom.' She pauses, then adds, 'Tell you what, I'll buy you some more wind chimes, if you like.'

'Very funny.'

'Well honestly, Bex, you must be nuts. What happened about Elinor's surgery, anyway?'

'It was cancelled,' I say, reading the third text again. 'It was only a minor procedure on her toe.'

'Her *toe*?' Suze stares at me. 'I thought she was dying!'

'So did I,' I admit.

'Well, I think you should cancel her. Say you made a mistake and you won't be here.' She prods my shoulder. 'Turn round. There's one more hook to do.'

I turn round, thinking hard. That's the obvious option. The easy solution. I could text Elinor back. Tell her not to come; make some excuse. We'll probably never see her again. But is that really what I want? Is that really for the best for all of us? For Luke? For Minnie?

Suze fixes the last hook in place. 'There. Done.' Then she adds, 'Or you could always say Minnie was ill. I do that all the time if I want to get out of things. Ernie's had whooping cough about five times, poor little love—'

'I'm not going to cancel.' I'm feeling resolute. 'Elinor and Luke have to sort things out, and I really think I can help them, and the longer I put it off, the harder it'll be.'

'God help us.' Suze stares at me, incredulous. 'You *are* going to stage an intervention.'

'Why not? I'm sure I can do it. With or without help,' I say pointedly.

'Who needs help?' comes Luke's voice from the corridor, and I stiffen. I hastily turn off my phone and paste on a casual smile.

'Oh hi!' I say brightly, as he comes in, all smart in black tie. 'Just talking about . . . kettlebells.'

'Marvellous,' says Luke, shooting me an odd look. 'What *is* a kettlebell? I keep hearing about them.'

'It's an exercise device,' I improvise. 'It's modelled on a kettle. And a bell, obviously. Both. So, what time shall we leave?' I add hurriedly.

'Oh God, is that the time?' Suze suddenly sounds fractious. 'Where's Tarkie?'

'Haven't seen him.' Luke glances at his watch. 'We'll need to go in about twenty minutes.'

Luke wasn't originally intending to come to the ASAs, but then suddenly Sage announced she wanted to go, and her whole entourage had to come too. Apparently she wanted to bring a monkey as a publicity stunt and Luke had to talk her out of it. A monkey! Imagine if it made a mess everywhere.

Now Luke's eye has fallen on a shiny-cardboard carrier bag lying on the bed, out of which is poking a diamanté-encrusted clutch.

'Another bag, Becky?' He raises an eyebrow. 'I thought the bag you bought at the weekend was so perfect you would use it for ever and it would be your signature look and people would call you "The Girl with the Lara Bohinc Bag"?'

I feel a dart of righteous indignation. Husbands should *not* memorize conversations, word for word. It's against the whole spirit of marriage. But in this case I don't mind, because whatever he's thinking, he's wrong.

'That clutch isn't for *me*. I bought it in my role as a stylist. It's tax-deductible,' I add smartly.

I don't actually know if that's true but it must be, surely?

'Right. Of course. The styling.' Luke looks quizzical. 'How's that going, then?'

'Great!' I say robustly. 'Lots of potential. Lots of irons in the fire.'

Luke sighs. 'Becky, sweetheart, I wish you'd let me help you. I'm sure I could get you a couple of introductions—'

'I don't need your help!' I reply, stung. 'I'm on the case.'

This is why I don't want to mention Lois Kellerton yet. I want to show him. The bag's for Lois, of course. It's a one-off from a vintage shop and has an Art Deco design which I think she'll love. Lately, Lois has taken to wearing really subtle, muted shades, which is all very well, but I think she needs to 'pop' more and this bag will be perfect. Especially against all that lovely dark hair. I'm planning to give it to her tonight, as an ice-breaker, and hopefully we can take things from there.

'Where *is* he?' Suze is tapping at her phone. 'Honestly, this bloody Golden Peace . . .' She shoots me an accusing look, which is totally unfair. 'I told him to get back in good time,' she mutters as she presses Send. 'He totally loses track of time. What's he *doing*?'

I know Suze thinks Tarkie attends Golden Peace far too much. But she's just prejudiced. The truth is, Tarkie is having a brilliant time hanging out with his volleyball gang, being one of the guys. No one pesters him about listed gables or investments in South Africa. Nor do they keep trying to pitch him movie ideas, because that kind of thing is totally banned at Golden Peace. I think it's the first place he's ever been where he's just him. Tarkie. The person.

From outside comes the sound of car doors slamming. A moment later I hear the front door opening and closing, followed by footsteps in the hall. There we go. I knew Tarkie would turn up.

'You see? He's here.' I grab my Lara Bohinc clutch bag and the diamanté one. 'Let's have a titchy while he gets ready.'

Suze is stepping into her teetering high heels, which make her look even taller and more willowy than usual. Her blonde hair, piled high in snaky curls, gives her yet more height, and she basically looks amazing: all golden suntanned limbs and fake lashes and imperious frown. No one can frown like Suze. She's really quite scary, especially when she's towering above you in her Louboutins. She gets it from her mother, who is equally formidable. Apparently she can trace her ancestry back to Boudicca. (Or do I mean Boadicea? The fierce fighty woman, anyway.)

Now Suze grabs her clutch (Tory Burch, snakeskin, on sale at Bloomingdale's) and strides out of the room, calling, 'Tarkie! Where have you *been*? We have to go!'

I hurry after her along the galleried landing, and stop dead at the same time as she does. Tarkie is in the hall below, but he's not alone. He's with Bryce, who is looking as tanned and crinkly-eyed as ever. They're both in baggy surfer shorts and bandanas, and Tarkie is holding a Frisbee. I've seen Tarkie holding many weird things in my time – a First World War gun, an antique stuffed owl, an ancient scythe – but somehow seeing him with a Frisbee makes me want to burst into giggles.

As I glance at Suze, I can tell she isn't thrilled.

'Hello, Bryce,' she says, overly pleasant, walking down the stairs. 'How lovely to see you again. Please don't let us keep you. Tarkie, you'd better get changed.'

Ouch. Suze's clipped, polite tones are like little shards of glass landing, one by one. Her smile is icy, and the atmosphere is distinctly uncomfortable.

'Darling, I'd rather not come tonight, if you don't mind,' says Tarkie, apparently oblivious. 'Bryce's organized an evening hike with some of the chaps. Sounds rather fun.'

'But, *darling*, we're going to the Actors' Society Awards. Remember? We arranged it?' Suze's voice is so flinty that even Tarkie seems to realize something's up.

'Oh Suze, you don't need me there, do you?' he says pleadingly. 'It'll be full of ghastly people.'

Only Tarkie could describe the pick of A-list Hollywood celebrities as 'ghastly people'.

'Yes, I do need you there!' exclaims Suze. 'And I could have done without you disappearing all day, too. Where've you been, anyway?'

'We played volleyball,' says Tarquin, looking a bit shifty. 'And we had lunch . . . and we talked . . .'

'All *afternoon*?' Suze is sounding shriller and shriller.

'My apologies,' says Bryce charmingly, in that smooth, hypnotic voice of his. 'I waylaid Tarquin. We got talking and never stopped.'

'Don't apologize! It was a wonderful day.' Tarkie turns eagerly to Suze. 'Suze, darling, Bryce has so many brilliant insights. I'd love us all to have supper one night. And Bryce—' He turns back to him. 'I'd love to come to that class you were talking about. Meditation, was it?'

'Mindfulness.'

'That's it! Sounds . . . ahm . . . fascinating.'

'I'm brilliant at that,' I put in helpfully. 'It's really easy.'

'You don't need to go to any classes, Tarquin!' snaps Suze.

'I agree,' says Bryce, surprisingly. 'It's not at all essential. Tarquin, I think you're someone who will heal himself through a slow, natural process. Just don't be afraid to talk.'

'Right. Ahm . . . absolutely.' Tarquin looks uncomfortable. 'The thing is, it's not terribly easy—'

'I know.' Bryce nods. 'It's hard. But it'll come. Remember, it doesn't have to be *with* anyone. The sea will hear you. The air will hear you. Just express yourself, and let your soul find the answers.'

I'm listening, totally mesmerized, but Suze is bristling.

'Talk to the sea?' she scoffs. 'What, and have everyone think you're mad?'

'"Mad" is a word I try not to use,' says Bryce, unruffled. 'And yes, I think talking to other people can bring its own unhelpful baggage. Sometimes you just need to talk to an entity. The void. Your god. We do a lot of healing work with animals.'

'Tarkie doesn't need *healing*!' Suze sounds outraged.

'That's your opinion.' He shrugs in a kind of all-wise, all-knowing, *I have perspective because I have more experience of human problems and neuroses and stress than you could possibly guess at, even though I'm bound to secrecy and will never blab any celebrity details* kind of way.

Well, that's what I picked up, anyway.

'I'm his *wife*,' says Suze stonily.

'Of course.' He lifts his hands. 'Suze, I respect you.'

There's a really weird chemistry between Suze and Bryce. She's practically sparking as she squares up to him . . .

Oh my God, does she fancy him? I mean, everyone kind of fancies Bryce, you'd have to be inhuman not to . . . but does she *really* fancy him?

'Come on.' At last Suze swivels and addresses Tarkie. 'We need to go.'

'I'll see you, Tarquin,' says Bryce, apparently unoffended.

'Call me, Bryce,' says Tarkie. 'If you and the chaps are playing volleyball, or if there's another hike . . .' He's so eager and hopeful, he reminds me of a little boy running after the cool kids in the playground.

'I'll call.' Bryce nods kindly, then turns and leaves.

'Well!' Suze exhales as the door closes.

'Interesting guy,' says Luke noncommittally. 'What's his background, Tarquin?'

'I don't know,' says Tarkie. 'And it doesn't matter.' He turns on Suze. 'I think you could be a bit more polite to my friends.'

'He's not your friend,' retorts Suze.

'He is! He's more of a friend than most of the people in my life! He's cleverer, and kinder, and he understands more . . .' Tarquin breaks off and we all gape at him. I don't think I've ever heard Tarkie so impassioned in my life.

Oh my God. My heart suddenly starts bumping in my chest.

'Lois, may I introduce Rebecca Brandon?' says April. 'Rebecca, this is Lois Kellerton.'

Seeing celebrities in real life is like seeing a Magic Eye, I've decided. At first they seem totally unreal, like a magazine or a film hoarding come to life. Then your eyes gradually adjust and they take on 3D form. And at last they kind of turn into real people. Kind of.

Lois's face is thinner even than it was when I saw her before. Her skin is so fair it's almost translucent. Her wavy hair is caught up in a loose knot, and she's wearing a drifty, silky grey dress that makes her look like a shadow.

'Hi,' she says softly.

'Hi,' I say awkwardly, holding out my hand. 'Lovely to . . . meet you.'

She takes my hand – and I see something snap in her face. She's realized. She's recognized me. My stomach clenches in apprehension. How is this going to go?

All credit to Lois, she's totally kept her cool. Her pupils haven't even dilated. No one would have any idea we've met before. That's what acting training does for you, I expect.

'Becky,' she says slowly.

'Exactly.' I swallow. 'I'm Becky.'

Don't mention shoplifting, I tell myself firmly. *Do not even THINK about shoplifting.* The trouble is, the more I tell myself *not* to think about it, the more I can't help it. I feel like her secret is dancing up and down inside me, shouting 'Let me out!'

'I love macadamias,' I blurt out in desperation. 'Don't you?'

'I guess so.' Lois looks puzzled, then adds, 'So, you want to be a stylist, April tells me.'

'Becky is a stylist!' says Suze loyally. 'She used to work at Barneys as a personal shopper. She's brilliant. I'm Suze, by the way. I'm in the profession too,' she adds grandly. 'I'm a background artist.'

Honestly, what is Suze like? *I'm in the profession too.*

'I shopped at Barneys a couple times when I was filming in New York,' says Lois. 'I saw . . . Janet?'

214

'Janet was my boss!' I try not to sound too excited. 'She taught me everything!'

'Oh, OK.' Lois gives me an appraising look. 'So you know what you're doing, then.'

'Becky, I'm so sorry,' April turns to me, 'but Cyndi couldn't make it after all. I was going to get Becky and Cyndi together,' she explains to Lois.

'Oh.' I hide my disappointment. 'Well, in the meantime . . .' I reach for the Art Deco clutch. 'I brought this along for you.' I proffer it to Lois. 'I saw it and it seemed like your style, it's vintage . . .' I trail off and hold my breath.

There's silence as Lois considers the bag. I feel like I'm in the *MasterChef* final, and Michel Roux Jr is considering my profiteroles.

'I like it,' Lois declares at last. 'I *love* it. Sold.'

'Great!' I say, trying not to sound too joyful. 'Well, it's from this great vintage shop, I go there all the time, I could easily source some more stuff for you . . .'

'I'd like that.' Lois gives me that ravishing, understated smile of hers, the one she does in *Tess*, when Angel strips off and does a sexy dance for her. (Did that happen in the book? Something tells me maybe not.)

She seems totally sweet and low-key. I can't understand why people think she's tricksy. Now she's looking at her phone and frowning. 'My agent. I need to go talk to some people. I'll be back for this delightful thing.' She puts the bag down on the table. 'And we'll talk terms.'

'But what about Cyndi?' I say awkwardly. 'I don't want to tread on her toes.'

'You won't.' Lois gives a laugh. 'The truth is, Cyndi's really too busy to look after me anyway. April always said she would be.'

'She has too many clients,' April says ruefully.

'I don't have too many clients,' I say at once, and Lois laughs again.

'Great, well count me one of them.' She smiles once more, then heads away, across the crowded room.

'Next time you go shopping, I'm coming with you,' says April, smiling. 'You can find me a purse like that, too.'

'Of course! And thank you so much for introducing me to Lois.'

'My pleasure! Thank *you* so much for pointing out that the scene I was shooting made no sense. They're still rewriting it, I believe.' She winks at me. 'See you girls later.'

She melts away into the crowd, and I gleefully turn to Suze.

'Did you see that? Lois liked the bag! She wants to talk terms!'

'Of course she liked the bag!' says Suze, giving me a hug. 'Well done, Bex! Lois seems really nice,' she adds consideringly. 'I thought she was supposed to be horrible.'

I'm about to say that that's exactly what I was just thinking too, when Luke's voice hails me.

'Darling, are you all right?' I turn to see him with Aran and two women I don't recognize, and Sage, who is wearing a silver dress and matching shoes and her hair in a sixties beehive.

'If that bitch gets it,' she's saying furiously. 'If that crazy bitch gets it . . .'

'Sage, calm down,' Aran murmurs.

'Having fun?' says Luke.

'Yes!' I say, still glowing. 'We're having a great time! Hi, Aran; hi, Sage . . .'

While I'm introduced to the two women, Sage flops down on a chair, furiously tapping at her phone.

'What's up?' I say quietly to Luke.

'Lois Kellerton,' he murmurs back. 'Florence Nightingale. I have a feeling Lois's going to get the role. Just don't mention it, OK?'

'Oh.' I feel an uncomfortable twinge. 'All right.'

I can feel Suze's eyes burning into me, and I know what she's trying to say: I should tell Luke that I'm going to start working with Lois Kellerton. She's right. I should. Only I'm not quite sure how to do it in front of Sage.

Could I text him?

I get out my phone, open a text and start typing:

Luke. I have a new client. It's Lois Kellerton.

No. Too blunt. I delete the whole thing and try again:

Luke, I have an amazing new opportunity which I don't want to mention out loud. And I hope you'll be pleased for me. I THINK you'll be pleased for me. There may be a very slight conflict of interest, but we can always build Chinese walls, and

Damn. I've run out of room. I'm just backspacing again, when Sage looks up from her own phone.

'Cute purse,' she says, spying the Art Deco bag and pulling it towards her. 'Is that yours, Becky?'

Shit. *Shit.*

'Oh. Um . . .' As I'm working out how to answer, Luke plunges in.

'That's one of Becky's work purchases,' he says. 'You know she's a stylist, Sage? She's worked at Barneys and at a major store in London. Remember, I was telling you about her work yesterday.'

'I do,' says Aran, looking up from his phone. 'We couldn't get you to shut up about it.' He winks at me, then resumes tapping at his phone.

I can't help feeling touched. I had no idea Luke was bigging up my work.

Sage's brow has wrinkled as though she's recalling a distant memory from a past life.

'Sure,' she says vaguely. 'You told me. So who is this purse for?'

'I think it might, in fact, be for you!' Luke's eyes twinkle. 'Am I right, Becky?'

No. Nooooooo!

Disaster. Total disaster. Why didn't I hide it under the table?

'Um . . .' I clear my throat. 'Actually—'

'For me?' Sage's face lights up. 'How cool. It matches my dress.'

Is she crazy? It's totally the wrong silver.

'The thing is— It's not—' I reach for the bag, but it's too late. Sage has stood up and is trying it out, posing as though she's on the red carpet. I meet Suze's eyes – and she looks as horrified as I feel.

'I think you've scored a hit, Becky,' says Luke, looking delighted. 'Bravo.'

'The thing is, it's for a client,' I say awkwardly. 'I've promised it to her. Sorry. I can try to get you another one like it.'

'Which client?' Sage looks put out.

'Just a . . . um . . . this girl . . .' I'm knotting my fingers. 'You wouldn't know her . . .'

'Well, tell her you lost it.' Sage pouts winsomely. 'It's too cute. I *have* to have it.'

'But I've promised it to her . . .' I try to swipe it, but she dances away.

'Mine, now!'

Before I can stop her, she's moving into a cluster of guys in black tie. The next moment she's gone.

'Luke!' I let out all my stress by banging the table. 'How could you? You've ruined everything! That clutch wasn't for her!'

'Well, I'm very sorry, but I thought I was helping you!' he replies hotly. 'You've been telling me for weeks how you want to be Sage's stylist.'

'I do! But I've got this other client—'

'Who is this other client?' He doesn't look convinced. 'Does she even exist?'

'Yes!'

'Well, who is it?' He turns to Suze. 'Do you know this client?'

'I think Becky needs to tell you herself,' says Suze in disapproving tones.

'Er . . . Luke,' I say with a small gulp. 'Let's go to the bar.'

*

As we make our way to the bar, I'm lurching between two feelings. Glee that I've finally got a client, and dread at having to tell Luke. Glee–dread–glee–dread . . . My head is spinning and my hands are clenched and my legs are shaking, and altogether I'm glad when we reach the bar.

'Luke, I have something to tell you,' I blurt out. 'It's good but it's not good. Or it may not be good. Or . . .' I've run out of possibilities. 'I need to tell you,' I finish lamely.

Luke eyes me for a moment without saying anything.

'Is this a stiff drink kind of a something?' he says at last.

'It could be.'

'Two gimlets,' he instructs the barman. 'Straight up.'

Luke quite often orders for me, which is because I can never decide what to have. (Mum's the same. Phoning for a Chinese honestly takes about an hour in our house.)

'So, the good news is, I've got a client.'

'So you said.' Luke raises his eyebrows. 'Well done! And the bad news?'

'The bad news is . . .' I screw up my face. 'My client is Lois Kellerton.'

I'm bracing myself for Luke to explode, or frown, or maybe bang his fist on the bar and say, 'Of all the movie stars in all the towns . . .' and stare murderously into the middle distance. But instead he looks puzzled.

'So?'

I feel a little indignant. How can he look so calm when I'm tying myself up in knots?

'So! Sage will be livid! I'll be on Team Lois and you'll be on Team Sage and it'll all kick off and—'

'It will *not* kick off.' Finally, Luke does sound angry. 'I'm not having this any more! The so-called feud is *over*. Sage is a grown woman and she needs to start acting with a little dignity and maturity.' He glowers at me, as though it's my fault.

'It's not just her,' I say, to be fair. 'It's both of them. Lois wore the same dress as Sage to an event, and then Sage bailed out of this charity thing—'

'Whatever.' Luke cuts me off. 'It's over. And as for your

career, you are an independent woman, and if Sage has any problem at all with you working for Lois Kellerton, she can answer to me. OK?'

He sounds so forthright I feel a glow of pleasure. I knew all along he'd support me. (Well, I kind of knew.) Our drinks arrive, and Luke lifts his up to clink mine.

'To you, Becky. First client in Hollywood. Bravo. I hope for your sake she's not as nutty as my client.'

I can't help giggling. It's so unlike Luke to diss his clients – he's usually far too discreet.

'So, is Sage difficult to work with?'

Luke closes his eyes briefly, and takes a swig of his drink. As he opens them, he's smiling wryly.

'Trapped inside that gorgeous, curvaceous body is a spoiled teenage girl with arrested development and the biggest sense of entitlement I've ever come across. And I've worked with bankers,' he adds, rolling his eyes.

'She's worse than *bankers*?' I say, playing along.

'She thinks she should be able to do exactly as she likes. All the time.'

'Can't movie stars do what they like?'

'Some can. When they reach a certain level.' Luke takes another gulp. 'Sage thinks she's Hollywood royalty. But she's not. Not yet. Her trouble is, she had very easy, very early success and nothing since has quite matched up to it.'

'So how can she get that success again?'

'That's what we're working on. But it's a work in progress.' Luke gives that wry smile again. 'Believe me, even the most obnoxious hedge-fund types in London are less of a pain in the butt than Sage Seymour. When I speak to boards of directors, they listen. We agree an action plan. We put it in motion. When I speak to Sage . . . who knows if she's even listening?'

'Well, Aran thinks you're brilliant,' I say. 'He told me so the other day.'

'Aran's great.' Luke nods. 'We see eye to eye, at any rate.' He lifts his glass up again. 'And that's why, my darling, I hope for your sake that your client is less nutty than mine.'

I grin at him as I sip my drink. It's nice to have a proper chat, the two of us. These last few weeks have been such a whirlwind, I've barely seen Luke, let alone spent time together as a couple. I'm about to share this thought with Luke, when a guy in a tuxedo with long, glossy dark hair passes by. He must surely have used hair straighteners and about a whole bottle of product. I glance at Luke and see that he's noticed the guy, too.

'Shall I grow my hair like that?' he says, his mouth barely twitching.

'Yes!' I say with emphasis. 'Definitely! I loved it when you had long hair.' I lean over to stroke his hair. 'I adore your hair. The more of it, the better.'

When we went on honeymoon, Luke let his hair grow and even had little plaits. But as soon as we got back to London he whipped it all off again. I've always thought that Long-hair Luke was slightly different from Short-hair Luke. More relaxed.

'You should wear long hair and flip-flops to work,' I suggest. 'That's the LA way.'

'British men don't wear flip-flops to work,' he says firmly.

'You're an Angeleno now,' I retort.

'Hardly!' says Luke, laughing.

'Well, nearly. And Minnie's definitely a mini-Angeleno. She loves coconut water. And you know she has lessons in yoga at pre-school? She's *two* and she's doing Kundalini yoga. They start by studying Sanskrit and they waft saffron scent through the air and then the teacher asks each of them to vocalize what the session means to them.'

'What does Minnie say?' asks Luke, with interest.

'I've only sat in on one session,' I admit. 'She said, "Bum bum bum".'

'Bum bum bum!' Luke splutters into his drink. 'Our articulate child.'

'It was pretty accurate!' I'm starting to laugh myself. 'They were doing Downward Dog. You should do Kundalini yoga, too, you know,' I add to Luke teasingly. 'When you've grown your hair down to your waist and bought a pair of baggy trousers you'll fit in perfectly.'

'D'you *want* to fit in perfectly, Becky?' As Luke holds my gaze, he seems to be asking me a bigger question.

'I . . . don't know,' I say. 'Yes. Of course. Don't you?'

'Maybe,' says Luke, after a pause. 'Strange place, this. Some bits I relate to. Others, not so much.'

'Well, everywhere's like that,' I point out. 'Remember when you did that job with those designers in Hoxton? You kept telling me how different they were from City people.'

'Touché.' He grins, and finishes his gimlet. 'Had you better go and see to your client?'

'She won't *be* my client if I can't get that clutch bag back off Sage,' I say, anxiously scanning the crowds of people. 'Can you somehow distract Sage and I'll grab it?'

'I'll see what I can do. Come on.'

As we start back across the ballroom, there's a booming fanfare over the loudspeaker system and a deep voice says, 'Ladies and gentlemen! The Actors' Society Awards are about to start. Please take your seats.'

I'm searching all around for a flash of silver, but without any joy. People are pressing back into the ballroom from outside, and it's getting pretty chock-full. And now there's a crush of photographers as some major celeb enters the room.

'Ladies and gentlemen!' comes the boomy voice again. 'Please take your seats for tonight's awards!'

I feel a tap on my shoulder and wheel round sharply, hoping it's Sage. But it's Lois.

'Becky, I was looking for you,' she says in that soft voice. 'We were interrupted.'

I can't reply. I'm staring in shock. She's holding the Art Deco clutch. How did that happen?

'Where did you get that?' I blurt out.

'It was lying on a table. You know, there was a champagne glass balanced on top of it.' She smiles in mock reproof. 'You should take better care of such a lovely thing. I have to go present an award, but I'll see you later, OK?' She twinkles at me, then hurries off.

In a slight daze, I return to our table and sink into my seat.

'What happened?' demands Suze. 'You've been ages!'

'It's OK. Luke's fine with everything and Lois's got the clutch.'

'Nicely done,' applauds Luke.

'Thanks.' I beam at him, finally relaxing. 'So, what are these awards all about?' I reach for the programme and flip through it. 'Best Debut. Suze, you could win that!'

'They should have Best Background Artist,' says Suze, looking up from her programme in dissatisfaction. 'We're the backbone of the film industry. Why don't we have our own Oscar? Tarkie!' she exclaims as he sits down. 'I want you to sponsor a new awards ceremony. For background actors.'

'Ahm . . .' Tarquin looks wary. 'Maybe.'

'The big corporations don't care about us. But where would they be without the talent and commitment of the background artist?' Suze sounds like she's about to organize a rally. 'Where would their blockbusters be then? We need recognition. We need respect!'

'And you want to win a prize,' I put in.

'It's not *about* that,' she says severely. 'I'm simply speaking out on behalf of my community.'

'But you would win a prize.'

'I might do.' She preens herself. 'We could have statues like the Oscars, but silver.'

'And call them "Suzes".'

'Shut up!' She pokes me. 'Although, actually . . . why not?'

'Ladies and gentlemen!' The deep boomy voice is back, and spotlights start circling the whole room. 'Welcome to this year's Actors' Society Awards. Please welcome your host, Billy Griffiss!'

Applause breaks out as music erupts from the loudspeakers, and Billy Griffiss comes running down a set of lit-up steps, on to the stage. (I'm not *exactly* sure who he is. Maybe a comedian.) He starts his speech, but I'm only half listening.

'Sage!' says Aran, as she approaches the table, all glittery under the circling spotlights. 'We lost you there. You need a drink, honey?'

'I've been looking for my purse,' says Sage, looking cross. 'I just had it. I put it down, and it was gone.'

'Never mind,' says Suze quickly. 'I don't think it went with your dress, actually.'

'And now, to present our first award, may I introduce a young lady who has done more for the share price of Kleenex than any other actor. We've seen her on the scaffold, we've seen her marooned in space, and now we're going to see her right here. The queen of the weepie . . . Miss Lois Kellerton!'

The theme tune to *Tess* blasts through the loudspeakers, and Lois appears at the top of the lit-up steps. She looks slim and ethereal and beautiful . . . and she's holding the Art Deco bag.

Shit.

OK. Think. Quickly. The important thing is that Sage doesn't look at the stage and see the clutch.

'Sage!' I say wildly. 'I need to speak to you. Now.'

I can see Suze clocking the silver bag in Lois's hand, and her eyes widen in comprehension.

'Ow!' She rubs at her chest vigorously. 'I don't feel great. Sage, have I got a rash? Could you look at my skin?'

Puzzled, Sage peers at Suze's chest.

'You're good,' she says, and turns back to the stage.

'Sage!' I hurry over to her chair and kneel down, forcing her to look away from the stage. 'I've had a brilliant idea for a dress! With a fishtail and a kind of . . . bodice . . .'

'Sounds great.' Sage turns away. 'We'll talk about it later. I want to watch Lois mess this up.'

'And the nominations are . . .' Lois is saying. She's standing at the lectern by now, and the clutch is resting on top of it in plain view.

'She's so skinny,' Sage is saying pityingly, plumping up her own cleavage. 'She has such a sad little body. She's—' Her eyes suddenly narrow. 'Wait. Is that my purse?' She gasps so loudly, heads turn at the next table. 'Is that *my* purse? *Did that witch steal my purse?*'

'No!' I say hastily. 'It was just a mix-up, I'm sure . . .'

'Mix-up? She stole it!' To my horror, Sage leaps to her feet. 'Give me back my purse, Lois!' she yells.

'Oh Jesus,' says Aran, and meets Luke's eyes.

'What is she *doing*?' Luke looks absolutely appalled.

Lois pauses in the reading, and peers uncertainly out into the audience. Sage is striding to the stage, her eyes flashing. To my disbelief she mounts the podium, her dress sparkling under the spotlights.

'That's my purse,' she says, grabbing it off the lectern. 'You're a thief, Lois. A common little thief.'

'*No.*' Aran bangs his head down on the table, as all the photographers rush forward and start snapping.

'I didn't steal anything.' Lois looks flabbergasted. 'This was given to me by my stylist, Rebecca.'

'She gave it to *me*,' Sage retorts, opening it up. 'Oh, look. *My* phone. *My* lipstick. *My* lucky charm. Now are you going to tell me this is *your* purse?'

Lois stares in bewilderment at Sage's stuff. Then she glances up, her eyes huge and anxious.

'I was given it,' she said. 'I don't understand.'

My legs trembling, I rise to my feet and call out, 'It's my fault! I promised it to both of you! I'm really sorry . . .'

But no one takes any notice, even though I'm waving my arms, trying to get their attention.

'Now, ladies, I'm sure this is just a misunderstanding,' Billy Griffiss is saying. 'It reminds me of the calendar thief. Did you hear about him? He got twelve months and they say his days are numbered.' He laughs loudly at his own joke, but if he's hoping for anyone to join in, he's out of luck. Everyone is watching Sage, riveted. Two guys in headsets have approached her, but she keeps batting them off.

'Excuse me?' I try waving my arms again. 'Sage?'

'People should know the truth about you, Lois,' she spits.

'You act so high and mighty, but you're nothing but a criminal. You're a thief! You're a shoplifter!'

There's a shocked murmuring from the audience at this. Someone shouts, 'Boo!' and someone else, 'Get her off!'

'Now, now.' Billy Griffiss sounds pretty shocked, too. 'I think that's enough—'

'It's true! She's a shoplifter! From . . . Pump!, wasn't it, Lois?'

Lois looks like she wants to throw up.

'There's CCTV footage,' says Sage in satisfaction. 'Take a look.'

'You don't know what you're talking about,' says Lois in a trembling voice.

'Yes I do. Becky saw her. Becky, you saw Lois shoplifting, didn't you? Tell them! This is the witness!' She gestures theatrically at me.

I'm still on my feet, so I'm totally identifiable. In one instant, everyone in the room seems to have turned to look at me. Photographers are pointing their cameras this way. A few flashes are already going off, and I blink.

'You saw Lois shoplifting, didn't you?' says Sage, her voice rising clearly through the room, her smile curving cruelly. 'Tell them, Becky. Tell the truth.'

Blood is rushing in my ears like a freight train. I can't think properly. The whole world is looking at me and I need to decide what to do and I'm too confused and the seconds are ticking by . . .

I've lied plenty of times in my life. I've said my leg was broken when it wasn't. I've said I had glandular fever when I didn't. I've said my boots cost £100 when it was actually £250. But those were lies about *me*. I've never lied about someone else.

I can't tell the world Lois is a shoplifter.

But I can't tell the world she *isn't* a shoplifter.

'I . . .' I glance desperately at Lois. 'I . . . no comment.'

I sink down in my chair, feeling ill.

'That proves it!' Sage crows. 'Look at the CCTV footage!

Becky saw it all. She's your witness. Get her on the stand!' She curtseys to the audience and sweeps off the stage.

Aran and Luke are just staring at each other, aghast.

'Becky.' Luke reaches over and squeezes my hand hard. 'Are you OK?'

'Yes. No.' I swallow. 'What was I supposed to do?'

'It was an impossible situation.' Luke's mouth is tight with anger. 'A situation you shouldn't have been put in.'

'They're coming.' Aran glances up at the photographers heading our way. He gives me a sympathetic look. 'Watch out, girl. Your life just changed for ever.'

'Becky!' A journalist is holding out a voice recorder at me. 'Becky! Did you see Lois stealing?'

'Did you catch her in the act?' chimes in another.

'Becky, look this way please!'

'This way, please, Becky!'

'Leave her alone!' commands Luke furiously, but the crowd of press is getting even bigger.

'Becky! To your right, please!'

I've always wondered what it's like to be in the glare of the paparazzi. Now I know. It's like being in a thunderstorm. It's all white light and noise and whooshing in my ears. Voices are calling at me from all directions. I don't know which way to look or what to do. All I'm aware of is my name, being shouted out, over and over.

'Becky!'

'Becky!'

'Beckeeeeeee!'

FOURTEEN

I suppose in the old days, we would have waited for the first editions to come out. We might even have got some sleep. But this is the 24-hour internet age. The news was right there, instantly.

It's 6 a.m. now, and none of us has been to bed. I've read about two hundred different pieces online. I can't stop. The headlines have been changing every hour, as more bits of news filter in:

Lois is 'Shoplifter'!!!
ASAs ceremony disrupted
Sage accuses Lois of theft, interrupts awards
Store assistant confirms shoplifting, police 'pressing no charges as yet'
Sage: I feel betrayed by former friend

And there's a whole load, just about me.

Witness Becky 'saw everything'
Becky 'may testify in court'
Stars fight over bag from stylist Becky

They just go on and on. The most extraordinary one is this one I found on a gossip site:

Becky 'drank cocktails' before row, bartender reports

I mean, for God's sake. What does that have to do with anything? They might as well write, 'Lois and Sage visited bathroom on day of row.' They probably *will* write that.

We've all given up saying how bizarre it is. Suze and Tarkie are on the sofa with all the children, eating cornflakes and watching the coverage on E!, which is basically a loop of Sage screaming at Lois and a shot of me looking bewildered. I've seen it about forty-seven times. I don't need to see it any more.

Luke and Aran are in the kitchen, talking grimly. Somehow they persuaded Sage to stop giving interviews, go home and promise to go to bed. Aran delivered her personally into the care of her housekeeper, handed over a huge tip and said, 'This girl needs to sleep.' But I bet she's stayed up all night, too. I bet she loves it.

As for Lois, I have no idea. Her people surrounded her and hustled her out of the place almost instantly. It was like seeing a caged animal again. Every time I think of it my insides squirm with guilt.

'Want watch *Barney*!' Minnie barges into me, interrupting my thoughts. 'Want watch *Barney*, not Mummy. Not *Mummy*,' she repeats disparagingly.

I suppose it is a bit boring, watching your mother on a loop on the TV when you were hoping for a big purple dinosaur.

'Come on.' I lift her up, all cosy in her rabbit dressing gown and slippers. 'Let's find you *Barney*.'

I settle her upstairs, watching *Barney* on our bed with a bowl of sugar-free spelt puffs. (Totally tasteless but, unbelievably, her favourite snack. She really is becoming a child of LA.) Then I pull back the curtains and do a double-take. There's a camera crew outside our gates. An actual camera crew! The next minute I hear the entrance buzzer sounding. Someone's pressing it, over and over. I bolt along the landing and start running down the stairs, but Luke is at the bottom, waiting for me.

'*Don't* answer it!' he says. 'Aran will take care of it.'

He shepherds me away from the door, into the kitchen. 'You're going to have to keep a very low profile over the next few days,' he says. 'Which is boring, but that's how these things go. We'll draft a statement and release it mid-morning.'

'Becky!' I can hear a man's faint voice from outside. 'Becky, we want to offer you an exclusive!'

'Should I maybe give an interview?' I turn to Luke. 'Like, make things clear?'

'No!' says Luke, as though the idea is anathema. 'A statement is enough. We don't want to feed the frenzy. The more you give them, the more they'll want. Coffee?'

'Thanks. I just need to . . . get my lip gloss . . .'

I dart into the hall again and run halfway up the stairs. There's a window from where I can see out to the front, and I peer through the glass. Aran is at the gates, talking to the camera crew. He's laughing and looks relaxed and even high-fives one of them. I can't imagine Luke behaving like that.

'Sorry, guys,' I hear him say, and then he turns back towards the house. 'I'll let you know as soon as.'

'Aran!' I say, as the front door opens. 'What's going on?' I walk back down the stairs to talk to him.

'Oh, nothing much.' He smiles easily. 'World's press descending: same old same old.'

'And they want to interview me?'

'They sure do.'

'What did you say to them?'

'I said don't scratch the gates, you miserable bloodsucking low-life.'

I can't help smiling. Aran seems so relaxed about things. The buzzer sounds again and he peers out of a side window.

'What do you know,' he observes. 'ABC just turned up. This story is going mainstream.'

'Luke says I should stay inside and ignore them,' I venture.

'And we'll just give out a statement later.'

'If you want this to go away, that's the best thing you can do,' he says, in neutral tones. 'Totally. Keep your head down and they'll get bored.'

I can sense a 'But' hovering in the air. I look at him questioningly and he shrugs noncommittally.

He's not going to say a single word more unless I press him, is he? I walk a little way off, in the opposite direction from the kitchen, and wait for Aran to follow me.

'But?' I say, and Aran sighs.

'Becky, you're Luke's wife. I'm not here to advise you.'

'But?'

'It all depends on what you want. And what Luke wants.'

'I don't know what I want,' I say, confused. 'I don't even know what you mean.'

'OK. Let me explain.' He seems to marshal his thoughts. 'I've watched you trying to make it in Hollywood as a stylist. Without a whole lot of success, right?'

'Right,' I say reluctantly.

'You know what people need to make it in Hollywood? They need heat. Right now, you have heat. All that attention, that buzz . . .' He gestures out to the front. 'That's heat. And call me an environmentalist, but I don't like to see heat go to waste.'

'Right,' I nod uncertainly. 'Me neither.'

'Whether you like it or not, getting ahead in this place isn't about talent or hard work. OK, maybe ten per cent is talent.' He spreads his hands. 'The other ninety per cent is catching a lucky break. So here's your choice. You can see last night as a weird little moment to hush up and move on from . . . or you can see it as the luckiest break you ever caught.' He focuses on me, his eyes suddenly intense. 'Becky, last night was Providence giving you a fastpass. You can jump to the head of the line if you want to. You can go the distance. Do you want to?'

I stare back, utterly mesmerized by his words. I can jump to the head of the line? Go the distance? Why on earth wouldn't I want to do that?

'Yes!' I stutter. 'Of course I do! But— but what do you mean, exactly? What should I do?'

'We can make a plan. We can use this heat. But you have to know what you're getting into. You have to be prepared to see it through.'

'You mean, use the media?' I say hesitantly. 'Do interviews?'

'Channel the energy, is all I'm saying. Your profile just went through the roof, but the world knows you as Becky Brandon, Witness to a Shoplifting. How about if you transformed that into Becky Brandon, Celebrity Stylist? Becky Brandon, Hollywood's fashion maven. Becky Brandon, the go-to girl for a great look. We can brand you any way we like.'

I stare back at him, too dazzled to speak. Brand? Celebrity stylist? *Me?*

'You know that bag you picked out is all over the internet?' he adds. 'Do you realize how hot you are right now? And if it goes to court, they'll be all over you. You'll be the star witness and, believe me, the world will be watching.'

I feel a fresh tingle of excitement. Star witness! I'll have to have a whole new wardrobe! I'll wear little Jackie O suits every day. And I'll straighten my hair. No, I'll put my hair up. Yes! Maybe I could have a different style every day, and people will call me The Girl with the Amazing Up-dos, and—

'Are you starting to realize what you have here?' Aran interrupts my thoughts. 'People would kill for this exposure.'

'Yes, but . . .' I try to calm my whirling thoughts. 'What do I do? Now? Today?'

'Well.' Aran sounds suddenly more businesslike. 'We sit down and we make a plan. I can pull in some colleagues, you'll need an agent . . .'

'Stop!' I say, as reality suddenly swoops in. 'This is all too fast.' I lower my voice a little. 'Don't you understand, everything you're saying, it's the exact *opposite* of what Luke was saying. He wants it all to go away.'

'Sure.' Aran nods. 'Becky, what you have to remember is, Luke doesn't see you as a client. He sees you as his wife. He's very protective of you and Minnie. Of course he is. Me? I see everyone as a client. Or potential client.' He grins. 'We can discuss that later.'

The buzzer sounds again and I jump.

'Leave it,' says Aran. 'Let them wait.'

'So, what will all this mean for Sage?'

'Sage!' He gives a short bark of a laugh. 'If that girl goes any further off the rails she'll find herself in the ravine. She'll be OK. We'll haul her back on track, Luke and I. She'll kick and scream and it won't be pretty. But then, nothing about Sage is. Except her face. When she's been in make-up,' he adds. 'You don't want to see her before that.' He grimaces. 'Brutal.'

'Rubbish!' I give a shocked giggle. 'She's beautiful!'

'If you say so.' He raises his slanty eyebrows comically.

He's so irreverent and so unruffled. It's like he's *enjoying* all of this. I gaze at him, trying to work him out.

'You don't seem as angry about all this as Luke. Hasn't Sage messed up your strategy?'

'Quite possibly. But I like a challenge.' He shrugs. 'Stars are like any other investment. May go up, may go down.'

'And Lois? Do you think this will . . .' I can hardly bear to say it. 'Ruin her?' I feel a fresh clench of guilt in my stomach. If I'd just kept my mouth closed. If I'd just kept my promise. I'm haunted by the sight of Lois swaying in shock on the stage. She looked so desperate. And it was all my fault.

'Depends how she plays it,' says Aran cheerily. 'She's a bright one, Lois. I wouldn't put it past her to come out on top.'

I can't believe he's so heartless.

'Didn't you see her?' I exclaim. 'She looked like she was about to collapse! I thought she was going to faint right there on the stage!'

'Probably didn't eat enough at dinner.' Aran's phone buzzes. 'I must go. But we'll talk. And Becky . . .' He gives me a significant look. 'Don't leave it too long. Remember, if you want to capitalize on this moment, you need the heat. And the heat won't last for ever. Hi,' he says into the phone.

'Wait! Aran.' I lower my voice and glance towards the

kitchen. 'If you were going to give me some advice on how to play it today . . . what would it be?'

'Hold on a moment,' says Aran into the phone and comes back towards me. 'I'm not advising you officially, you understand, Becky.' He glances towards the kitchen.

'I understand,' I practically whisper.

'But if I had a client in your situation who wished to make the most of her exposure, I'd advise her to be seen. Get out there. Don't say *anything*. Stay dignified, pleasant, going about your daily business. But be seen. Be photographed. And think about what you wear,' he adds. 'Be casual but cool. Make your outfit a talking point.'

'OK,' I say breathlessly. 'Thanks.'

While Aran takes his call, I head to the window on the stairs again and peep out. There are more press gathered outside the gates. Waiting for me. I'm hot! Aran's words keep going round my head. I mean, he's right. All this time, I've been trying to make it in Hollywood and now, here's a golden opportunity, right in my lap, and if I don't take advantage of it I may never have the chance again . . .

'Becky?'

Luke's voice makes me jump. 'Made you that cup of coffee.'

'Thanks,' I say, and smile nervously at him as I take it. 'This is all a bit weird, isn't it?' I gesture to the crowd of journalists.

'Don't worry. It'll all die down.' Luke gives me a quick hug. 'Why don't you and Minnie and the others watch movies in the basement? Then you don't even have to see them.'

'Right,' I say after a pause. 'Yes. We could do that.' I glance out of the window again. I can see a camera with NBC on it. *NBC!*

My mobile rings yet again, and I pull it out, expecting to see 'Unknown Number'. I've already had about six journalists leaving messages on the phone today; God knows where they got my number from—

But it's not a journalist, it's Mum.

'It's Mum!' I exclaim as Luke walks away to take another

call. 'At last! Hi, Mum. I've been trying to get in touch with you all night! Where are you?'

'I'm in the car! I told you about our mini-break with Janice and Martin, didn't I? The Lake District. No signal. But lovely views, although the hotel *was* a little chilly. We had to ask for extra blankets, but they couldn't have been more charming about it—'

'Right.' I try to get a word in. 'Er, Mum, something's happened—'

'I know!' says Mum triumphantly. 'We'd just got on to the M1 when I had a call from someone at the *Daily World*. She said, "Do you know your daughter has been causing a sensation in Hollywood?" Well! I said I had no idea, but it didn't surprise me. I always knew you'd be a sensation. Janice has just found a picture of you on her smartphone. We've all had a look. Lovely frock. Where did you get that, love?'

'Mum, you didn't talk to them, did you? Only Luke says not to speak to the press. Just ring off.'

'I wasn't going to ring off!' says Mum indignantly. 'I wanted to hear all about it, for a start. Such a pleasant girl. She gave me every detail.'

'How long did you talk for?'

'Ooh, I'd say . . . How long was I on the phone, Janice? About forty minutes?'

'Forty *minutes*?' I echo, aghast.

There's Luke saying 'Don't speak to the press' and even Aran advising me 'Don't say anything', and now Mum has given an in-depth interview to *the Daily World*.

'Well, don't say any more!' I instruct her. 'Not till you speak to Luke, anyway.'

'She wanted to know if you'd ever shoplifted yourself,' says Mum. 'The idea! I said absolutely never, unless you count the time you came home from Hamleys with six pairs of dollies' shoes in your pockets. But you were only three, bless you. We sent them back in an envelope, remember?'

'You *didn't* tell her that!' I wail. God knows what they'll write now. 'Mum, can I speak to Dad? Is he driving?'

'No, Martin's doing this stretch. I'll put you on.'

There's a scuffling noise, then I hear my father's voice, deep and reassuring.

'How's my little Becky? Plunged into another kerfuffle, I see! Are the media stationed outside your house as we speak?'

'Pretty much.'

'Ah. Well, you know the only thing worse than being talked about, don't you?'

'*Not* being talked about,' I answer, with a smile. Dad always has some little saying for each occasion.

'If you need us to fly over and give you our support, I'm sure your mother will be only too happy to buy a new outfit for the occasion.'

'Dad!' I can't help laughing.

'Seriously, Becky.' His voice changes. 'Are you all right? And Minnie?'

'We're fine.'

'Because we will come, if you need us. The next flight we can.'

'I know,' I say, touched. 'Don't worry, Dad. But can you stop Mum talking to the press?'

'I'll do my best,' he says. 'Now, apart from foiling shoplifters and becoming a global media sensation, is life all right in Hollywood? Sun not too warm? Sky not too blue?'

'It's all fine.' I laugh again.

'I don't suppose you've had a chance to look up that old friend of mine?'

Damn. *Damn.* I totally meant to do that. This is the second time he's had to remind me. I feel terrible.

'Dad, I'm really sorry,' I say. 'It just slipped my mind. But I will, I promise . . .'

'Darling, please don't worry! You're very busy. I know that.'

He's so understanding, I feel worse than ever.

'I'll do it,' I say. 'I absolutely promise.'

As I put the phone down, I'm thinking hard. I can see another news van pulling up outside the gates and Aran's words are running through my brain: *Don't leave it too long. The heat won't last for ever.*

'Your parents OK?' says Luke, coming back into the hall.

'Yes, fine. Except my mother gave an interview to the *Daily World*. It's OK,' I add quickly at his appalled expression. 'I've told her not to say any more.'

'Right, well.' He sighs. 'Can't be helped. Now, I've drafted a statement which I think we should release in an hour or two. I'll send it over to Aran's legal team, check for any holes. If you don't want to watch a movie why don't you go and have a nice bath?' he adds. 'Take your mind off things.'

'Actually, I have to go out,' I say, trying to sound casual.

'Out?' Luke stares at me as though I'm insane. 'What do you mean, *out*?'

'I have to do something for my father. I have to look up his old friend Brent Lewis. Remember, he asked me to?'

'Well, yes, I do, but . . . *now*?'

'Why not now?' I say, a little defiantly.

'Because, look at that rabble!' expostulates Luke, gesturing at the window. 'If you set foot outside the gates, they'll descend on you!'

'Well, maybe I don't care! Maybe it's more important to me to do this favour for my father. Why should the press stop me leading my normal life?' I'm getting quite stirred up here. 'Why should I be trapped in my own home? What am I, a prisoner?'

'Hardly a prisoner,' says Luke impatiently. 'I simply think that, just for today—'

'I made my father a promise, Luke!' I say, in an impassioned voice. 'I'm going to see that promise through, whatever it takes. And no one's going to stop me, not the press, not you, not no one!'

'Fine,' says Luke at last. 'Whatever. If you really insist on doing this, then just get straight in the car and drive out. Don't talk to the press.'

'I won't,' I say.

'Even if they try to get a rise out of you, ignore them.' He shakes his head. 'Becky, I still think you should stay inside.'

'Luke,' I say, my voice quivering a little. 'You don't understand. I have to do this. For my father. For myself. And for all of us.'

Before he can ask what I mean by that (I have no idea), I head up the stairs, feeling all noble, like a prince about to go into battle. Which, actually, this kind of is. And the point is: I have to win. This is my chance. My big, Hollywood, one-in-a-million, photo-opportunity chance.

Oh my God. What am I going to *wear*?

OK. It took me an hour and three mirrors and about two hundred pictures on my phone, but I've finally worked out the perfect, casual-but-cool outfit for facing the press. My most flattering white Stella McCartney cropped trousers with the little zips. Killer heels by D&G, and a bright-pink shell top from J Crew which will really stand out. And the *pièce de résistance*: these stunning oversized sunglasses which I found in the same shop I bought the diamanté clutch bag. They're vintage Missoni and the frames are pink and green swirls. You can't miss them. They'll definitely be a talking point.

What I must do is make sure I stand in a flattering way as I'm opening the car door. Yes. And say things like, 'Please leave me alone, no press, please, I'm just going about my day.'

I take out my Velcro rollers, give my lips a final touch-up, and examine my reflection. OK. Good. I must get outside quickly, before the press get bored and decide to leave. Luke has already gone out with Aran, to see Sage, and I heard the journalists all shouting as they drove away. And now it's my turn! I feel like a gladiator about to go into the ring.

I tracked down an address for Brent Lewis after about six phone calls. Of course, his family doesn't live at the address Dad gave me. But someone there had a number for his mother, and someone at that number said she'd moved to Pasadena, and there they said she'd gone to Florida, and so it went on, till I discovered that she actually died seven years ago. But by then I'd also been given a number for a sister called Leah, and through her I finally got an address for Brent – somewhere called the Shining Hill Home Estate, off the San Fernando Road. I've looked on the map and it's in an area of LA I've never been to before. But that's fine. I've got sat nav.

Minnie is playing some very disorganized ball game with the Cleath-Stuarts in the basement. I put my head round the door and say casually, 'I'm just running an errand. See you later.'

'Mine sunglasses,' says Minnie at once, clocking the vintage Missonis. 'Miiiiiiine.'

'Minnie!' I say sternly. 'We don't say "Mine"!'

'Please,' she amends at once. 'Pleeeeeeease!'

'No, darling.' I give her a kiss. 'They're Mummy's.'

'*Pleeeeease!*' She makes a determined swipe for them.

'You have . . . er . . .' I cast around and find a toy handbag, which I hand to her. 'This.'

Minnie looks at it disdainfully. 'So over,' she enunciates carefully and throws it on the floor.

Oh my God. Did Minnie just say 'So over'? I meet Suze's eyes and we both give shocked giggles.

'I didn't teach her that,' I say.

'Nor did I!' says Suze.

I glance at Clemmie – but she's happily playing in a vest with one of Minnie's skirts on her head. The Cleath-Stuart children wouldn't have the first idea what 'So over' meant.

'It was Ora,' I say with sudden conviction. 'She's a bad influence on Minnie. I knew it!'

'You don't know it!' objects Suze. 'It could have been anyone.'

'I bet it was her. Minnie, this bag is *not* over.' I pick the bag up and hand it back to Minnie. 'It's a timeless classic. And we don't throw our bags on the floor, even if they *are* over.'

'Where are you going?' Suze is looking me up and down. 'Nice shoes.'

'Just looking up this guy for my dad.'

'You know the place is still crawling with journalists?'

'Yes.' I try to sound nonchalant. 'Never mind. I'll just have to . . . er . . . ignore them.'

Suze gives me a sharp look. 'Bex, have you curled your hair?'

'No!' I say defensively. 'I mean . . . a bit. Just to put some body in. Is there anything wrong with that?'

Her eyes focus on my face. 'Are you wearing *false eyelashes*?'

'Just a couple,' I say, flustered. 'What is this, the third degree? Anyway, I have to go and run this errand. See you!'

I turn and rush up the stairs. At the front door I take three deep breaths, then push it open. Here we go. Celebrityville, here I come.

At once a barrage of voices hits me.

'Becky! Beckeee! This way!'

'Becky, have you been in touch with Lois?'

'Have you spoken to the police?'

'Becky! This way!'

Oh my God. There are twice as many journalists as there were before. The gates are about twenty metres away from the front door – tall, with iron bars and swirls – and there are camera lenses pointing at me through every gap. Just for an instant I want to duck back inside the house – but it's too late now. I'm out.

The thing about having lots of photographers pointing their cameras at you, is they might take a picture *at any time*. I have to do everything in a flattering way. Sucking in my stomach and throwing my shoulders back, I make my way slowly towards the car, trying to ignore all the shouts.

'Becky, can we have an interview?' one man keeps yelling.

'I'm just going about my daily life,' I call, tossing my hair back. 'Thank you.'

My car keys are in my pocket and I manage to get them out in a seamless move. I open the car door – making sure that my legs are crossed over in a Victoria Beckham-type pose – then get in. I close the door, and exhale. There. Done.

Except . . . What if none of them got a good shot?

Should I have gone closer to the gates? Should I have walked more slowly?

This is my *one chance* to be photographed by the world's press in an iconic, defining picture that will be a talking point and launch my career as a Hollywood stylist. I think I need to get out of the car and do it again.

I ponder hard for a few seconds, then open the door and get out, as elegantly as I can. Trying to look as though I'm ignoring the photographers, I stroll right to the front of the drive and start to examine a hedge intently.

'Becky! Beckee! This way!'

'No press,' I say, smoothing down my hair. 'No press, thank you. I'm just going about my daily business.'

Casually, I take off my sunglasses and do my best sucked-in-cheeks, pouty expression. I swivel this way and that a few times, swinging my arms. Maybe I should open the gates, so they get a better view of my shoes. I zap the gates, and they slowly start to swing open.

'Becky!' A woman is waving a microphone in my direction. 'Sharon Townsend, NBC. Tell us about seeing Lois shoplifting!'

'Please respect my privacy,' I say. 'I'm just going about my daily business.'

A brilliant new idea hits me and I head over to the car. I heave myself up on to the bonnet, adopt a casual pose and get out my phone – I can be having a phone call in my own drive, while sitting on my car! What could be more natural than that?

'Hi,' I say into the phone. 'Yes. Absolutely.' I cross my legs at a more flattering angle and gesticulate animatedly with my sunglasses. 'I know. Awful.'

The sound of cameras snapping is getting more and more frantic. I can't help beaming with exhilaration. It's really happening! I'm famous!

'Becky, who are your shoes by?' someone yells.

'Please don't intrude on my life,' I reply graciously. 'I'm just going about my daily business.' I lift up my feet so everyone can see the cool silver heels, and turn them from side to side.

'They're by Yves Saint Laurent,' I hear a woman say.

'No they're not!' I forget my plan to say nothing, and hurry towards the open gates. 'They're Dolce and Gabbana. My top is J Crew and my trousers are Stella McCartney. And my sunglasses are vintage Missoni.' Should I add 'I'm available for styling at reasonable prices, please enquire within, no job too small'?

No. Too much.

'What's your message to Lois?' A cluster of microphones arrives right in front of my nose.

'Who did the clutch bag really belong to, Becky?'

'Were there drugs in the bag? Is Lois an addict?'

OK, this is getting out of hand.

'Thank you so much,' I say, a little shrilly. 'I'm just going about my daily business. I have an important errand to run. Thank you for respecting my privacy.' Suddenly I remember about posture. I adjust my legs so they'll look thinner, and put one hand on my hip like a supermodel.

'What about your phone call?' says a sardonic-looking guy in jeans.

Oh yes. The phone call. I'd forgotten about that.

'Er . . . bye, then!' I say into the phone, and hastily put it away. 'Thank you,' I add to the journalists. 'Thank you so much. No press, please.' Feeling a little hassled, I head towards the car, get out my keys and immediately drop them on the ground. Damn.

No *way* am I stooping down in front of a bank of cameras, so I cautiously bend my knees as though in a curtsey, keep my back dead straight and manage to hoik the keys up. I sink into the car, start the engine and carefully drive forward. The mob of journalists parts to let the car out, but the flashes and shouts keep coming, and someone even bangs on the roof.

As I finally escape, I sink back and exhale. That was only five minutes – and I'm exhausted. How do celebrities *do* it?

Anyway. The point is, I did it. Ten minutes later, my heart has stopped thumping and I'm feeling rather pleased with myself.

I'm driving along the Hollywood Freeway, saying aloud, 'Drive on the *right*. Drive on the *right*,' and my sat nav is telling me to keep going straight on. Which is handy as I'm not in the correct lane to turn off anyway. The whizzy no-hands car phone suddenly buzzes with Luke's number, and I press green for Answer.

'Sweetheart. Hi. Did you get out OK?'

'Yes, all good,' I say. 'I'm on the road.'

'The press weren't too aggressive?'

'Er . . . no! They were fine.'

'And you just got straight in the car and drove away?'

'Pretty much.' I clear my throat. 'I mean, they might have got a *few* shots of me . . .'

'I'm sure you did brilliantly, darling. It's not easy, keeping your cool when you're surrounded by cameras.'

'How's Sage?'

'Manic,' says Luke. 'She's had lots of offers already, and she wants to say yes to all of them.'

'Offers of what?'

'You name it. Interviews, film roles, nude magazine spreads, endorsement campaigns. All what you might call low-rent. Very much *not* what our strategy was all about. Not that she can see that.'

He sounds so exasperated, I want to giggle. I should imagine Sage Seymour is a bit of a change, after he's been used to dealing with sensible businessmen in suits.

'Well, good luck!'

'You too. See you later.'

I ring off, and then dial Dad's number.

'Becky?'

'Hi, Dad! Listen, I'm going to see your friend Brent. I'm in the car right now.'

'Darling!' Dad sounds surprised. 'That was quick. I didn't mean for you to drop everything.'

'It's no trouble,' I say. 'He's based somewhere called the Shining Hill Home Estate, does that sound right?'

'Sounds rather grand!' says Dad. 'That'll be right. I'm sure

243

he's done very well for himself. He probably lives in a mansion.'

'Really?' I say, my interest piqued a little. 'What does he do?'

'I'm not sure. Back then, he was a postgraduate student.'

'So how do you know he lives in a mansion?' I object.

'Oh, I'm certain he's done all right for himself.' Dad chuckles. 'Let's say, he was on the right path already— Oh, Becky!' Dad interrupts himself. 'Mum says, there's a new picture of you on her phone on the internet! Standing outside your house. Is that you this morning, darling?'

'Yes!' I say in excitement. 'Have they uploaded them already? What does it say?'

'*Witness Becky is pretty in pink*,' reads Dad carefully. '*Brit set to testify in court*. That's on the *National Enquirer* website.'

National Enquirer! Pretty in pink! I feel a jolt of excitement. Although what's this about testifying in court? I never said anything about that.

'Do I *look* all right?' I demand. That's the main point.

'You look wonderful! Ah now, Mum's found another one: *Becky steps out in YSL shoes.*'

For God's sake. I *told* them my shoes weren't Yves Saint Laurent.

'Darling, you're quite the celebrity!' says Dad. 'Don't forget us, will you?'

'I won't!' I laugh, then jump as I see *Luke* flash up on the screen.

'I'd better go, Dad. Talk to you later.' I punch Answer. 'Hi, Luke.'

'Becky, my darling,' he says, in that deadpan, patient tone he uses when he's actually quite pissed off. 'I thought you said you walked straight to the car and got in?'

'Er . . . yes. Kind of.'

'So why am I looking at a picture of you on the *Daily World* website, sitting on the car bonnet, brandishing your sunglasses and beaming at the camera?'

'I was making a phone call,' I say defensively. 'I just happened to sit on the car. They must have snapped me.'

'You happened to sit on the car?' says Luke disbelievingly. 'How does one *happen* to sit on a car?'

'I was going about my daily life,' I insist. 'It's not my fault if I'm being stalked and harassed by the press.'

'Becky.' Luke exhales. 'What kind of game are you trying to play here? Because it's a dangerous one. Once you invite these people into your life, it's very difficult to shut them out again.

I don't want to shut them out, I think mutinously. *I want to grab my chance while I'm hot.*

But Luke wouldn't understand, because he's totally warped by his job. I've heard his personal views before, when he's had a couple of glasses of wine. He thinks fame is overrated and privacy is the greatest luxury of the modern world and the tsunami of social media is going to lead to the permanent disintegration of human interaction. (Or something. I sometimes stop listening, to be honest.)

'I'm not playing any game,' I say, trying to sound righteously indignant. 'I'm just dealing with a situation, the best way I know how. And what you could do, Luke, is support me.'

'I *am* supporting you! I'm advising you! I told you to stay indoors! Now you're all over the papers—'

'It's for my career!' I say defensively.

There's silence down the phone and suddenly I realize my sat nav is talking to me.

'Right turn *not* taken,' she's saying sternly. 'Make a U-turn as soon as possible.'

Damn. I missed my exit. It's all Luke's fault.

'Look, I have to go,' I say. 'I need to concentrate on the road. We'll talk about it later.'

I ring off, feeling all cross and prickly. Any other husband would be *proud* of his wife. I want to talk to Aran. He'll understand.

'Make a U-turn as soon as possible,' the sat nav persists.

'All right! Shut up!'

I really have to focus on the road. I have no idea where I am, except that I'm going in the wrong direction. Truthfully, I'm still a bit hazy about most of LA. I mean, how on earth are you supposed to get to know the whole city? LA is so *big*. It's about the size of France.

OK, maybe not France. Maybe Belgium.

Anyway, I need to step on it. Finally I reach a point where I can U-turn. I swing the car round, ignoring the hoots from some other totally unreasonable drivers who shouldn't have been driving so fast, and set off, this time in the right direction. Shining Hill Home Estate, here we come!

As I get near my destination, I'm looking out for some beautiful shining hill, but I can't see one. All I can see is a great big road with motels either side and lorries thundering past, and billboards. This isn't at all what I was expecting.

After a while, my sat nav takes me off the main road and up an even less inspiring side road, and I peer around warily. There aren't any mansions. There aren't any expensive cars. There's a crummy-looking gas station and a motel offering rooms for $39. Is this really where Dad's friend lives?

'Destination two hundred yards ahead on the right-hand side,' my sat nav is saying. 'Destination one hundred yards ahead . . . You have arrived at your destination.'

I pull up at the side of the road and stare out of the window, my jaw slack with disbelief. The sat nav is right: I've arrived at the Shining Hill Home Estate. But it's not a mansion. It's a trailer park. There's a faded sign chained to a galvanized pair of gates and beyond it I can see rows of mobile homes stretching into the distance. I check my piece of paper again: 431 Shining Hill Home Estate. Brent Lewis must live in trailer no. 431.

Part of me wants to phone Dad instantly and tell him how wrong he's got it about his friend, but I decide to investigate first, so I lock the car and proceed cautiously into the trailer park. No one stops me, and I soon work out where number 431 is from a map on a board. As I make my way down a line of trailers, I get stares from some people sitting outside their mobile homes, and I can't help glancing around curiously myself. Some of the trailers are really nice-looking and

246

well kept, with plants and pretty curtains, but some are awful. One has broken patio furniture piled high outside it, almost blocking the door. Another has the sound of screaming coming from it. Another has all its windows broken in.

I arrive at no. 431 and approach it. It's a very plain trailer – not run-down but not very appealing, either. The door is shut and the blinds are down and there are no signs of life. There's a piece of paper taped to the door and I glance at it as I knock. It says: *Notice of Eviction.*

I scan the notice, which is all about Mr Brent Lewis of 431 Shining Hill Home Estate and his failure to pay six months' overdue rent, and the steps which must therefore be taken, signed *Herb Leggett, Manager*.

'You a friend of Brent?' A voice hails me and I turn to see a skinny woman standing on the steps of the trailer opposite. She's wearing black jeans with her hair thrust into a ponytail and holding a small boy on her hip.

'Is Brent around?' I say. 'I'm not a friend exactly, but I'd like to see him.'

'You a social worker?' Her eyes narrow. 'Police?'

'No!' I say, shocked. 'Nothing like that. I'm just . . . my dad knew him years ago.'

'You British?'

'Yes. My dad is too.'

The woman sniffs and nods. 'Well, you just missed him. He took off yesterday.'

He *took off*? Oh God. What's Dad going to say?

'Do you have a forwarding address?' I ask.

She shrugs. 'Said his daughter was stopping by next week, clear things out. I can ask her.'

'Could you?' I say, eagerly. 'I'm Becky Brandon, this is my number . . .' I get out one of my business cards and hand it to her. 'If she could ring me, that would be great, or maybe you could ring me. Or . . .'

The woman shrugs again, and tucks the card into her jeans. Immediately the small boy pulls it out and throws it on the ground.

247

'No!' I leap forward. 'I mean . . . let's not lose that. Shall I put it somewhere safe for you?'

The woman shrugs yet again. I really don't have high hopes that she's going to talk to Brent's daughter. All the same, I tuck the card safely into the window frame of her door.

'So, I'll look forward to hearing from Brent's daughter,' I say as brightly as I can. 'Or you. Whichever. I'd be really grateful. Anyway . . . er . . . lovely to meet you. I'm Becky, by the way.'

'You said.' She nods, but doesn't volunteer her own name.

I can't keep babbling on at this woman, so I give her one last friendly smile and turn on my heel to leave. I still can't believe this is where Dad's friend has ended up. It's such a shame.

As soon as I'm on the road again, I dial Dad's number.

'Dad!'

'Darling! Did you see him?'

'Not exactly.' I wince. 'Dad, I'm afraid you were wrong. Brent Lewis has been living in a trailer park, and now he's just been evicted because he didn't pay his rent. I couldn't get an address.'

'No. No!' Dad gives a short laugh. 'Darling, that's not right. It can't be the same Brent Lewis. I'm sorry you wasted your time, but—'

'Well, it was the address I got from his sister. It must be him.'

There's a longish silence.

'He lives in a trailer park?' says Dad at last.

'Yes. I mean, his trailer's quite nice,' I say hastily. 'Not broken or anything. But now he's been evicted.'

'This can't be right.' Dad sounds almost angry. 'You must have got it wrong, Becky.'

'I haven't got it wrong!' I say, nettled. What does he think I am, an idiot? 'I saw the eviction notice myself. Brent C. Lewis. It didn't say what the C was for.'

'Constantine. He had a Greek mother.'

'Well, there you are.'

'But . . .' He exhales. 'This is impossible.'

'Look, Dad,' I say kindly. 'It's been a long time. Who knows what happened in Brent Lewis's life? He could have gone into business, he could have had six divorces, he could have turned into a criminal—'

'Becky, you don't understand,' he says hotly. 'It shouldn't have happened. This shouldn't have happened.'

'You're right, I don't understand!' I exclaim. 'If he was such a close friend of yours, why didn't you stay in touch?'

There's silence, and I sense I've touched a nerve. I feel a bit mean, confronting Dad like that, but honestly, he drives me mad. First he won't use Skype or Facebook or anything normal. Then he sends me off on a wild goose chase to see his friend, and *then*, when I report back, he doesn't believe me.

'I'll text you his sister's number, if you like,' I say. 'But honestly, I'd just forget about it if I were you.'

My screen starts flashing with the word *Aran* and I realize I've got a call waiting.

'Dad, I have to go,' I say. 'We'll talk later, OK? I'm sure Brent Lewis is fine,' I add, trying to sound reassuring. 'I wouldn't worry about him any more.' I ring off and press Answer. 'Aran! Hi!'

'Becky.' His easy voice comes down the phone. 'How're you doing? You shaken off the paparazzi yet?'

'Just about!' I laugh.

'So, that was quite the photocall you had this morning. Cute outfit. Great sunglasses. You made a splash. Good work.'

'Thanks!' I beam. I *knew* Aran would appreciate my efforts.

'As a result, the phone has been ringing off the hook.'

'Really?' I feel a tweak of excitement. 'What, like, journalists? Fashion editors?'

'Journalists, producers, all kinds of people. Like I said, you're hot. And I have a great offer for you. I took the liberty of dealing with it myself, although if you like, I can hand over everything to Luke—'

'No.' I answer a bit too quickly. 'I mean . . . he's my husband. He's a bit too close, don't you think?'

'I agree. So, the offer is, a segment on *Breakfast Show USA*. The producer just called, and she's very anxious to have you on the show. I told her you're a stylist and she said great.

They're very happy for you to film a styling segment. New trends, new looks, whatever. We'll work out the details.'

'Oh my God.' I feel breathless. A styling segment on *Breakfast Show USA*. This is huge. This is mammoth!

'Now, you're going to need an agent,' Aran is saying. 'I'm going to set up a meeting with our friends at CAA. My assistant will call you with the details, OK?'

CAA! Even I know that CAA is the biggest name in Hollywood. They represent Tom Hanks. They represent Sting! I feel giddy. Never in a million years did I expect to be catapulted into all of this.

A sudden thought strikes me. 'Does Luke know everything?'

'Sure, of course.'

'What did he say?'

'He said it's your decision.'

'Right.'

I feel a bit hurt. It's my decision. What kind of lame response is that? Why didn't he say, 'My God, this is amazing, I always knew my wife would be a star'? Why isn't he on the phone telling me my whole life is going to change here and he'll be with me every step of the way?

'So, what's your decision?' prompts Aran.

Does he even need to ask?

'It's yes, of course!' I say joyfully. 'It's yes! It's a great big yes!'

FIFTEEN

I've never been anywhere like CAA in my life. The building is like some sort of spaceship in which all the men are from *Men in Black* and all the girls are from *Vogue* and all the sofas are from *Architectural Digest*. Just sitting in the lobby for five minutes was a better Hollywood experience than the entire Sedgewood Studios tour. I saw three girls from *Gossip Girl*, and a cool rapper guy feeding his tiny puppy with a milk dropper, and two famous TV comedians having a huge, *sotto voce* row about something called 'back end', while continuing to smile at a very pretty girl on reception. (I'm not sure of their names. I think maybe they're both called Steve Something.)

And now I'm sitting in this very smart boardroom-type place, at a smooth, pale wooden table, and listening to two women talk to me. One's called Jodie and the other's called Marsha and they're both 'talent' agents. Apparently I'm the 'talent'. Me! 'Talent'! Wait till I tell Luke that.

They're very smart and very intense. They're both dressed immaculately in a sleek-navy-Prada-ish-high-maintenance sort of style. One has got a vast diamond on one finger and I'm so mesmerized by it, I can barely concentrate on what she's saying. Except I keep being jerked back to attention by words like 'fanbase' and 'global appeal'.

'Reality,' says the dark-haired woman, who is either Jodie or Marsha. 'What's your opinion on that?'

'Er . . .'

I want to reply, 'I've totally lost my grip on it,' but I sense that's not the right answer. I sip my iced water, which is so freezing it gives me an instant headache. Why do Americans like their drinks so cold? Are they descended from Eskimos or something? Ooh, maybe they are. Maybe they migrated down from Alaska, millions of years ago. It makes total sense. Have I hit on a whole new theory of human evolution?

'Becky?'

'Yes!' I come back to the room. 'Definitely! Um, what exactly do you mean by "reality"?'

'A reality show,' says Jodie-or-Marsha, patiently. 'We think we could package a great show as a vehicle for you, your family, your quirky British friends . . .'

'You mean, cameras would be following us around the whole time?'

'It would be semi-scripted. It's less intrusive than you might think.'

'Right.'

I try to imagine sitting in the kitchen with Luke, acting out a semi-scripted scene for the cameras. Hmm.

'I'm not *totally* sure my husband would like that,' I say at last. 'But I can ask him.'

'Another format we have available is "BFFs in Hollywood",' says Marsha-or-Jodie. 'You would be working with a young actress named Willa Tilton. The concept is, two best friends making it in Hollywood, confiding in each other, shopping for clothes, appearing on the red carpet, getting into scrapes. You would be the married one and Willa would be the single one. I think it would have a lot of appeal.'

'I think they'd work well together as best friends,' Jodie-or-Marsha agrees.

'But Willa Tilton isn't my best friend,' I say, confused. 'I've never met her. My best friend is called Suze.'

'She would be your best friend *for the camera*,' says

Marsha-or-Jodie, as though I'm slightly subnormal. 'It's a *reality* show.'

'OK,' I say, still confused. 'Well, I'll think about it.'

I take another sip of water, trying to get my head together. Somehow I can't take any of this seriously. Me? On a reality show? But as I look from Jodie to Marsha (or the other way round), I realize they're genuine. They wouldn't give me the time of day unless they meant it.

'In the meantime, we have the *Breakfast Show USA* segment,' says Jodie-or-Marsha, 'which will be very high profile. Now, do you have an assistant?'

'No,' I say, and the two women exchange looks.

'You might think about getting yourself one,' says Marsha-or-Jodie.

'Your life is going to start feeling a little different,' adds Jodie-or-Marsha.

'Make sure you have some camera-ready outfits.'

'Consider getting your teeth whitened.'

'And you could lose a pound or two.' Marsha-or-Jodie smiles kindly. 'Just a thought.'

'Right.' My head is whirling. 'OK. Well . . . thanks!'

'It's a pleasure.' Jodie-or-Marsha pushes back her chair. 'Exciting, huh?'

As I'm walking along one of the museum-style corridors with an assistant called Tori (dressed head to toe in Chloé), I hear a little shriek behind me. I turn and see Sage skittering along the corridor, her arms outstretched.

'Beckeeeeee! I've missed youuuuuu!'

I blink in astonishment. Sage is wearing the skimpiest outfit I've ever seen. Her bright-blue polka-dot top is basically a bikini top, and her tiny frayed hot pants are more like knickers.

Plus, what does she mean, she's missed me?

As she throws her arms around me, I inhale the smell of Marc Jacobs Grapefruit and cigarettes.

'It's been so long! We have so much to talk about! Are you done here? Where are you going now?'

'Just home,' I say. 'I think they're organizing me a car.'

'Noooo! Ride with me!' She takes out her phone and punches something into it. 'My driver will take you home, and we can chat.'

'Becky, are you OK with Sage?' says Tori. 'You don't need a car?'

'I guess not,' I say. 'But thanks.'

'We're good now,' says Sage to the girl who was accompanying her. 'We'll see ourselves out. We have to talk!' Sage hits the button for the lift and links arms with me. 'You are *so* hot right now. We're both hot,' she adds with satisfaction, as we get in. 'You know they're begging me to do Florence Nightingale? Your husband thinks I should take it. But you know, I have a lot of propositions right now. *Playboy* offered me a *gazillion*.' She takes out some gum and offers it to me.

'*Playboy?*'

'I know, right?' She shrieks with laughter. 'I need to hit the gym if I'm doing that.'

I blink in surprise. She's doing it? I can't believe Luke or Aran want Sage to do *Playboy*.

'Cute shades,' she adds, looking at my Missonis, which are propped up on my head. 'You were wearing them on Saturday, right? The press was all over them.'

She's right. There were pictures of me in my Missonis in all the tabloids, and on millions of websites. It's all so surreal. When I look at the photos, it doesn't feel like me. It feels like some other person out there, posing as 'Becky Brandon'.

But that *is* me. Isn't it?

Oh God, it's too confusing. Do celebrities ever get used to being two people, one private and one public? Or do they just forget about the private one? I'd ask Sage, only I'm not sure she's ever had a private life.

'They're so unique.' Sage is still fixated on my shades. 'Where did you get them?'

'They're vintage. You can have them, if you like,' I add eagerly, and hand them over.

'Cool!' Sage grabs them and puts them on, admiring her reflection in the mirrored wall of the lift. 'How do I look?'

'Really good.' I tweak her hair a bit. 'There. Lovely.'

At last! I'm styling a Hollywood film star, just like I wanted to in the first place.

'You're smart, Becky,' Sage says. 'This is a *great* fashion story. I'm wearing the shades you had on two days ago. The press will love it. This will be everywhere.'

That's not why I gave them to her, but I suppose she's right. I suppose she thinks about everything in terms of the press. Is that how I have to start thinking, too?

We emerge on the ground floor, and Sage leads me straight to a big guy in a blue blazer, who is sitting on a chair in a corner. He has Slavic features and huge shoulders and doesn't smile. 'This is Yuri, my new bodyguard,' says Sage blithely. 'Do you have security, Becky?'

'*Me?*' I laugh. 'No!'

'You should totally think about it,' she says. 'I had to hire Yuri after I got mobbed at home. You can't be too careful.' She glances at her watch. 'OK, shall we go?'

As we head out of the building, I feel a jolt of shock. A cluster of waiting photographers immediately start calling out, 'Sage! This way, Sage!' They weren't there earlier.

'How did they know you'd be here?' I say in bewilderment.

'You give them your schedule,' Sage explains in an under-tone. 'You'll get into it.' She hooks her arm more firmly around mine, and dimples in a smile. Her long, golden legs look amazing, and the Missoni shades clash brilliantly with her polka-dot top.

'Becky!' I hear a shout. 'Becky, over here, please!' Oh my God, I've been recognized! 'Beckeee!'

The shouts are growing into a chorus. All I can hear is, 'Becky! Sage! Here!' Sage is playfully adopting pose after pose, most with her arm around me. A couple of tourists approach, and with a charming smile, Sage scribbles autographs for them. It takes me a moment to realize they want mine, too.

After a while, a blacked-out SUV appears, and Sage skips along to it, accompanied by Yuri. We get in, the photographers still clustering around us, and the driver manoeuvres away.

'Oh my God.' I sink back into the leather seat.

'You should hire security,' says Sage again. 'You're not a civilian any more.'

This is unreal. I'm not a civilian any more! I'm one of them!

Sage is flipping through channels on the in-car TV, and she pauses as her own face comes into view, with the headline, *Sage speaks out.*

'Hey! Check it out!' She cracks open a Diet Coke, offers one to me and turns up the volume.

'I feel personally betrayed by Lois,' the on-screen Sage is saying. 'I feel she's let me down, not just as a fellow actor but as a woman and as a human being. If she has problems, then I feel for her, but she should deal with those in an appropriate manner, not inflict them on others. You know, we were once friends. But never again. She's let down the entire profession.'

'That's a bit harsh,' I say uncomfortably.

'She stole my purse,' says Sage, unmoved. 'She's a psycho.'

'She didn't steal it. It was a *mistake.*'

'Tough talk there from Sage Seymour,' a TV presenter is saying on-screen. 'With us in the studio to discuss the scandal is Hollywood commentator Ross Halcomb, film critic Joanne Seldana, and . . .'

'Sage,' I try again. 'You do know it was a mistake, don't you?'

'Sssh!' says Sage, waving a hand impatiently. We sit in silence as a whole bunch of people in a studio discuss whether Sage Seymour's career will now go stellar, and then as soon as they've finished, Sage flicks to another news piece about herself. I feel more and more uncomfortable, but Sage won't let me speak. The TV airways seem to be filled with coverage of her, on every channel – until she clicks on to a new channel and Lois's face suddenly appears.

'Lois!' Sage leans forward animatedly.

The camera pans away and I see that Lois is being filmed outside her house, which is a huge, Spanish-style mansion. She's wearing a billowy white nightshirt and has bare feet, and seems to be shouting at someone, but there's no sound.

'What is she *doing*?' Sage is gazing at the screen.

'Why isn't she inside?' I wince. 'She doesn't look well.'

Lois looks terrible. I mean, *terrible*. Her skin is pale, her eyes are hollow, her hair is lank and she's twisting it between her fingers.

I wonder if she's heard from the police. No one knows if they're going to press charges; no one knows anything yet. I keep expecting to be summoned to a police station, but so far, nothing. When I mentioned it to Aran, he said, 'Becky, don't worry. Your profile is up there, even without a court case.'

But that's not what I meant. I was thinking about Lois.

'Leave me alone.' Her voice suddenly becomes audible. 'Please leave me alone.'

And now we can hear the shouts from the photographers and journalists outside the gate.

'Are you a thief, Lois?'

'Did you take Sage's bag?'

'Have you been charged?'

'Do you have a message for the American people?'

Lois's eyes are dark and despairing and she's biting her lip so hard I can see specks of blood appearing. She looks totally on the edge – just like she did when I first caught hold of her in the street. She goes back inside, the front door slams and the picture flashes back to a studio, where a woman in a tailored red jacket is watching a screen seriously.

'And there we can see the first shots of Lois Kellerton since this scandal,' she says. 'Dr Nora Vitale, you're an expert on mental health. Would you say Lois Kellerton is experiencing a breakdown?'

'Well, now.' Dr Nora Vitale is a thin woman in a surprisingly frivolous pink dress, with a serious expression. 'We don't use the word "breakdown" these days . . .'

'Jeez.' Sage switches off the TV. *'That'll* be all over Hollywood in twenty seconds. You know what they're saying?'

'What?'

'They're saying this goes back years. She's been stealing all her life.'

'What?' I say in horror. 'No! I'm sure it was just a one-off. She was under great strain, she made a mistake . . . anyone can make a mistake!'

'Well.' Sage shrugs comfortably. 'Whatever you think, people are coming forward. People she's worked with. Make-up artists, assistants, saying she stole from them, too. She's going to drown in lawsuits.'

'Oh God.'

Guilt is squeezing me inside. I'm going hot and cold with remorse. This is all my fault.

'So, when am I going to *see* you again?' To my surprise, Sage throws her arms around me when we stop outside my house. 'I want you to style me for my next appearance. Head to foot.'

'Wow,' I say, taken aback. 'I'd love to!'

'And we have to have lunch. Spago, maybe. Sound good?'

'Yes! Fab.'

'We're in this together, Becky.' She squeezes me again, as the back doors magically slide open.

There's a cluster of photographers outside my gates. I'm almost getting used to them. I check my reflection in my compact, then carefully slide out of the SUV. I zap open the gates with my remote control, and wave goodbye to Sage. The next minute, Minnie is running down the drive towards me. She's wearing her gorgeous little yellow dress and clutching a painting she must have just done. I've kept her off pre-school today, because she was complaining of earache this morning. (Although it could just have been that her Alice band was too tight.)

'Mummy!' She's brandishing the painting triumphantly at me as I sweep her into a hug. 'Schlowers!'

Minnie is obsessed with flowers at the moment, which she calls 'schlowers'. She weeps if Luke won't wear his one-and-only 'schlowers' tie, so he puts it on every morning and then takes it off again in the car. Her painting doesn't look very much like flowers to be honest, just big red splodges, but I gasp admiringly, and say, 'What beautiful red flowers!'

Minnie regards the red splodges stonily. 'Dat not de schlowers. *Dat* de schlowers.' She jabs her finger at a tiny blue stripe which I hadn't even noticed. 'Dat de schlowers.' Her brows are lowered and she's giving me an imperious frown. 'DAT DE SCHLOWERS!' she suddenly yells, sounding like a commandant ordering an execution.

'Right,' I say hastily. 'Silly me. Of course that's the schlowers. Lovely!'

'Is that your daughter?' To my surprise, Sage has got out of the SUV after me. 'I have to say hello. Too cute! Listen to her little British accent! Come here, sweetie.' She lifts Minnie up and swings her around till Minnie starts squealing with delight. The photographers are all clicking away so fast, it sounds like an insect infestation.

'Sage,' I say. 'We don't want Minnie to be photographed.'

But Sage doesn't hear me. She's running around the drive with Minnie, the two of them in fits of laughter.

'Pleeeeease!' Minnie is reaching out for the swirly Missoni sunglasses. 'Pleeeeease!'

'No, these are mine! But you can have some.' Sage rummages in her bag and produces another pair of sunglasses. She gives Minnie a kiss on the nose, then puts the sunglasses on her. 'Adorable!'

'Sage!' I try again. 'Stop it! I need to get Minnie inside!'

My phone suddenly bleeps with a text, and feeling hassled, I pull it out. It's from Mum.

Becky. Very urgent. Mum

What? What's very urgent? I feel a spasm of alarm, mixed with frustration. What kind of message is 'Very urgent'? I speed-dial her number and wait impatiently for the connection.

'Mum!' I say as soon as she answers. 'What is it?'

'Oh, Becky.' Her voice is wobbling. 'It's Dad. He's gone!'

'Gone?' I say stupidly. 'What do you mean, gone?'

'He's gone to LA! He left a note! A *note*! After all these years of marriage, a *note*! I've been to Bicester Village with Janice for the day – I got a lovely bag at the Cath Kidston outlet shop – and when I came back he'd gone! To America!'

I stare at the phone, flabbergasted. 'But what – I mean, where—'

'In the note, he said he needed to track down his friend. Brent Lewis? The one you looked up?'

Oh, for God's sake. Not this again.

'But why?'

'He didn't say!' Mum's voice rises hysterically. 'I have no idea who this friend is, even!'

There's a slight edge of panic to her voice, which I can understand. The thing about my Dad is, he seems like this very straight-down-the-line, normal family man. But there's a bit more to him than that. A few years ago we all discovered that he had another daughter – my half-sister Jess – about whom nobody had known a thing.

I mean, to be fair to Dad, he hadn't known either. It's not like he'd been keeping a massive secret. But I can see why Mum might be a bit paranoid.

'He said he had something he needed to "put right",' Mum is continuing. '"Put right"! What does that mean?'

'I don't know,' I say helplessly. 'Except he was very shocked when I told him Brent Lewis lives in a trailer.'

'Why shouldn't he live in a trailer?' Mum's voice is shrill again. 'What business is it of Dad's where this man lives?'

'He kept saying, "It shouldn't have happened,"' I say, remembering. 'But I have no idea what that meant.'

'I don't know what flight he's on, or where he's staying . . . Do I follow him? Do I stay here? It's Becky,' I hear her saying in a muffled voice. 'The sherry's on the second shelf, Janice.' She returns to the line. 'Becky, I don't know what to do. Janice said it's his mid-life crisis, but I said, "Janice, we already *had* that with the guitar lessons. So what's this?"'

'Mum, calm down. It'll be fine.'

'He's bound to come to you, Becky. Keep an eye on him, love. Please.'

'I will. I'll call you as soon as I hear anything.'

I ring off and instantly start texting Dad.

Dad. Where are you? Call me!!! Becky xxx

God, what a drama. What is Dad *doing*? I send the text and turn round, wondering why I can hear laughter. At once my heart plunges in horror.

Sage is posing for the cameras in an exaggerated starlet way, and Minnie is copying her perfectly. Her hand is on her hip, her head is cocked at an angle and she's tilting her shoulders back and forth, just like Sage. Everyone is roaring and the cameras are snapping.

'Stop!' I say furiously. I scoop Minnie up, and press her head against my chest, out of sight. 'Please don't use those pictures!' I say to the photographers. 'She's only a little girl.'

'Want do waving!' Minnie struggles to escape from my grasp. 'Want do WAVING!'

'No more waving, darling,' I say, kissing her head. 'I don't want you waving at those people.'

'Becky, relax!' says Sage. 'She better get used to it, right? Anyhow, she loves the limelight, don't you, cupcake?' She ruffles Minnie's hair. 'We need to get *you* an agent, munchkin. Aren't you launching your own family reality show, Becky?' she adds to me. 'That's what Aran said. Smart move.'

'I don't know,' I say, feeling harassed. 'I need to talk it over with Luke. Look, I'd better take Minnie inside.'

'Sure,' says Sage gaily. 'We'll talk soon, OK?'

As Sage disappears off in her SUV, I hurry into the house and shut the huge front door. My heart is thumping, and my thoughts are all confused. I don't know what to focus on first; my brain is skittering about so madly. Dad. Reality show. Minnie. Press. Sage. Lois. Dad.

I can't believe Dad is coming to LA. It's insane. Dad doesn't belong in LA, he belongs at home. In the garden. At his golf club.

'Bex!' Suze comes into the hall and eyes me in surprise. 'Are you OK?'

I realize I'm backed up against the front door as though I'm sheltering from attack.

'My dad's coming to LA.'

'Oh, brilliant!' Her face lights up. 'And your mum?'

'It's not brilliant. He's run off, and only left a note for Mum.'

'*What?*' She stares at me, incredulously. 'Your dad ran off?'

'There's something going on.' I shake my head. 'I don't know what. It's all to do with this trip he went on when he was much younger. He's trying to track down one of his friends from it.'

'What trip? Where did they go?'

'I dunno.' I shrug. 'Round California and Arizona. They had this map. They went to LA . . . Las Vegas . . . maybe Utah too. Death Valley!' I suddenly remember. 'I've seen pictures of them in Death Valley.'

I wish I'd listened a bit harder now. Every Christmas Dad used to tell me about his trip and pull out his old map, with the red dotted line showing where they'd been.

'Well, I expect he'll turn up,' says Suze reassuringly. 'He's probably just having a mid-life crisis.'

I shake my head. 'He's had that. He took guitar lessons.'

'Oh.' Suze thinks for a moment. 'Is there such a thing as a later-life crisis?'

'God knows. Probably.'

We head into the kitchen and I open the fridge to pour us each a glass of white wine. I don't care what time it is, I need it.

'Juice,' says Minnie at once. 'Juuuuuuice! Juuuuuuuice!'

'OK!' I say, and pour her a cup of Organic Carrot and Beetroot Juice Mix. They got her into it at the pre-school. It's the most revolting thing I've ever tasted, and it costs $10.99 for a tiny carton, but apparently it's 'detoxing and low sugar', so we've been asked to provide it instead of fruit juice. And the worst thing is, Minnie loves it. If I'm not careful, she's going to turn into some junior Juicing Nazi and I'll have to hide all my

KitKats from her and pretend that chocolate oranges are macrobiotic.

'So, where's Tarkie?' I ask as I hand Minnie her juice.

'Do you have to ask?' Suze's jaw tightens. 'You know he's started going out at six a.m. every day for a Personal Validation session with Bryce? I barely see him any more.'

'Wow. What's Personal Validation?'

'I don't know!' Suze erupts. 'How would I know? I'm only his *wife*!'

'Have some wine,' I say hurriedly, and hand her a glass. 'I'm sure it's good for Tarkie to be doing all this. I mean, it's got to be positive, hasn't it? Personal validation? It's better than *im*personal validation, anyway.'

'What *is* validation?' counters Suze.

'It's . . . er . . . being yourself. Kind of thing.' I try to sound knowledgeable. 'You have to let go. And . . . be happy.'

'It's bollocks.' Suze's eyes flash at me.

'Well . . . anyway. Cheers.' I lift my wine glass and take a swig.

Suze takes a massive gulp, then another, then exhales, seeming a bit calmer. 'So, how was the agent?' she asks, and my spirits instantly rise. At least something is going well.

'It was amazing!' I say. 'They said we need to plan my future carefully, and they'll help me juggle all my offers. And I need to hire security,' I add, importantly.

'Hire security?' Suze stares at me. 'You mean, like, a bodyguard?'

'Yes.' I try to sound casual. 'It makes sense now I'm famous.'

'You're not *that* famous.'

'Yes I am! Haven't you seen the photographers outside the gate?'

'They'll get bored soon enough. Honestly, Bex, you're only going to be famous for, like, five minutes. I wouldn't waste money on a bodyguard.'

'Five minutes?' I say, offended. 'Is that what you think? If you want to know, I've been offered a reality show. I'm going to be a global brand. This is only the beginning.'

'You're doing a reality show?' She seems gobsmacked. 'Has Luke agreed to that?'

'He . . . well, it's under discussion,' I prevaricate.

'Does Luke know about the bodyguard?'

'He doesn't need to know!' I'm feeling more and more scratchy. At CAA, everything seemed so shiny and exciting, and now Suze is putting a damper on it all. '*I'm* the celebrity, not Luke.'

'You're not a celebrity!' says Suze scoffingly.

'Yes I am!'

'Not a proper one. Not like Sage.'

'Yes I am!' I say furiously. 'They all said I was at CAA. Even Sage said so. And I need a bodyguard. In fact, I'm going to sort it out right now.' And I head out of the kitchen, full of indignation. I'll show Suze. I'm going to phone Aran's assistant and get the name of the top Hollywood security company and hire a bodyguard. I don't care what she thinks.

From: Blake@firstmovesecuritysolutions.com
To: Brandon, Rebecca
Subject: **Your security requirements**

Dear Rebecca

It was good to talk to you earlier and I attach a link to our online brochure of our products and services. I'm sure we can provide you with the range of security solutions you will need in your new, high-profile position, whether this be in the form of personnel, or home security/surveillance equipment.

As regards the DF 4000 Deluxe X-ray body scanner we were discussing, please be assured, I have never known a case of a husband 'using it to track down shopping parcels hidden about his wife's person'.

I look forward to hearing from you and fulfilling your security needs.

Best wishes

Blake Wilson
Security Facilitation Vice-President

SIXTEEN

It's fine. It's all good. We'll get used to this.

I'm sure every family finds it tricky at first, having a bodyguard.

It only took twenty-four hours to fix myself up with a security team. The company couldn't have been more helpful, and they *totally* understood that I need extra protection now I'm in the public eye. After a bit of discussion we decided that I maybe didn't need an armed twenty-four-hour squad, but I could start with what they call 'Mid-Level Protection'. My team began work this morning, and so far they've been brilliant. There's Jeff and Mitchell, who are both dressed in dark suits and shades. And there's Echo the German shepherd dog, who was trained in Russia, apparently. We've had a briefing meeting to discuss my requirements, and we've discussed my itinerary for the day. Now Mitchell is touring the house with Echo in order to check the 'ongoing security of the premises', while Jeff sits in the kitchen in order to provide 'personal integrity reinforcement'.

The only thing is, it's a bit awkward having Jeff in the kitchen at breakfast. He just sits there at the side of the room and looks unsmilingly at everyone, and mutters things into his headset. But we'll have to get used to it, now we're a celebrity family.

There's still no word from Dad, beyond a text he sent Mum late yesterday, saying:

Landed fine in LA. Have some things to take care of. Remember to water the roses. Graham xxx

Remember to water the roses. I mean, honestly. Mum nearly had a fit. I've already spoken to her today on the phone, and I've got lots of messages to pass on to Dad, should I see him. (Most would result in instant divorce, so I think I might forget about those.) I just hope he's OK. I mean, I know he's a grown man, but I can't help worrying. What 'things' is he taking care of? Why hasn't he told Mum? What's the big secret?

I pour myself some coffee, and offer the coffee pot to Tarquin, but he doesn't notice. He's munching a piece of toast and listening to his iPod, which is his new thing. He says he has to start the day with an hour of guided meditation, and it drives Suze mad.

'Tarkie!' She pokes him. 'I said, I might meet my agent this afternoon. Can you pick the children up?'

Tarkie gives her a blank look and takes another bite of toast. He looks so different these days. He's tanned, and his hair is cropped really close to his head (Suze hates that too) and he's wearing a soft grey T-shirt with a logo of the sun on it. I've seen them in the gift shop at Golden Peace. There's a special course called *Turn to the Sun*, and lots of merchandise to go with it, only I don't know what it's all about, because I never did it.

It has to be said, I'm just a *tad* less into Golden Peace than I was. I think I've grown out of it. It's a natural process: you gain everything you can from a place and then you move on. I mean, I'm totally cured of shopping now, so what's the point of going back? (Plus the gift shop is online, so if I need anything from it I can just log on.)

'Tarkie!' Suze rips an earbud out of Tarkie's ear, and he flinches in irritation.

'Suze, I need to concentrate,' he says, and pushes his chair back with a scraping sound.

'You don't! What does that thing say anyway? "Stop listening to your wife"? "Stop engaging with the real world"?'

Tarkie glares at her. 'It's a tailor-made meditation recorded by Bryce. He says my psyche is battered by the world and I need to retreat.'

'I'll batter *him*,' mutters Suze.

'Why are you so negative?' Tarkie clutches his head. 'Suze, you're toxic. Finally I'm getting my head together and you have to . . . to . . . to *sabotage* me.'

'I'm not sabotaging you!' Suze yells. 'Don't you dare call me toxic! Who brought you to LA in the first place? Who said you needed a break? Me!'

Tarkie isn't paying any attention to her, I realize. He's focusing on a far corner of the kitchen, breathing deeply.

'Tarkie?' Suze waves a hand in front of his face. 'Tar-*quin*.'

'Bryce said this would happen,' he says as though to himself. 'People outside the method are afraid of it.'

'What method?' expostulates Suze.

'You need to strip yourself bare to build yourself back up again,' says Tarquin, as though the very fact of having to explain it pains him. 'You need to strip away every level. Do you know how many levels we all have?' He rounds on Suze. 'Do you realize how much work I still have to do?'

'You've done enough work,' says Suze savagely.

'No I haven't! You're obstructing me!' He sweeps the whole kitchen with his gaze. 'You're *all* obstructing me!' He shoves his earbud back in his ear, swivels on his heel and stalks out of the room.

I'm open-mouthed in astonishment. I've never seen Tarkie so antagonistic. He was practically snarling at Suze. I mean, in some ways it's great, because for a long time I've felt he was too timid. On the other hand, Suze looks like she wants to murder him. No, correction: she now looks like she wants to murder me.

She turns on me. 'This is all your fault.'

'*My* fault?'

'You introduced him to that place! You introduced him to

Bryce! Now he's calling me "toxic"! His own wife! He won't talk to me, he won't listen, he just moons around with that wretched iPod, God knows what it's saying to him . . .'

'It's probably just saying really positive, helpful stuff,' I say defensively. 'I mean, I went to zillions of classes at Golden Peace and I'm fine.'

'You're not vulnerable like Tarkie!' snaps Suze. 'Honestly, Bex, I could kill you!'

Instantly Jeff is on his feet.

'Are we having some trouble here?' He advances on Suze, reaching for his holster thing. (It's not a gun. It's a baton.)

Suze stares at him in disbelief.

'Are you *threatening* me? Bex, is this for real?'

'Just checking we don't have any trouble, ma'am,' says Jeff implacably. 'Rebecca, are you OK?'

'Fine, thanks,' I say, embarrassed. 'It's OK, Jeff.'

As he takes his seat again, Ernie, Clementine and Wilfie come running into the kitchen. They adore the new bodyguard team. They've been following Mitchell around the garden and now they come to a halt in front of Jeff. Ernest is leading the way and Clementine is hanging back a little, her thumb in her mouth.

'Where's your dog?' says Wilfie to Jeff.

'Jeff doesn't have a dog,' I explain.

'Sarabande at school has got a bodyguard all the time,' says Ernest importantly. 'Her father's a billionaire. Her bodyguard is called Tyrell and he can do magic tricks.'

'Well,' says Suze tightly. 'Lucky Sarabande.'

'If people attack you, then your bodyguard stops them,' adds Ernie knowledgeably. 'Help! Jeff!' He clutches at his throat. 'I'm being attacked by aliens! Help!'

'Help!' chimes in Wilfie. He falls to the floor and starts writhing. 'A snake is eating me! Save me! Jeff!' He turns agonized eyes on Jeff. 'Jeff! My legs have gone!'

'Stop it, boys,' says Suze, giggling. 'Wilfie, get up.'

Jeff hasn't moved a muscle. He looks supremely unamused. Now Wilfie gets up and surveys him closely.

'Do you have special powers?' he says. 'Can you go invisible?'

'Of course he can't go invisible,' says Ernie scathingly. 'He can do kung fu. Ha-ya!' He emits a high-pitched cry and starts doing kung fu moves all over the kitchen.

'Can I sit on your knee?' says Clementine, prodding Jeff's leg. 'Can you tell me a story? Why do you have a moustache? It looks like a caterpillar.'

'Clemmie, do you want some orange juice?' I say quickly. 'Come and sit at the table.' I'm about to pour her a glass when Jeff leaps to his feet. Before I know it, he's at the door of the kitchen, barring the way and muttering urgently into his headset.

'Sir, can I ask you to verify your identity?' he's saying. 'Sir, could I ask you to remain there?'

'I'm Luke Brandon,' I hear Luke saying testily, outside the kitchen door. 'I'm the master of the house. This is my daughter, Minnie.'

'I don't have you on my list, sir. Could you please step to one side?'

'It's OK!' I call hurriedly. 'He's my husband!'

'Rebecca, he's not on the list.' Jeff gives me a reproachful look. 'We need everyone to be on the list.'

'Sorry! I thought he went without saying.'

'When it comes to personal security, no one goes without saying,' says Jeff severely. 'All right, sir, you may step forward.'

'You didn't put me on the list?' As Luke enters the kitchen, holding Minnie's hand, he's goggling with disbelief. 'You didn't put *me* on the list?'

'I meant to! I mean . . . I didn't think I needed to.'

'Becky, this is ludicrous. *Two* bodyguards?'

'Sage recommended it,' I say defiantly. 'She said you can't be too careful.'

'Doggie!' Minnie points joyfully at the window where Mitchell is leading Echo past, talking feverishly into his headset. 'See doggie!'

'You're not going near that doggie,' says Luke firmly. 'Becky, that dog is going to maul Minnie.'

'She won't. She's under control. She was trained in Russia,' I add proudly.

'I don't care where she was trained! She's an attack dog!'

The buzzer sounds and Jeff instantly stiffens.

'I'll take care of this.' He mutters into his headset, 'Mitch, do you read me? Secure Area A for delivery arrival. Repeat, secure Area A.'

As Jeff strides out of the kitchen, Luke and Suze exchange looks.

'We can't live like this.' Luke pours himself a cup of coffee. 'Becky, how long have you booked these clowns for?'

'Don't call them clowns! And I've booked them for a week.'

'A *week*?'

'Package for you.' Jeff comes back into the kitchen, heaving a large crate with *First Move Security Solutions* on the side.

'Security Solutions?' Luke stares at the crate. 'What's this?'

'It's . . . er . . . some stuff I bought.'

'Oh Christ.' He closes his eyes. 'What have you done now?'

'You don't need to sound like that! It was recommended by the experts!' I reach for a knife and jemmy off the top of the crate. 'They said I might like to consider investing in extra security for my family. So I bought . . .'

I hesitate as I peer into the crate, slightly losing my nerve. They look a bit more *military* than I was expecting.

'What?' demands Luke. 'What did you buy?'

'Body armour.' I try to sound casual. 'Just as a precaution. Loads of celebrities wear it.'

'Body armour?' Luke's voice rises incredulously. 'You mean, bullet-proof vests?'

'Bullet-proof vests?' Suze spits out her tea. 'Bex, you *didn't*!'

'This one is for you.' I pull out the Panther model in taupe, which I thought would really suit Suze.

'I'm not wearing a bullet-proof vest!' she says in horror. 'Get that thing away from me!'

'How much did these cost?' Luke is holding up the Leopard model in khaki green, with a finger and thumb.

'It doesn't matter how much they cost,' I say defensively.

271

'Who can put a price on the safety of loved ones? And anyway, there was a special offer. Buy four garments and get a stun gun free.'

'A *stun gun?*' Luke recoils.

'Every family should have a stun gun,' I say, more confidently than I feel.

'You've gone insane.' Luke turns to Suze. 'She's insane.'

'Luke, I'm not a civilian any more!' I exclaim. 'Life has changed! Don't you understand that?'

I feel so frustrated. Why don't they get it? Sage understands, and the man at the security company totally understood. In fact, he thought I should buy a door-frame X-ray scanner, too, *and* change all our locks to 'panic hardware'.

'Becky, my darling,' says Luke kindly. 'You are totally and utterly deluded, if you think—'

He breaks off as a frantic barking comes from outside. The next minute, Jeff is on his feet, listening furiously to his earpiece.

'Stay where you are,' he says gruffly to me. 'We have a situation.' As he hurries out of the kitchen, I hear him ordering, 'Describe the intruder.'

Situation? *Intruder?* My heart spasms in fear.

Well, if I'm honest, half in fear and half in triumph.

'You see?' I say to Luke. 'You *see*? Minnie, darling, come here.' I draw her protectively towards me, my voice quivering. She gazes up at me, her eyes huge and questioning, and I stroke her brow. 'Children, stay away from the windows. We'll be fine.' I try to sound brave and positive. 'Let's just keep calm and sing "My Favourite Things".'

We need a panic room. *That's* what celebrities have. And maybe more dogs.

'Is it a burglar?' Clemmie starts to cry.

'I'll fight him,' says Ernest boldly. 'Ha-ya!'

'Luke,' I say quietly. 'Get the stun gun out of the crate.'

'Are you out of your mind?' Luke rolls his eyes. He takes a piece of toast out of the toaster and calmly spreads butter on it, then takes a bite. I stare at him in indignant disbelief. Is he heartless? Doesn't he care about our safety?

'Let go!' A male voice is shouting from outside. Oh my God, it's the intruder. 'Call off that dog! Call it off!'

'Identify yourself!' Mitchell's voice is booming through the air, and Echo is barking more loudly than ever. I can't help feeling terrified and exhilarated, all at the same time. This is like something off the TV!

'The burglar's here!' Clementine bursts into fresh, terrified sobs, and after a nanosecond, Minnie joins in.

'For God's sake!' says Suze, and glances balefully at me. 'Happy now?'

'Don't blame *me*!'

'He'll get us!' Clementine wails. 'He's coming!'

There's the sound of scuffling coming from the hall and men's shouts, then a thump and a furious exclamation from one man, who suddenly sounds just like—

Hang on a minute. That's not—

'*Dad?*' I yell incredulously, just as Jeff and Mitchell appear at the kitchen door, manhandling my father as though they're cops in a movie and he's the double-crossing vice-president who was found trying to climb out of a window.

'Becky!'

'That's my *dad*!'

'Grandpa!'

'We found this suspect prowling in the drive—'

'I wasn't prowling—'

'Let go of him!'

We're all speaking at once, and poor Wilfie has put his hands over his ears.

'Let go of him!' I yell again, above the hubbub. 'He's my father!'

Reluctantly, Mitchell lets go of Dad's arm, which he had twisted behind his back. I mean, honestly. How could they think Dad was an intruder? You couldn't see anyone less suspicious-looking than my dad. He's wearing summer trousers and a blazer, and a panama hat, and he looks as though he's about to go to a cricket match.

'How's my Minnie?' he says in delight, as Minnie throws herself at him. 'How's my little sweetheart?'

'Dad, what's going on?' I demand. 'Why are you here? Mum's so worried!'

'Are you sure this is your dad?' Mitchell says mistrustfully to me.

'Of course I'm sure!'

'Well, he's not on the list.' Jeff gives me his reproachful look again. 'Rebecca, we need comprehensive information to work effectively.'

'I didn't know he was coming!'

'So how did he access the drive? How did he open the gates?' Jeff is still frowning suspiciously at Dad.

'It's the same code as the garage at home,' says Dad cheerily. 'I thought I'd chance it, and hey presto.'

'I always use the same code,' I explain to Jeff. 'It's the same as my pin number, too. And my mum's. That way, we can get money out for each other. It's really handy.'

'You use the same code for *everything*?' Jeff looks aghast. 'Your mother has the same code? Rebecca, we *talked* about code safety.'

'Oh, right,' I say guiltily. 'OK. I'll change it. One of them. All of them.'

(I'm so not going to change anything. Four numbers is hard enough to remember as it is.)

'Welcome, Graham.' Luke is shaking Dad's hand. 'Would you like some breakfast? You'll be staying with us, of course.'

'If that's all right.'

'Dad, where've you *been*?' I chime in impatiently. 'What's going *on*? Why are you in LA?'

There's silence in the kitchen. Even Jeff and Mitchell look interested.

Dad gives me a guarded smile. 'I just have some business to take care of. That's all. I stayed at a hotel last night, and here I am.'

'It's Brent Lewis, isn't it? Dad, what's the mystery?'

'No mystery,' says Dad. 'Simply . . .' He hesitates.

274

'Something I have to put right. Might I make myself a cup of tea?' He reaches for the kettle and peers at it, puzzled. 'Does this go on the stove?'

'That's how they do it in America,' I explain. 'They don't understand electric kettles. But then, they don't really understand tea, either. Here, I'll do it.' I fill the kettle with water, plonk it on the hob, then immediately text Mum: **He's here!!!**

Dad has sat down at the table with Minnie on his lap, and is playing Incy Wincy Spider with her. Soon all the other children are clustering around too, and he doesn't even notice me texting. A minute or two later, my phone rings, and it's Mum.

'Where is he?' she demands shrilly. 'What's he doing? Does he know how worried I've been?'

'I'm sure he does,' I say hurriedly. 'I'm sure he's really sorry. There'll be a brilliant explanation, I know it.' Dad glances up, his expression blank, and I make vigorous hand gestures which are supposed to mean 'It's Mum!'

'Well, put me on!'

'Er, Dad,' I say. 'It's Mum. She wants to talk to you.' I hold out the phone gingerly and take a step backwards.

'Jane,' says Dad, as he takes the phone. 'Now, Jane. Jane, listen. Jane.'

I can hear Mum's tinny voice coming through the phone in a constant, high-pitched stream. Dad clearly can't get a word in.

Suze raises her eyebrows at me and I shrug back helplessly. I've never felt at quite such a loss.

'You mustn't concern yourself,' Dad is saying. 'I've told you, it's simply an issue with a couple of old friends.' He pours boiling water into the teapot. 'No, I'm not coming home on the next flight! I must do this.' He sounds suddenly resolute.

I look questioningly at Luke, who also shrugs. This is driving me mad.

'She wants to talk to you, darling,' says Dad, handing the phone back to me. He seems quite unruffled by Mum's tirade.

'Why won't he tell me what he's doing?' Mum's voice blasts in my ear. 'He keeps saying he's got "something to sort out" with that Brent Lewis. I've Googled him, you know. Can't find anything. You said he lives in a trailer. Did you actually meet him?'

'No.' I glance at Dad, who's sipping tea now.

'Well, keep an eye on Dad.'

'I will.'

'And I'm coming out, as soon as I can make arrangements. It *would* be the same time as the church bazaar.' Mum gives a gusty sigh. 'I preferred the guitar lessons to this. At least he did them in the garage.'

As I put the phone down, I turn to Dad and see that he's looking at my necklace with a kind of rueful expression. It's the Alexis Bittar one that he got me with his BB.

'I love this,' I say, touching it. 'I wear it all the time.'

'Do you, darling? That's good.' He smiles, but there's something wrong in his smile. I want to scream. What is *up*?

He finishes his tea, then gets to his feet.

'I must be off.'

'But you've only just got here! Where are you going? To Brent's trailer? Did you call his sister?'

'Becky, it's my business.' He sounds final. 'I'll be back later.'

Nobody says anything until he's left the kitchen – then everyone seems to breathe out.

'What is he *doing*?' I almost squeak with frustration.

'Like he said,' Luke comments, 'that's his business. Why don't you leave him to it? Come on, poppet,' he adds to Minnie. 'Teeth. Come on, you lot,' he adds to the Cleath-Stuarts. 'You can all do your teeth too.'

'Thanks, Luke,' says Suze gratefully. As the children all pile out of the kitchen with Luke, Suze gives the most almighty sigh. She's staring out of the window, and I can see a little frown between her brows that wasn't there before.

'Are you OK?'

'I'm tired of LA,' she says. 'It's not good for us.'

I stare at her in astonishment. 'Yes it is! Look at you! You're working as an extra, and Tarquin's a total VIP, and you're all thin and tanned, and—'

'It's not good for us as a *family*.' She cuts me off. 'In England, yes, we had loads of headaches, but we dealt with them together. I feel like I'm losing Tarkie.' Her voice suddenly wobbles. 'Bex, I don't know him any more.'

To my horror, her eyes are welling up with tears.

'Suze!' I rush over and give her a hug. 'You mustn't worry! He's just going through a funny patch. He's finding himself.'

'But he doesn't talk to me! He looks at me as though I'm the enemy!' Suze gives a shaky sigh. 'Bex, when the children are at school, d'you feel like going for a walk and just chatting? We could go to Runyon Canyon, maybe have lunch . . .'

'Suze, I would,' I say regretfully. 'But I've got to go shopping for Sage's outfit.'

An odd flicker passes over Suze's face. 'Right.' She breathes out. 'Of course. You have to go shopping.'

'It's not shopping for *me*!' I say, stung. 'I have my TV segment coming up! I have to source pieces for Sage! I have to go to vintage shops and build up some relationships! It's a massive job. Suze, this is my big chance. This is *it*!'

'Of course it is,' she says, in a tone I can't quite read.

'Another time?'

'Another time.' She nods, and gets up from the table.

I'm left alone in the kitchen with Jeff, and I glance over at him. He's sitting in silence, staring implacably ahead, but even so, I feel judged.

'I *do* have to go shopping,' I say defensively. 'This is my big chance to be a Hollywood stylist.'

Jeff says nothing. But I know he's judging me. They're all judging me.

This is what it's like to be a celebrity. Your family don't understand. No one understands. No wonder they say it's lonely at the top.

On the plus side, it turns out that shopping for a movie star is the *perfect* way to shop. I just wish I'd known a movie star before.

There's the most fab vintage shop on Melrose Avenue, and the owner, Marnie, is absolutely on my wavelength. By mid-morning, I've been on the fastest, most efficient shopping spree of my life. I've bought three new clutch bags, two stoles and a vintage diamanté headdress. I've got three evening coats on hold, and five dresses, and this fantastic velvet cloak, which, if Sage doesn't want, I am totally getting for myself.

I've also bought myself a couple of tiny things – just a sequined evening dress and a few pairs of shoes, because I'll need them for my new lifestyle. I even used my notebook from Golden Peace, just to make sure I wasn't shopping in an unhealthy way. In answer to the question, 'Why am I shopping?' I wrote, 'Because I am a celebrity stylist now.' I mean, you can't argue with that.

When I head out of the shop, the blacked-out SUV is waiting by the kerb. Mitchell is standing to attention, his shades glinting in the sun, and Jeff escorts me to the SUV door. I can see some shoppers looking at me curiously, and I put my hand up to shield my face, just like a proper A-lister.

As I get into the SUV, surrounded by bags, I feel elated. I'm totally on track with my new career! The only slight worry I have is that my *Breakfast Show USA* segment is tomorrow, and I *still* haven't heard from them what sort of styling they want. How can I prepare a fashion piece if I don't have a brief? I've left a zillion messages for Aran about this already, but I decide to try him again anyway, and this time he picks up.

'Oh hi, Aran,' I say. 'Listen, did you ever hear back from *Breakfast Show USA* about what sort of clothes I should prepare? Because it's tomorrow! I need to get some pieces together!'

'Oh!' Aran laughs. 'My bad. Yes, I meant to tell you. They say don't worry about the clothes. They'll take care of all that. Your job is just to go on the show and talk.'

Don't worry about the clothes? I stare blankly at the phone. How can I not worry about the clothes when I'm the stylist?

'But how will that work? How will I prepare?'

'Becky, you'll be great,' says Aran. 'You can comment on the clothes, engage in some general chat, get your personality across.'

'Oh,' I say. 'Well, OK. Thanks.'

I ring off, still puzzled. This is all very weird. But maybe they do things differently in the States. In fact, maybe I should do some research. I zap on the TV to see if there are any fashion items I can watch, and flick through the channels, until an image suddenly stops me. For a moment I can't even make sense of what I'm seeing.

It's a fuzzy picture of Lois's house in the dark. There's an ambulance flashing in her driveway and paramedics wheeling a hospital gurney and the headline is *BREAKING NEWS: Lois in suicide bid?*

Suicide?

Suicide bid?

Oh God, oh God, oh God . . .

My heart thumping, I turn the volume up and lean forward anxiously to hear the voice-over.

'There are unconfirmed reports that Lois Kellerton was rushed to the hospital last night, in what one commentator described as "the desperate act of a desperate star". Over to our reporter Faye Ireland.'

The picture switches to a reporter standing outside what I recognize as Lois's house, talking gravely into a microphone.

'Neighbours confirm that at around midnight last night, an ambulance was summoned to the house, and one witness saw Lois Kellerton being placed in the ambulance, on a gurney. Some time in the early hours of the morning, Lois Kellerton appeared to return to the house and has not been seen since.' The screen shows a fuzzy, long-lens picture of a girl covered in a sheet being bundled into the house. 'Friends have been worried about the state of mind of the award-winning actress, since her apparent exposure as a thief.' The picture flashes to the familiar sight of Lois at the ASAs, crumpling in shock on the stage. 'Ms Kellerton's spokesman refused to comment on these latest troubling events. Back to the studio.'

'And now to sports . . .' says a woman in a purple dress, and I switch off. I'm quivering all over. I never thought in a million years anything like this would happen. I never imagined – I never expected—

I mean, it isn't *my* fault.

It isn't. It really isn't.

Is it?

On impulse, I dial Sage's number. Of all people, she must know how I feel. In fact, she must feel even worse.

'Sage,' I say, as soon as she answers. 'Did you see the news about Lois?'

'Oh.' She sounds unconcerned. 'That.'

'Sage, we did that to her!' My voice is trembling. 'I can't believe it's gone so far. Have you been to see her or called her or anything?'

'See that maniac?' Sage retorts. 'You have to be kidding!'

'But shouldn't we do something? Like . . . I don't know. Go and apologize?'

'No,' says Sage flatly. 'Not happening.'

'Just "no"?'

'This is her problem, Becky. She'll sort it out. I gotta go.' And she rings off.

Sage sounds so sure of herself. But I can't feel like that. Doubts are crawling all over me like insects. I can't bear it. I want to do something. I have to do something. Make amends.

But how can I make amends?

I close my eyes, thinking hard for a moment, then open them and whip out my phone. I still have April Tremont's number and she answers after the second ring.

'Rebecca?'

She doesn't exactly sound delighted to hear from me.

'Um, hi, April,' I say nervously. 'Sorry to bother you. It's just, I saw the news about Lois. I feel terrible about everything that happened and I'd really like to apologize to Lois and somehow make amends. Maybe help her. Or something . . .' I tail off lamely.

'*Help* her?' April's voice is so sarcastic, it makes me wince. 'You helped enough already, don't you think?'

'I know you're her friend,' I say humbly. 'You must think I'm an awful person. But you have to know, I never realized it would turn out like this, I never meant to expose her. And I wondered if you could help me get to see her, maybe? To say sorry?'

'Lois isn't talking to anyone,' says April curtly. 'I've phoned a million times but she won't reply. And even if she were, you're the last person I'd bring along. Yes, she needs help. She's needed help for a long time, if you ask me. But not from opportunistic users like you.'

'I'm not an opportunistic user!' I say in horror.

'Don't tell me you're not doing nicely from this,' snaps April, and rings off.

I stare at my phone, my cheeks hot, feeling as though I've been slapped. As I lift my eyes, I see Jeff's thick neck ahead of me and feel a fresh twinge of shame. Here's me, riding along in an SUV with bodyguards and shopping bags, my career transformed. And there's Lois, being rushed to hospital.

Jeff hasn't said a word all this time, but I know he's been listening. And judging me again. I can see it from the muscles in his neck.

'I'm not opportunistic,' I say defensively. 'I could have sold the story weeks ago, couldn't I? But I didn't. It's not my fault Sage blabbed. And I've wanted to be a Hollywood stylist for ever. Can you blame me if I leap at the chance? It doesn't mean I'm opportunistic.'

Again Jeff is silent. But I know what he's thinking.

'Well, what *can* I do now?' I say, almost angrily. 'If April won't take me to see Lois, then it's impossible! I can't say sorry, or offer help, or anything. I don't even know where she—'

I break off. I'm remembering something that April said, when we were sitting in her trailer. *We've both lived on Doheny Road for ever.*

281

'Mitchell,' I say, leaning forward. 'Change of plan. I want to go to Doheny Road.'

It takes us about thirty minutes to reach Doheny Road, and as soon as we arrive it's obvious which house is Lois's. Journalists are camped outside the gates and prowling up and down the street, and I can see two vox-pop interviews going on. We pull up some way further on, outside a mansion that looks like a Greek temple.

'Stay in the car, Rebecca,' says Mitchell. 'We need to survey the area.'

'OK.' I try to sound patient as they clunk the car doors shut and head towards Lois's house, looking conspicuous in their dark suits. All this 'surveying' and 'securing' is starting to get on my nerves. Once you get over the novelty, having a body-guard is a real pain.

I have to sit for ages while they scout around the whole neighbourhood. As they return to the car, their faces are even more sober than usual.

'The building is currently compromised with the strong presence of media,' says Mitchell. 'We foresee a high-risk situation developing. We recommend you do not proceed.'

'D'you mean not go into the house?' I clarify.

'We recommend you do not proceed.' Mitchell nods. 'At this time.'

'But I want to proceed.'

'Well, we recommend that you do not.'

I glance from Jeff to Mitchell. They look identically serious, with their dark glasses masking any expression they might have (which is probably non-existent to begin with).

'I'm going to proceed,' I say defiantly. 'OK? I need to see Lois Kellerton. I can't live with myself if I don't at least try.'

'Rebecca,' says Mitchell sternly. 'If you approach the front of the house, we cannot guarantee your security.'

'It's a situation,' chimes in Jeff, nodding.

I look over their shoulders at the crowd of journalists. It is a bit of a mob. They might have a point.

'Well, then, I'll have to break in at the back,' I say. 'Will one of you give me a leg-up?'

Jeff and Mitchell exchange glances.

'Rebecca,' says Jeff. 'Under the terms of our contract, we are not permitted to aid you, the client, in any endeavour deemed as law-breaking.'

'You're so *square*!' I say in frustration. 'Don't you get bored, driving around in dark jackets and pretending everything's serious all the time? Well, OK, I'll do it by myself. And when I'm arrested, I'll say: "Mitchell and Jeff had nothing to do with it, Officer." Happy?'

I grab my bag, slither out of the car and start heading towards Lois's house, my heels clicking on the road.

'Rebecca, wait.' Jeff's voice follows me.

'What now?' I turn. 'I know, you think I shouldn't proceed. You're worse than the bloody sat nav.'

'Not that.'

'What, then?'

He hesitates, then says in a low voice, 'There's a weak point in the fence by the pool house. CCTV just misses it. Try there.'

'Thanks, Jeff!' I beam at him and blow him a kiss.

Lois's property is so huge, it takes ages to find my way to the back. As I hurry along a side road, I start feeling more and more nervous. I've never met anyone suicidal before. I mean, not *really* suicidal. Shouldn't I have training or something? Anyway, too late now. I'll just have to be really gentle. And uplifting and positive. And apologetic, obviously.

What if she blames me for everything?

I feel an uncomfortable twinge. I really, really want Lois to understand that I didn't tell everyone. OK, I blabbed to Sage, but *I told her to keep it a secret*.

But what if Lois won't see it? What if she screams at me? What if she picks up a knife and says she's going to stab herself right there, in front of me, and I throw myself at her to save her but it's too late? Oh God . . .

Feeling slightly ill with all these lurid thoughts, I force myself to keep going. At last I arrive at an eight-foot-high fence, with what must be the pool house on the other side. There's no way I could climb over it on my own, but after walking back and forth a few times, I see what Jeff meant. Two of the slats are loose. I prise them to one side, exposing a gap. I peer at it incredulously. I'm meant to climb through that? What size does he think I am, minus 20?

But there's no other option, so I bend down and start squeezing myself through the gap. I can feel the wood scraping my back, and my hair gets caught a few times, and for one awful moment I think I'll be stuck there for ever. But at last I manage to pop through. (Simultaneously breaking another two slats. In fact, I've kind of wrecked this little area of fence. I expect Lois will sue me for that.)

The pool house is about the size of my parents' house in Oxshott. The pool is pretty huge, too. Then there's a kind of ornamental hanging garden which looks very weird and out of place and a lawn and a great big terrace with sofas and chairs and then, finally, the house. Which is vast, needless to say.

OK. What do I do now? I suddenly remember Jeff mentioning CCTV and it occurs to me that I'm probably being filmed right now. Argh. I need to move fast, before the attack dogs reach me. I hurry to one side of the plot and make my way cautiously towards the house. My heart is beating fast and I'm expecting to be stopped at any moment. But the way I see it, if I can just get to speak to Lois – even for a second – she'll know I tried. She'll know I was thinking of her.

Panting, I reach the terrace and crouch down behind a massive pot containing a fern. Five yards away are the French windows. They're open. Do I just walk in? What if I freak her out?

Or maybe I should just write a note. Yes. Much better. I don't know why I didn't think of that before. I'll write a note and leave it on the terrace and creep away, and then she can read it in her own time. I rummage in my bag for my notebook and pen, which I've been using to make styling notes. I carefully tear out a page and write the date at the top.

Dear Lois

Oh God. What do I write? How do I put it?

I'm so, so sorry for everything that's happened. But you must know, I was as shocked as you when Sage exposed you. I told her IN CONFIDENCE.

I underline the last two words several times, and am sitting back on my heels to take stock, when something attracts my attention. It's a pair of sunglasses, lying on a chair. A pair of Missoni sunglasses. They're pink and green and swirly and they look exactly like the ones I gave Sage yesterday morning.

They can't be the same ones. Obviously they can't be. But—

I stare at the sunglasses, totally baffled. One part of my brain is saying, 'It's a coincidence,' and the other part is saying, 'It can't be a coincidence.' At last I can't bear it any longer. I have to see. I edge forward and grab the sunglasses off the chair – and there's no doubt about it. They're the ones I bought. They have the same rubbed-away bit on the gilt 'M' and a tiny chip on one arm.

What are they *doing* here? Did Sage send them to Lois? But why? And wouldn't she have mentioned it on the phone earlier? And why would she send sunglasses to Lois, anyway?

My head spinning, I creep forward to put them back – and then freeze. Through the glass of the French windows I can see straight into Lois's living room. There's Lois, sitting on a sofa, laughing. And there's Sage, sitting next to her, passing her a bowl of nachos.

My whole body feels paralysed with shock. *Sage?* In Lois's *house?* But— but— but—

I mean—

That's just—

I've leaned so far forward, trying to see, I suddenly lose my balance, and the sunglasses go clattering on to a glass table. Shit. *Shit.*

'Who's there?' says Sage sharply, and comes to the French windows. 'Oh my God, *Becky?*'

I stare helplessly up at her, unable to reply. I feel as though the world has turned upside down. A few minutes ago, Sage was telling me she didn't want to see Lois. But she must have been in Lois's house *even while she was talking to me*. What is going on? What?

'Get in here,' says Sage, glancing around. 'There aren't any press following you, are there? What did you do, break in?'

'Yes,' I say, getting to my feet, still dazed. 'I made a bit of a mess of the fence. Maybe someone should see to that. Sorry,' I add to Lois, who has followed Sage to the French windows. Lois doesn't look the dishevelled mess I was expecting. She's wearing long, pale-green wide-legged trousers and a black halter top and her hair is smoothed into a side ponytail. She's also smoking, which is a bit of a shock. Lois Kellerton doesn't smoke. I've read it in magazines a million times.

'You look so freaked!' Sage bursts into laughter as she closes the French windows behind me.

Finally I find my voice. 'I *am* freaked! What do you expect?'

'Poor Becky,' Sage says kindly.

'What . . . I mean . . .' I don't even know where to begin. 'Don't you . . .'

'You thought we hated each other, right?' says Sage.

'Everyone thinks you hate each other!' I expostulate. 'Everyone in the world!'

'Well, we kinda do.' Sage pushes Lois, whose mouth turns up in a little smile.

'Everything's a game,' she says. 'We're playing the game. The long game,' she adds.

'Lois's really smart,' chimes in Sage.

They're both nodding, as though that explains everything.

'I don't get it,' I say, feeling more bewildered than ever. 'I just don't. You have to start from the beginning.'

'Oh well, the *beginning*.' Lois leads me into the kitchen, where a huge oak table is covered in laptops, magazines, coffee cups and take-out boxes. I even see a box of Krispy Kremes, which makes me double-take. I thought Lois hated white sugar? 'That would be when we were . . . what, ten?'

'We were on *Save the Kids* together,' Sage nods.

'Then we had a big fight.'

'But we made up.'

I'm totally lost. 'Was that recently?'

'No! We were, like, sixteen,' says Sage. 'I was so mad at Lois, I trashed her car. Remember?'

Lois shakes her head ruefully. She's a lot more composed than Sage. In fact, I can't stop staring at her. Her nails are perfect. Her hands aren't shaking one little bit as she makes coffee. She doesn't look anything like a suicidal head-case.

'Did you really try to commit suicide?' I blurt out, and she gives another secretive little smile.

'Becky, none of this is real!' says Sage. 'Don't you realize that? You're in on it too now.' She gives me a squeeze. 'Lois will tell you what to do. She has the whole thing planned.'

'What do you mean?' I say in bewilderment. 'What whole thing?'

'Redemption,' says Lois. 'Reconciliation ... forgiveness ... *Camberly*.' She pauses, then says it again with relish, '*Camberly*.'

'*Camberly*.' Sage nods. 'We just heard. We're doing it, the two of us. A special. It's gonna be huge.'

'*Huge*.' Lois agrees.

'They're gonna plug it everywhere. The big truce. Sage and Lois confront each other.' Sage's eyes are sparkling. 'Who's not going to watch that? Lois has this whole remorseful-sinner thing going on, too. You're going to wear white, yes?' she adds to Lois.

'White shift and flats.' Lois confirms. 'Penitent angel. They may get the store owner on, apparently. So I can apologize to him.'

'That would be good TV,' says Sage. 'I'm gonna offer Lois help,' she tells me. 'And we're both gonna cry. I need to talk to you about a dress,' she adds. 'Something innocent-looking. Maybe Marc Jacobs? Maybe, like, a soft pink?'

I can't believe what I'm hearing. It's like they've practically written a script. They probably *will* write a script.

287

'Do the *Camberly* people know about this?' I stutter. 'That it's all fake?'

'No!' Sage seems shocked. 'Nobody knows. Lois even fired her media team to keep them out of the way, so they have no idea.'

'I knew we had a big chance,' says Lois. 'But my people would never have gone along with it. They're so *conventional*.' She shakes her head impatiently.

'So . . .' I rub my head, trying to get things clear. 'So you're not really a shoplifter? But I caught you red-handed!'

'That was an experiment,' says Lois. She sits down at the table, one leg crossed elegantly over the other. 'I wasn't expecting to get caught. But it all worked out.'

'Lois's really imaginative,' says Sage admiringly. 'The feud was her idea. She came up with the cancer-victim line. She came up with the two green dresses. I mean, those were just tiny little ideas between ourselves. They didn't get us huge attention. But now this suicide thing is on a whole new level. Genius. It's put us right back on the front pages.'

As I look at Lois's calm face, I feel revulsion. She actually faked a suicide attempt?

'But how could you do that? People have been really worried about you!'

'I know,' says Lois. 'That's the point. The farther you fall, the more they love you when you bounce back.' She sighs at my expression. 'Look. It's a competitive world. We need exposure. All the public craves is a good story. Don't *you* love a good story? Don't you read *US Weekly*?'

'Well, yes, but—'

'Do you think every word is true?'

'Well, no, but—'

'So what's the difference?'

'Well, *some* of it has to be true!' I say hotly. 'Otherwise what's the point?'

'Why? Does it matter? As long as we entertain our audience?'

I'm silenced for a while, thinking about all the stories Suze and I have read in the gossip magazines. Does it matter if they're true or not? Like, I've always taken it as gospel truth that the cast of *Our Time* all hate one another. What if they don't? What if Selma Diavo isn't really a bitch? I've read about the stars for so long, I feel like I *know* them. I feel familiar with their worlds and their friends and their ups and their downs. I could probably write a thesis on Jennifer Aniston's love life.

But the truth is, all I really *know* is images and headlines and 'quotes' from 'sources'. Nothing real.

'Wait a minute,' I say, as something occurs to me. 'If everyone thinks you're a suicidal wreck, how will you get any work?'

'Oh, I'll get work,' says Lois. 'The offers are already coming in. Lots of shoplifting roles.' She gives a sudden burst of laughter. 'I'll be punished and then I'll be forgiven. That's how Hollywood operates.'

She looks so relaxed, I feel a spurt of anger. Does she realize how worried I've been about her? And I don't even know her! What about her friends? What about her parents?

Oh, actually, her parents are dead. And she doesn't have any friends. (At least, that's what *National Enquirer* said. But who can I believe any more?)

'I thought you were about to have a breakdown,' I say accusingly. 'You were shaking . . . you were collapsing . . . you couldn't even breathe . . .'

'I'm an actor,' says Lois with a shrug.

'We're actors.' Sage nods. 'We act.'

I cast my mind back to the Lois I caught shoplifting all those weeks ago – the timid wraith in the hoody. The trembling hands, the whispering voice, the flinching expression . . . That was *acting*? I mean, OK, I know I shouldn't be surprised. Lois is one of the top actors in the world. But still. She looked so *real*. I almost want to ask her to do it again.

'What about Luke?' I turn to Sage. 'Does he have any idea?'

'I don't think so,' says Sage, after a pause. 'Although he's smart. He asked me straight out, was any of this fabricated? Of course I told him no. Has he said anything to you?'

'Nothing.'

'He mustn't know,' says Lois. 'He mustn't know anything. Every attempt to fool the American public needs a level of plausible deniability.'

'*The President's Woman*,' chimes in Sage, and high-fives Lois.

I knew I'd heard Lois say that somewhere before. It was when she played the Vice-President and wore all those pin-stripe suits.

'Luke is our level of plausible deniability,' she's saying now. 'He and Aran both. They're credible, they're trustworthy . . .'

'Luke's great,' says Sage, turning to Lois. 'When this has simmered down, you should totally hire him. He has, like, all these ideas for strategy. And he's such a gentleman.'

'But Sage . . .' I don't quite know how to put it. 'Inventing a feud with Lois can't be part of Luke's strategy, surely?'

'So I had to go a little off the path.' She tosses her hair back. 'It worked, didn't it? You *mustn't* tell him,' she adds. 'You know what he thinks I should be doing? Charity work. Like, some trip to Darfur.' She makes a disparaging face. 'I told him I was researching landmines today. In fact, you can back me up!' Her face brightens. 'Tell him you called me and I was totally on the internet looking at charity websites.'

'I can't lie to Luke!' I say in horror.

'Well, you can't *tell* Luke,' retorts Sage.

'Becky, you're in this now,' says Lois sternly. 'And if you're in it, you're in it.'

That's a quote from one of her movies, too, but I can't remember which one. The Mafia one, maybe?

'We'll give you a break in styling,' she continues. 'You can dress us both for events. You'll make contacts, it'll be the real deal. But you cannot tell anyone.' Her eyes are flashing at me. She's got up from her chair and looks suddenly quite intimi-dating, like she did when she played that partner in a law firm who was also a serial killer. '*You cannot tell anyone*,' she repeats.

'Right.' I swallow.

'If you do, we'll trash you.'

I have no idea what she means by 'trash' but it can't be good.

'Right,' I say again, nervously.

Lois has already turned away and is tapping at a laptop. '*Lois and Sage to appear on* Camberly,' she reads aloud. 'It's up! You should go, Becky,' she adds to me. 'Call your driver. The guard will let him in and he can back the SUV right up to the door. The press won't see you. That's what Sage did yesterday. And if your driver asks, tell him I wasn't available. I was too ill. That'll get around.'

'Drivers know everything,' chimes in Sage. 'Hey, look, we made Fox News!'

The two of them are totally engrossed in the laptop. There's no point me sticking around.

'Well . . . bye then,' I say, and reach for my phone. A few minutes later Mitchell and Jeff arrive at the front door in the blacked-out SUV and I slide in seamlessly, just as Lois described. It's like the house was designed for discreet exits. As we make our way out of the gates, journalists start banging on the sides of the SUV and flashing cameras, shouting 'Lois! Lois!' until we manage to break free and drive off.

They thought I was her. The world has gone nuts. My head is still spinning and the blood is pulsing in my ears. What just happened there? *What?*

From: Kovitz, Danny
To: Kovitz, Danny
Subject: **i'm so collld**

---

so cooooooooooolllld. can'ttt tyyype fingers agonynnn this issssn't howexxpcteted

dddanananyyyy

SEVENTEEN

By the time Luke gets home that evening, I'm feeling calmer. The thing is, this is what Hollywood is like and you just have to get used to it. Yes, it seems completely freaky and messed up at first, but gradually it starts to feel more normal. They're right. It *is* all a game. Everyone's playing it, the stars, the journalists, the public, everyone. And if you don't want to play, maybe you shouldn't come to Hollywood.

On the plus side, Sage has been texting me all afternoon, and I've been texting back, and it's like we're best friends. I'm totally in the gang! Lois even texted me too, a few times. The forthcoming *Camberly* interview is already huge news, just as they said it would be. It's been featured on every news website, and it's all over the TV too, and the Sage-and-Lois soap opera is Topic A again.

They've been really clever. (At least, Lois has been really clever.) And now I'm part of it too! The best bit was this afternoon, when I was picking up the children from school. I'd already made quite an impression, what with Jeff and Mitchell and the blacked-out SUV. But then, when I was waiting at the pre-school door to get Minnie, Sage rang and I said, 'Oh, hi Sage, how are *you*?' just a bit more loudly than usual, and everyone turned to stare.

The only not-so-A-list thing is, all the photographers have disappeared from our gates, which is a bit disloyal of them. At least, not *all*. There's one geeky Asian guy who is still hanging around. He has bleached-blond hair and today he was wearing a pink bomber jacket with tight black jeans and rubber ankle boots. I started to pose and he took a few snaps, then he beckoned me over and said excitedly, 'You're a friend of Danny Kovitz, right? The designer? Could you get me his autograph?' It turns out his name is Lon and he's a fashion-design student and he worships Danny. And now he worships me too because I'm a friend of Danny.

And OK, maybe I did play up to it a bit. Maybe I did promise to come out tomorrow morning wearing a vintage Danny Kovitz outfit (i.e. two years old) which never even hit the catwalks, and let him take a picture of it. The thing is, I *like* having photographers outside the house. It's boring not to have any around.

I'm in the kitchen preparing an A-lister-type supper when Luke comes in. Dad must have come back at some point and he and Tarquin have gone out sightseeing – they left a note – and Suze is nowhere to be seen, so I guess she's with them too. All the children are in bed and I've sent Jeff and Mitchell out for supper, so it's just me and Luke, which is nice.

Now that I'm a rising Hollywood celebrity, I have to cook appropriately. We'll probably need to get a chef or private juice-maker or something, but for now I'm making a very of-the-moment dish. Grain soup. It's the latest thing. All the A-listers have it, plus I need to look thin for all my forthcoming appearances, and apparently it's got some magic combination that boosts the metabolism.

'Hi!' I greet Luke with a kiss and a wheatgrass smoothie, which is also very healthy and A-list.

'What's that?' He sniffs it and recoils. 'I'm having a glass of wine. Want one?'

'No thanks,' I say, self-righteously. 'I'm trying to follow a clean diet.' I ladle grain soup into two bowls and put it on the table. 'This is totally organic and macrobiotic. It has chia,' I add.

Luke looks dubiously at it and pokes it with his spoon.

'OK,' he says slowly. 'What are we having with it?'

'This is it! It has protein and sprouty things and everything. It's a meal in a bowl.' I'm about to take a spoonful, when I remember something. I push my chair back and start doing squats.

Luke stares at me in alarm. 'Becky, are you all right?

'I'm fine!' I say breathlessly. 'You should do squats before you eat. It boosts the metabolism. All the stars do it. Nine . . . ten.' I take my seat again, panting slightly. Luke surveys me silently for a moment, then takes a spoonful. He munches it, but doesn't say anything.

'Isn't it great?' I say cheerily, and take a massive spoonful myself.

Argh. Blurgh. Akk.

Seriously? This is what the film stars eat?

It's really watery, and what little taste it has is like a mix of mushrooms and sawdust and earth. I force myself to swallow it down, and take another spoonful. I don't dare look at Luke. A bowl of this won't fill him up. Nor me. It wouldn't even fill up Minnie.

How do the A-listers stay so cheery when they have to eat grain soup the whole time? It must be mind over matter. They must sit there grimly, telling themselves, 'I'm ravenous . . . but I'm in a movie! My stomach is rumbling and I feel faint . . . but I'm friends with Leonardo DiCaprio!'

I take another mouthful and try to chew it a hundred times, as recommended in the blog I read. But honestly. How can this be good for you? My jaws are aching and all I can taste is sprouty things. I would kill for a KitKat—

No, stop it. A-listers don't eat KitKats. If I'm going to be in their crowd I need to learn to love grain soup.

'Luke, maybe we should buy a yacht,' I say, to take my mind off the grain soup.

'What?' He looks flabbergasted.

'Just a little one. And then we could hang out with other

people on yachts. Like Ben and Jennifer,' I add casually. 'Those kinds of people.'

Sage was talking about Ben today as though they're best friends. Well, if she can be friends with him, why not me, too?

'Ben?'

'Ben Affleck.'

'Ben *Affleck*?' Luke puts his spoon down. 'Why on earth would we hang out with Ben Affleck?'

'We might!' I say defensively. 'Why shouldn't we? We live in LA now, we're in the movies . . . you're bound to meet Ben Affleck at a party or something . . .'

'I doubt it,' says Luke, dryly.

'Well, I will, then! Maybe Sage will introduce us. Or maybe I'll style him or one of his friends.'

And I'll become best friends with Jennifer Garner, I think secretly. I've *always* thought I would hit it off with her.

'Becky, this conversation makes no sense.' Luke is shaking his head and I look at him impatiently. He's so slow sometimes.

'Don't you realize everything's changed? I'm in the public eye now. I'm in a whole new zone.'

'You're hardly an A-lister,' he snorts, and I feel a dart of indignation.

'Well, I will be! I have paparazzi outside the house . . . Sage Seymour calls me all the time . . .'

'The paparazzi have gone,' says Luke, unmoved. 'And Sage calls *me* all the time, too. That doesn't make me an A-lister.'

'*Aran* believes in me,' I say pointedly. 'He says I'm going to be huge. He says I could have my own network show by next year.'

Luke sighs. 'Darling, I don't want to rain on your parade – but don't believe every word Aran says. He's a great guy, but he just says whatever the conversation of the moment seems to require. Maybe he believes it, maybe he doesn't. It's the Hollywood way.' He sips his wine. 'And another thing: we need to get rid of those goons. We can't live with them lurking around the place all day.'

'Mitchell and Jeff?' I put down my spoon in dismay. 'I couldn't live without Mitchell and Jeff.'

Luke peers at me incredulously for a moment, then throws back his head in laughter. 'Darling, you've only had body-guards for a day. You can't be dependent on them already. And if you are, I'm afraid you need a reality check.' He gets up from the table. 'I'm making myself a sandwich. Sorry.' He starts slathering mayonnaise on to bread, and I watch in secret envy. 'Since you're talking to your best friend Sage non-stop,' he adds, 'you can tell me something. I'm convinced she's up to some lunatic plan or other. What has she said to you?'

I feel a tweak of alarm. I wasn't expecting him to ask me straight out.

'What do you mean?' I say, playing for time.

'She's hiding something.' He sits down with his monster sandwich and takes a bite. 'Truthfully, Becky, I'm nearly at the end of the line with Sage. I thought we could work together, but . . .' He wipes a blob of mayonnaise off his chin and takes another huge bite.

'But what?'

'If she can't play straight with me, then it's not going to work.'

'You mean . . .' I feel a sudden foreboding. 'Luke, what *do* you mean?'

'I don't know yet.' He opens a bag of crisps, which he must have bought himself. *I* certainly didn't buy them. 'Here's the thing, Becky. A lot of issues are up in the air.'

'What kind of issues?'

'I spoke with the London office today and there's some intriguing stuff going on back there. We've just had a call from the Treasury. I'm going to have to fly back to take a meeting. And if we progress with that association, then I'll need to be on board.'

'In London?' I can't hide my dismay.

'Well, it makes sense. This LA jaunt was always temporary. It's been fun and interesting, but frankly, I'd take ten bolshie Treasury officials over one obstreperous movie star any day.'

Luke laughs but I don't join in. I'm feeling a rising rage. He's talking about moving back to London? Without even consulting me?

'We can't move back to London!' I blurt out. 'What about me? What about my new career?'

Luke looks taken aback. 'Well, you can be a stylist in London, surely? It's the home of style.'

'I can't be a *Hollywood* stylist in London.'

'Darling, there's a film industry in Britain. I'm sure you can get some contacts together, talk to the right people . . .'

How can he be so dense?

'But it isn't Hollywood!' I cry out. 'I want to live in Hollywood and be famous!'

As soon as the words are out, I feel a bit stupid. But even so, I don't want to take them back. I mean them. I've only had the teeniest taste of being famous. How can I give it up?

Luke is looking at me, an odd expression on his face.

'Are you sure about that?' he says at last.

This is the final straw. How can he even ask that?

'I want it more than anything!' I cry out. 'You know what my dream is? To be standing on the red carpet in my own right! Not shuffled along like a second-class citizen, just filling up the space . . . but there as me. *Becky.*'

'I didn't realize it was so important to you,' says Luke, in a toneless way which infuriates me.

'Well, it is. It's always been my dream.'

'No it hasn't!' Luke gives a short laugh. 'Are you trying to pretend this is the fulfilment of a childhood ambition?'

'Well . . .' I flounder briefly. 'OK . . . maybe it's a new dream. Does it matter? The point is, if you *respected* me, Luke, you wouldn't drag us all out to LA, then drag us back to London without any warning. I know you're the big-shot Luke Brandon, but I have a career too! I'm my own person! I'm not only "Mrs Brandon"! Or would you like me to turn into some corporate wifey-wifey? Maybe that's what you secretly wanted, all along! I'll go and learn how to make profiteroles, shall I?'

I break off, slightly shocked at myself. I didn't mean to say all that: it just came out. I can tell I've hurt Luke by the way his eyes are flickering. I want to say, 'Sorry, I didn't mean it,' and give him a hug – but that wouldn't feel quite right, either.

The truth is, I meant *some* of it. I'm just not sure which bit.

For a while there's silence in the kitchen. Neither of us is looking at the other, and the only sound is coming from the sprinklers in the garden outside.

'I'm not dragging anyone anywhere,' Luke says at last, his voice tight. 'This is a marriage and we do things by agreement. And if after all these years together you think I don't respect you, then . . .' He breaks off and shakes his head. 'Look, Becky, if you really feel that your career path lies in LA and can't be anywhere else, then fine. We'll work it out. I want you to have what makes you happy. Whatever that might be.'

Everything he's saying is positive and supportive. I should feel pleased. But his face is so distant, it unnerves me. Usually my intuition tells me exactly what Luke is thinking – but right now, I'm not at all sure.

'Luke . . .' To my horror my voice is a bit wobbly. 'It's not that I don't want us to be together. I just— I need—'

'It's fine.' He cuts me off. 'I get it, Becky. I have to make some calls.'

Without giving me another glance, he picks up his sandwich and strides out of the kitchen, his steps resounding down the corridor. Slowly, I stir my grain soup, feeling a slight shock. One minute we were talking normally, and the next, we were . . . what? I don't even know how things have been left.

I don't see Luke for the rest of the evening. He's talking on the phone in his office and I don't want to disturb him, so I sit in the kitchen flicking through TV channels, my head full of dark, circular thoughts. This is the biggest chance of my life. Luke should be *excited*. I mean, Aran is more excited than he is. How can that be right? And anyway, why did he give me that look? Just because he thinks fame is overrated.

And the Treasury. The *Treasury*. Who would choose the

Treasury over Hollywood? Is he insane? I've been to the Treasury, and believe me, it has nothing to recommend it. I bet if you asked all the Treasury officials, 'Would you rather be in Hollywood?' they'd all march out in an instant.

And why did he have to make me feel guilty? I shouldn't feel guilty, but I do. I don't even know *why* I feel guilty. I've done nothing wrong except become the celebrity of the moment and want to take advantage of that. If Luke can't see that, then maybe he shouldn't work in the media. He should be *excited*.

I'm just summoning up my name on Google for the billionth time, when the door opens and in walk Dad and Tarkie. No, in *lurch* Dad and Tarkie. They're arm in arm, and Dad bumps into the table and Tarkie bursts out laughing, and then he trips up on a chair.

I goggle at them in astonishment. They're drunk? My father and Tarquin have gone out and got *drunk*? Why didn't Suze stop them?

'Where's Suze?' I demand. 'Dad, what happened today? Did you meet Brent?'

'I have no idea where my wife is,' says Tarkie, talking with elaborate carefulness. 'I have my friends and that is all I need.' He claps Dad on the back. 'Your father is a very, very, very . . .' He seems to run out of steam for a moment. 'Very interesting man,' he resumes. 'Wise. He understands. Nobody else understands.'

Dad lifts a finger as though he's about to make a speech. '"The time has come," the walrus said, "to talk of many things."'

'But Dad, where did you *go*? Is everything OK?'

'"Of shoes – and ships – and sealing wax" . . .' continues Dad, totally ignoring me.

Oh God, surely he's not going to recite the whole of *Alice in Wonderland*, or whatever it is.

'Fab!' I say brightly. 'Good idea. Would you like some coffee, Dad?'

'"Of cabbages – and kings".' Tarkie nods gravely.

'We know where the secrets are buried.' Dad abandons Lewis Carroll and suddenly looks serious.

'We know where the *bodies* are buried,' chimes in Tarkie.

'And the secrets.' Dad turns to face Tarkie and taps his nose with his finger.

'And the bodies.' Tarkie is nodding earnestly.

Honestly, I can't follow a word they're saying. Dad gives a sudden gurgle of laughter, and Tarkie joins in. They look like two small boys playing truant from school.

'Coffee,' I say briskly. 'Sit down.' I head over to the kettle, and reach for our strongest espresso blend. I can't believe I'm trying to sober up my dad. What is going on? Mum would be livid.

As I'm pouring hot water into the French press, I can hear Dad and Tarkie murmuring to each other behind me. I turn sharply, but they don't even notice me. I hear Tarkie saying, 'Bryce,' and Dad saying, 'Yes, yes. *Yes*. He's the man. Bryce's the man.'

'Here you are!' I put the cups down sharply, trying to shock them into sense.

'Oh, Becky.' As Dad looks up, his face is wreathed in fondness. 'My little girl, a star in Hollywood. I'm so proud of you, Becky, my love.'

'You're famous,' chimes in Tarkie. 'Famous! We were in a bar and you came on the TV. We said, "We know her!" Your father said, "That's my daughter!"'

'I did.' Dad nods drunkenly.

'He did.' Tarkie regards me solemnly. 'What does it feel like, being famous, Becky? Fame!' he suddenly sings loudly. For a dreadful moment I think he's going to start singing the *Fame* song and dancing on the table, but he clearly doesn't know the rest, so he just sings 'Fame!' again.

'Drink your coffee,' I say, but less sternly than before. I feel quite mollified by their interest. You see? *They* get it. *They* realize I'm famous. 'It feels . . . well, I suppose I've got used to it now.' I shrug carelessly. 'I mean, obviously life will never be the same . . .'

'You're one of them.' Dad nods sagely. 'She's one of them.' He turns to Tarkie, who nods back. 'She mingles with the famous people. Tell me who you've met, darling.'

'Heaps of people,' I say, basking in their admiration. 'I hang out loads with Sage, and I met Lois, obviously, and . . . er . . .' Who was that ancient guy at the benefit? 'I met Dix Donahue, and I've got April Tremont's phone number, she's in that sitcom *One of Them*, and—'

'Dix Donahue!' Dad's face has crinkled up with delight. 'Now, he's a big name. One of the greats. Your mother and I used to watch him every week.'

'We got on really well,' I boast. 'We chatted for ages. He was such a nice man.'

'Did you get his autograph for me?' Dad's face is all lit up with excitement. 'Show me the book, love. It must be full by now!'

It's as if something cold trickles down my back. Dad's auto-graph book. Shit. *Dad's autograph book*. I'd forgotten all about that. I don't even know where it is. Still in a suitcase some-where? I haven't given it one single thought since I arrived in LA.

'I . . . um . . .' I rub my nose. 'Actually, I didn't get his autograph, Dad. It . . . it wasn't the right time to ask. I'm sorry.'

'Oh.' Dad looks crestfallen. 'Well, you know best, Becky. Whose autographs have you got?'

'I haven't . . . actually . . . got any.' I swallow. 'I thought I'd get to know the place first.' I make the mistake of looking at Dad, and I can see from his face that he knows I'm lying. 'But I will!' I add hastily. 'I'll get loads! I promise.'

I get to my feet and start stacking plates from the dish-washer, trying to fill the silence in the kitchen. Dad doesn't speak. At last I dart another look at him, and he's just sitting there, his face craggy with disappointment. Tarquin seems to have fallen asleep with his head on the table, so it's only me and Dad, not saying anything.

I feel all prickly with guilt and resentment and frustration as

I crash the plates into their piles. Why does everyone keep making me feel *bad* about stuff? At last Dad draws in breath and looks up at me.

'Becky, love, there's something I'd like to say—'

'Sorry, Dad,' I cut him off. 'I need to go and check on the children. I'll be back in a while, OK?'

I cannot face one of Dad's Little Talks. Not right now. I head upstairs and tuck all the children in, then lurk in Minnie's darkened room for a long while, sitting with my head against her cot bars, listening to her twirly-ballerina music box.

I don't want to see Dad. I don't want to see Luke, either. Where's Suze? I try her number, but her phone's switched off. In the cot, Minnie gives one of her sleepy snuffles and turns over, sucking her rabbit, all cosy under the covers. I eye her enviously. Life is so simple for her.

Maybe I can fake some autographs in Dad's book. Yes! Genius idea. I'll pretend I bumped into a load of famous people at the filming. Maybe I could even forge Dix Donahue's signature. I mean, Dad will never know the difference, will he? I'll fill his books with autographs and he'll be happy and it'll all be good.

Feeling better, I switch on Minnie's night light and reach for *Each Peach Pear Plum*. It's one of my favourite books. I'll read this, and perhaps *Guess How Much I Love You* too, and then I'll go and check on my notes for the filming tomorrow. It's a 6 a.m. call, so I need to get an early night.

And on the plus side, I'm totally prepared for the show. I've made about twenty pages of notes, with pictures and mood boards and everything. I've worked on every single fashion story I can think of, so I'll be able to talk, whatever pieces they've chosen. Just thinking about it makes my stomach flutter. I mean, it's *Breakfast Show USA*! It's going to be huge! My career will be launched! And *then* everyone will see.

GREENLAND ENDEAVORS
... where challenge and adventure meet inspiration ...

OFFICIAL REPORT

Client: **Danny Kovitz**
Subject: **Medical Emergency/Airlift**

The client began to exhibit signs of distress early on Monday. Despite encouragement from the Team Leader and other team members, he finally stopped skiing, threw down his pack, and began sobbing. The client was airlifted at 15.00 hours, and taken to Base Camp on Kulusuk.

A full medical examination was undertaken and the client was found to be in good health, with no signs of frostbite or respiratory disorder. However, the client was in significant mental distress. Nurse Gill Johnson observed him for three hours, during which time she noted down the following remarks: 'My toes have gone'; 'My fingers will have to be amputated'; 'My lungs have frozen'; 'I have snowblindness'; 'Why me?'; 'I'm ebbing away'; 'Tell the world I was brave at the end'. Despite her reassurances, he remained convinced for several hours that he was about to die.

The client subsequently enjoyed a substantial meal, viewed several episodes of *America's Next Top Model* on the sanatorium TV, and slept a comfortable night before being transported the following day to Reykjavik and thence to New York.

Greg Stein
Team Leader

From: Kovitz, Danny
To: Kovitz, Danny
Subject: **don't know how i survived**

---

dearest friends

despite my best endeavors my trek across the ice sheet ended
prematurely when, against my own wishes, i was airlifted to safety. i
wanted to continue but was told by the team leader that to do so
would endanger myself and the others. you will be shocked to hear I
was <u>near death</u>.

i feel heartache at leaving the expedition but i will always
remember the soaring landscape and will recreate this in a series of
winter white dresses for my next a/w collection, it will be called ice
and pain and will use textured quilted fabrics with raw bone, nb
tristan, plse have list of raw bone sources ready for my return.

i am now, on medical advice, checking in to a place of rest and
recuperation. you can send flowers and presents to me via my new
york office.

kisses

danny xxx

EIGHTEEN

They weren't interested in any of my notes. They didn't even have any clothes in the studio. We didn't talk about fashion at all. I'm sitting in the limo, numb with shock, driving away from the studios with Aran. How did that happen?

At first it all seemed perfect. The limo arrived at 6 a.m., and Jeff 'secured' it, while I posed for pictures taken by Lon and all his friends, who were yelling 'Becky! Beckeeee!' I was wearing my exclusive Danny Kovitz dress with a little shrug over it, and I felt just like a top-notch celebrity. Then we whizzed off to the studios, and I had my make-up done next to Ebony-Jane Graham, who is totally famous if you watch weight-loss programmes.

The host was called Marie and she was very smiley with enormous pearls. (And also a fairly enormous bottom, only you don't see that as she sits on the sofa the whole time.) I was all set to start filming at 7.20, and I was dying of excitement, except my one niggle was: where were the clothes? When I asked the assistant producer, she just looked at me blankly and said, 'You're on to talk about Lois, right?' There wasn't time to protest because she bustled me on to the set, where I found not just Marie, but a kleptomania expert called Dr Dee.

Even then, I didn't realize. I kept thinking, 'They'll ask me about styling soon. Maybe the clothes are on-screen. Maybe some models will appear, wearing the latest outfits.'

I was so *stupid*. The segment started, and Marie read out an introduction all about Lois and Sage, and then she turned to me and said, 'So, Becky. Let's go back to basics.'

'Absolutely!'

I beamed at her, and was about to explain that this season's trends are all about clean lines and playful accessories, when she continued, 'You were actually in the shop when Lois – for whatever reason, and we'll go into that later with Dr Dee – shoplifted some items. Could you relive that moment for us?'

I stumbled through some awkward account of seeing Lois take the socks, and then she asked me about the awards, and then she turned to Dr Dee and said, 'So, Dr Dee. Why does an A-list movie star like Lois Kellerton turn to crime?'

And that was it. My part was over. Dr Dee talked endlessly about self-esteem and childhood issues, blah blah (I tuned out), and then the segment was finished. Not one fashion reference. Not one mention of me being a stylist. They didn't even ask me who the diamanté clutch bag was by.

'So.' Aran looks up from his phone and smiles his Hollywood smile. 'That went well.'

'Went *well*?' I echo in disbelief. 'It was awful! I thought I was going to be styling clothes! I made all these notes, and I was all prepared, and it was supposed to launch me as a stylist . . .'

'OK.' Aran looks at me blankly, then shrugs. 'But it was great exposure. We'll build up to the styling thing.'

Build up to it?

'You said it would be a styling segment,' I say as politely as I can. 'That's what you told me.'

I don't want to be a diva. I know Aran's really helping me and everything. But he did promise styling. He did promise clothes.

'Sure.' He's got that blank look again, as though he's already tuned out what I just said. 'So, we'll work on that. Now, I have a couple of new offers, one of which is huge. *Huge.*'

'Really?' I can't help feeling hopeful.

'You see? I told you you'd be the queen of the moment. The first thing is a nice invitation to the *Big Top* premiere tomorrow. They want you to do the red carpet.'

'Do the red carpet?' I feel a sudden glittery excitement. 'Like . . . do interviews?'

'Sure. I think you should do it.'

'Of course I'll do it!' I say in elation. 'I can't wait!'

I'm going to do the red carpet at a premiere! Me! Becky! In my own right! 'What's the other thing?'

'This is shit-hot, totally confidential.' He nods at his phone. 'I should not even be sharing this with you.'

'Really?' I feel fresh sparks of excitement. 'What is it?'

'It's reality. But it's a whole new *breed* of reality.'

'Right.' I feel a bit hesitant at the word 'reality', but I'm not going to give that away. 'Cool!' I say determinedly. 'That sounds fab!'

'What it is—' He interrupts himself. 'OK, it's not for the squeamish. But you're not squeamish, are you, Becky?'

'No! Definitely not!'

Oh God. Please don't say he wants me to go on a show where you have to eat bugs. I can't eat a worm. I *can't*.

'I didn't think you were.' He flashes that smile at me again. 'What this show is about is aesthetic improvement. The working title is *Even More Beautiful*. Each celebrity will have a mentor in the form of another celebrity, and that mentor will carefully guide a process of aesthetic alteration. The American public will follow each process and vote on the result. Obviously medical professionals are on hand to consult at all times,' he adds blithely.

I blink at him, not sure if I heard right.

'Aesthetic alteration?' I say at last. 'You mean, plastic surgery?'

'It's a pioneering show.' Aran nods. 'Super-exciting, huh?'

'Yes!' I say automatically, although I can't quite get my head around this. 'So . . . I'd decide what kind of plastic surgery some celebrity has and then it gets voted on? But what if I get it wrong?'

Aran is shaking his head.

'We see you as one of the celebrity participants who would *undergo* the journey. You would be assigned a celebrity mentor who would aim to make you the most beautiful swan. Not that you're not already a swan,' he adds charmingly. 'But everyone can do with a little improvement, right?' He twinkles. 'The surgery alone would be worth thousands, together with the fee and the prime-time exposure ... like I said, it's a great opportunity.'

My head is spinning. He can't be serious.

'You want me to have plastic surgery?' I falter.

'Believe me, this is going to be the biggest TV show ever to hit our planet,' says Aran confidently. 'When I tell you who's already signed up . . .' He winks. 'Let's just say, you will be in stellar company.'

'I'll . . . I'll think about it.'

I stare out of the window, feeling dazed. Plastic surgery? Luke would be absolutely— Oh God. I can't even *tell* Luke about this. There's no way I'm doing it.

'Aran.' I turn back. 'Listen. I don't think . . . I mean, I know it's a great opportunity and everything—'

'Sure. You think it's grotesque. You're shocked I even asked.' Aran twinkles again. He opens a box of gum and offers me some and I shake my head. 'Becky, you want a shortcut to fame? This is your quickest route.'

'But—'

'I'm not telling you what to do, I'm just giving you the information. Think of me as your GPS. There are slow routes and there are quick routes to fame. Appearing on this show would be a super-fast route.' He tips three pellets of gum into his mouth. 'Now, if you don't like the *look* of the super-fast route, that's another story.'

He's so matter-of-fact. He's so detached. As I survey his smooth, immaculate face, I feel more confused than ever.

'You said I was hot already. You said my profile had gone

through the roof. So why do I need to do a reality show?'

'Becky, you don't *do* anything,' Aran says bluntly. 'You're not on a TV show. You're not dating a celebrity. If Lois pleads guilty there won't even be a court case. If you want to stay out there, you need to be out there.'

'I want to be out there, *styling*.'

'Well then, style.' He shrugs. 'But that is not the super-fast route, I can tell you.'

The car pulls up in my drive and he leans over to kiss me lightly on each cheek. 'Ciao, ciao.'

I get out, followed by Jeff, and the car drives off, but I don't approach the house. I go and sit on a low wall, thinking hard and chewing my lip. I let my thoughts simmer down into a decision, then determinedly pull out my phone and jab in a number.

'Becky?' comes Sage's sleepy voice down the phone. 'Is that you?'

'Listen, Sage, are you going to the *Big Top* premiere tomorrow? Only I'd love to put an outfit together for you. Remember, you said you wanted me to style you? Remember we were talking about it?'

'Oh.' Sage yawns. 'Sure.'

'So . . . are you going to the premiere? Can I dress you?'

I'm crossing my fingers tightly. *Please say yes, please say yes . . .*

'I guess so.'

'Great!' I exhale in relief. 'Fantastic! Well, I'll put some looks together. I'll call you later.'

As I head into the house, my spirits are higher. So what if the interview today wasn't brilliant? I've taken charge. I'm styling Sage Seymour. I'm doing the red carpet. Everything's coming together!

I can hear Luke in the kitchen, and my stomach gives a twinge of apprehension. I haven't spoken properly to Luke since yesterday. He came to bed after I'd fallen asleep, and I left him dozing when I got up for the TV show. So we haven't seen each other since our row.

No, not *row*. Discussion.

'Why don't you sit there for now,' I say to Jeff, and point to one of the big chairs in the hall. 'I guess Mitchell's patrolling the garden.'

'You got it,' says Jeff, in that expressionless way he has, and settles his huge frame down on the chair. I take a deep breath, then saunter into the kitchen, humming, like someone who's totally OK with everything, and didn't have a tense moment with their husband last night.

'Hi!' My voice is a little too high-pitched.

'Hi.' Luke looks up from some document in a plastic binder. 'How was the interview?'

'It was . . . good. How's things with you?'

'How's things?' Luke gives a short, humourless laugh. 'To be honest, things have been better.'

'Really?' I look at him in alarm. 'What's up?'

'I *thought* that wretched Sage was up to something and now, sure enough, I discover that she is.'

'Oh really?' I say, my heart pumping a little faster. 'Um, what?'

'Both of them. Sage and Lois.' He glances at the door. 'Shut that, will you? I don't want your goons hearing.'

I do as he says, my mind working quickly. What's he found out? How did he find out?

'They staged the whole thing. The whole feud, the stealing, the row at the awards . . . Fake. The whole lot of it.'

'No!' I exclaim, trying my best to sound shocked. 'You're joking!'

'Aran discovered it last night. We're meeting later on. Obviously this goes no further—' He breaks off and his dark eyes suddenly narrow. 'Wait a minute. Becky?'

'Er . . . yes?' I falter. He comes right up near and eyes me closely. I can feel my cheekbones quivering under his scrutiny. And my lips. I think my hair is shaking, too.

'Becky?' he says again, and I feel a horrible sense of foreboding.

Oh *God*. The thing about Luke is, he knows me really, really

311

well. How am I ever supposed to keep anything from him?

'You knew?' he says at last. 'You *knew* about this?' He seems so scandalized that I gulp inwardly.

'Kind of. I mean, I only found out yesterday afternoon.'

'And you didn't tell me? Even when I asked you directly?'

'I couldn't! I mean, Sage said . . . I promised her . . .'

I trail off feebly. Luke doesn't just look angry, he looks hurt. And weary. He looks like he's had enough, I think with a lurch. But enough of what? Of Hollywood? Of me?

'Don't worry, I get it,' he says, sounding tired. 'You rate your loyalty to Sage above your loyalty to me. That's fine. I know where I stand.'

'No!' I say in dismay. 'That's not . . . I just . . .' Again I trail off, twisting my fingers miserably. I can't find the words. Maybe there aren't any words, except the ones I don't want to say because he'll think I'm shallow, which I'm *not*.

Well, OK, maybe I am. A little bit. But then, everyone in Hollywood is shallow. I mean, compared to lots of people here, I'm deep. I'm profound! Doesn't he realize that?

'They've been really clever,' I say at last. 'You have to admit that. Lois thought up the whole thing. No one has any idea.'

'I think you'll find they've been less clever than you think,' says Luke dryly. 'When this gets out, neither the press nor the public will be very impressed.'

'Maybe it won't get out.'

Even as I'm saying it, I know I'm being naive. Everything gets out.

'It'll get out. And then I think they'll both have even more trouble finding the kind of work they want.' Luke shakes his head. 'Becky, I have to tell you, I won't be working with Sage any longer than I have to. I'll wrap up our work properly, stay professional – but it's over. There's no point my advising some-one who's going to ignore everything I say. I've never met anyone so unprincipled, so capricious, so *stupid* . . . And I'd advise you not to get too mixed up with her either. She won't do you any favours.'

'Yes she will!' I say, hotly. 'She's my friend! She's my—'

'Your passport to fame and fortune. I get it.'

'It's not "fame and fortune",' I say, over-defensively. 'It's my *work*. It's my *career*. I'm styling her for a premiere. It's my big chance! Aran says—'

'Aran doesn't love you.' He cuts me off again, this time so fiercely that I take a step back in shock. 'I do. I love you, Becky. I *love* you.'

His eyes are only inches away from mine. And as I gaze into their dark depths, it's as though I can see our whole life together. I can see Minnie being born. Our wedding at my parents' house. Luke whirling me on the dance floor in New York. My Denny and George scarf.

I don't know what he can see in my eyes, but he's gazing just like me, unblinking, as though he's trying to drink me in.

'I love you,' he says again, more quietly. 'And I don't know what's gone wrong here, but . . .'

I feel suddenly close to tears, which is just stupid.

'Nothing's gone wrong,' I say, gulping. '*Nothing*.'

'OK. Well.' He shrugs and moves away. There's a flat silence which seems to weigh on my shoulders. I can't bear it. Why doesn't he understand?

Then Luke turns, and there's a new animation in his face.

'Becky, listen. I have to go back to London for a few days. It's the Treasury stuff I told you about. I'm flying tomorrow. Why don't you come? We could pull Minnie out of pre-school, spend some time together, regroup, talk things over, have breakfast at the Wolseley . . .'

I feel a little pang. He knows breakfast at the Wolseley is one of my favourite things in the world. 'If your mother would have Minnie for the night, we could even take a room at the Ritz,' he adds, his eyes twinkling. 'How about that?'

The Ritz is where we spent our first ever night together. It's a fabulous idea. I have a sudden vision of us waking up in some beautiful, luxurious bed, all relaxed and content, as though none of these arguments had ever happened. Luke has put his hands on my shoulders. He gently pulls me towards him and his hands travel down my back.

'Maybe we could make that little sibling for Minnie,' he says, in that soft growly voice that normally makes me go weak. 'So, shall I book three tickets for tomorrow?'

'Luke . . .' I gaze up at him, agonized. 'I can't. I just can't. It's this premiere, and I've said I'll dress Sage, and it's my—'

'I know.' Luke exhales sharply. 'Your big chance.' I can see him making a supreme effort to stay good-natured. 'OK, another time.' He steps away and my skin feels cold where he's let go of it. I wish he'd hold me again. I wish the premiere wasn't tomorrow. I wish . . .

Oh God, I don't *know* what I wish.

'Anyway, there's my father to think about,' I point out, relieved to have another reason to grab on to. 'I can't just leave him with no warning.'

'Fair enough.' Luke has retreated into his detached, every-day mood. 'Oh, I meant to tell you. Your mother called me. She asked what's going on. Apparently you didn't ring her back yesterday?'

I feel another guilty twinge. My mum's left so many messages on my phone, I can't keep track of them any more.

'I'll call her. She's just stressing about my dad. She can't stop.'

'Well, she's got a point,' says Luke dryly. 'What's up with your father? Why is he here, anyway? Have you got to the bottom of it?'

'Not yet,' I admit. 'I haven't had a chance to talk to him.'

'You haven't had a chance?' says Luke incredulously. 'He's staying with us, for God's sake!'

'I've been really busy!' I say, stung. 'I had my filming this morning, and I had to prepare for it, and I've got to put together some looks for Sage now . . . I've been frantic. And it doesn't help that he went out with Tarquin and got drunk! They made no sense at all when they got in last night.'

'Well, I'd talk to him when you have a chance.'

'I will. I'm totally planning to. Is he here?'

Luke shakes his head. 'I haven't seen him. Or Tarkie. They must have gone out.' He glances at his watch. 'I must get some things ready. See you later.' He kisses me briefly and heads out. I slump into a chair, feeling totally and utterly deflated.

So far, today has been pretty much the *opposite* of what I hoped. I thought I'd do an amazing TV interview. I thought I'd arrive back from the studios in clouds of glory. I thought Luke would be waiting, proud and beaming, maybe toasting me with champagne. My phone bleeps with a text and I reach for it despondently. It's probably Luke saying, **And by the way, your outfit looked crap, too.**

But it's not from Luke. It's from Elinor.

I sit bolt upright, my heart suddenly beating fast. *Elinor*. I open the text and read the message:

Dear Rebecca, I have arrived in Los Angeles.

Oh my God. She's here? Already?

A moment later, a whole load more text appears:

I look forward to my meeting with Luke and I trust you have prepared the ground with him. Perhaps you could contact me at your earliest convenience. I am staying at the Biltmore. Kind regards, Elinor Sherman.

That's *so* Elinor. She writes texts as though she's using a quill pen on parchment.

I read the message through a few more times, trying not to panic. It's fine. It's all fine. I can handle this. In fact, this is good timing. This could be the answer to everything. Luke and I need to clear the air; Luke and Elinor need to clear the air; everyone needs to clear the air. We need one big honest, cathartic session, and then everyone will be a lot happier.

Maybe this will even bring me and Luke together. He'll realize that I *do* care about more than being on the red carpet. He'll realize that, all this time, I've been thinking about his welfare and happiness. And then he'll be sorry for calling me

315

shallow. (OK, maybe he didn't actually call me shallow. But he thought it, I know he did.)

I haven't prepared any ground with Luke, but how can I? If I mention Elinor's name he just shuts down. The best thing is just to get them in the same room and lock the door. That's what you do with interventions: you take people by surprise.

What I *have* done is write a letter. Because that's the other thing you do with interventions. You write down all the ways in which the individual is hurting you by their behaviour, and you read it out and they say, 'My God, *now* I understand,' and immediately give up alcohol/drugs/rifts with family members. (Well, that's the idea.)

I'll buy some candles and some calming room spray, and . . . what else? Maybe we should all chant first. I did a brilliant chanting class at Golden Peace, except I never quite learned what words we were supposed to be saying. So I usually just chanted 'Pra-daaaaa . . .' over and over. No one seemed to notice.

And maybe I should coach Elinor. Because if she arrives and gives Luke that icy look and says, 'You need a haircut,' then we might as well not bother.

I consider for a moment, then type a reply:

Dear Elinor, I will be glad to meet you later today. Perhaps we could have tea together before seeing Luke in the evening. Shall we say 3 p.m.?

I've sent it before I realize that I have no idea where to have tea in LA. In London it's easy. You can't move for teapots and silver tiered plate stands and scones with cream slathered on them. But in LA?

I think for a second then text Aran:

Do you know the best place to have afternoon tea in LA?

Immediately his reply pings back:

Sure. The Purple Tea Room. Latest place. Always booked up. Shall I get you a reservation?

After a few more texts it's all set up. I'm meeting Elinor at 3 p.m. and we'll talk everything through. And then she'll come here to see Luke at 7 p.m., and I guess we'll take it from there.

The trouble with Luke is, he's so stubborn. He's decided he hates his mother and that's it. But if he only *knew*. If he'd only give her a *chance*. Elinor may have done all kinds of terrible things when he was growing up, but while we were planning his birthday party I saw how much she regrets it. I saw how much she wants to make amends. I even saw how much she loves him, in her own chilly, Vulcan weirdo way. And the thing is, she won't live for ever, will she? Does Luke really want to be estranged from his own flesh and blood?

As I'm gazing through the kitchen window, Suze's car turns into the drive, and I watch her park carefully under a tree. Thank God. Suze will help me. I haven't seen Suze properly for ages, I realize. I've missed her. What's she been up to? Where was she last night?

I'm about to yell 'Suze!' out of the kitchen window when, to my surprise, the front passenger door opens and two long legs in capri leggings emerge, followed by a sinewy body and unmistakable blonde hair.

I stare, discomfited. It's Alicia. What's Suze doing with Alicia?

Suze is just in jeans and a black top, but as usual, Alicia is wearing an amazing yoga outfit. There are slits in the side of her orange top and I can see her tanned, lean torso. Urgh. She's such a show-off. The two are talking earnestly. Then to my horror, Suze leans forward and gives Alicia a big hug. Alicia is patting her back and seems to be talking soothingly. I feel outraged at the sight. In fact, I almost feel sick. Suze and Alicia Bitch Long-legs? Hugging each other? How *can* she?

Suze turns and heads towards the house, and a moment later I hear her key in the lock.

'Suze!' I call, and I hear her turn her footsteps towards the kitchen.

'Oh, hi.' She stands in the doorway, but doesn't rush up or smile, or anything normal. She looks strained. She's clutching on to the door frame and I can see the tendons in her hand standing out.

'How was the TV?' she says, as though she really couldn't care less. 'Are you even more famous now?'

'It was fine. Suze, where on earth have you been? Were you out last night with Alicia?'

'Yes I was – but why do you care?' she says, with a taut little smile. 'If you're lonely, why not hang out with Sage? Or you must have some celebrity event you should be at, surely?'

'Don't be like that!' I say, feeling hurt. 'I need you. Guess what's happened. Elinor's arrived, and I've got to stage my intervention, and I'm not nearly ready, and—'

'Bex, I really don't care.' Suze cuts me off roughly. 'I have other things to worry about. In fact, I'm just here to pick up a couple of things and then I have to go.' She turns on her heel and I hurry after her.

'Where are you going?' I demand, following her up the stairs.

'To Golden Peace.'

'Is that why you're with Alicia?' I try not to let myself sound resentful, but I can't help it. 'I saw you with her. I saw her hugging you.'

'I expect you did.'

'You were hugging Alicia Bitch Long-legs? On *purpose*?'

'That's right.' Again, Suze couldn't sound less interested. She grabs a jacket and puts it in her tote bag, followed by a set of notes that look like they're in Tarquin's handwriting. 'OK, I'm off.' She pushes past me and strides out of the room.

I stare after her, mortified. She's behaving as though I don't exist. What's wrong?

'Suze!' I run down the stairs behind her. 'Listen. What time will you be back? Because I'd really like to talk. Things haven't been great with Luke, and now Elinor's here, and it's going to be really tricky, and I'm just feeling a bit—'

'Things haven't been great with Luke?' She wheels round, her blue eyes suddenly blazing with anger, and I take a step back in alarm. 'You know what, Bex? Things haven't been great with Tarquin, either! But you weren't interested in that, were you? So why should I be interested in your stupid problems?'

For a moment I'm too shocked to reply. She looks livid. In fact, she looks in a terrible state. Her eyes are bloodshot, I now notice. Has something happened that I don't know about?

'What are you talking about?' I say anxiously.

'I'm talking about the fact that he's been taken away from me by that evil man,' she says, trembling. 'I'm talking about the fact that he's been brainwashed.'

She's not still on about that, is she?

'Suze,' I say as patiently as I can. 'Bryce's not evil—'

'You don't get it, Bex!' Suze explodes. 'They've fired him!'

'*What?*' I gape at her.

'The wellbeing committee think he's introduced unhealthy practices into Golden Peace. They're really worried. They want Tarkie to come into Golden Peace and tell them what's been going on in all those one-to-one sessions. I'm going to see an expert on cults today. He's going to advise me. I'm on my way there right now with Alicia. She's been totally supportive and brilliant,' she adds tremulously. 'In fact, it was Alicia who alerted her husband and pushed for Bryce to get fired.'

I'm speechless with shock. My head's spinning with all this new information. Bryce fired? Alicia brilliant? Tarquin *brainwashed*?

'Suze,' I falter at last. 'Suze, I had no idea—'

'Of course you didn't,' she says with an edge which makes me flinch. 'You were too busy choosing clutch bags.'

'That was for work,' I say defensively. 'It wasn't fun!'

'Oh, yes, *work*. I forgot.' She sounds even more scathing. 'Your super new career which we all have to tiptoe around because you're famous. Well, I hope you're enjoying your dream, Becky. I'll just get on with sorting out my nightmare.' She reaches for her car keys, her hands shaking.

'Suze!' I say in horror. 'Wait! Look, let's have a cup of tea . . .'

'It's beyond a cup of tea!' she almost shrieks. 'Don't you get that? No, of course you don't. Luckily I had Alicia. She's been amazing. So helpful and so kind . . .' Suze's voice gives a sudden wobble. 'I knew something was wrong, I *knew* it . . .'

I gaze at Suze, stricken. I've never felt so bad in all my life. This is all my fault. I introduced Tarquin to Golden Peace, I didn't listen when Suze was worried . . .

'I'm so sorry . . .' I swallow. 'I didn't realize . . . Suze, whatever I can do to help I'll do . . .' I move forward to give her a hug, but she bats me off.

'I have to go. Alicia's waiting.'

'Where's Tarkie?'

'I don't know. With Bryce, I should think. Being told a load of vile rubbish.' She opens the front door but I jam a foot across it.

'Suze, please,' I say desperately. 'Tell me. What can I do?'

Suze surveys me silently, and for one hopeful moment I think she's going to relent and treat me like her oldest, best friend again. But then, with a weary sigh, she shakes her head.

'No, Bex. You deal with your problems. I'll deal with mine.'

She's gone. I peep through the little side window, staying out of sight. I can see her hurrying to the car. I can see her face relaxing as she calls something to Alicia. My throat is tight and there's a hotness in my chest.

The car moves off down the drive and I press my head against the window, breathing a cloud on to the glass. What's happening to my life? Ever since that awards evening when everything kicked off, I've felt like I'm living in a kaleidoscope. It's whizzing around, making different patterns every moment, and as soon I get used to one, it shifts again. Why can't things stay the same for *just one second*?

The electric gates are slowly shutting. The car's gone. My heart feels full to bursting, except I'm not sure what it's most full of: stress about Luke, worry for Tarkie, longing for Suze to come back, or hatred for Alicia. Because I don't care what Suze says – I don't believe Alicia's changed. She plays games. If she's being nice and supportive to Suze now, it's only because she wants to damage her in some way later. She's got some poisonous plan up her sleeve, I know it. And Suze trusts her more than me . . . Suze likes her more than me . . .

Tears are welling up in my eyes and one suddenly trickles down my nose. Another is following it as my phone rings, and I hastily wipe them both away as I answer.

'Aran! Hi! How are you?'

'Hey, babe,' comes his easy voice. 'I hear you're styling Sage for the *Big Top* premiere. Congratulations, that's pretty big!'

'Thanks!' I try to sound as bright as I can. 'I'm so excited!'

'Did you tell Luke? Is he psyched?'

'Kind of,' I say after a pause.

Not only is he not psyched, I want to say miserably, he isn't even a tiny bit proud. He thinks I should fire the bodyguards. He won't eat grain soup. He doesn't want to be an A-lister. I mean, if you don't want to be an A-lister, why come to Hollywood in the first place?

'Well, guess who wants to meet you at the premiere? Nenita Dietz.'

'No!' I gasp. 'Nenita Dietz has heard of me?'

In spite of everything, my spirits rocket up. I spent that whole stupid studio tour trying to find Nenita Dietz. And now she's trying to find me!

'Of course she's heard of you.' Aran laughs. 'We'll set up a meeting, a photo opportunity on the red carpet, maybe you guys can chat at the party . . . How does that sound?'

'Amazing!' I breathe.

As I ring off I feel heady. Me and Nenita Dietz on the red carpet. Making friends and talking fashion. I couldn't even have *dreamed* that.

'Hey, guess what?' I call out, before I realize that there's no one to hear me. A moment later, Jeff appears around the door.

'You OK?' he says.

'I'm going to meet Nenita Dietz!' I say. 'On the red carpet! *She's* asked to meet *me*. Do you know how important she is?' Jeff's face is blank, but I can see his eyes reading my expression for clues.

'Awesome,' he says at last, and nods. He disappears again, and I quell a feeling of disappointment that he wasn't more excited. No one's proud of me, not even my bodyguard. Another tear suddenly rolls down my cheek and I brush it away impatiently. This is stupid. *Stupid*. Life is great. Why am I feeling like this?

I'll call Mum. The solution hits me out of the blue. Of course. Mum will make me feel better. I should have thought of this ages ago. And I can reassure her about Dad, too. It's evening in the UK. Perfect. I lean back in my chair, dialling the number, and as I hear her familiar voice answering, I feel a relief all over my body.

'Mum! How are you? Listen, I'm styling Sage for a premiere tomorrow! And I'm meeting Nenita Dietz! She especially called Aran to say she wanted to meet me! Can you believe it?'

'That's lovely, Becky.' Mum sounds tense and distracted. 'Listen, darling, where's Dad? Can I speak to him?'

'He's out at the moment. I'll get him to call you back.'

'Well, where is he?' I hear a shrill of alarm in her voice. 'Where's he gone? Becky, you said you'd keep an eye on him!'

'I *am* keeping an eye on him!' I retort, a bit impatiently. Honestly, what does she expect, that I stalk my own father? 'He's been out with Tarquin, Mum. They've really bonded. It's so sweet. Yesterday they went out sightseeing and had supper together and—' I break off just before I say 'got drunk'. 'They had a good time,' I amend. 'Mum, you mustn't worry.'

'But what's this all *about*? Why did he suddenly fly to LA?' She still sounds distressed. 'Have you found out? What's he said to you, love?'

I feel a huge twinge of guilt. I should have made more time to talk to Dad yesterday. I really should. And I should have got those autographs for him. I feel terrible about that.

'He hasn't said *that* much,' I admit. 'But we'll have a big old talk tonight. I promise. I'll wheedle it out of him.'

As I put the phone down ten minutes later, I feel both better and worse. Better, because it's always good to talk to Mum. But worse, because I can see how I've let things unravel. I've been too distracted. I should be more on the case with Dad . . . I should have been there for Suze . . . I close my eyes, burying my face in my palms. Everything feels painful and wrong. I've messed up in all directions, all at once, and I didn't even realize I was doing it, and now I don't know where to start to put things right . . . What am I going to *do* . . .?

For what seems like ages I simply sit there, letting my thoughts whirl around and gradually settle. Then, full of determination, I grab a piece of paper from the kitchen notepad, and write a heading: *Resolutions*. I'm going to make my life work for me. I'm not going to let it whirl around like a kaleidoscope any more. It's *my* life, which means *I* get to choose how it goes. Even if that means wrestling it to the floor and bashing it on the head and saying, 'Take, that, life!'

I scribble hard for a while, then sit back and look at my list with resolve. It's quite a lot – it'll be a challenge – but I can do it all. I *have* to do it all.

Resolutions:

1. *Bring peace to Luke and Elinor. (Like St Francis.)*
2. *Go on the red carpet and get a million autographs for Dad.*
3. *Come up with perfect outfit for Sage and get hired by Nenita Dietz .*
4. *Make friends with Suze again.*
5. *Save Tarkie from cult.*
6. *Find out reason for Dad's trip and reassure Mum.*
7. *Buy strapless bra.*

OK, so the last one isn't quite as life-changing as the others, but I really do need a new strapless bra.

NINETEEN

By 3 p.m. I'm feeling a lot calmer. I've bought my new bra and I've sent over three dresses, six pairs of shoes and a tuxedo suit for Sage to try on. (I don't think she'll go for the tuxedo suit, but she should. She'd look amazing.) I've also taken Minnie out of pre-school early, and dressed her up in her sweetest smocked pink-lawn frock, with a big sash and puffed sleeves. It has matching pink-lawn knickers, too, and I'm actually quite envious. Why don't grown-up dresses have matching knickers? Everyone would buy them. I might write to a few designers and suggest it.

Jeff has driven us to the Purple Tea Room, which is halfway along Melrose Avenue and has a big hand-painted sign with swirly letters. I help Minnie down from the SUV, shake out her skirts and say, 'See you later, Jeff. I'll call.' Then we head towards the sign and push open the glass-paned door.

Crikey.

OK, so I don't think Aran and I mean quite the same thing by 'afternoon tea'. When I say 'afternoon tea' I mean silver teapots and waitresses in frilly white aprons and tiny cucumber sandwiches. I mean starched tablecloths and maybe a harp playing and Miss Marple-type ladies sitting at the next table.

The Purple Tea Room is nothing like that. For a start there aren't any chairs or tables, only cushions and bean bags and odd-shaped stools made out of wood. The room is big, but it's dimly lit, with candles casting a wavery glow over the walls. There's music playing, but it's Eastern sitar music, and the air smells scented, but not of scones or cinnamon. More of . . .

Well. Hmm. You'd think they'd be more subtle; I mean, this isn't Amsterdam, is it?

Everywhere I look I can see hip young people lying around, sipping at tea cups, typing on Apple Macs and having their feet or shoulders rubbed by what seem to be therapists in baggy Indian trousers. And in the middle of it all is sitting Elinor, bolt upright, wearing her usual stiff bouclé suit and chilly expression. She's perched on a stool in the shape of a mushroom, holding a glass of water and looking around as though she's Queen Victoria and these are the savages. I bite my lip, trying not to giggle. Poor Elinor. She was probably expecting starched tablecloths, too.

She's looking rather pale and wan, but her dark helmet of hair is as immaculate as ever, and her back is ramrod straight.

'Ladeee!' shrieks Minnie as she spots Elinor. 'Mummy!' She turns to me in joy. 'Is *Ladeeee*!' Then she wrenches herself out of my grasp, runs to Elinor and hurls herself affectionately against Elinor's legs. Everyone in the place turns to watch and I can hear a few 'Aaahs'. I mean, whatever you think of Elinor, it's a very sweet sight.

In fact, I can't remember the last time I saw Minnie quite so thrilled. Her whole body is shaking with excitement and her eyes are bright and she keeps glancing up at me as though to share the wondrous moment. Elinor looks pretty delighted to see Minnie, too. Her cheeks have turned a kind of almost-pink and her frozen face has come alive.

'Well, Minnie,' I can hear her saying. 'Well, now, Minnie. You've grown.'

Minnie is delving in Elinor's crocodile-skin bag, and triumphantly produces a jigsaw puzzle. Every time Elinor sees

Minnie, she brings a different jigsaw puzzle, and puts it together while Minnie watches in awe.

'We'll do it together,' says Elinor. 'It's a view of the Wellesley-Baker Building in Boston. My great-grandfather used to own it. Your ancestor, Minnie.' Minnie nods blankly, then turns to me.

'Mummy, Ladeeeee!' Her joy is so infectious that I find myself beaming, and saying, 'Yes, darling! Lady! Isn't that lovely?'

The whole 'Lady' thing began because we had to keep Minnie's meetings with Elinor a secret from Luke, and we couldn't risk her saying, 'I saw Granny Elinor today.'

I mean, they still are secret. This meeting today is secret. And as I watch Minnie and Elinor gazing at each other in delight, I feel a sudden fresh resolve. This rift is stupid and sad and it has to end now. Luke and Elinor have to make up. They have *family* together.

I know Elinor said something tactless, or worse, about Luke's beloved stepmother which he was upset by. (I never got the exact details.) That's how this whole argument began. But life can't be about holding on to the bad things. It has to be about grabbing on to the good things and letting the bad things go. Looking at Elinor as she opens the jigsaw with an ecstatic Minnie, I know she's a good thing. For Minnie, and for me, and for Luke. I mean, she's not perfect, but then, who is?

'Can I offer you some tea?' A drifty girl in a linen apron and baggy white trousers has come up so silently, she makes me jump.

'Oh, yes please,' I say. 'Lovely. Just normal tea for me, thanks. And milk for my daughter.'

'"Normal tea"?' the girl echoes, as though I'm speaking Swahili. 'Did you look at the tea menu?' She nods at a booklet on Elinor's lap which seems to be about forty pages long.

'I gave up,' says Elinor crisply. 'I would like hot water and lemon, please.'

'Let's just have a look . . .' I start to skim through the booklet, but before long my eyes are blurring with type. How can there be so many teas? It's stupid. In England you just have *tea*.

'We have teas for different needs,' says the girl helpfully. 'We have Fennel and Peppermint for digestion, or Red Clover and Nettle for skin complaints . . .'

Skin complaints? I eye her suspiciously. Is she trying to say something?

'The white teas are very popular . . .'

Honestly, tea isn't supposed to be *white*. I don't know what Mum would have to say to this girl. She'd probably produce a Typhoo teabag and say, '*This* is tea, love.'

'Do you have a tea for making life totally brilliant in every way?' I say, just to wind the girl up.

'Yes,' she says, without missing a beat. 'Our Hibiscus, Orange and St John's Wort tea promotes an improved sense of wellbeing through mood enhancement. We call it our happy tea.'

'Oh,' I say, taken aback. 'Well, I'd better have that one, then. Would you like that, Elinor?'

'I do not wish to have my mood enhanced, thank you.' She gives the girl a stern look.

That's a shame. I'd love to see Elinor on happy pills. She might smile properly, for once. Except then she'd probably crack, it occurs to me. White powder would fall from the corners of her lips and suddenly her whole face would disintegrate into plaster dust and whatever else they've patched her up with.

The girl has given our order to a passing guy in what looks like a Tibetan monk's outfit, and now turns back.

'May I offer you a complimentary reflexology session or other holistic therapy?'

'No thanks,' I say politely. 'We just want to talk.'

'We're very discreet,' says the girl. 'We can work with your feet, or your head, or the pressure points in your face . . .'

I can see Elinor recoiling at the very idea. 'I do not wish to be touched,' she says stiffly. 'Thank you.'

'We can work without touching you,' persists the girl. 'We can do a tarot reading, or we have a humming meditation, or we can work with your aura.'

I want to burst into giggles at Elinor's expression. Her aura? Do they mean that chilly cloud of disapproval that follows her around like her own atmosphere?

'I do not possess an aura,' she says, her tones like icicles. 'I had it surgically removed.' She glances sidelong at me and then, to my utter astonishment, she gives the faintest of winks.

Oh my God. Did Elinor just make a joke?

At her own expense?

I'm so gobsmacked I can't speak, and the girl seems a bit nonplussed as well, because she backs away without trying to press any more therapies on us.

Minnie has been surveying Elinor intently throughout all of this, and now Elinor turns to her.

'What is it, Minnie?' she says, uncompromisingly. 'You shouldn't stare at people. Aren't you going to sit down?'

Elinor always talks to Minnie as though she's another adult, and Minnie loves it. Minnie doesn't answer, but leans forward and picks a tiny thread off Elinor's skirt.

'All gone,' she says dismissively, and drops the thread on the floor.

Ha! Ha-di-ha!

How many times has Elinor picked me up for some tiny bit of fluff or speck on my clothes? And now Minnie's got her revenge. Only, Elinor doesn't look remotely put out.

'Thank you,' she says to Minnie gravely. 'The housekeeper at my hotel is somewhat lax.'

'Lax,' agrees Minnie, equally gravely. 'Lax bax . . . *Guess* how much I love you,' she adds inconsequentially.

I know that Minnie's quoting from her bedtime book, but Elinor doesn't – and I'm stunned by her instant reaction. Her cheekbones start to tremble and there's a sheen to her eye.

'Well,' she says in a low voice. 'Well, Minnie.'

It's almost unbearable, watching her tight, chalky-white face struggle with emotion. She puts her lined, beringed hand on Minnie's head and strokes it a few times, as though that's the most she can bring herself to do.

God, I'd love to loosen her up. I should have ordered the

Mind-Altering Tea for Repressed Older Women in Chanel Suits.

'Elinor, we have to reconcile you with Luke,' I say impulsively. 'I want you to be part of the family. Properly. I'm going to stage an intervention at our house and I'm not letting either of you go till you're friends.'

'I don't believe "friends" is the appropriate term,' she says, looking puzzled. 'We are mother and son, not contemporaries.'

OK, this is why she doesn't help herself.

'Yes it is!' I say. 'It's totally appropriate. I'm friends with my mum and you can jolly well be friends with Luke. When I tell him everything you did for the party—'

'No.' Elinor cuts me off, a sudden steel to her voice. 'I have told you, Rebecca. Luke must never know of my involvement.'

'But you did such an amazing thing!' I say in frustration. 'And he thinks it was Suze and Tarkie! It's crazy!'

'He must never know.'

'But—'

'He must never know. I am not buying his love,' she adds, so quietly I can barely hear her.

'Elinor, it's not "buying his love",' I say gently. 'It wasn't just about the money. It was about all the thought and effort you put into it.'

The girl arrives with our drinks, and we're both silent as she arranges teapots, cups, strainers and little sugar crystals on a trolley made out of bamboo. I pour Elinor her hot water and she picks it up without drinking it.

'So, Elinor,' I say, in soft, coaxing tones. 'Will you tell him?'

'No,' she says in final tones. 'And you will not tell him, either. You made me a promise.'

Argh. It's like she's made of granite. This intervention is not going to be an easy matter.

'OK, then. Well, we'll find another way.' I reach in my bag for my 'conflict resolution' notes. I printed them off from Google and they've been quite helpful, except I realized a bit too late they were about conflict resolution in an industrial-action situation. I skim through the pages, trying to find something useful. *Picketing*, no . . . *union representation*, no . . . *Health and Safety Executive*, no . . . *cooperation techniques* . . . ooh, that's more like it. *Win-win negotiating strategy.*

Yes! That's very good. Win-win is exactly what we need. In fact, I'm not sure why anyone would ever choose anything *except* win-win. I mean, why would you opt for lose-lose?

I read the paragraph, and the phrase that keeps popping out is 'common ground'.

'We need to find common ground,' I say, looking up. 'What common ground do you have with Luke?'

Apart from being totally stubborn, I *don't* add.

Elinor looks at me silently. It's as though she hasn't understood the question.

'Charity work,' she says at last.

'OK . . .' I wrinkle my nose dubiously. 'Anything else? Have you ever done anything fun together? You must have done! When he was in New York.'

When I first met Luke, he was really close to Elinor. Unhealthily close, actually, although I'd never say that. I mean, I don't want him to go back to worshipping her, but can't they recapture any of that relationship?

'Did you ever go on holiday together?' I ask with sudden inspiration. 'Did you have any fun times then?'

I have an image of Elinor limbo-dancing at some Caribbean resort while Luke cheers her on, cocktail in hand, and force myself not to giggle.

'We stayed in the Hamptons,' she says after some thought. 'My old friend Dirk Greggory had a beach cottage there. I took Luke on a number of occasions.'

'Great. So, you could reminisce about that . . . maybe plan another trip . . .'

'If we did, it would have to be soon,' says Elinor with asperity. 'Dirk passed away two years ago, and his daughter is selling the beach cottage. A mistake in my opinion, as was the ghastly work she did to the porch—'

'Wait,' I cut her off, my head spinning. 'Wait. So there's a cottage in the Hamptons that you and Luke have happy

330

memories of . . . and it's about to be sold . . . and this is your last chance to go back there? Why didn't you say that in the first place?'

'Brown bear, brown bear,' puts in Minnie, looking up from her milk. 'What do you see?'

'I fail to understand.' Elinor's brow creases as much as it can, i.e. hardly at all.

'What do you see, Mummy?' demands Minnie imperiously. 'What do you seeeeee?'

It's a good thing I know all her little books off by heart.

'A red bird.' I turn back to Elinor. 'This is perfect. You can say that's why you've come to see Luke. He's bound to listen.'

'Red bird, red bird, what do you see?'

'A blue horse.'

'No!' cries Minnie, crashing down her beaker. 'Not blue horse! Yellow duck!'

'OK, yellow duck,' I say, hassled. 'Whatever. Elinor, this is definitely the way to go! Try to remember all the great times you had together and mention them to Luke. Try to find that bond again.'

Elinor looks dubious, and I sigh. If only she'd present herself better. (By which I *don't* mean having immaculate nails and matching shoes.)

'Could you wear something a little less formal tonight?' I suggest. 'And maybe loosen your hair? And talk differently?'

Basically, have a personality transplant, is what I'm really saying.

'Talk differently?' Elinor seems affronted.

'Try repeating this after me.' I lean forward. '"Luke, my love, if we can just spend some time together—"' I break off at Elinor's rigid expression. I can see she isn't going to go for 'Luke, my love'. 'All right, let's try it a different way. You could say, "Luke, my angel . . ."' Her face grows yet more rigid. '"Luke, my sweetheart . . . my darling—"' I break off. 'OK, what *would* you say?'

'Luke, my son,' says Elinor.

'You sound like Darth Vader,' I say bluntly. Elinor doesn't even flinch.

'So be it,' she says, and sips her water.

That is *totally* a Darth Vader thing to say. Next she'll be ordering the destruction of a thousand innocent Jedi younglings.

'Well, do your best.' I reach for my tea, feeling exhausted. 'And I'll do my best. That's all we can do.'

From: Yeager, Mack
To: Brandon, Rebecca
Subject: Re: **Darth Vader**

Dear Rebecca

Thanks for your email.

There are many theories regarding the inspiration for Darth Vader, as outlined in my book *Whence Anakin?*, available from all good bookshops.

Whether he was based on a 'real-life person' as you suggest, and whether that person left 'real-life genes swirling around in the gene pool for anyone to come across', I think doubtful.

In short, I think it unlikely that your mother-in-law is related to Darth Vader.

All my best wishes and may the Force be with you,

Mack Yeager
President, SWGS
STAR WARS GENEALOGY SOCIETY

TWENTY

We've arranged that Elinor will come to the house at 7 p.m., and by ten to seven I'm swigging wine, trying to stay calm. I never knew being a peacemaker would be so nerve-racking. Does the Dalai Lama get this stressed out before he spreads peace throughout the world? Does he apply his lip gloss three times because he's so flustered? (Not very likely, actually.)

At least Minnie went to bed without a fuss, and the older children are happily watching *Wall-E*. The intervention should be over by the time they have to go to bed. Or I suppose it should. How long does an intervention take?

Oh God, why did I ever decide to do this?

On the plus side, the Intervention Room (i.e. kitchen) looks brilliant. I've lit about twenty candles for a mellow, calming atmosphere, and I've got soft music playing and I'm wearing a green dress which is very soothing. At least, it would be soothing if it weren't for the fact that it cost me $280 last week in Intermix and today I saw it marked down to $79.99! They could have warned me. They could have given me some secret sign. That assistant must have been laughing her head off as she wrapped it up.

Anyway. Never mind. Luke doesn't need to know all of that.

The point is, the room is ready and I'm ready and now all we need is for Elinor to arrive. I can't pretend I'm not tense. And I can't pretend the atmosphere isn't tense. I keep glancing at Luke, wondering how he'll react.

He's sitting at the kitchen table, sipping a beer, and his face is resolutely turned away from me. As I look at him, I feel a kind of plunging inside. We aren't right. We aren't *us*. It's not that we've rowed again, it's almost worse. We're not making proper eye contact, and neither of us has mentioned our talk this morning. The only time I've seen Luke smile today was earlier on, when he was on the phone with Gary, his colleague.

Gary is in New York right now but flying back to London tomorrow morning. They were talking about the Treasury meeting and Luke seemed all fired up. He kept dropping in 'Number 10' and 'policy' and I could tell his brain was whizzing with ideas. He kept laughing at things that Gary said, and he seemed in a better mood than he has been for days.

I really, *really* hate to say it . . . but I think the truth is that high finance suits him better than movie stars.

Dad is still out, which I'm a bit relieved about, because he'd only want to join in the intervention and start telling Elinor she'd be a nice-looking girl if she'd get a bit of meat on her bones. And I haven't heard from Suze since I saw her this morning, except for one text asking me to pick up the children from their activity clubs. I know she came back again to the house earlier, because Mitchell told me. Apparently she was still with Alicia and still looking for Tarquin. She went around the house yelling, 'Tarkie! Tarquin, where are you?' and then she drove off again. That's all he had to say about Suze. He then proceeded to give me a full report on all the security breaches he had identified that day (two, both consisting of the little boy next door throwing his Frisbee into our garden).

I think Mitchell will be glad to leave. He was so bored today, he mended our barbecue, which he showed me proudly. I didn't even know it was broken, to be honest. In fact, I must tell Luke.

'By the way, Mitchell mended the barbecue,' I say, awkwardly breaking the silence.

'I was going to do that,' says Luke at once, his jaw tight. 'You didn't have to ask Mitchell.'

'I didn't ask Mitchell! I didn't even know it was broken . . .' I trail off, in slight despair. I've got to get him in a better mood before Elinor arrives.

'Look, Luke . . .' I bite my lip. 'Are we OK?'

There's a pause, then Luke raises his shoulders in a shrug. 'What do you mean?'

'I mean this!' I say in frustration. 'Not looking at each other! Being all prickly!'

'Are you surprised?' says Luke heatedly. 'I've spent the day managing fall-out from Sage and Lois's stunt. A job which might have been easier if I'd known all along that it was a fake.'

'Shhh!' I say, glancing at the open door. 'Jeff might hear!'

'Right at this moment, I couldn't care less who hears,' says Luke curtly.

He looks totally fed up, and I know a lot of it is my fault.

'Luke, I feel really bad for you,' I say, reaching a hand out to his. 'And I'm so sorry. I should have told you about Sage and Lois when you asked. But please look at me.'

Luke takes another slug of beer and finally meets my eyes.

'Becky, life is tricky enough without us having secrets from each other,' he says. 'We should be on the same side.'

'I am on your side!' I say fervently. 'Of course I am. I just wasn't thinking. I've been trying to be independent . . . trying to get my career going . . .'

'I get that.' He sighs. 'And I don't mean we can't be our own people. If you have to spend time out here for your career, then that's what you have to do and we'll make it work.' He gives me a strained smile. 'I can't pretend I look forward to life without you – but if it's really your dream, I'm not going to stand in your way.' He hesitates, spinning the beer bottle round in his fingers, then plants it firmly on the table. 'But we have to be honest with each other. We *have* to, Becky. Honesty is the foundation of everything.'

'I know,' I gulp. 'I know it is.'

Oh God, should I quickly tell him about Elinor coming here tonight? Explain everything? Give him my reasons, tell the whole story, try to make him understand . . .

But it's too late. As I'm drawing breath, the doorbell rings shrilly and I feel a clutch of nerves at my stomach. She's here. Help. She's here.

'I'll go,' I say breathlessly, and make for the door before Luke can move. 'Jeff, I'll go!' I call as I hear his heavy tread coming from the TV room. 'I know who it is!'

I gave Elinor the code for the gate earlier and told Mitchell to put Echo away for the night.

My heart is hammering as I swing open the heavy front door. And there she is. My mother-in-law. The first thing I see is the nervous look in her eye. The second thing I see is the dress. She's in a dress. A wrap dress. Elinor Sherman is wearing a *wrap dress*?

I blink in astonishment. I've never seen Elinor in anything other than a suit, or perhaps a very structured evening gown. Where did she even get this? She must have gone out to buy it specially.

It's not the greatest fit. She's so skinny, it swathes her body a little too loosely. And I wouldn't have chosen that brown and cream print for her. But the point is, she's in it. She made the effort. It's as if she's taken off her armour.

Her hair is different, too. I can't quite work out how, because Elinor's hair has always been a mystery to me. It's not so much hair as a helmet. (Sometimes I even wonder if it's a wig.) But tonight it's looser in some way. Softer.

'You look great!' I whisper, and squeeze her bony hand. 'Well done! OK. Ready?'

As we walk towards the kitchen I feel sick with apprehension, but I force myself to keep going. I can do this. I need to do this. We can't go the rest of our lives with Elinor an outcast.

And we're in. I retrieve the heavy key from the drawer where I've been keeping them safe from Minnie and hastily lock the door. Then I turn to face Luke, breathing hard.

I don't know what I was expecting . . . I don't know what I was hoping . . .

OK, I *do* know what I was hoping. I was secretly hoping that Luke would look up, and his face would turn from shock to rueful understanding to wise acceptance, and he'd say something simple like, 'Mother. It's time for peace. I see that now.' And we wouldn't need the intervention at all.

But that's not what happens. He stares at Elinor in shock, but his expression doesn't change. Or if it does, it gets worse. As he turns to me, shock veers to icy fury. For the first time ever, his expression actually scares me.

'You're joking,' he says, his voice colder than I've ever heard it. 'You're fucking joking.'

'I'm not joking,' I say, my voice trembling.

Luke gazes at me a moment more, then strides to the kitchen door, without even glancing at Elinor.

'I've locked it,' I call after him. 'This is an intervention!'

'A what?' He wheels round, his hand on the door handle.

'An intervention. We have a problem and we need to fix it and we're not leaving this room till we do,' I say more bravely than I feel.

For a while no one moves. Luke has fixed his eyes on mine and it's as though we're having a private, silent conversation. It's as though I can hear his words: *You didn't. You didn't.*

And I'm replying: *I did. I so did.*

At last, Luke swings round to the fridge and pulls out a bottle of wine. He pours a glass and hands it to Elinor, saying abruptly, 'What do you want?'

My heart sinks. He sounds like a sulky toddler.

'She's your mother,' I say. 'Don't speak to her like that.'

'She's *not* my mother,' says Luke harshly.

'I'm *not* his mother,' echoes Elinor, even more harshly, and I see the surprise flash through Luke's eyes.

They're so similar. I mean, that's the irony. They look like

338

they've come out of the same Russian-doll set, standing rigid, their chins tight and their eyes steely with determination.

'I forfeited the right to be your mother many years ago,' Elinor says, more quietly. 'I know that, Luke. But I would like to be Minnie's grandmother. And your . . . friend.' She glances at me and I give her an encouraging nod.

I know how hard this must be for Elinor. It *so* doesn't come naturally. But honestly, with her hair loosened, holding a glass of wine, using the word 'friend', she sounds almost normal. She takes a tentative step towards Luke, and I long for him to see her the way I do. But he's prickling all over with suspicion. He doesn't *want* to see.

'I still don't get it,' he says. 'Why are you here?'

'She's here because this is nuts!' I say, unable to stay quiet. 'You're flesh and blood. You're connected, OK, whether you like it or not. And one day you'll both be dead!'

OK, that just popped out. Not sure where I was going with that.

'We'll both be *dead*?' says Luke disbelievingly. 'Why the hell is that relevant?'

'Because . . .' I flounder for a moment. 'Because you'll be in heaven or floating around in the sky, or wherever, OK?'

Luke raises an eyebrow. 'Floating in the sky.'

'Yes. And you'll look back at your life, and you won't remember any one argument or one hurtful comment, you'll remember the *relationships* you had. You'll see a great big pattern to your life. And your pattern is all wrong, Luke. Don't let one false stitch spoil your pattern.'

Luke doesn't react. Is he even listening?

'Do you realize that by cutting off contact with your mother, you're spoiling Minnie's pattern, too?' I warm to my theme. 'And what about my pattern? You know, life isn't just about your own pattern, Luke. All the patterns weave together, and they make, like, a worldwide web of patterns, like, an *über*-pattern, and—'

'Jesus Christ!' Luke expostulates. 'Enough with the bloody patterns!'

I stare at him, feeling hurt. I was rather proud of my pattern theory. Then, out of the corner of my eye, I see Elinor retreating towards the door. She's not trying to escape, is she?

'Where are you going?' I grab her. 'Tell him about the cottage.'

'Cottage?' Luke manages to make the word 'cottage' sound highly suspicious and sinister. I nudge Elinor to speak. Honestly, these two really don't help themselves.

'Dirk Greggory has died,' says Elinor. 'You were fond of his cottage, I think. It will be possible for us to visit one last time before his daughter sells it. But I will have to let the family know.'

'Oh.' Luke sounds taken aback. 'I see.'

'I have a photograph of you there,' says Elinor to my surprise, and opens her bag.

She produces an ancient-looking crocodile case, and snaps open the stiff clasps. I immediately see an old black-and-white print of some gorgeous-looking man, which Elinor bundles out of view. She leafs past about five more pictures, then removes a photo and hands it to Luke. 'You remember this?'

I peer at the photograph with curiosity and see a younger-looking Luke standing on a wide, sandy beach, dressed in a polo shirt and rolled-up cotton trousers, with bare feet. He's holding a wooden spade and laughing. His hair is longer than it is today, and it's rumpled in the wind. I feel a tiny stab of jealousy. I wish I'd known him then.

Luke gives the photo the barest glance. 'That was a long time ago.'

'You were twenty-three. It feels like only a year or two ago.' Elinor places a different photo on top, without saying anything. This time Elinor is in the shot too. She's wearing *such* a hideous-looking mustard-coloured halterneck and slacks combo, I nearly gasp. But her sunglasses are quite cool, and the setting is amazing. The pair of them are standing on a boat, with nothing but ocean in the background.

'You carry photographs around with you?' I can't help saying incredulously. Elinor immediately looks as though I've tapped into her secret source of weakness.

'A few,' she says, her face closing up. 'On occasion.'

She's like a snail, I think in fascination. Every time you touch her, she retreats. But the point is, snails can be tamed.

Actually, *can* snails be tamed? OK, she's not a snail, she's a ... tortoise. No. A meerkat? No. Oh, fuck knows what she is. The point is, this picture seems to have gripped Luke. I can't tell if he's gazing at the sea or the boat or Elinor's revolting out-fit, but something has got to him.

'Minnie would love it there.' He glances up at me. 'So would you. It's a magical place. The sand, the sea ... You wouldn't believe it.'

'You could easily charter a boat,' puts in Elinor.

'Minnie should learn to sail.' Luke has that gleamy, distant look he gets when he's making plans. 'Becky, you need to learn to sail too.'

Luke's mentioned the whole sailing thing quite a few times in our marriage, and so far I've managed to avoid it.

'Can't wait!' I say brightly.

The oven pings and we all jump. It's as though we've come back to life. For an awful moment I think Luke's going to snap back into his cold, angry self and tell Elinor to leave. But instead he looks up from the photo and surveys each of us in turn. He walks over to the window, heaves a deep sigh and rubs his face with the flat of his hands.

I know it's all going on inside his head. He hates to be rushed; we just have to let him get there. Elinor is following my lead. She's standing absolutely still, barely even breathing.

'Look ... maybe this has gone on long enough,' Luke says at last. 'I'd like to ... start again.'

As the words leave his mouth, I practically collapse in relief. Elinor doesn't move very much at all, but I've learned to read her too. The two lines at her jaw have relaxed, which is the equivalent of her going 'Phew!'

'I would like that,' she says in a low voice. 'I meant what I said.'

'I know. And I didn't mean what I said.' Luke smiles, a rue-ful boyish smile that makes my heart constrict. It hasn't been easy for him, losing one mother and loathing the other. 'Come here.' He pecks Elinor on the cheek. 'You'll stay for supper?'

'Well . . .' Elinor shoots a questioning look at me and I nod.

'May I have the key back now?' Luke says to me.

'I *suppose* so,' I say teasingly, and hand it to him.

'And you must meet Minnie,' he adds to Elinor. 'She won't be asleep yet; I'll get her up. Minnie!' he calls, unlocking the kitchen door. 'There's someone for you to meet! You haven't seen her since she was a baby,' he adds to Elinor as he strides out. 'You'll get such a shock.'

Minnie.

Shit. Minnie. As far as Luke is concerned, Minnie and Elinor are strangers. Elinor and I meet eyes, and I can tell we've had exactly the same thought.

OK. Don't panic. It'll be fine. I just need to think quickly . . . I need to head this off . . . think . . . think . . .

I can hear Minnie pattering down the stairs, and Luke following her and saying, 'Now, Minnie, I've got a surprise for you.'

'Surprise!' replies Minnie. 'Present?'

'No, not a present, a person, and here she is . . .'

The kitchen door opens and Minnie stands in the doorway, a tiny figure in her frilled white nightdress and rabbit slippers.

'Ladeeeeee!' she cries joyously.

'This is your grandmother!' says Luke with a flourish. 'Minnie, this lady is *my* mother. Would you like to say hello?'

Minnie isn't listening. She rushes over, flings herself at Elinor's legs and then starts trying to open her bag.

'Ladeeeeee!' she says. 'Daddy, is Ladeeeee!' She finds a puzzle in Elinor's bag and pulls it out in triumph. 'Puzzle, Ladeee! Do it at the table,' she enunciates carefully as she climbs on to a chair. 'At the *table*.'

Luke is staring at them both in utter bewilderment.

'She . . . knows her,' he says. 'Minnie, darling, do you know your grandmother?'

'Not "gran-mudder",' says Minnie scornfully. 'Is *Ladeee*.'

'She knows you.' He addresses Elinor directly. 'How

could she know you? She hasn't seen you since she was a baby.'

'She doesn't know Elinor!' I say quickly. 'Don't be ridiculous! She's just being friendly.' But my voice sounds false even to my own ears.

I can see the truth dawning on Luke's face.

'She used to talk about seeing a "Lady",' he says slowly. 'We didn't know what she was talking about.' He whips round to me, suddenly pale with fury. 'That was my mother, wasn't it? Becky, what have you been doing behind my back? And no more lying.'

He sounds so self-righteous, I feel a surge of outrage. He has no idea. *No bloody idea.*

'OK, I did take Minnie to see Elinor!' I cry. 'Because she's her grandmother and they should get to know each other! But before you get so high and mighty, do you want to know what else we were doing, Luke?'

'Rebecca,' says Elinor, in a tone of dreadful warning, but I ignore her.

'We were planning your surprise party! You thought that was Suze and Tarquin? Well, it wasn't! It was your mother. She organized the whole thing and paid for it, and she wouldn't take any credit, but she should! Because it was her. It was Elinor.'

I break off, breathing hard. At last. At *last*. I've been carrying that secret around like a heavy weight, ever since the night of the party.

'Is this true?' Luke sounds shaken. I'm not sure if he's asking me or Elinor, but in any case, Elinor doesn't answer. She looks dry-frozen. All the warmth has vanished and her eyes have dwindled to dark, burning points.

'That is not why I came here, for you to discover that fact, Luke,' she says, her voice an angry rasp. 'It is *not* why I came here. You were *not* supposed to discover . . . you were *never* supposed to know . . .' Her face is trembling and as I watch I'm suddenly appalled. Is she—

No.

Is she about to *cry*?

'Elinor,' I say desperately. 'Elinor, I'm sorry, but he had to know—'

'No.' She won't meet my eye. 'No, Rebecca. You have undermined everything. Goodbye, Minnie.'

To my utter horror, she grabs hold of her bag with shaking hands and walks out.

'Ladeeee!' cries Minnie. 'No go!'

I watch, paralysed, unable to bring myself to go after her. Only when I hear the heavy front door slam do I move. A horrible guilt is growing inside me, and I can't stop myself lashing out at Luke.

'Happy now?' I round on him. 'So you've destroyed your mother's life. I hope you feel good.'

'Destroyed her life? I don't think so.'

'You have! All she wants is to make amends and be part of the family and see Minnie. Don't you get that, Luke? She doesn't want to buy your love. She wouldn't let me tell you about the party. She was watching the whole thing from a hiding place, but she wouldn't come out. And then you went overboard, thanking Suze and Tarkie. *They* knew it was Elinor. They felt terrible.'

'So everyone knew except me,' says Luke tightly. 'Of course they did.'

'Ladeeee!' wails Minnie, as Luke's BlackBerry bleeps with a text. 'Where Ladeee?' She gets down from the table, looking determined. 'Find Ladeeee.'

'Minnie, Lady had to go to her own home,' I say hurriedly. 'But I'll tell you a bedtime story about Lady, how about that? And then you can go to sleep and then tomorrow we'll do something nice—' I break off, noticing a weird flicker pass over Luke's face. 'What is it?'

Luke says nothing. He's just gazing at his phone. He glances at me, then focuses on his screen again. OK, I don't like this.

'What?' I say. 'Tell me!'

Silently, Luke turns his phone round. I squint at the screen and see a picture of Minnie, standing in our drive, in a sexy, grown-up pose.

'It's on the *USA Today* website,' he says, and my heart plummets.

'Let me see.' I grab the phone and wince at the image. They've managed to make Minnie look all grown-up and knowing and . . . awful. I'm *sure* they've touched up her mouth so she looks like she's wearing make-up.

'That was Sage's fault,' I say, handing the phone back. 'She encouraged Minnie. I stopped her as soon as I saw what they were doing. Who sent it to you?'

'Aran. But I think he got our numbers mixed up, because the message is to you. He seems to think you'll be pleased. It's "all raising the family profile", as he puts it.'

There's an accusing note to Luke's voice, I suddenly realize.

'*Pleased?*' I echo in horror. 'Of course I'm not pleased. I was livid! I told them to stop! Luke, you can't think—' I stop at his expression. He's staring at his phone again, with a look of revulsion.

'Aran's just sent me another text for you by mistake,' he says. 'You really must tell him your correct number.'

'Oh,' I say nervously. 'What does he say?'

'He's set up the meeting you discussed with the producers of *Even More Beautiful*,' says Luke in an odd, toneless voice. 'He's told them you're super-excited, and they can't wait to meet you.'

I don't believe it. I *told* Aran I wasn't interested.

'That's nothing,' I say hurriedly. 'Don't worry about it. It's just a—'

'I know exactly what it is,' says Luke, still in the same odd voice. 'It's a reality show involving plastic surgery. Are you so desperate for fame, Becky? Are you willing to butcher your body to become a celebrity? Are you willing to leave Minnie and put yourself at risk of injury, or death, just so you can stand on the red carpet?'

'No!' I say, appalled. 'Luke, I wouldn't actually *do* it—'

'So why are you having the meeting?'

'I'm not! I told Aran I didn't want to do it! This is all a mix-up.'

'Why would Aran set up a meeting unless you'd expressed interest?' His voice is inexorable.

'I don't know!' I say desperately. 'Luke, please believe me! I told Aran I wasn't interested. I wouldn't lie to you—'

'Oh really? That's a good one, Becky.' He gives a short, ill-humoured laugh. 'You wouldn't lie to me. That's a brilliant one.'

'OK.' I clutch my hair. 'I know I fibbed about Minnie seeing Elinor. And Sage and Lois. But that was different. Luke, you *can't* think I'd be willing to have plastic surgery on TV!'

'Becky, to be absolutely honest,' he says, his face hard, 'I have no idea how your mind works any more.'

'But—'

'Where Ladeee?' Minnie interrupts. 'Where Ladeee gone?'

Her little face is so innocent and trusting that with no warning, I burst into tears. I would never, *ever* use her for publicity. I would never, *ever* put myself at risk for some stupid reality show. How could Luke think that?

He's shrugging on his jacket and now he heads to the kitchen door, still with that distant expression. 'Don't worry about supper for me.'

'Where are you going?' I say.

'My assistant had a place held for me on the midnight flight to New York. Then I decided I didn't want to go till the morning. But I don't know why I'm waiting around. I'll see if she can still get me out tonight, then I can hook up with Gary.'

'You're leaving?' I say, stricken.

'Do you care?'

'Of course I care!' My voice wobbles perilously. 'Luke, you're not listening! You don't understand!'

'No,' he lashes back. 'You're right. I don't. I don't know what you want or why you want it or what your values are any more. You're lost, Becky. Completely lost.'

'I'm not!' I give a sudden sob. 'I'm not *lost!*'

But Luke has gone. I sink back into my chair, feeling shaky

with disbelief. So much for my intervention. Elinor stalked out. Luke stalked out. I've made everything a zillion times worse.

How could he think I'd have plastic surgery? How could he think I'd use Minnie?

'Where Ladeeeee?' says Minnie again. She looks curiously at my face. 'Mummy crying,' she adds dispassionately.

'Come on, darling.' With a huge effort I force myself out of my chair. 'Let's get you to bed.'

Minnie isn't too keen on the idea of bed, and I don't really blame her, to be honest. It takes ages to cajole her back under the blankets, and I end up reading *Guess How Much I Love You* about ten times, because each time we finish, she says, 'Again! More! Moooooore!' and I can't resist her pleas. Reading the familiar words is soothing me as much as her, I think.

And then just as I'm creeping out of her darkened room, I hear the front door slam down below. It's like a stab in the heart. He's gone and he didn't say goodbye. He *always* says goodbye.

I feel dazed. I don't know what to do with myself. At last, I head back into the kitchen, but I can't bring myself to eat, and that's not only because it's revolting quinoa bake from that stupid Eat Good & Clean website which I am never, ever visiting again. So I just sit at the table, my mind circling round and round, trying to work out where exactly I went so disastrously wrong.

And then there's the sound of a key in the front door, and my heart lifts. He's back. He came back! I knew he would.

'Luke!' I go running into the hall. 'Luke— Oh.'

It's not Luke, it's Suze. She's looking tired, and as she takes off her jacket I can see she's been nibbling the skin on her fingers, which she does whenever she's stressed.

'Hi,' she says shortly. 'Are the children OK?'

'Watching *Wall-E*.' I nod. I have a feeling they might have put it on for a second time, although I won't mention this to Suze. 'What happened about Tarkie? Did you find him? Is he OK?'

Suze surveys me silently for a moment. She looks as if I've

made some joke, which isn't that funny; in fact, is quite taste-less.

'I have no idea if he's OK, Bex,' she says at last, in a strange manner. 'Because it turns out Tarkie wasn't at Golden Peace. He's not in LA at all. He texted me from some roadside diner.'

'A roadside diner?' I echo in astonishment. 'Where?'

'He didn't say.' I can tell Suze is trying to keep it together, but she's not really succeeding. 'He didn't tell me anything. And now he won't answer the phone at all. I have no idea where he is, I have no idea what he's doing, he could be any-where . . .' Her voice rises to an accusing roar. 'And it's all your dad's fault!'

'My *dad's* fault?' I say, staggered.

'He's dragged him off on some wild goose chase.' Suze's eyes blaze at me accusingly. 'Apparently he's got to "put some-thing right". What is it? What's he got to put right? Where've they gone?'

'I don't know.'

'You must have some idea.'

'No! I don't!'

'Didn't you talk to your dad, Bex? Don't you know what he's doing here? Weren't you *interested*?' Suze sounds so scathing that I flinch. First Mum, then Luke, now Suze.

'I was going to talk to him.' I know how feeble this sounds, and a warm shame creeps over me. *Why* didn't I sit down properly with Dad? 'All I know is it was something to do with some old friend from a trip, years ago.'

'Some old friend,' repeats Suze sarcastically. 'Could you be any more vague?'

Her tone is so lacerating, I suddenly find myself lashing back. 'Why are you blaming me? It's not *my* fault!'

'It is your fault! You've totally ignored your dad, so he's latched on to Tarkie! They were drunk last night, you know that? Tarkie's in a vulnerable place at the moment. He shouldn't be getting drunk. Your dad's a total alkie.'

'No he isn't! If anything, Tarquin got *him* drunk.'

'Rubbish.'

348

'It's not rubbish!'

We're both glaring at each other, and I suddenly realize we'll wake Minnie, standing here and yelling.

'Look,' I say more quietly. 'Look, I'll find out. I'll find out where they've gone. We'll track them down.'

'Where's Luke?'

I feel a spasm of pain, but hide it. I don't feel like sharing this evening's events with Suze right now.

'Gone back to the UK,' I say matter-of-factly. 'He has to talk to the Treasury.'

'Great. Just great.' Suze lifts her hands and drops them despairingly. 'I thought he'd be able to help.'

She looks so devastated, I feel instantly nettled. So what if Luke's away? We don't need him. We don't need a man. I may have messed up on this, but I can put things right.

'I'll help,' I say, with determination. 'I'll do it. I'll find them, Suze. I promise.'

PLEASEGIVEGENEROUSLY.COM

Give to the world . . . share with the world . . . enhance the world . . .

YOU HAVE REACHED THE PLEDGE PAGE OF:

DANNY KOVITZ

Personal message from Danny Kovitz

Dear Friends

As many of you know, this is my year of 'giving back', of 'challenging myself', of 'taking myself to a whole new place'.

Due to circumstances beyond my control, I have sadly had to cancel my planned schedule of endeavors. However, I am now going to undertake a different – though equally taxing – set of challenges, which I list below. Please follow the links and pledge generously, my darling, wonderful friends.

Miami cocktail challenge
Spa challenge (Chiva Som)
Spa challenge (Golden Door)
Cruise challenge (Caribbean)

If any of you would like to join me in these endeavors, please do. Let's change the world together.

Big love

Danny xxx

TWENTY-ONE

Where am I supposed to start? I mean, how do you find a middle-aged man and a slightly troubled aristocrat who could be anywhere in LA, or California or . . . *anywhere*?

Suze rang the police last night, but it wasn't a success. They didn't exactly rush round to the house with their sirens blaring. In fact, they didn't rush anywhere. Suze didn't tell me what they said, but I could hear her getting quite shirty down the phone. I think they implied that Dad and Tarkie were probably just at a nightclub and would reel back in the morning and she should stop stressing out.

Which, you know. Might be true.

I've searched Dad's room for clues, of course. The first thing I found was a jolly note on his pillow, telling me that he was off on a 'little trip' and he had 'something to put right', but that I wasn't to worry and he would be back with Tarquin in 'two shakes of a duck's tail'. Apart from that, my findings consist of:

1. The map from his trip, all those years ago.
2. A copy of Vanity Fair from 1972.
3. A napkin from Dillon's Irish Bar. (Relevant?)

I look yet again at the map. I'm holding it really carefully, because it's pretty fragile, and I'm tracing my finger over the ancient red-biro line marking their route. Los Angeles . . . Las Vegas . . . Salt Lake City . . .

What is he 'putting right'? What's been going on?

I wish for the millionth time that I'd listened more carefully when Dad was telling me about his trip. I can remember vague details and stories – like the time they staked their hire car in a poker game, and the time they got lost in Death Valley and thought they were going to die – but nothing solid. Nothing that actually helps us.

Mum had no idea about it when I spoke to her on the phone, either. In fact, she was in such a state that I couldn't get much sense out of her at all. She was packing, and Janice was helping, and the two of them were getting in a total tizzy about how to carry their money without being mugged. She and Janice are both coming out on the next possible flight to LA, leaving Martin to 'man the phones at home' as Mum put it. She's convinced that Dad is dead in a ditch somewhere, and kept talking about 'If the worst should happen' and 'If he's alive, God willing' until I finally snapped and yelled, 'Mum, he's not dead!' Then she accused me of being insensitive.

I've left about five messages for Brent Lewis's sister, Leah, but she hasn't replied. The only thing I can think of doing now is going back to that trailer park where Brent Lewis lived. I know he's been evicted, and I haven't heard from his daughter, but maybe some neighbour will have a number for him, or something? He's my only connection with Dad's trip, or any of it.

'If you'll take the children to school, I'll head over to the trailer park straight away,' I say to Suze. 'Jeff will drive me.'

'Fine.' Suze doesn't look at me properly. She hasn't looked at me properly since last night. Her phone is clamped to her ear, and she's stirring her tea obsessively with her other hand, round and round and round.

'Who are you phoning?' I venture.

'Alicia.'

'Oh.' I turn away.

'Hi,' says Suze into the phone. 'No. Nothing.'

I feel a tweak of hurt. She's talking in the kind of intimate shorthand you use when you're really close to someone. Like the way we talk. Used to talk.

I can almost feel tears rising at the thought of Suze and Alicia being that close, but then I have only had about two hours' sleep. I kept checking my phone for messages from Luke, but there weren't any. I've composed a million texts to him, but I haven't sent any of them. Every time I even picture him, I feel such a tidal wave of hurt that I don't know where to start.

I rub my eyes and drain my coffee. 'OK, Jeff,' I call. 'Shall we go?'

As Jeff comes into the kitchen, his demeanour is gloomier than ever. He hasn't reacted well to the news of Dad and Tarkie disappearing. He seems to feel it's all his fault, even though I keep reassuring him that it isn't.

'The site's secure,' he says. 'Mitchell's on patrol in the yard with Echo.'

'Great,' I say. 'Thanks.'

Jeff heads to the kitchen door and checks it, then goes to the window and runs a finger along the glass. He murmurs into his headpiece, then goes back to check the door again. God, he's making me edgy.

'The kitchen's fine!' I say. 'We're safe! Look, Jeff, my dad just took off. It wasn't your fault.'

'Shouldn'ta happened,' he says heavily. 'Not on my watch.'

'Well, let's go, and maybe we'll find something out.' I push my chair back with a scrape. 'Suze, I'll keep you posted.'

'Fine.' Suze's eyes are fixed resolutely beyond me. Her jaw is tight and her hair is lank. I know she didn't get any sleep at all.

'Look, Suze,' I say tentatively. 'Please don't worry. I'm sure everything's fine.'

She doesn't even answer. I can see her mind grimly whirring around all the worst possibilities. There's nothing more I can say.

'OK.' I bite my lip. 'Well . . . I'll talk to you later.'

*

We've been driving twenty minutes or so when my phone rings and I reach for it eagerly. But it's not Suze or Dad, or even Luke, but Sage.

'Oh, hi Sage.'

'Hey, Becky!' Her voice peals happily down the phone. 'Are you super-excited?'

'What?' I say blankly.

'Our *Camberly* show! It airs in, like, ten minutes! I'm totally psyched. Aran was just on the phone. He was, like, this is huge already, babe. I mean, have you *seen* the hits on YouTube? And that's just the trailer!'

'Right. Right.' I try to wrench my head away from Dad and into the world of Sage. 'Yes, I saw that. It's phenomenal!'

It's true, it is pretty phenomenal. There have been wall-to-wall trailers for the last two days, for what they're calling *The Big Showdown: Lois Meets Sage*. They were on this morning while I was making coffee, but we turned the telly off because it was all getting a bit too much.

(Well, in fact, Suze threw her phone at the telly and yelled, 'Shut up! Shut *up*!' So I zapped it off.)

'So are you watching?'

'I will be!' I say, hastily turning on the in-car TV. 'I'm in the car but I'll be watching it in here. I can't wait. I'm sure you're amazing in it.'

'I'm awesome,' says Sage in satisfaction. 'So the other thing is, I had this great idea for my premiere outfit tonight. You have to come over and help me with it. Where are you now? Could you be here in, like, fifteen minutes?'

'Fifteen *minutes*?' I stare at the phone. 'Well . . . no. Sorry. I have some stuff I have to do this morning. It's kind of a family emergency.'

'But you're styling me!' says Sage, sounding affronted.

'I know. I'm coming round later, remember? Can we discuss it then?'

There's silence down the phone. Oh God. Is Sage pissed off?

'What's the idea?' I say hastily. 'I bet it's brilliant.'

'I can't *tell* you. I have to *show* you.' She gives a huffy little sigh. 'OK, if you really can't come now I guess we'll meet later. You'll be, like, totally oh my God.'

'Wow! Sounds amazing. I'll see you later. OK?'

I ring off and turn up the volume on the TV. It's showing a weather report for the East Coast and I find myself wondering if Dad and Tarkie could have got on a plane.

No. They wouldn't do that. Would they?

Even though I'm sure both Mum and Suze are overreacting to the situation, I feel a little chill. People you love shouldn't disappear, simply telling you vaguely they have 'something to put right'. They shouldn't do that.

Suddenly I realize the *Camberly* show is starting. The familiar titles are zooming over the screen and shots of Camberly in evening dress and running along the beach with her dog are flash-cutting with shots of her famous white house, where it's 'filmed'. (It's really filmed in LA, on a studio set. Everyone knows that.) Normally, there are several sections in the show. There's an interview and a song and a cooking slot, and often a competition. But today is a 'special'. It's all about Lois and Sage. As soon as the music dies away, the camera focuses on Camberly, looking sombre, and a backdrop of Sage's and Lois's faces blown up, glaring at each other. It all looks very dramatic.

'Welcome to my home,' Camberly says, in serious tones. 'And to a unique and momentous hour-long special. Sage Seymour. Lois Kellerton. Meeting for the first time since their infamous encounter at the ASAs. We'll be back after this.'

Music plays again, and the titles swoosh around the screen. I stare at it in slight outrage. An ad break *already*? I will never get used to American telly. Yesterday I started watching an advert and it went on for twenty minutes. Twenty whole minutes! (It was quite good, though. It was all about this brilliant barbecue grill thing, which gives you a 'restaurant-quality finish' with none of the calories. I wrote the number down, actually.)

I sit impatiently through a zillion ads for pain relievers, and then watch as Sage appears on the screen, sitting on the sofa with a rapt Camberly. At first, it's very boring, because she gets Sage to tell her exactly what happened at the awards ceremony, in every detail, and shows the video clip about ten times, and asks Sage over and over, 'And how did that make you feel?'

Sage is acting devastated. She keeps using phrases like 'I felt so betrayed' and 'I just don't understand Lois' and 'Why me?' in a broken voice. I think she's overdoing it, myself.

Then it's *another* ad break – and then it's time for Lois's appearance. And even though I know they've cooked all this up, my heart is beating faster at the thought of them together on the sofa. God knows what the American public is feeling. This really is a TV event.

Suddenly we're back in the studio, and Lois walks on to the set, wearing skinny cigarette pants and a billowy white silk shirt and . . . holding the clutch bag! I can't help gasping, and Jeff looks in the rear-view mirror.

'Sorry,' I say. 'Just watching the telly.'

Sage and Lois are staring at each other like two hostile cats, with a kind of crackling, unsmiling tension. The cameras keep switching from close-up to close-up. Camberly is watching silently, her hands to her mouth.

'Have your clutch bag.' Lois throws the bag down on the floor. Camberly jumps in shock and I make a squeak of protest. She'll damage the diamanté!

'You think I want it?' says Sage. 'You can keep it.'

Hang on. I'm a bit offended, here. That's a really nice clutch bag. Which, by the way, no one has ever paid me for.

'You two girls haven't seen each other since the awards ceremony,' says Camberly, leaning forward.

'No,' says Sage, not taking her eyes off Lois.

'Why would I want to see *her*?' chimes in Lois.

And suddenly I lose patience with the whole thing. It's so unreal. They're going to fight and be mean and then they'll probably hug each other and cry at the end.

'We're here,' says Jeff, pulling the car over. 'You wanna keep watching?'

'No thanks,' I say, and switch off the TV. I look out of the window, trying to get my bearings. There are the galvanized gates. There are the rows of mobile homes. OK. Let's hope I find some answers here.

'This is really the address?' says Jeff, who is peering out of the window dubiously. 'You sure about that?'

'Yes, this is it.'

'Well, I think it's advisable I come along with you,' he says firmly, and gets out of the car.

'Thanks, Jeff,' I say, as he opens my car door.

I'm going to miss Jeff.

This time I walk straight to no. 431, without looking right or left. The eviction notice is still on the door, and the trailer opposite is shut up. I can see my card, still stuck in the window frame. Great. Clearly that woman didn't pass it on.

I walk past an old man sitting outside a trailer about three along but I don't feel like approaching him. Partly because he keeps giving me funny looks, and partly because he has a massive dog on a chain. I can't see any neighbours other than him. So what do I do now? I sit down on a plastic chair which seems to be randomly in the middle of the path, and heave a big sigh.

'Are you visiting with someone?' says Jeff, who has followed me without comment.

'No. I mean, yes, but he's been evicted.' I gesture at the notice on the door. 'I want to find out where he's gone.'

'Uh-huh.' Jeff digests this for a few moments.

'I was hoping to speak to a neighbour,' I explain. 'I thought I could get a forwarding address or something . . .'

'Uh-huh,' says Jeff again, then nods at the trailer. 'He might be in there. Back door's open.'

What? That hadn't even *occurred* to me. Maybe he's come back. Maybe Dad's in there with him! In excitement, I hurry to the trailer door and bang on it.

'Hello?' I call. 'Brent? Are you there?'

There's a pause, then the door swings open. But it's not

Brent. It's a girl. She's a little older than me, I'd say, with wavy sandy hair and a freckled, weatherbeaten face. She has pale-blue eyes and a nose ring and an unfriendly expression. I can smell toast and hear Michael Jackson's *'Beat It'* playing faintly in the background.

'What?' she says.

'Oh, hi,' I say hesitantly. 'Sorry to disturb you.'

A little dog comes running out of the door and licks my toes. He's a Jack Russell, and he's wearing the cutest lime-green harness.

'Gorgeous!' I say, and squat to pat him. 'What's he called?'

'Scooter.' The girl doesn't unbend a millimetre. 'What do you want?'

'Oh. Sorry.' I rise up and give her a polite smile. 'How do you do?' I extend a hand and she cautiously takes mine. 'I'm looking for someone called Brent Lewis. Do you know him?'

'That's my dad.'

'Oh!' I exhale in relief. 'Great! Well, he was a friend of my father, and I think my dad's gone off looking for him, but I don't know where's he's headed.'

'Who's your dad?'

'Graham Bloomwood.'

It's as though I've said 'the Antichrist'. Her whole body jolts in shock. But her eyes stay on mine, unwavering. There's a gimletty hardness to them which is starting to freak me out. What's wrong? What have I said?

'Your dad is *Graham Bloomwood*?' she says at last.

'Yes! Do you know him?' I say tentatively.

'So, what, you've come here to gloat? Is that it?'

My mouth falls open a little. Have I missed something here?

'Er . . . gloat?' I echo, at last. 'No. Why would I come here to gloat?'

'Who's that guy?' Her eyes suddenly fix on Jeff.

'Oh. Him.' I cough, feeling a bit embarrassed. 'He's my bodyguard.'

'Your bodyguard.' She gives a bitter, incredulous laugh and shakes her head. 'Figures.'

It figures? Why does it figure? She doesn't know anything about me—

Oh, she's recognized me! I *knew* I was famous.

'It's just been since the whole ridiculous business on TV,' I say, with a modest sigh. 'When you're in my position you have to hire security. I mean, I'm sure you can imagine what it's like.'

She might want an autograph, it occurs to me. I really should get some of those big shiny pictures to carry about with me.

'I could sign a napkin,' I suggest. 'Or a piece of paper?'

'I have no idea what you're talking about,' says the girl, her tone unchanged. 'I don't watch TV. Are you a big deal?'

'Oh,' I say, feeling suddenly stupid. 'Right. I thought . . . Well . . . no. I mean, kind of . . .' This conversation is excruciating. 'Look, can we talk?'

'Talk?' she echoes, so sarcastically that I wince. 'It's a bit late to *talk*, don't you think?'

I stare at her in bewilderment.

'I'm sorry . . . I don't follow. Is something wrong?'

'Jesus H. Christ.' She closes her eyes briefly and takes a deep breath. 'Look, just take your little bodyguard and your little designer shoes and your little prinky-prinky voice and go. OK?'

I'm feeling more and more upset by this conversation. Why is she so angry? I don't even know her. Why did she say I'd come here to gloat?

And what 'prinky-prinky voice'? I don't have a prinky-prinky voice.

'Look.' I try to stay calm. 'Please can we start again? All I want is to track down my father and I'm quite worried about him, and this is the only place I can think of, and—' I break off. 'I'm sorry, I haven't even introduced myself properly. My name's Rebecca.'

'I know.' She looks at me strangely. 'Of course it is.'

'And what's your name?'

'Rebecca too. We're all called Rebecca.'

It's as though time stands still. I gape at her blankly for a few seconds, trying to process her words. But they make no sense. *We're all called Rebecca.*

We're all . . . what?

What?

'You knew that.' She seems puzzled by my reaction. 'You had to know that.'

Am I missing something? Have I moved into some weird, parallel universe? Who's *we*?

What the bloody hell is going ON?

'Your dad did see my dad. Couple days ago.' She gives me a challenging stare. 'I guess they had it out at long last.'

'Had it out about what?' I say in despair. *'What?* Please tell me!'

There's a long silence. The other Rebecca is just staring at me with her narrow blue eyes, as though she can't work me out.

'What did your dad tell you about that trip?' she says at last. 'The trip in seventy-two.'

'Nothing much. I mean, just little stuff. They went to the rodeo, they ate ice-cream, my dad got really sunburned . . .'

'That's all?' She seems incredulous. 'Sunburn?'

'Yes,' I say helplessly. 'What else was there to tell? What do you mean, we're all called Rebecca?'

'Jesus H. Christ.' She shakes her head. 'Well, if you don't know I'm not telling you.'

'You have to tell me!'

'I have to tell you *nothing*.' She looks me up and down, and I can feel the contempt in her eyes. 'I don't know where your dad is. Now fuck off, princess girl.' She picks up the little dog, and to my horror, bangs the trailer door shut. A moment later I can hear the back door being locked, too.

'Come back!' I beat furiously on the door. 'Please! Rebecca! I need to talk to you!'

As if in answer, the sound of *'Beat It'* from inside gets louder.

'Please!' I can feel tears rising. 'I don't know what you're talking about! I don't know what happened!'

I bang on the door for what seems like for ever, but there's no answer. Suddenly I feel a huge, gentle hand on my shoulder.

'She ain't opening that,' says Jeff kindly. 'I say you leave it. I say we go home.'

I can't reply. I stare at the trailer, a painful fullness in my chest. Something happened. And I don't know what, and the answer's in there, but I can't get at it.

'I say we go home,' repeats Jeff. 'Nothing you can do now.'

'All right,' I say at last. 'You're right. We should go.'

I follow him past the mobile homes, past the man with the scary dog, out of the gates. I don't know what I'm going to say to Suze. I don't know what I'm going to do, full stop.

As Jeff starts up the car, the TV comes on, and I'm assailed by the sound of sobbing. Lois and Sage are in each other's arms on-screen, mascara dripping down both their faces, while Camberly watches, her hands clasped in delight to her mouth.

'I've alwaaaays respected you ...' Sage is hiccuping.

'I've had such a damaaaaged life,' Lois sobs back.

'I love you, you know that, Lois?'

'I will always love yoooooou ...'

They both look absolute wrecks. They must have worn non-waterproof mascara on purpose.

Lois cradles Sage's face between her hands and says tenderly, 'You have a beautiful spirit,' and I can't help snorting with laughter. Is anyone going to believe in this 'reconciliation'? I have no idea. And right now, I don't care. All I can think is: where's Dad? What's going on? What on earth is going *on*?

When I get back, Suze is out. Presumably she's with Alicia. Presumably they're having really long, heartfelt conversations, because Suze can't talk to me, her oldest friend, who helped her have her first baby, does she remember *that*? And spent a whole week jiggling him in my arms while Suze slept, does she remember *that*? Where was Alicia then? She was swigging cocktails and planning how to ruin my life, that's where she was.

Anyway. If Suze wants to be best friends with Alicia, then fine. Whatever. Maybe I'll make friends with Robert Mugabe, to match.

I leave her a voicemail, giving her the bare bones of what happened, and do the same for Mum. But then I feel at a loss. I can't just head off randomly in search of Dad. I don't have a single other clue.

So at last I pack up my bag and get Jeff to take me to Sage's house, which is surrounded by paparazzi. (Proper paparazzi, not just Lon and his mates.) As we approach, I realize they won't be able to see inside the blacked-out SUV. I wind down the window and they start snapping away at me inside the car, while I ignore them elegantly and Jeff shouts, 'Wind that window up!' (He doesn't have to be so cross. I only wanted some *air*.)

When I finally get inside, the whole place is pumping with music, and there are about ten assistants milling around, making smoothies and telling people on the phone that Sage is not available. Sage herself is dressed in grey leggings and a T-shirt reading *SUCK ON THAT*, and seems totally hyper.

'So, wasn't *Camberly* awesome?' she says about five times before I can even say hello. 'Wasn't it incredible?'

'It was amazing! Did you wear non-waterproof mascara on purpose?' I can't help asking.

'Yes!' She points her finger at me as though I've got an answer correct on a quiz show. 'That was Lois's idea. The make-up people were all like, "You might cry, people often do on this show," and we were like, well so what? We want to be *honest*, you know.' She blinks at me. 'We want to be *truthful*. Mascara runs and that's the truth, and if it's not your perfect put-together look, then too bad.'

I clamp my lips together so I won't laugh. *Truthful?* Only I can't say anything because she's my client, so I just nod earnestly.

'Wow. You're so right.'

'I know,' she says in satisfaction. 'So, some dresses arrived. Where did I put them?'

After some searching, I find a Danny Kovitz box in the corner of the room. It was sent over this morning from Danny's LA showroom and contains three dresses. He's such a star. (I talked to Adrian at the Danny Kovitz headquarters today. Apparently Danny has checked into the Setai in Miami and says he's never going anywhere colder than 75 degrees Fahrenheit again. I never *thought* Greenland would suit him.)

I shake out the white beaded dress, which is absolutely gorgeous, and head over to Sage.

'This is amazing.' I drape the dress over my arm so she can see. 'It's very fitted, though, so you'll need to try it.'

'Cool!' Sage strokes it. 'I'll try it on in a minute.'

'So, what was your brilliant idea?'

'Oh, that.' She gives me a secretive smile. 'I'm not going to tell you.'

'Really?' I stare at her, disconcerted. 'Not at all?'

'You'll see it tonight.'

Tonight? Is it a hair do? Or a new tattoo?

'OK!' I say. 'Can't wait! So, I have some other options as well as the white—'

'Wait.' Sage is distracted by a TV on the wall. 'Look! The interview's on again. Let's watch it. Hey, guys!' she calls to her assistants. 'The show's on again! Get popcorn!'

'Whoo!' shout a couple of assistants. 'Go Sage! Awesome!'

'Let me call Lois. Hey, babe,' she says as soon as she's put through. 'We're on again. Becky's here. We're going to watch it.' She high-fives me as she speaks, and I notice a tongue stud which wasn't there before. Is that her new thing?

'Come!' Sage beckons me to her enormous white squashy sofa. 'Relax!'

'OK!' I surreptitiously glance at my watch. It'll be fine. We'll watch the show and then we'll get to work.

Except we don't just watch it once, we watch it four times.

Each time, Sage keeps up a running commentary, saying things like, 'See how I really nail the emotion here?' and, 'Lois looks so good from that angle,' and once, 'Where did Camberly have her *boobs* done? They're pretty great.' Whereupon a young assistant leaps up and says, 'I'm on it,' and immediately starts tapping at his BlackBerry.

By the fourth go I'm numb with boredom. The weird thing

is that if I could see myself, I'd be mad with jealousy. I mean, look at me! Lounging on a squashy white sofa with a movie star . . . sipping smoothies . . . listening to her little in-jokes . . . You'd think it would be paradise. But all I really want to do is go home and see Suze.

I can't, though, because we still haven't got to the clothes. Every time I mention them, Sage says 'Sure', and absently waves a hand at me. I've told her about fifty times that I'll need to go and pick up Minnie from pre-school soon and I don't have all day, but she doesn't seem to have registered that.

'OK, let's go have our nails done!' Sage suddenly gets up from the sofa. 'We have to get to the spa. We all have reservations, right?'

'Right!' says an assistant. 'We have the cars waiting outside.'

'Cool!' Sage starts searching around the coffee table. 'Where are my *shoes*? Did they slide under the sofa? Christopher, find my shoes,' she says prettily to the most handsome of her assistants and he instantly starts grovelling on the floor.

I'm not following any of this. How can she be going off to a spa?

'Sage?' I try to get her attention. 'Aren't we going to decide on your look for tonight? You were going to try on the dresses?'

'Oh, sure,' says Sage vaguely. 'We'll do that too. We'll talk about it at the spa.'

'I can't come to the spa,' I say as patiently as I can. 'I have to pick up my daughter from her class trip to the Museum of Contemporary Art.'

'Her kid is *so* sweet,' Sage announces to her assistants, and they all croon back, 'Oh cuuuute! Adorable!'

'So what about the dresses?'

'Oh, I'll try them on myself.' She suddenly seems to focus. 'I don't need you to be there. You did a great job, Becky, thanks! And thank you, Christopher, angel!' She slides her pumps on.

She doesn't need me? I feel like she's slapped me in the face.

'But I haven't explained each look yet,' I say, bewildered. 'I was going to try them on with you, talk you through the accessories, see if we need to alter anything . . .'

'I'll figure it out.' She spritzes herself with scent, then catches my eye. 'Go! Have fun with your daughter!'

'But . . .'

If I don't help her create her look, then I'm not a stylist at all. I'm a delivery girl.

'Your car will take you, right? See you tonight!' Before I can say anything else, she's skipped out of the door. I can hear a roar from the paparazzi outside and the sound of engines and the general mayhem that surrounds Sage.

I'm alone, apart from a housekeeper, who walks silently around, picking up bowls and brushing popcorn off the sofa. And just for an instant, I feel totally deflated. This isn't how I pictured it at all. I had so many ideas I wanted to share with Sage, yet she doesn't even seem *interested* in the clothes.

But as I pull out my phone and dial Jeff's number, I force myself to look on the positive side. Come on. It's all still good. I've still been to her house, I've still given her the bones of her outfit. When people ask who styled her, she'll say, 'Becky Brandon.' It's still my big chance. I have to hold on to this. Whatever else is going on, this is still my big Hollywood chance.

As we approach the house, Lon is still hanging around outside the gates, and he gesticulates wildly at the car. He's wearing a lime bandana today, and thigh boots.

'Pirate!' cries Minnie, who is clutching the 'Rothko-inspired' painting she did at the museum. (It's really good. I'm going to put it in a frame.) 'See pirate!'

'Becky!' I can hear him shouting as we drive past. 'Becky, wait! Listen! Guess what?'

The thing about me is I'm a total sucker for anyone who says 'Guess what?'

'Hey, Jeff,' I say, as the gates start opening for us. 'Stop a minute.'

'*Stop* a minute?'

'I want to talk to Lon. That guy.' I point.

Jeff halts the car and turns round in his seat. He's got his 'disappointed' face on.

'Rebecca, we've talked about street interactions,' he says. 'I do not recommend that you get out of the vehicle at this time.'

'Jeff, honestly.' I roll my eyes. 'It's Lon. He's a fashion student! I mean, it's not like he's hiding a *gun*.'

OK, saying 'gun' was a mistake. At once Jeff stiffens. He's been on hyper-alert ever since Dad and Tarkie disappeared.

'If you wish to approach this person . . .' he says heavily, 'I will secure the area first.'

I want to giggle at his disapproving expression. He's behaving like he's some stiff and starchy 1930s butler and I've said I want to talk to a tramp.

'Fine. Secure the area.'

Jeff gives me another reproachful look, then gets out of the car. The next minute I can see him frisking Lon. Frisking him!

But Lon doesn't seem to mind. In fact, his face is all shiny and excited, and I can see him taking pictures of Jeff with his phone. At last Jeff returns to the car and says, 'The area is secure.'

'Thank you, Jeff!' I beam, and bound out of the car. 'Hi Lon!' I salute him. 'How are you? Nice boots! Sorry about all the security and stuff.'

'No, that's fine!' says Lon breathlessly. 'Your bodyguard is so cool.'

I nod. 'He's really sweet.'

'I guess you have to be super-careful of nut jobs,' says Lon reverently. 'I've seen your guard dog, too, patrolling the grounds and everything?'

Lon is so starry-eyed, I can't help blossoming under his gaze.

'Well, you know.' I toss my hair back. 'When you're in my position, you have to be careful. You don't know who's out there.'

'Have you had many attempts on your life?' Lon is agog.

'Er, not *that* many. You know. Just the normal amount.' I quickly change the subject. 'Anyway, so what did you want to say?'

'Oh, right!' Lon nods animatedly. 'We saw your special

delivery from Danny Kovitz. The van came earlier, and I got talking to the guy. He works at the showroom. He knew all about it. It's a dress for you to wear tonight.'

'Danny sent over a dress for me?' I'm so touched, I can't help grinning.

'It's from the new collection, *Trees and Wires*? Like, the one that hasn't even been shown yet?' Lon seems beyond ecstatic. 'The one that Danny said came straight from his soul?'

All Danny's recent collections have been called *Something and Something*. One was *Metal and Philosophy*. Another was *Envy and Scarlet*. The fashion journalists and bloggers write screeds on what the titles mean, but if you ask me, he just picks two random words out of the dictionary and chooses two different fonts and calls it meaningful. Not that I'll say this to Lon, who looks like he's going to expire with excitement.

'No one has seen anything of this collection,' Lon is babbling. 'There are rumours online, but nobody *knows* anything. So, like, I was wondering, will you wear it tonight? And can we take some pictures? My friends and me?'

His face is scrunched up in hope and he's folding his bandana into ever-decreasing squares.

'Of course!' I say. 'I'm leaving at six but I'll come out five minutes early and you can all see the dress.'

'Yay!' Lon's face relaxes into a beam. 'We'll be there!' Already he's tapping at his phone. 'Thanks, Becky! You're the greatest!'

As we head inside, my spirits are higher than they have been for ages. Danny sent me a dress! I'm going to be a fashion story! Nenita Dietz is bound to be impressed when she sees me. But my momentary euphoria freezes into icy fog as soon as I see Suze. She's sitting in the kitchen, surrounded by papers, on which I can see her scribbled writing. Her hair is shoved into a dishevelled knot. I can hear *The Little Mermaid* playing in the next room, and smell toast, which is clearly what she's given her children for their tea.

On the table is a fancy-looking Golden Peace tote bag, which is new. Alicia must have given it to her, as well as that sweatshirt sticking out of it. I know what she's doing. She's trying to buy Suze's love.

'Nice bag,' I say.

'Thanks,' says Suze, barely looking up. 'So you're back.' She sounds accusing, which is hardly fair.

'I was back earlier,' I reply pointedly. 'But you were out.' *With Alicia*, I refrain from adding. 'Any news?'

I know there isn't any news, because I've been checking my phone every five minutes, but it's worth asking anyway.

'Nothing. I've been on the phone to all of Tarkie's friends, but none of them has any leads. What have you done? Have you spoken to your dad's friend?'

'I went to the trailer park. I did some investigating there.'

'Oh yes, I got your voicemail.' She stops scribbling, and draws her feet up to her chair, hugging her knees. Her face is drawn with worry, and I feel a sudden urge to hug her tight and pat her back, like I would have done any other time. But somehow . . . I can't . . . Everything feels too stilted between us. 'You met another Rebecca? That's so strange.'

I tell her all about the trailer park, and she listens in silence.

'Something's going on with my dad,' I finish. 'But I have no idea what.'

'But what does it *mean*?' Suze rubs her brow. 'And why has he got Tarquin involved?'

'I don't know,' I say helplessly. 'Mum will be in the air by now, so I can't ask her, and anyway, she doesn't know anything . . .' I grind to a halt. My attention has been grabbed by something on the kitchen counter. It's a big box with *Danny Kovitz* printed on the side.

Obviously my dress isn't the priority right this second. On the other hand, I can't wait to see it. I don't even know if it's full-length, or mid-length, or a mini-dress . . .

'I tried the police again,' Suze is saying. 'Absolutely useless! They said I could file a report. What good is a report? I need them *out* there, searching! They kept saying, "But where would we search, ma'am?" I said, "That's for you to find out! Put some detectives on it!" Then they said, "Could these two gentlemen have just gone on a little trip?" I said, "Yes! They *have* gone on a trip. That's the whole *point*. But we don't know *where*!"'

As Suze is talking, I edge over to the counter. I lift the lid a little way and hear a rustle of tissue paper. There's a lovely waft of scent, too. Danny always has his clothes sprayed with his signature fragrance before they're sent out. I push aside the silvery-grey tissue paper and glimpse a shoulder strap made out of linked copper hoops. Wow.

'What are you doing?' says Suze tonelessly.

'Oh.' I jump, and drop the lid. 'Just having a look.'

'More "essential shopping" for Sage, I suppose.'

'It's not for Sage, it's for me. I'm wearing it tonight. Danny sent it over specially. It's from his *Trees and Wires* collection . . .' I trail off, registering the sharp silence in the kitchen. Suze is staring at me with a look I can't quite work out.

'You're still going to the premiere,' she says at last.

'Yes.'

'I see.'

There's another long silence. The atmosphere is getting edgier and edgier, until I want to scream.

'What?' I say at last. 'What? Don't you think I should go?'

'Jesus, Bex! Do you really have to ask?' Suze's sudden vehemence takes me by surprise. 'Your dad is missing and Tarkie too, and you're going to a bloody premiere? How can you be so selfish? I mean, what kind of priorities do you have?'

Resentment is rising inside me. I'm tired of Suze making me feel bad. I'm tired of *everyone* making me feel bad.

'Your dad's disappeared without a trace and taken Tarkie with him!' Suze repeats, still on her tirade. 'There's obviously some mystery; they could be in big trouble—'

'Well, what am I supposed to do about it?' I explode. 'It's not my fault if they just took off! I've got one chance in Hollywood, Suze, *one chance*, and this is it! If I don't grab it, I'll always regret it.'

'The red carpets will always be there,' says Suze scathingly.

'The TV interviews won't always be there! Nenita Dietz won't always be there! I don't see why I should just sit around, doing nothing, waiting for news. You can do that if you like. Maybe Alicia could keep you company,' I can't help adding bitterly. And I grab the Danny Kovitz box and march out of the kitchen before Suze can say anything more.

As I get ready, there are two voices arguing in my head. One is mine and one is Suze's. Or maybe one is Luke's. Or maybe they're both mine. Oh God, I don't know *whose* they are, but by quarter to six I'm sick of both of them. I don't want to have to think about whether I'm doing the right thing. I just want to do it.

I stare at myself boldly in the mirror and adopt a red-carpet pose. I look good. I think. I've put on a bit too much make-up, but I don't want to look washed out next to all the celebrities, do I? And Danny's dress is genius. It's short and slinky in a flattering black fabric, and the single shoulder strap is made of a mass of unpolished copper hoops. (They're digging into my skin a bit, and they'll probably leave marks, but I don't care.) I'm wearing the spikiest ever black stilettos and my bag is a little copper-framed clutch (it was in the box with the dress). I definitely look like a top celebrity stylist.

Adrenalin is pumping through my body. I feel like I'm about to go into a boxing ring. This is it. This is *it*. As I'm carefully painting my lips, my phone rings, and I put it on speaker.

'Hello?'

'Becky.' Aran's voice fills the room. 'Psyched for tonight?'

'Definitely!' I say. 'Can't wait!'

'Great! I just wanted to let you know the run-down. You are in demand tonight, girl.' He laughs. 'You'll be talking to NBC, CNN, Mixmatch, that's a fashion channel . . .'

As he continues, I can barely concentrate. It all seems so sur-real. I'm going to be on NBC!

'So just stay bright and positive,' Aran is saying. 'Ooze your British charm and you'll do great. See you later!'

'See you there!' I give myself a final spray of perfume and look at my reflection. British charm. How do I ooze British charm?

'Cor, strike a light, guv'nor!' I say aloud.

Hmm. Maybe not.

As I walk downstairs, I can hear Suze approaching. I start prickling with defiance, and clench my bag tight. She appears in the hall, holding Minnie on her hip, and looks me up and down dispassionately.

'You look amazing,' she says flatly.

'Thanks.' I match her tone.

'Thin.' She manages to make this sound like an accusation.

'Thanks.' I take out my phone and check for texts. There's one from Jeff telling me he's waiting outside, but nothing from Luke. Not that I was really expecting it, but still my heart drops in disappointment. 'I'll have my phone on the whole time,' I add. 'In case you . . . you know. Hear anything.'

'Well, enjoy yourself.' She hoists Minnie to the other hip and I glare at her resentfully. She's only carrying Minnie to make me feel bad. She could easily put her down on the floor.

'Here are the details of where I am.' I hand her a printed sheet. 'Thanks for looking after Minnie.'

'Oh, any time.' Her voice is so sarcastic I wince. She doesn't mean it, I tell myself. She's just stressed out about Dad and Tarkie.

I mean, I'm stressed out, too. But there's a bigger emotion overriding the stress. It's excitement. NBC . . . red carpet . . . exclusive designer outfit . . . How could I *not* be excited? How can Suze not understand?

'Well, I hope you have the time of your life,' she says as I open the door.

'I will,' I say mutinously. 'See you later.'

I step outside and hear a roar from outside the gates. I stop dead and blink in astonishment. Oh my God. Lon must have brought his entire class to see the dress. There's a whole crowd of them, clustered together, pointing cameras and phones at me through the iron bars of the gates.

'Open the gates,' I instruct Jeff, and I approach the throng, waving graciously, feeling like a princess.

'Becky!' Lon is calling.

'Beckeeeee!' shouts a girl in a black shift dress. 'Over here!'

'You look amazing!'

'How does the dress feel?'

'Can we get a back view?'

'Did Danny tell you anything special about the dress? What was his inspiration?'

As I pose, looking this way and that, I keep darting glances back at the house. I hope Suze is watching out of the window and can hear all the yelling. *Then* maybe she'll understand.

TWENTY-TWO

At last everyone has taken their photos and I've done two little interviews about Danny for fashion blogs, and I'm in the car, on the way to the premiere. I feel a bit giddy. It's going to be brilliant. It already *is* brilliant.

The premiere is being held at El Capitan, and I know we're getting near from the noise. The thumping music is practically rocking the SUV, and there are shouts from the crowd, and as we slow down, someone bangs on the car, which makes me jump, startled.

'You OK?' says Jeff at once.

'Fine!' I say, exhilarated. 'It's pretty big, isn't it?'

The film is an action movie about two circus performers who foil a terrorist attack. Apparently they use all the animals and their circus skills to help them, and it was nearly derailed when an elephant went a bit crazy during the filming.

Jeff has to show all kinds of passes to officials, and as he does so, I peer out of the window. I can see faces pressing up against the glass, trying to see through the tinted windows. They probably think I'm Tom Cruise or something.

'Jeez!' Jeff says, trying to negotiate a path through the hubbub. 'Place is chaos. You wanna go through with this?'

Honestly. Not him too.

'Yes,' I say firmly. I reach in my bag for my dad's autograph book. I've brought it with me and I'm determined to get him as many autographs as I can. *Then* Suze won't be able to call me selfish.

We're in a queue of cars, and I can see how the process works. The car pulls up to the dropping-off point, and the door opens and the celebrity gets out and the crowd goes wild. There are two limos ahead of us. Soon it'll be me!

'So, you text as soon as you need to get out of here,' says Jeff. 'Or call. Any kind of trouble, you just call.'

'I will,' I promise, and check my reflection one last time. My heart is starting to beat fast. This is really it. I need to get out of the car elegantly, I need to stay calm, I need to remember who made my dress . . .

'OK, you're on.' Jeff pulls up and a guy in a headset yanks open the door and I'm out. I'm standing on the red carpet. On the proper red carpet. I'm one of them!

I'm so transfixed by the atmosphere I don't move for a moment. The music is even louder, now I'm outside. It's all so big and bright and spectacular. The entrance to El Capitan is done up like a circus big top, and there are circus performers wandering about everywhere. There are fire-eaters and jugglers and a contortionist girl in a jewelled bikini, and a ring-master cracking his whip. And there's an elephant! An actual elephant, walking back and forth with its trainer. The crowd is going wild over some young guy in jeans, who I think is in a band, and I can see Hilary Duff about ten yards away . . . and is that Orlando Bloom signing autographs?

'Rebecca?' A girl in a black trouser suit approaches me with a businesslike smile. 'I'm Charlotte. I'll be escorting you on the red carpet. Let's keep moving.'

'Hi, Charlotte!' I beam at her as we shake hands. 'Isn't this *amazing*? Look at the jugglers! Look at the elephant!'

Charlotte seems puzzled.

'Right,' she says. 'Whatever. Let's go.'

Cameras are flashing everywhere as we proceed along. I've been practising the proper film-star pose for days, only now I have to walk, too. I never practised film-star walking. Damn. How do they do it?

I think they kind of glide seamlessly along. I'll glide too. Perhaps with my legs slightly bent?

'Are you OK?' Charlotte gives me a strange look and I hastily straighten my legs. Maybe that's not such a good look. 'So, we have your photocall and then your interviews . . .' She glances at her watch and consults her clipboard. She seems totally unimpressed by the elephant, or the fire-eaters, or the celebrities. In fact, she seems unimpressed by the whole event. 'So, you're on.'

With no warning, she pushes me into an empty patch of red carpet, in front of a bank of photographers, who all start shouting, 'Becky! Becky, over here!'

Hastily I get into position. Legs crossed, chin tucked, radiant, celebrity-type smile . . .

I'm waiting to feel the glee I did before . . . but it's weird. I feel a bit nothingy. And then, almost before they've started, it's over, and Charlotte is tugging me along again, towards the rows of TV cameras.

It was more fun when it was me and Suze, giggling at the whole thing, flashes through my mind.

No. Don't be stupid. This is fantastic. I'm a proper celeb! I'm part of it! I've loads to say about Sage's outfits, and my own dress, and fashion . . . I can't wait.

'So, the first interview is with Fox News,' says Charlotte in my ear, and pushes me towards a TV camera. I quickly straighten my hair, and hope my lipstick hasn't come off on my teeth, and put on my brightest, most intelligent expression.

'Hello, Betty!' says a very coiffed woman in a trouser suit. 'We're delighted you could join us!'

'Thanks!' I smile. 'Although actually, it's *Becky*.'

'Betty,' she continues as though she didn't hear, 'you are, of course, the witness to Lois Kellerton's shoplifting incident. Have you seen Lois since then?'

I'm flummoxed for a moment. What do I say? I can't reply,

'Yes, I broke into her house and found her plotting how to fool the American public.'

'Um . . . no,' I say, feebly.

'If you see her tonight, what will you be saying to her?'

'I'll be wishing her well.'

'Lovely! Well, thank you, Betty! Enjoy the movie!'

To my astonishment, Charlotte grabs my arm and shunts me onward. That was it? That was the interview? Don't they want to know what I do for a living? Don't they want to know who my dress is by?

'And the next one is TXCN,' says Charlotte in my ear.

Another TV camera is pointing at my face, and a guy with red hair grins at me.

'Hi there, Betty!' he says in a Southern accent. 'How're you doin'?'

'It's *Becky*,' I say politely.

'So, shoplifting. Is it a crime or is it a disease?'

What? How on earth would I know? I stammer some answer, feeling like a total moron, and before I know it, I'm moving on to the next interview. That guy wants to know if Lois put up a fight when I confronted her, and the next woman asks me if I think Lois might have shoplifted because she was pregnant. I haven't had a chance to mention my dress, or the fact I've styled Sage. And they all call me Betty.

'I'm called *Becky*!' I exclaim to Charlotte as we're moving on. 'Not Betty!'

'Oh,' she says, unmoved. 'I guess it might have been written wrong in the press pack.'

'But—' I stop, mid-sentence.

'But what?'

I was going to say, 'But don't they all *know* my name?' Looking at Charlotte's expression, though, I change my mind.

Maybe I'm not quite as famous as I thought I was. I feel a bit crushed, even though I think I manage to hide it quite well. Charlotte leads me on to another reporter, who shoves a radio mic in my face, and I've just babbled a few lines about how I'm really glad that Lois and Sage have reconciled and yes, I did see the interview . . . when there's the most almighty roar and I can't help looking round.

It's Sage.

She's standing in front of the photographers and they are going wild. I mean, nuts. The level of shouting is going up and up and up, and the flashes are like some kind of lightning storm, and the crowd is surging in her direction, pressing against the metal barriers and holding out phones and autograph books.

Sage looks absolutely delighted. She's posing in Danny's white dress, which looks sensational, and she's flicking her hair around, and blowing kisses to the crowd. And then it happens. She blows a particularly energetic kiss . . . and somehow the side seam of her dress comes apart. I watch in shock as the whole thing unravels, exposing the entire side of her body.

Sage gives a huge gasp, and clutches at the dress, and the photographers nearly have fits, trying to get a shot of her.

I'm slack-jawed in horror as white beads start rolling all over the red carpet. That dress was fine this afternoon. It was *fine*. She must have doctored it. That was her secret plan which she didn't want to tell me. A deliberate wardrobe malfunction. A girl in a black trouser suit is trying to offer Sage a coat, but she's ignoring the offer, and beaming at the cameras.

Danny's going to *kill* me. He's got a particular sore spot about his clothes falling apart, ever since an unfortunate incident in Barneys when he hadn't sewn up his seams properly. He'll ask me why I didn't make sure she was dressed properly, and I'll have to say she wouldn't let me near her, and he'll say I should have insisted . . .

I can't tell anyone I'm Sage's stylist now. It hits me with a fresh blow. They'll laugh at me. My whole plan is ruined.

Charlotte has been listening to her earpiece and now looks up.

'Rebecca, you're done,' she says with a professional smile. 'You can go in now. Enjoy the movie.'

'Oh,' I say, taken aback. 'Is that all?'

'That's all,' she says politely.

'But I thought I was doing loads of interviews.'

'The plan changed. If you make your way into the movie theatre, someone will show you to your seat. Have a good evening!'

I feel a pang of dismay. I don't want to go into the movie theatre. Once I go in, it's over.

'Can I stay out here a bit longer?' I say. 'I want to . . . you know. Soak it all up.'

Charlotte looks at me as though I'm crazy. 'Sure.' She shrugs, and turns away, leaving me alone. I feel a tiny bit awkward, with nothing to do, but I determinedly swivel round and survey the rows of surging people and TV cameras and celebrities talking to interviewers. Come on, Becky. Here I am on the red carpet. Maybe Sage has derailed my plan a little, but I can still enjoy myself. I can still be positive.

The entire line-up of Heaven Sent 7 has just appeared on the red carpet, and a bunch of teenage girls is screaming hysterically. I can't help feeling a thrill. They're huge! I so want to share this with someone. I automatically pull out my phone, and start to text – and then stop, mid-word. I can't share it with Luke. Or Suze. Or Mum.

Or Dad, obviously.

Or . . . anyone.

Without meaning to, I heave a miserable sigh, then immediately plaster a wide smile on, to compensate. I can't be sighing on the red carpet. That's a ridiculous idea! It's all good. It's all fab. It's—

Oh, there's Aran, looking immaculate in a black tuxedo and open-collared blue shirt. Feeling a surge of relief, I hurry over to him. His hands are in his pockets and he's watching Sage, with that wry, detached expression he has. Sage has found a little mini trench coat from somewhere, and has put it on over her dress and is talking eagerly to a queue of interviewers.

'Hey, Becky.' Aran kisses me lightly on each cheek. 'Having a good time?'

'Yes!' I say automatically. 'It's wonderful!'

378

'Good.' He smiles. 'I'm glad.'

'Although, did you see Sage's dress? It totally collapsed.'

He rolls his eyes. 'Believe me, I saw that.'

'She was lent that dress by a friend of mine. He's a really famous designer. And she ruined it on purpose.' I'm trying not to sound accusing, but I can't help it.

'Ah.' Aran winces. 'Well, I'm sure we can figure out compensation—'

'It's not the money! It's just so inconsiderate. And now I can't let anyone know I'm her stylist. I mean, that was the point of tonight; to launch myself as a stylist! I sourced her that dress and she would have looked amazing, but then she goes and deliberately sabotages it . . .' My voice is trembling. I think I'm more upset than I quite realized.

'Uh-huh.' Aran surveys me as though he's working something out. 'Did you meet Nenita yet?'

'No.'

'Well, we'll fix that up.'

'OK. Thanks.' To my dismay, a tear has come to one of my eyes. I wipe it hastily away and smile, but Aran has noticed.

'You all right, Becky?'

'Kind of.' I gulp. 'Not really. My dad's gone missing and I had a row with Luke, and then I had one with my best friend, too . . . No one *gets* it. This.' I spread my arms around.

'You don't surprise me,' says Aran.

'Really?'

'It happens. You're not a civilian any more, remember?'

He sounds totally unmoved, and I suddenly feel a pang of frustration at his easy-going, Teflon manner. If the world ended, he'd probably just shrug and say, 'That's the way it rolls.'

And what did he mean, *You don't surprise me?*

'Let me find Nenita.' He pats me on the shoulder.

As Aran heads off, I look around again, trying to savour the experience, but suddenly I'm finding it a bit jarring. Everything's so bright. The white smiles, the cameras flashing, the sequins and jewels and shrieking. It's like, even the air is alive with electricity. My hair is prickling with it, and my leg is tingling . . .

Oh. Actually, that's my phone, buzzing. I grab it out of my clutch, and it's Suze. I feel a dart of terror and jab the Answer button.

'Is everything OK?' I demand. 'Has anything happened?'

'Oh God, Bex.' Suze sounds despairing, and I feel a lurch of fright. 'Alicia's found out some information. They've gone off with Bryce.'

'*Bryce?*' I stare at the phone, not quite understanding. 'Bryce from Golden Peace?'

'Your dad had some mission and he asked Tarkie to help him carry it out. And Tarkie asked Bryce to come with them. Bryce! Alicia reckons he's just after our money. He wants to set up some rival centre, and he's going to brainwash Tarkie into funding it, and we have no idea where they've gone . . .'

'Suze, calm down,' I say desperately. 'It'll be fine.'

'But he's evil!' She sounds almost hysterical. 'And they've driven off into the desert with him!'

'We'll find them. We will. Suze, just try to get as much information as you can . . .' She's trying to say something else, but I can't make it out. Her voice is crackling and breaking up. 'Suze?'

My phone goes dead and I stare at it in dismay. Bryce. Tarquin. My dad. In the middle of nowhere. What's Mum going to say? What are we going to do?

'Becky.' Aran is at my side again. 'Let me take you to meet Nenita.' His eyes twinkle. 'She's a pretty big deal in your world, huh?'

'Um . . . yes. Massive.' In a daze, I follow him across the red carpet, stumbling slightly in my heels. This is the biggest moment of my career. Meeting Nenita Dietz. I have to put my personal life aside. I have to focus.

Nenita Dietz is holding forth to a group of people, and we wait patiently at the side until she pauses. She looks *amazing*. She's in a massive blue fur coat and spiky metallic boots. Her long, dark wavy hair is shining with red and gold highlights under the spotlights and she must be wearing at least three pairs of false eyelashes. From here she looks like a fairy princess.

'Nenita Dietz,' Aran says pleasantly. 'Let me present Becky Brandon.'

'Becky!'

As I take her hand I feel like I'm meeting the queen. I mean, she *is* the queen of Hollywood stylists.

'Hello!' I gabble nervously. 'I love your work. Actually, my background's fashion, too. I was a personal shopper at Barneys and I'd love to get into styling and I'm such an admirer of yours. Especially of *Clover*. The clothes were exquisite.'

I've mentioned *Clover* because it's a very low-budget film that she did a few years ago, which most people haven't even heard of, and I'm hoping to get some Brownie points. But Nenita doesn't seem interested in my opinion of *Clover*.

'You.' She points at me with narrowed eyes. 'You're the young woman who saw Lois stealing and told the world.'

'Um, yes. I mean, no. I only told one person . . . or maybe two . . .'

'Lois is a *wonderful girl*,' she says with emphasis. 'You should be ashamed of yourself.' Her words feel like a slap, and I start backwards.

'I didn't mean to cause any harm,' I say hastily. 'And I honestly didn't tell the world . . .'

'You'll bring bad karma into your life, you realize that?' As she leans forward, I can see that her eyes are all yellowed, and her hands are a lot older than her face. She actually looks quite intimidating.

'Lois's doing fine, Nenita,' says Aran. 'You know that.'

'Bad karma.' She fixes me with her yellow gaze and jabs a finger at me again. 'Bad karma into your life.'

I'm trying not to recoil in horror. I feel like she's putting a curse on me.

'Also, your dress is dated,' she adds disdainfully, and I feel a prickle of outrage on Danny's behalf. 'Nevertheless,' she says, as though bestowing on me a massive honour, 'I can see that you, young woman, are like me. When you really want something, you have to have it.' Her eyes run appraisingly over me again. 'You may call me.'

She hands me a silver-edged card with a telephone number on it, and Aran raises his eyebrows.

'Well done, Becky!' he murmurs. 'Nice job!'

I stare down at the card, feeling a bit dizzy. I've done it. I've actually made contact with Nenita Dietz.

The crowd is moving towards the movie-theatre entrance, surging around us, and a bulky man bumps into me, causing me to drop my bag. As I stand, I see I've been split up from Nenita and Aran and the crush is increasing. Girls in black suits are circulating, telling everyone that the movie will start soon, could they please take their seats. Feeling a bit like a zombie, I follow them in. The foyer is crowded with people and cameras and journalists, and I just let the throng propel me forward. A pleasant young man shows me to a seat in the auditorium, where I find a complimentary bottle of water and some popcorn and a circus-themed goodie bag.

I'm here! I'm one of the in-crowd! I'm in a top seat at a premiere! I have Nenita Dietz's card and an invitation to call her!

So . . . why do I feel so hollow? What's wrong?

My leather seat seems chilly and the air conditioning is making me shiver. As music starts blasting through the speakers, I jump. This should be the biggest treat ever, I keep telling myself. Suze's voice is ringing in my ears: *I hope you have the time of your life* – and my own defiant reply, *I will.*

But the truth is: I'm not. I'm sitting in a cold, dark room full of strangers, about to watch a movie I don't want to see, without any friends or family to share it with. I'm not famous. Everyone was calling me Betty. I'm not Betty, I'm *Becky.*

I finger Nenita's card to reassure myself. But even that feels toxic in my fingers. Do I want to work with that scary witch? Do I want to be her? I feel as though I've reached the oasis mirage in the desert. I'm scooping up sand and I'm telling myself it's fresh and pure water . . . but it's not.

I'm breathing harder and harder; my thoughts are whirling around my head; I'm gripping the armrests of my seat until my fingers hurt. And suddenly I've had enough. I can't stay here. I don't want to be here. I have other, far more important things in my life than a red carpet and celebrities. I have my family and my friends, and a problem to sort out, and a husband to win back, and a best friend to help. *That's* what I have. And I can't believe it's taken me so long to see that.

I have to leave. Right now.

Muttering apologies to the people around me, I get up and make my way to the side of the auditorium. The seats are full by now and a man in a dinner jacket has just started making a speech at the front, and all the attendants are giving me odd looks . . . but I don't care. I need to get out. I need to talk to Suze as soon as I can. She probably hates me. I don't blame her. I hate me, too.

Nenita is still standing in the lobby with Aran and a few others, and as I look at her anew, I feel a sudden revulsion. No, worse: outrage. How dare she try to curse me? How dare she diss Danny? As she's turning away to enter the auditorium, I tap her on the shoulder.

'Excuse me, Nenita,' I say, my voice shaking slightly, 'I'd just like to rebut a couple of things you said. Maybe I shouldn't have betrayed Lois – but you should know, she isn't exactly the girl you think she is. Second, I reckon people who try to give other people bad karma get bad karma *themselves*. Third, my dress is not dated. Danny Kovitz is a very talented designer and all the young fashion bloggers are going wild over it, so maybe if you don't like it, *you're* the one who's dated.'

I hear a couple of gasps from Nenita's acolytes. But I don't care. I'm on a roll.

'As for us being similar . . .' I hesitate. 'You're right. When I know what I want in life, I go after it.' I look around at the PR girls, the cameras, the rows of glossy *Big Top* goodie bags with striped handles, waiting to be collected. I would have gone wild about those goodie bags, once upon a time. But now it feels as though they're somehow contaminated. 'And the truth is . . . I don't want this.'

'Becky!' says Aran, with a laugh.

'I don't want it, Aran.' I look him square in the eye. 'I don't want the fame and I don't want the heat.'

'Sweetheart, don't overreact!' He puts a hand on my arm. 'Nenita was joking about your dress.'

Is that all he thinks I care about? My *dress*?

But then . . . why wouldn't he?

Suddenly I can see myself as everyone else has seen me over the last few weeks. And it's not a great sight. I have a horrible thickness in my throat, and I can feel tears rising. But there's no way I'm losing it in front of Nenita Dietz.

'It's not just about my dress,' I say, as calmly as I can, and shake off his arm. 'Bye, Aran.'

A bunch of black-suited girls are gossiping in a clutch by the doors, and as I approach, one springs to life.

'Did you leave the movie already? Are you OK?'

'I'm fine.' I attempt a smile. 'But I need to go. It's an emergency. I'm going to call my driver.'

I fumble for my phone and text a message to Jeff:

Can we go now? Thx love Becky x

I stand awkwardly by the doors for a while, wondering where Jeff will pull up – and then I can't stand waiting any longer. I'll go out and see if I can spot the car.

I push the doors open and head back out on to the red carpet. It's empty now, littered with a couple of discarded pro-grammes and a Coke can and a cardigan that someone must have put down. I can see some white beads from Sage's dress still glimmering on the red pile. I don't know *how* I'm going to explain that to Danny. It was hand-sewn. It must have taken ages to make. All ruined in an instant.

And as I look at the beads, my spirits plunge further. I feel like *everything* has been ruined tonight. My stupid Hollywood dreams, my plan to be a celebrity, my friendship with Suze . . . I feel a fresh crush of pain and take a deep, shaky breath. I need to hold it together. I need to find Jeff. I need to . . .

Wait.

I gulp, and stare, unable to move. I can't believe it.

Coming up the red carpet – the empty red carpet – is Luke. He's walking steadily but purposefully, and his eyes are fixed on mine. He's wearing his dark Armani overcoat, and I can see that underneath he's in black tie.

As he gets near I start to tremble. His face is taut and stern, giving nothing away. There are tiny shadows under his eyes and as he reaches me, he doesn't smile. For one awful moment I think he's come here to divorce me.

'I thought you went to New York,' I falter, my voice barely above a whisper.

'I did.' He nods gravely. 'I did. And then I turned straight round and came back again. Becky, I behaved atrociously. I'm sorry. To you and to my mother. It was unforgivable behaviour.'

'It wasn't!' I say at once, flooded with relief.

'You have every right to be angry with me.'

'I'm not. Honestly, I'm not.' I gulp. 'I'm just . . . I'm so pleased to see you.'

I reach for his hand and clasp it tight. I never expected to see Luke here. Not in a million years. His hand is warm and firm and feels like it's anchoring me. I never want to let it go.

'Why aren't you inside?' He jerks his head towards the auditorium. 'Has the evening been a success?'

Part of me longs to say, 'Yes! It's been brilliant!' and regale him with my triumph. But there's a bigger part of me that can't lie. Not to Luke. Not when he's standing here. Not when he flew back from New York. Not when he's the only person at this premiere who actually cares about me.

'It's not what I thought,' I say at last. 'Nothing's what I expected.'

'Mm.' He nods, as though he can read my mind.

'Maybe . . .' I swallow. 'Maybe you were right. Maybe I am a bit lost.'

For a moment Luke doesn't say anything. Those intense, dark eyes of his meet mine and it's as though we don't have to talk. He can sense it all.

'I was brooding about that all the way to New York,' he says finally, his voice deep and gravelly. 'And then it hit me. I'm your husband. If you're lost, it's up to me to come and find you.'

With no warning, tears start to my eyes. After everything I did to annoy and upset him. He came to find me.

'Well . . . here I am,' I manage, a lump suddenly in my throat, and Luke sweeps me into his arms.

'Come here,' he says against my wet cheek. 'No one should have to go to a premiere on their own. I'm sorry, my darling girl.'

'*I'm* sorry,' I mumble back, sniffling against his white collar. 'I think I lost the plot a bit.'

Luke offers me his handkerchief, and I blow my nose and try to repair my eye make-up a little while he waits patiently.

'All the interviewers called me Betty,' I tell him. '*Betty.*'

He raises his eyebrows. 'Betty? No, I can't see it.' He glances at his watch. 'Now, what shall we do? You want to go back inside?'

'No,' I say with resolve. 'I want to find my dad. I want to make up with Suze. I want to hug Minnie. I want to do anything *but* go inside.'

'Really?' He meets my eyes . . . and I can see he's asking me a bigger question. The same question he was asking me before. It seems so long ago, now.

'Really.' I nod. 'It's . . . it's over.'

'OK then.' His eyes soften. 'OK.' He takes my hand, and slowly we start to walk back down the empty red carpet.

TWENTY-THREE

They talk about rose-tinted spectacles. Well, I think I've had red-carpet-tinted spectacles. I mean, this red carpet is actually quite tatty, now it's empty of celebrities. As Luke and I walk along, hand in hand, there are cameras still banked along the barriers, but we have the carpet to ourselves. It reminds me of strolling along the Walk of Fame, weeks ago, when we were new to LA and it was a big adventure ahead of us. I can't believe how much has happened since then.

'I need to build bridges with my mother,' says Luke.

'Yes, you do.' I nod. 'And you will. It'll be wonderful. Luke, you should see your mum with Minnie. They're amazing! They're actually very similar.'

'I can imagine.' He shoots me a wry smile, and I have a sudden vision of sitting with Luke and Elinor and Minnie, a happy family around the tea table. It'll happen, I tell myself. Soon. Everything will change.

'Buy her a jigsaw,' I suggest. 'She loves jigsaws.'

'OK.' Luke smiles. 'I'll do that. Or maybe I should buy her a hundred. I have a lot to put right.'

'Oh God, so do I.' I wince, as all my troubles flood back into my brain. Suze . . . Tarquin . . . My dad . . . 'I had this big row with Suze.' I wring his hand. 'It was awful. She's really angry with me—'

'Becky.' He cuts me off gently. 'Listen. I have to tell you something. Suze is here.'

'What?' I turn my head, puzzled. 'What do you mean? Where?'

'I left the car a few streets away. She's parked there right now. She wants to drive into the desert after your father and she wants you to come too.'

'What?' I stare at him. 'Are you serious?'

'Absolutely. When I told her where I was going, she begged to come along with me. If I didn't succeed, she was going to come and drag you out of the premiere herself.'

'But . . .' I can't process this. 'Into the *desert*?'

Luke sighs. 'Suze is in a real state. We think your father and Tarquin are heading to Las Vegas. Suze is worried about Tarquin, and, to be fair, I think she has good reason to be.'

'Right.' My head is spinning. 'So . . . where are the children?'

'Mitchell is babysitting right now. Obviously we'll have to decide what the best plan is. We need to get home, work out what we know, put together a route . . . And you need to think hard, Becky. I mean, he's your father. If anyone can figure out where he's gone . . .'

'I've got that old map of my dad's.' My mind starts to whir. 'We might be able to work out something from that, maybe?'

'Becky!' A voice hails us, and I whip round to see Jeff a few yards away, leaning out of the driver's window and waving. 'I can't get any closer!'

'Jeff!' I hurry towards his friendly face. Within a minute, both Luke and I are in the back seat of the SUV, and Luke is instructing him on where to go.

'Movie finished early?' says Jeff, as he manoeuvres the car out.

'I just decided I'd had enough.'

'Smart.' Jeff nods.

'I did everything I needed to. Except . . . wait.' I turn to Luke, stricken. 'The autographs! I never got any!'

'Becky, it doesn't matter—'

'It does! I promised Dad I'd get him some autographs, and I haven't got a single one.' I stare at Luke miserably. 'I'm so *crap.*'

'Sweetheart, it's not the priority right now—'

'But I promised. And I let him down *again*.' Remorse is pouring through me. 'He wanted Dix Donahue's autograph, and I never got it, and now I've forgotten again, and—'

'You want some signatures? I'll fill your dad's book.' Jeff's voice comes from the front of the car, and I blink in astonishment.

'*You* will?' I say, stupidly.

'You name a celebrity, I've worked for them. They all owe me one. I'll get your autographs.'

'Really?' I say, agog. 'Like who?'

'Name a celebrity,' repeats Jeff.

'John Travolta.'

'I couldn't say.'

'Brad Pitt!'

'I couldn't say.'

His face is blank but his eyes are twinkling in the rear-view mirror. I think I love Jeff.

'That would be amazing. Thank you so much.' I carefully take out Dad's precious autograph book and put it on the front passenger seat. What seems like thirty seconds later, Jeff is pulling up in a side street and Luke is saying, 'We're parked just here. Thank you, Jeff.'

'Bye, Jeff.' I lean over and give him a hug. 'You've been so wonderful.'

'You're a nice family,' says Jeff gruffly. 'I'll see you again with those autographs.'

We get out of the SUV and a breeze ruffles my dress. I glance at my reflection in the car window, and my own eyes stare back at me, huge and over-made-up, and a bit wired. I suddenly feel really nervous at the idea of seeing Suze. I feel as if I've been in some other, alternate universe. But I can't run. I can't dodge this. The car door is opening and she's getting out.

For a moment we just stand there, staring at each other through the evening air. I've known Suze for many years, and she hasn't changed a bit. Same blonde hair; same endlessly long legs; same huge, irreverent laugh; same way of nibbling her thumb when she's stressed. I can only imagine the state of her skin right now.

'Bex, I know you're really busy.' Her voice is husky. 'I know you've got all these big chances and everything. But I need you. Please. I need you.'

I'm so taken aback that she isn't shouting at me, tears spring to my eyes again.

'I need you too.' I skitter to her on my heels, and envelop her in a huge hug. When's the last time I hugged Suze? Ages ago.

She's crying too, I realize. She's really sobbing on my shoulder. She's been totally wiped out by all the worry, and I wasn't there for her. I feel a horrible gnawing in the pit of my stomach. I was a bad friend. A bad, bad friend.

Well, I'm going to make up for it now.

'I missed you,' she mumbles into my hair.

'I missed you too.' I squeeze her tight. 'The red carpet wasn't the same without you. I didn't have the time of my life at all; in fact, it was awful.'

'Oh, Bex. I'm sorry.'

And I can tell she truly is. Even though I've been so crap to her, she still wishes I'd had a nice time. That's how lovely Suze is.

'They've gone to Las Vegas,' she adds.

'I heard.'

She lifts her face and wipes her nose with her sleeve.

'I thought we could follow them?'

'OK.' I squeeze her hands tight. 'Let's do it. Whatever you want to do, Suze, I'm right behind you.'

I have no idea what I've just signed myself up for, but I don't care. This is Suze and she needs me, so I'm in.

'I've been texting Danny,' she adds, her voice a bit snuffly. 'He's coming, too.'

'Danny is?' I say in astonishment.

She turns her phone to show me the screen.

Suze, my darling, do you even need to ASK??? I will be there in a nanosecond and we will find that husband of yours. Danny xxxxx

Danny is such a star. Although how we're going to keep tabs on him in Las Vegas, I have no idea.

'Well, there we are then.' I give her another hug. 'We're sorted. We have a team. We'll do it, Suze. We'll find them.'

How? I can't help thinking. How are we going to find them? This whole idea feels a bit nutty to me. But Suze wants me to do it, so that's all that matters.

I'm about to suggest that we all go home, order take-out and pool our ideas when the other passenger door opens. I feel a massive shock as another blonde head appears. Alicia? Seriously? *Alicia?*

'Alicia's going to come too.' Suze wipes her eyes. 'She's been so lovely. She was the one who found out about Las Vegas. Bryce told one of his friends at Golden Peace that's where he was going. Alicia had every single member of staff interviewed until she got some information . . . Honestly, Bex, she's been amazing.'

'Great!' I say after a pause. 'How . . . fabulous of her.'

'You two will be friends, won't you?' Suze looks anxious. 'You have put all that stuff in the past behind you?'

What can I say? I can't add to Suze's stress.

'Of course,' I say at last. 'Of course we have. We'll be great friends, won't we, Alicia?'

'Becky.' Alicia comes forward, her footsteps silent in her trendy soft-leather yoga flip-flop things; her face in that composed, serene expression she puts on. 'Welcome.'

Instantly my hackles rise. She doesn't get to say welcome. *I* say welcome.

'And welcome back.' I smile sweetly at her. 'Welcome to *you*.'

'This is a challenge we have.' She looks at me seriously. 'But

I'm sure if we all work together, we can find Tarquin, your father and Bryce before—' She breaks off. 'Well. We're worried that Bryce is . . . predatory. That's our concern.'

'I get it.' I nod. 'Well, let's get back to the Batcave and make a plan. Don't worry, Suze.' I give her another squeeze. 'We're on the case.'

'You get in.' Suze is tapping at her phone. 'I'll just be a second.'

I climb into the car, followed by Alicia, and we sit in silence for a moment. Then, just as Alicia is drawing breath to speak, I turn to her.

'I know you haven't changed,' I say in swift, low, furious tones. 'I know underneath all that sweetness and honey you have some agenda of your own. But just know, if you hurt Suze one tiny bit, I will burn you.' I'm glaring at her so hard, I think my eyes might pop out. 'I will burn. You.'

The car door opens and Suze climbs into the front passenger seat. 'Everything OK?' she asks breathlessly.

'Fine!' I say brightly, and after a moment, Alicia echoes, 'Fine.' She looks a bit shell-shocked. Well, good. I don't care about me, she's already hurt me enough. But I'm not having her hurt Suze.

Luke gets into the driver's seat, slams the door and turns to make a comical face at me. 'Ready, Betty?'

'Ha ha.' I make a face back at him. 'Funny. Let's head home.'

He starts the engine, and as we move off I look back through the rear window, craning my neck, slightly blinded by the streetlamps. We're driving away from the TV cameras, the bright lights, the celebrities. We're driving away from everything I was so excited about. I may never get to walk on a red carpet again, it hits me. That could have been my last chance. Maybe this is farewell to Hollywood.

But I don't care. I'm heading the right way. And I've never felt better in my life.

FROM THE OFFICE OF DIX DONAHUE

To Graham Bloomwood

With greatest appreciation for you and your
wonderful daughter Rebecca.

You're welcome to come to a show and visit me
back stage any time.

With very best wishes

Your pal

Dix Donahue

PS: Thank Jeff for this!

PPS: I heard you went missing. Hope you're back
safe and sound by now??

Becky will return soon!

CREDITS

Associate Producers (UK)
Araminta Whitley, Peta Nightingale, Jennifer Hunt,
Sophie Hughes

London Unit
Linda Evans, Bill Scott-Kerr, Larry Finlay, Polly Osborne,
Claire Evans, Suzanne Riley, Sarah Roscoe and her team,
Claire Ward, Kate Samano and Elisabeth Merriman,
Jo Williamson, Bradley Rose

Associate Producers (US)
Kim Witherspoon, David Forrer

New York Unit
Susan Kamil, Deborah Aroff, Kelsey Tiffey, Avideh Bashirrad,
Karen Fink, Theresa Zoro, Sally Marvin, Loren Novek,
Benjamin Dreyer, Paolo Pepe, Scott Shannon, Matt Schwartz

Associate Producers (rest of the world)
Nicki Kennedy
Sam Edenborough & all the team at ILA

Best Boys: Freddy, Hugo, Oscar and Rex
Best Girl: Sybella
Key Grip: Hestia the Labrador
Catering: Carol and Edith
Childcare: Greena and Grub-Grub
Miss Kinsella's nutritional supplements supplied by: Rolo &
Mint Aero
Production Manager: #HenrytheManager

Lifetime Achievement Award: Barb Burg RIP, 29 April 2014

THE SHOPAHOLIC SERIES

Starring the unforgettable Becky Bloomwood,
shopper extraordinaire . . .

The Secret Dreamworld of a Shopaholic

(also published as *Confessions of a Shopaholic*)

Meet Becky – a journalist who spends all her time telling people
how to manage money, and all her leisure time spending it. But the
letters from her bank manager are getting harder to ignore. Can she
ever escape this dream world, find true love . . . and regain the use of
her credit card?

Shopaholic Abroad

Becky's life is peachy. Her balance is in the black – well, nearly –
and now her boyfriend has asked her to move to New York with
him. Can Becky keep the man *and* the clothes when there's so much
temptation around every corner?

Shopaholic Ties the Knot

Becky finally has the perfect job, the perfect man and, at last, the
perfect wedding. Or rather, *weddings* . . . How has Becky ended up
with not one, but two big days?

Shopaholic & Sister

Becky has received some incredible news. She has a long-lost sister! But how will she cope when she realizes her sister is not a shopper . . . but a skinflint?

Shopaholic & Baby

Becky is pregnant! But being Becky, she decides to shop around – for a new, more expensive obstetrician – and unwittingly ends up employing Luke's ex-girlfriend! How will Becky make it through the longest nine months of her life?

Mini Shopaholic

Times are hard, so Becky's Cutting Back. She has the perfect idea: throw a budget-busting birthday party. But her daughter Minnie can turn the simplest event into chaos. Whose turn will it be to sit on the naughty step?

OTHER BOOKS

Sophie Kinsella's hilarious, heart-warming
standalone novels

Can You Keep a Secret?

Certain she's going to die in a plane crash, Emma blurts out her
deepest, darkest secrets to the sexy stranger next to her. But it's OK,
because she'll never have to see him again . . . will she?

The Undomestic Goddess

Samantha works all hours, has no home life and thrives on adrenalin.
Then one day it all falls apart. She finds herself a new life as
housekeeper in a country house. Will her old life ever catch up with
her? And if it does, will she want it back?

Remember Me?

What if you woke up and your life was perfect? Somehow Lexi's
life has fast-forwarded three years, and she has everything she's ever
wanted – the job, the house, the man. Or does she? What went on in
those missing years, and can she cope when she finds out the truth?

Twenties Girl

Lara has always had an overactive imagination. But even she finds it hard to believe when the ghost of her great aunt Sadie shows up, asking for her help. Is Lara losing her mind? Or could two girls from different times end up helping each other?

I've Got Your Number

First Poppy loses her engagement ring – a priceless heirloom – and then she misplaces her phone. The only alternative seems to be to take a mobile she finds in a bin. Little knowing that she's picked up another man in the process . . .

Wedding Night

Lottie is determined to get married. And Ben seems perfect – they have history, he's gorgeous and he's willing to do it now. They'll iron out their little differences later. All that's left to do is seal the deal. But their families have different plans . . .